JANA OLIVER

MACMILLAN

First published in the US 2012 by St. Martin's Press

First published in the UK 2012 by Macmillan Children's Books
a division of Macmillan Publishers Limited
20 New Wharf Road, London N1 9RR
Basingstoke and Oxford
Associated companies throughout the world
www.panmacmillan.com

ISBN 978-0-330-51949-6

1 3 5 7 9 8 6 4 2

A CIP catalogue record for this book is available from
the British Library.

Printed and bound by CPI Group (UK) Ltd, Croydon CR0 4YY

To Jean Marie Ward,
who knows that high heels and
Armageddon have much in common

Acknowledgements

Writing a story about the end of the world (or the near miss thereof) isn't for wimps. This book required many countless hours to bring it to the final version that you (hopefully) have just enjoyed. So it's time to list my accomplices, who joined me in this merry battle of words.

My many thanks to Rachel Petty, who helped me smooth out the rough edges and make the story sing. Meredith Bernstein (my literary agent) deserves a shout-out as well for keeping me sane during the revisions.

Michelle Roper, Jean Marie Ward, Haley Vornholt and Danita Hodges all weighed in on the story, some more than once, and I owe them big time for all their comments, insights and support. Atlanta and Oakland Cemetery take some serious hits in this book, so once again I thank both for providing such a wonderful canvas on which to paint this series.

Finally a hug to all my readers, who have taken Riley, Beck and company into their lives and into their hearts. Bless you all!

'Hell begins on the day when God grants us a clear vision of all that we might have achieved, of all the gifts which we have wasted, of all that we might have done which we did not do.'

– Gian Carlo Menotti

Chapter One

2018
Atlanta, Georgia

Riley Blackthorne's tears were no more. She'd cried herself dry, yet she still lingered in the arms of a dead man. If given the chance, she would remain in her father's arms for the rest of her life.

When she looked up, sad brown eyes gazed back. Master Trapper Paul Blackthorne was a reanimated corpse now, summoned from his grave by none other than the Prince of Hell. Like the day he'd been buried, he wore his best suit and favourite red tie, the one she'd given him as a present.

On the run from the Vatican's team of Demon Hunters, Riley had taken refuge in the home of Mortimer Alexander, a summoner of the dead. She had not expected to find her father waiting for her. Now, as they huddled together, she laid her head on his chest, seeking solace in his embrace.

'I've missed you,' she whispered.

'I've missed you too, Pumpkin.'

This isn't right. We're just borrowing time.

Her dad should be in his grave. Then he would never

know that Riley wasn't his innocent little girl any longer, that she'd given up her virginity the night before.

I was a fool. Why did I let Ori do that?

She'd spent that night in the arms of someone who said he would protect her. Who said she was special and that he cherished her because she reminded him of Heaven. Morning brought the bitter truth – Ori's protection came with a big price tag. Her lover, the fallen angel, would watch over her only if she consigned her soul to Hell. Then Lucifer, the Prince, had arrived and turned Ori into a statue for failing to follow his orders.

Riley wiped a bead of sweat off her forehead. Her body felt like a war zone, some unknown fire burning inside her now.

What if I'm pregnant? She shuddered at the thought. Ori had said that wasn't possible, but that could have been a clever lie. Is that why the demon hunters wanted her? What would the child of a Fallen and mortal be like? Normal? Evil? Somewhere in between?

What would the Church do to me and the baby?

When she shivered, her father broke the embrace.

'Come with me,' he said, taking her hand and slowly rising to his feet. 'I need to feel the sunlight again.' He stopped in the kitchen and poured her a tall glass of apple juice, then they entered a walled garden where cardinals and raucous blue jays flitted around a well-stocked birdfeeder. Water cascaded from the fingers of a nude stone nymph perched in the centre of a broad fountain. They settled on a stone bench still covered with frost, and Riley's behind immediately reacted to the cold. Her father didn't seem to notice it.

He handed her the juice. 'Drink. You look awful.'

It wasn't a good sign when a dead guy said you looked bad.

Riley took a long sip. It was cold and it tasted good. Clutching the glass in her hands, she gave in to the questions that careened around inside her.

'What's it like to be . . . dead?' she asked, her voice barely above a whisper.

'Very peculiar.'

'You can't tell me, can you?'

'No. Not like I thought,' he murmured.

The next question was harder. 'Did you see Mom?'

He shook his head as his eyes clouded with sadness. 'No.'

Riley's heart fractured into smaller pieces. 'Lucifer told me what you did. How you gave up your soul for me.'

Her dad's eyes widened. 'You spoke with the Prince?'

'He was in the graveyard this morning after . . .' Riley paused, biting down on her lip. *No, can't go there.* Maybe someday she'd have the courage to admit what she'd done, but not now. 'Lucifer said you pledged your soul to him so that Archfiend wouldn't kill you. So you could take care of me.'

Her dad issued a resigned nod. 'Your mother understood why I did it.'

'Mom knew?' she blurted. 'Why didn't you guys tell me?'

'You were too young.'

'That's crap and you know it,' she retorted. 'I was old

enough. What else haven't you told me, Dad? What else is going to fall on my head when I'm not looking?'

He didn't reply, his eyes not meeting hers now. Which meant there *was* more.

It was so unfair. Her father was supposed to remain alive until she became a master trapper.

'Lucifer didn't keep his bargain,' she complained. 'Your soul should be yours.'

'He said he wouldn't release it, that I owed him a debt, but he wouldn't say what.'

'So you're stuck in Hell until he decides you're not?'

Her father winced. 'Don't be angry. I did what was best. My soul isn't important.'

It was so important that Lucifer wasn't willing to give it up even when her dad had died before his time.

'Does Mort know who summoned you?' There was a faint nod. 'And he's OK with that?' she asked, surprised.

'He was shocked, but he hasn't thrown me to the wolves yet.'

'What about Beck?'

Her father shook his head. 'I don't look forward to the day he learns the truth. It's going to tear him apart.'

Denver Beck, her dad's trapping partner, had considered Paul Blackthorne a mentor. To learn he was aligned with Hell would be as devastating as when Beck had found out she'd slept with a Fallen.

Her father touched her arm. 'I'll see if our host has some place for you to sleep. You need rest.'

Riley blinked to hold back the tears. 'In a little bit,' she said, not wanting to be separated from him. Closing her eyes, she leaned against him, inhaling the confusing scents of oranges and cedar chips. Desperate to find some good in all this disaster, she took his hand and squeezed it, remembering what it had been like before he died. When his hands were warm and his heart beating. When there had been all the time in the world.

The spare bedroom in Mort's house was bright, decorated with cream walls and peach accents. It felt like a girl's room, which made Riley wonder if he had a sister or a niece. She yawned, then pulled the curtains to reduce the light. As she pulled off her shirt, her long brown hair fell over her face. With it came the unmistakable scent of crisp night air. *Ori's scent.*

'Damn you,' she swore, flinging her clothes in all directions as if that might reverse the dark echoes of the angel's touch. She fled into the shower stall, adjusting the temperature as cold as she could stand to combat the inferno inside her veins. As the water cascaded, she scrubbed her skin until it turned red. The memories refused to be washed away.

When Riley finally climbed into the bed, she curled into a foetal position, sleep tugging at her. She wasn't the first to give up her virginity to a guy who said he'd always care for her. Riley had heard other girls admit the same mistake during whispered confessions in school restrooms. From this point on, she would always divide her life into *Before* and *After the Angel*. Statue or not, Ori would be inside her heart, affecting every chance at love for the rest of her days.

Just like Beck.

To Denver Beck, there were many ways to welcome a new day – spread-eagled on his own lawn, wrists secured by flex-cuffs wasn't the best of them.

'What the hell is goin' on?' he bellowed into the dirt.

The response was the sound of combat boots tromping around inside his house as their owners' voices called out to each other in Italian. When there was a sharp shatter of glass, he swore. Beck closed his eyes to keep the dirt out of them and forced himself to relax. If he fought back, the demon hunter behind him might feel the need to make this his last day on earth.

I'll be damned if I die like this.

His only choice was to remain here until the Vatican's elite team finished their search. Which, from all the commotion, involved tearing his house apart.

When he heard a name in the midst of the voices flowing around him, he sighed into the dirt. They were searching for Riley Blackthorne, the seventeen-year-old daughter of Beck's dead trapper buddy, Paul.

The day had sucked even before this paramilitary-style raid, one Beck was sure his neighbours were enjoying with their morning coffee. Right after dawn Riley had arrived on his doorstep, weeping and shell-shocked. Through tears and sobs she'd admitted her blackest sin: she'd spent the night with a Fallen, one of Lucifer's own.

Beck had known this Ori guy was bad news from the first moment he'd seen him with Riley, but he'd never expected the bastard to be a fallen angel.

Why him? Even now he could see her huddled on the couch, weeping, as he'd shouted that very question at her. After all Beck had done for her, she'd taken up with that *thing*.

When he'd spat insults at Paul's daughter, she'd responded in kind. Fearing how bad it might get between them, Beck had bolted from the house. When he'd returned a short time later, he'd found his front door wide open and the Vatican's team on the prowl.

More rapid-fire conversation bounced around him now: Beck didn't need to speak the language to hear the frustration. Since Riley wasn't lying in the dirt beside him, this raid made the hunters look bad. They would need a scapegoat and Beck would do just fine. A new voice cut in – it was the hunters' captain. Apparently he'd finally decided to join the party.

Without warning, Beck was hauled roughly to his knees. Once he was up, he tried to wipe his mouth on his arm: it proved impossible with the flex-cuffs in place. The demon hunter with the rifle circled round to the side now, the weapon pointed at Beck's chest.

The captain of this unit squatted in front of him, his dark eyes flinty. Elias Salvatore was thirty-two, a decade older than Beck. He had a Mediterranean complexion, black hair and a goatee, coupled with an athletic build. His navy turtleneck sported epaulettes and the Demon Hunters' emblem – St George slaying the dragon. Crisply pleated trousers tucked neatly into polished combat boots.

'Mr Beck,' he said evenly.

'Captain Salvatore. What the hell is goin' on?'

'We were informed that Riley Blackthorne was here.'

Who told ya that?

'She was here a while ago. Must have left.'

The man's eyes narrowed further. 'Where is she?'

'No idea.' It was a safe bet one of the neighbours had heard them shouting at each other, so he went with the truth in case the hunters bothered to check. 'We had words.'

'About what?'

'That's none of yer business,' Beck said. A second later he was face down in the dirt, a heavy boot pressing on his back.

The captain issued a crisp command and Beck was hauled up again. He gave a look over his shoulder and found the boot belonged to Lieutenant Amundson, the captain's second-in-command. He was a tall man, Nordic, and not known for his manners.

Beck spat dirt. 'Get these damned cuffs off me.'

Salvatore gave a gesture. There was the snick of a knife then the cuffs fell away. Amundson had made sure to cut Beck's palm in the process.

Beck wiped his hands on his jeans, then inspected the wound.

The captain delivered a penetrating look over the

prisoner's shoulder then gestured for the lieutenant to move away. 'I apologize.'

Beck clamped down on his fury. Throwing punches wasn't a smart move right now.

Did the hunters know about Riley and the Fallen? *They have to. Why else would they be lookin' for her?* Still, he didn't dare make assumptions.

'What's this all about?' Beck asked.

The captain rose. 'Let's go inside.'

Beck stood, dusted off his jeans and retrieved his trapping bag where it lay near the driveway. He felt the bottom of the canvas and was relieved to find it wasn't wet, which meant none of the glass spheres inside had shattered when he'd been tackled by the hunters. He'd need those special magical globes to trap Hellspawn.

After ensuring they were alone, Salvatore closed the front door behind them. Beck had expected the place to have been turned inside out, but that wasn't the case. The only damage appeared to be a glass that had been knocked off the counter. He ignored the mess on the floor and dropped on to the couch in the same place that Riley had occupied when she'd delivered her devastating news.

Where are ya, girl? If she ran to her apartment, they'd find her there. If she was smart, she'd go to Angus Stewart, one of the two master trappers in the city. Stewart would watch over her.

The captain sat in a chair opposite him. He moved as if he hadn't had a decent night's sleep in days. 'We must find

Riley Blackthorne as quickly as possible.'

'Why?'

'There's a fallen angel in Atlanta. His name is Ori. We believe he has targeted Paul Blackthorne's daughter.'

Beck made sure he appeared shocked. It wasn't hard. He still couldn't believe that Riley had been with one of Lucifer's allies.

'Why would one of those want her?'

Salvatore shook his head. 'He is known for his seductions.'

Beck's jaw tensed, but he didn't reply.

'There is a strange pattern of events in this city, and that usually means there's an epicentre, a focus to that activity.'

'If yer sayin' that Riley's the reason for all this—'

'What other conclusion can we draw?' Salvatore retorted. 'Every demonic event in this city has centred on her: a Grade Five demon tried to kill her. The same fiend pressed its attack during the trappers' meeting at the Tabernacle and that ambush alone cost you a third of your Demon Trappers Guild.'

'I know the numbers, hunter,' Beck replied sullenly.

'If she is the nexus of this activity, we have to locate her and find a way to break that connection with Hell before more people die.'

Beck didn't want to think about what 'break that connection' meant. 'Why a commando raid on my house? Ya could have knocked on the door like anyone else.'

'You weren't home,' the captain observed. 'Do you usually leave your house unlocked?'

Beck hesitated. 'No. Why?'

'Both the front and back doors weren't bolted and your alarm wasn't engaged. The back door was partially ajar, indicating a hasty departure, perhaps?' The captain leaned forward, elbows on knees. 'Did you call Riley and warn her that we were coming?'

By now they'd have gone through his phone and know he'd called Riley after they'd quarrelled, so he opted for the truth. 'I didn't know ya were comin' here.'

'Yet you spoke to her.'

'Yeah. We argued about this Ori guy. He'd told her he was a freelance demon hunter and I told her to stay away from him. She wasn't listenin' so we had words. I called her to . . .' Why had he called her? Certainly not apologize, that was for sure.

'Where is she now?'

Beck shook his head. 'I don't know. Now I'm done talkin' to ya unless the Guild's lawyer is watchin' over me.'

The captain sighed. 'Look, I respect your loyalty to the girl's father. Paul Blackthorne trained you, brought you up through the Guild. You were there when he died at the hands of the same demon that tried to kill his daughter. I know what you're feeling, but we need your help.'

'Bite me.'

Salvatore scowled. 'So be it.' He triggered a radio on his shoulder and Italian filled the air. He'd barely finished giving the order when two hunters were through the front door.

The captain rose, his face set. 'Denver Beck, as representative of the Holy See, I arrest you for obstructing justice, additional charges to be filed at a later time. You are duly warned that if you are found to be aiding Hell in any manner, the ultimate penalty is death.'

'Go figure,' Beck muttered.

Chapter Two

Riley stood alone in a field of crisp, freshly fallen snow. There was nothing around her, no buildings, no people. High above a blood-red moon held court in the sky, thousands of stars paying homage.

A breeze tugged at her hair and it smelt of deepest midnight. She felt Ori's presence even before his arms slid round her waist, drawing her back against him. She knew it was a dream, but she didn't want to wake. Here it would be perfect. There would be no Heaven or Hell, no one to tell her what she was doing was wrong. It would just be Ori and her forever.

Turning in his arms, Riley gazed up at his black hair and those bottomless eyes. Eyes that had seen the beginning of the cosmos.

'I am sorry,' Ori murmured, his voice just as she remembered it. 'I hurt you and that is not what I wanted.'

'It didn't have to be that way,' she said. *It could have been so different.*

'Let me make it right between us. Let me show you what your future can hold.'

He gestured and a scene appeared in the air in front of

them. It was Riley, older now. She had a grace and strength that she never thought possible. She was teaching two apprentices how to trap demons and they were riveted on her words. This Riley was strong and confident, no hint of the troubled girl that lay within.

'You'll be a renowned master trapper, like your father,' Ori explained. 'The trappers will be in awe of your skills. All the while, my protection will keep you safe from harm.'

She could trap and be successful and everyone would think she was the best there was. *Just like my dad . . .*

His kiss reignited her desire for him. Her need for love, for someone to care for her. She melted against his body, savouring the touch and scent of him.

'I am yours,' the angel said. 'Give me your soul and we can be together forever, Riley Anora Blackthorne.'

'Do you love me?' she asked. That was what she wanted, what she craved. To be loved by someone as magnificent as an angel.

Ori did not reply, his face tormented. As if he wanted to lie, but could not. He tried to smile, but failed. 'Come with me,' he said, offering a hand. 'We will have eternity together. Is that not enough?'

Riley hesitated, her heart pounding hard. *If he doesn't love me . . .* Was she so desperate that she'd settle for an empty life? Caught in her doubts, she looked away and found that the field wasn't empty any longer. Her family's mausoleum now stood a short distance away, cloaked in snow and moonlight. Solid red stones, stained-glass windows, all testimony to the

Blackthorne legacy. The lion-winged gargoyles on the roof glared down at her, brilliant yellow flames pouring from their mouths, as if she was a threat to the dead within.

The double brass doors swung open and, instead of the stone interior lit by dancing candlelight, there was semi-darkness. Figures moved around inside, all talons and teeth and glittering ruby eyes. The emissaries of Hell awaiting her decision.

It was so tempting. She'd spend forever with her father. The demons couldn't hurt her and –

A voice cried out her name. She searched across the field and found Beck running towards her at top speed. He cried out again, his voice ragged as if he'd been shouting for hours and she'd not heard him.

'Do not listen to the trapper,' Ori warned. 'He is jealous of us. Of what we have.'

She hesitated, confused.

'Riley!' Ori called, more forceful now. 'Pledge me your soul. I promise you will never suffer another moment of your life.'

'What will we have?' she demanded. 'Some promises? None of which you will keep.' She shook her head. 'You never loved me. You only loved my soul and what it will buy you in Hell.'

'You are wrong,' the angel retorted. 'This was always about you.'

'Lies!' she shouted.

A searing cramp dug deep into her belly and she doubled

over in agony. Riley forced herself to straighten up, holding her stomach. The area around her had become a minefield of skulls, each inhabited by a demon. They taunted her, threatened her, spoke of the endless tortures that awaited her soul in Hell.

Ori was no longer near her but at the edge of the skull field now, pacing in agitation. 'You have to give your soul. It is the only way, Riley! Please, I beg of you!'

The snow around her turned crimson and began to boil.

'No,' she said. 'I have lost too much already.'

As the skulls massed for an assault, Beck charged into the minefield, bent on her rescue. He only made it a few steps before he cried out her name once more, then died in tormented agony as the demons tore him apart.

'NO!!!!'

Riley lurched upright in the bed, sweat pouring off her in streams. Her chest felt heavy and each breath only brought in a tiny stream of air. She bent over, clutching her stomach. Swallowing repeatedly to keep from vomiting, she struggled to regain her senses and break free of the nightmare.

With a groan, she wiped sweat off her brow. A vicious headache pounded in the very centre of her forehead. The room around her was quiet. There were no demons, no angel, no dying Beck. As the nightmare receded, the horror of it still clung to her.

Was this a sign of what her future held? Would Ori continue to push at her mind until she screamed for release? Would Beck throw away his life to save her soul?

With another groan, Riley rooted in her messenger bag and excavated two Advil and a bottle of water. She washed the tablets down, hoping they'd stay put, then leaned back against the headboard.

'This seriously sucks.' The verbal acknowledgement only made her head thump harder.

Once she'd shaken off the worst of the dream, she headed for the bathroom and made a totally useless attempt to do something about her hair. When she pulled on her clothes, she was relieved they smelt less like the lying angel now. It was a pity that the memory of his touch wouldn't fade as easily.

Out of habit she retrieved her cellphone, but a second before powering it on she hesitated: did she dare check her messages? Would the hunters be able to track her here?

'Better not,' she said, leaving the phone off. It felt weird to be so out of touch. How would she let her friends know what was happening? Her best buddy Peter freaked if he didn't hear from her regularly. Simi, her barista friend at the local coffee shop, would wonder what happened to her, especially since she insisted on updates every couple of days.

Staying with Mort was too dangerous for all of them. Eventually the hunters would come here. The only choice was for her and her dad to make a run for it, hide out until the Vatican's boys got bored and returned to Rome. *We'll have to start over. Find a place to live. I'll have to get a different job.* If they survived all that, eventually she'd have to convince Lucifer to put her dad back in the ground.

All because I wanted someone to love me.

*

While some would argue that the Westin Peachtree Plaza wasn't a jail, the earnest demon hunter parked near the hotel room's door told Beck he wasn't free to come and go as he pleased. Since it looked like he was here for the time being he made his way to the bathroom. Running a wet facecloth over his hair took most of the dirt out of the blond strands. He made sure to keep the bandage dry.

Riley's selfish actions had brought the hunters to his doorstep. That angered him, not only because of what she'd let that Fallen do to her, but because he'd promised her father he'd keep her safe. Still, Beck's wounded pride was the least of his worries: what would the hunters do to Paul's daughter when they caught her? Would they put her on trial? Lock her up? Or worse?

Knowing that his questions were not going to be answered by staring into the bathroom mirror, Beck returned to the bedroom. The hunter tracked his movements, vigilant as ever. Dusting himself off, which left a trail of dried grass on the carpet, Beck unlaced his work boots and dropped on to the king bed. It was one of those fancy ones you find in expensive hotels. He'd learned to sleep on some of the world's hardest surfaces during his stint in the army, so something this soft made him uncomfortable.

By his count there were two hunters guarding him: one in the corridor and one in the room with him. He could try to escape, but it'd probably buy him a bullet. Captain Salvatore had promised to call Master Stewart, and for some reason Beck trusted him to do just that. If he was patient, the Scotsman would get him out of here.

The guard in the room was Hispanic with dark, intense eyes and a fighter's bulk. He kept his attention riveted on his prisoner's every move.

'Can ya not do that?' Beck growled. 'Yer drivin' me crazy.'

The guy gave a shrug then settled back in the rolling chair, his attention a few feet to Beck's left. That was some improvement.

'How long is this gonna take?' No reply.

Knowing he wasn't going to be told anything of value until his captors were damned well ready, Beck pulled himself off the bed and went through his exercise regime to blow off steam. Fifty push-ups followed by fifty sit-ups. Then another fifty push-ups, a number of those one-handed. As he worked up a sweat, he tried hard to block the memories: Riley crying in his arms, the knowing smirk on that fallen angel's face. How disappointed Paul would be if he knew his daughter had been deceived like that.

Dammit. I did what I could, but it wasn't enough. It's never enough.

He lost count of the push-ups and finally slumped to the carpet when his arms grew too weak to support him and his back felt like it had been scorched by molten lead. The pain did as he'd hoped, blocking things he didn't want to think about. Muscles quivering, he returned to the bed, tucked his arms behind his head and stared up at the pebbled ceiling.

Someone had known Riley was at his house this morning

and that list was pretty short unless one of his neighbours was a spy for the hunters. Master Stewart knew she was there: Beck had called him the moment he'd left her at the house, seething in anger at what had happened between her and the angel.

Then there was Justine Armando, the woman he'd been with overnight. Justine was a new addition to Beck's life, a freelance journalist who'd arrived in Atlanta at the same time as the hunters. She trailed after their teams as they did the Vatican's dirty work across the world, writing up glowing newspaper accounts of their exploits. Beck had been interviewed by her . . . twice. Then they'd taken it a step further and he'd landed in her bed. That's where he'd been this morning, in this same hotel, when Riley's panicked phone call had reached him. When he'd heard that terrified voice, he'd bailed out of Justine's arms and bolted out of the door, sure Paul's daughter was in grave danger.

Had Justine told the hunters where Riley was? He had to admit he wasn't sure. All Beck could remember was the petulant frown on her face as he bent over to kiss her goodbye.

Couldn't be her. He wasn't willing to accept that, though he knew Riley would believe it in a heartbeat. He could still hear her warning him about Justine and how he was going to get hurt.

He huffed at the thought that he was responsible for Riley's problems. If she'd taken his advice, she wouldn't be in this world of hurt. He'd be the first to admit his words were at war with his heart. Everyone made mistakes and most didn't end up with Hell or the Church breathing down their necks.

When there was a knock at the door, the guard cautiously checked the peephole, then opened it, revealing Lt Amundson.

'Master Stewart knows you're in custody and that you're not leaving until we have the Blackthorne girl,' he said in his heavily accented English.

At least Stewart knows where I am. 'If that's the case, how about some breakfast?'

There was a grunt from the lieutenant and then the door shut behind him. Staring up at the ceiling, all Beck could think of was Paul's daughter, of her bitter tears and his unrelenting fury. How sick he'd felt when she'd told him what she'd done.

It was best he had no idea where Riley Blackthorne was hiding. The way he felt right now, he'd hand her over to the demon hunters himself.

Chapter Three

As Riley made her way back through Mort's house, she tried not to get lost. The place was larger than she'd first thought, the walls aged brick with exposed wooden roof beams overhead. Kind of cool in a warehouse-maze sort of way.

In the circular brick room Mort considered his office. The early afternoon poured down from the skylights, forming golden pools on the worn wooden floor. The summoner and her father were deep in conversation at a picnic table, sitting on benches across from each other.

About Riley's height and considerably wider, Mortimer Alexander had a pleasant round face and a bright smile, though behind all that was a fierce spirit. He'd chosen to become the Summoner Advocate of Atlanta, a job that earned him no respect from his fellow necromancers who spent most of their time luring the dead out of their graves and selling their bodies as unpaid slaves to rich people.

'Riley,' he said. 'Do you feel better?'

'Yes,' she said, politely lying. If anything, she felt worse now. The nightmare still hovered at the edges of her mind, like a monster hiding under a child's bed.

'There's my favourite daughter,' her father called out, a smile lighting his face.

He wore some of Mort's clothes now – a T-shirt and jeans – both hideously oversized. The jeans ended at his ankles and seemed out of place with his black socks and dress shoes. She had to find him clothes that fitted, but going to their apartment was going to be difficult: It was a good bet the hunters were watching the place.

The moment she plopped on to the bench seat near her father he put his arm round her. She leaned into him. Some things never changed, even if he was no longer among the living.

Mort cleared his throat. 'I put your car in my garage,' he said, pointing at her keys on top of the table. 'If the hunters are patrolling the streets, it's out of sight.'

She hadn't thought of that. 'Thanks.'

'The latest news is that Lord Ozymandias is furious someone stole your father right out from under his nose.'

As the most powerful summoner in Atlanta, Ozymandias had been after her father since the moment he'd died. During her cemetery vigil the necromancer had tried devious magic tricks to coerce her into breaking the sacred circle that protected her dad's grave. He'd not been successful and her dad's body had stayed put. *Until Lucifer came calling.*

'You know, that's just tough,' she said, totally pleased at the news. Then that happiness faded. 'Will Ozy come here?'

Mort cringed at the casual use of the senior necromancer's name. 'He will if he finds out your father's staying with me.'

Awkward silence fell after that. Her dad kept taking sips from a bottle filled with a luminescent liquid that looked like orange juice spiked with iridescent sparkles.

'Stabilizer,' Mort explained before she could ask. 'A basic potion with added magical oomph. It's why he smells like oranges. He has to drink a lot of it. A reanimate's vocal cords are difficult to keep hydrated.'

Riley really didn't want a lesson in Deader physiology, but she'd got one anyway. It came with hiding in a summoner's house.

'We talked while you slept and we both agree that Master Stewart is your best hope with the hunters,' Mort added. 'They'll listen to him.'

'Riiight,' Riley replied. 'They'll brand me a heretic and fry me. I know where this is going.'

Her father touched her hand. 'I wouldn't put you . . . in danger.'

But you did. You made a deal with Hell and when you died they came after me. Riley didn't dare say any of that, so she gnawed on the inside of her lip instead.

'I can get some money and we'll go somewhere else,' she suggested.

'But where? Paul said you have an aunt in Fargo, but the hunters will look there. You can't live on the streets. It's not safe for a girl your age.'

She looked at her father. 'I can't leave you here, Dad. Mort doesn't need the hassle from the hunters or the other summoners. We need to go somewhere else.'

'That's your choice, Riley,' the necromancer said solemnly, 'but I'd advise that Paul remain with me. He's safer here. I can take care of him, keep him in good condition.'

'And I can't?' she asked, too tired to be angry at what he was suggesting.

'You don't have magic behind you,' was the gentle reply. 'Your father's care involves certain spells, potions and a lot of finesse. If I don't watch over him, in a couple weeks the body will begin to disintegrate while the mind keeps working. He'll be safer with me than with anyone,'

It was a compelling argument, though Riley wished that wasn't the case. Next to her, her dad's eyes began to blink more rapidly now.

'What's going on? Are you really tired or something?' she asked.

It was Mort who answered. 'Reanimates have little or no life force behind them and they wear out quickly. He'll be going dormant here in a little bit. After a rest, he'll be back.'

'Oh. Can Master Stewart get the hunters to back off?'

'No,' Mort replied, 'but he can negotiate with them, act as the Guild's representative.'

The Scotsman would be a better choice than Master Harper, the trapper she was apprenticed to. Harper hated Riley and her dad. If he had the chance to bring both of them down, he'd jump at it.

'You sure Stewart will help me?' she asked.

'I've dealt with him as the Summoners' Advocate and

he's nothing but fair. However, you have to make a decision soon. The longer this goes on, the harder it will be to get the hunters to cooperate.'

Cooperate? What little she knew of the Vatican's boys, that wasn't a word those guys were familiar with. She'd seen their high tech equipment and their paramilitary work ethic. No matter her deal with Heaven, they would only be interested in her chat with the Prince of Darkness and her knocking boots with the Fallen.

'If I had something to bargain with . . .' she murmured.

Her father coughed, then took another long swig of the glowing potion. 'Holy . . . Water.'

The way he was fading she didn't have time to get into a lengthy discussion about the fake Holy Water that was being sold in the city. 'Who do you think is doing this?'

'No idea.' A few rapid blinks then he closed his eyes, like someone had flipped a switch to the Off position.

Riley looked over at Mort. 'It's like he's in screensaver mode. Is this going to happen a lot?'

'Plan on it. Your father has the ability to do high level cognitive reasoning which takes a heavy physical toll.'

'How did you find him?'

'I didn't. He arrived at my door late last night. For a while I thought it was because of that invitation spell I'd invoked, offering him refuge if he broke free of his summoner.' Mort's calm brown eyes met hers. 'But now I know that's not the case.'

He's not sure if Dad told me about Lucifer. Which he hadn't since that news items had come from the Prince himself.

'I know who summoned my father,' Riley replied. 'What I don't understand is why Lucifer set him free.'

Mort visibly relaxed. 'I'm just as confused. He owns your father's soul. Why does he need his body?'

Riley shrugged. Another question for which there was no answer.

Tereyza, Mort's housekeeper, appeared at that moment bearing a tray. Riley was presented with a full cup of something with a heady fruity aroma.

'Tea always helps clear the mind,' Mort said.

The only thing that cleared Riley's mind was hot chocolate, but that didn't seem to be on the menu, at least not here.

'I detect inner conflict,' the summoner said. 'Want to talk it out?'

Riley shook her head. No matter how much she'd like to push this disaster on to someone else, it was her mistake that had landed her in this situation. She needed a way to get to her house, collect the stash of money she had hidden there, then decide where she was going next. But to do that Riley had to get into the apartment complex unnoticed.

I wonder . . .

Riley retrieved her trapper's licence from the messenger bag. The photo had been taken when she'd sported a bizarre mishmash of teal, black and brown hair. After he'd seen the photo, her dad had insisted it return to its natural and boring brown.

'That's a devious smile,' Mort said over the top of his tea cup.

'The hunters are looking for this Riley,' she said, pointing towards her face. 'What if I looked completely different?' She held up the licence for contrast. 'If I get some hair dye maybe I can pull it off.'

'No need. I can do that with magic.'

Riley blinked. 'You can?' Why hadn't she thought of that? Probably because tea-sipping Mort didn't seem overly magical.

'Sure,' he replied. 'It's an easy spell. I can make your features look any way you want.'

That sounded like a plan, which meant there had to be a downside. 'What happens if the Vatican finds out I used magic to hide from them?'

'Nothing good,' their host admitted.

'Thought so.' Still, she felt it was worth the risk.

'Can I borrow your cellphone?' she asked. After he handed it over, she dialled her best friend, Peter.

'Riley? Where have you been? I tried calling—' her friend began.

She cut him off, told him what she needed.

'What is this all about?' he asked.

'The Demon Hunters are after me. If you help me, you could get in deep trouble with those guys.'

There was a very long pause.

'If you're not good with this, just say so, Peter. I won't be upset.'

'No, I'm good,' he said at last. 'My dad won't be home for another two hours and I'll need his car.'

'That's fine. I need to make a run to my place and it's best we do it closer to dark.'

'Then what?'

'I'm leaving town.'

More silence. Finally he spoke. 'When and where should I pick you up?'

Riley put the question to Mort and he came back with a location about a quarter of a mile away, near the heart of Little Five Points. She relayed the info to Peter, along with a time.

'Right. See you in a while.' Her best friend hung up.

Peter's going to help me. Maybe this will work out after all.

She handed her phone back to Mort and in return he offered her a plate loaded with baked goods. 'Strudel?' he said.

Riley took two thick slices and placed them on the small plate in front of her. If she was about to play cat and mouse with the Vatican's dudes, she needed serious fuel.

After about an hour's work, Mort's magical expertise resulted in a brown band, about two inches wide, with twin snaps and a few arcane symbols carved on the thick leather.

'Do those mean anything?' Riley asked.

He shook his head. 'All for show.' He handed it over. 'Prepare to be amazed.'

Riley swore she felt a tingling sensation as she snapped the band on her left wrist, then dutifully followed him to the closest bathroom mirror. And gasped. The new Riley had raggedy hair that looked like someone had chopped at it with a pair of kid's scissors. It was a breathtakingly mix of blue, black and stark white streaks. Two long micro-thin braids went to her waist – those were platinum white as well. There was a clear plastic barbell wedged in her left eyebrow, a blue gem in her nose, multi-piercings in her ears and a tongue stud: all the stuff she'd never been brave enough to try for real. Turning, she studied the blood-red tattoo that began on the back of her neck and wrapped round her throat. It was a vampire bat with enormous fangs.

'OK, that's different,' she said, shivering. *Kinda cool, actually*. And since a lot of kids in Atlanta had tats or piercings and bold hair colours she'd fit right in.

Mort nodded approvingly. 'The hunters might zero in on you because of your age, but with one glance they'll know you're not Riley Blackthorne.'

Not even close. Which was the whole point of using magic. 'How long does this last?'

'When you're wearing the bracelet, you're the Bride of Frankenstein. Take it off and you're the real Riley.'

'You could make a fortune on Halloween.'

The summoner chuckled. 'The downside is the magic uses some of your energy to power itself. You'll be more tired than normal, so only wear the bracelet when you need it, OK?'

'Can anyone use this?' It'd be fun to try it out on Peter.

'No. It's keyed to you. It's best the hunters not find you wearing this. They're pretty savvy about magic, even if they don't like it. They might figure out what the bracelet is and that won't go down well for you.'

'Understood.'

When they returned to Mort's office, a quick look proved her father was still in siesta mode.

'Tell Dad that I'll be OK and I'll let you know where I end up. Don't let him worry about me.'

'He would worry about you even if you were sitting next to him,' Mort replied softly.

The summoner was right. That was one of the reasons now was the best time go. It'd be hard when her father woke and found out she'd left him behind, but he'd understand. At least she hoped he would.

'I bought this while you were sleeping,' Mort said, handing her a cellphone. It was one of the cheap, pre-paid kind. 'It's not tied to you in any way and I'll keep refilling the minutes as you need. I programmed in my number if you have any trouble.'

This guy was amazing and she said so. A shy grin crept on to the summoner's face at her compliment, but he didn't deny it.

After Riley was sure she had everything she needed, she placed a kiss on her sleeping dad's forehead and took what might be her last look at him.

'Love you. Don't worry, I'll be good from now on.' *No more lying angels.* 'Who knows? Maybe I'll find a way to get you into Heaven with Mom.'

That was all bluff, though she owed Lucifer a favour and in return he'd said he'd grant her one wish. Could that be her father's *Get Out of Hell Free* card?

It was a small sliver of hope and she clung to it.

After one last kiss marred by tears, Riley followed the necromancer to a rear door that opened on to a gravelled alley.

'If you need to return, the bracelet is also your key back inside,' the necro said. 'Place it up against the door and it'll let you in.'

'Wow.' *Who knew magic could actually be helpful?*

Mort sobered. 'Please be very careful.'

'I will. Thanks, I owe you.' On impulse, she gave him a hug, though her hands wouldn't reach all the way round him. That got her an instant blush.

When the summoner closed the door behind her, the wood shimmered and then went solid again. Soon she'd be on her own, moving from town to town, trying to stay ahead of the demon hunters. And the demons.

Riley slipped the strap of her messenger bag over her shoulders. All she could think of was what her dad would say when he found out she was gone.

Chapter Four

The prisoner had expected room service, but Beck got a redhead instead. He rose off the bed as Justine Armando was escorted into his hotel room by one of the hunters.

'Hello, Beck,' she said, tossing her expensive black leather coat on a nearby chair, followed by a folded newspaper on the nightstand. 'I heard you were here in the hotel so I thought I'd pay you a visit.'

The guards were locked in full stare mode – apparently they'd never seen the reporter in action. Sporting a set of brilliant emerald-green eyes, Justine was a stunningly petite woman with shocking red hair that tumbled over her shoulders in wide curls. Her accent was hard to pin down, but it flowed like verbal honey no matter the subject.

Beck's attention moved to the hunters. 'Any way ya can give us some space?'

A conversation started between the men in Italian, and for a time it didn't look like the answer was going to be positive. Justine weighed in, also in Italian, and abruptly they changed their minds. She had that effect on men.

When the door closed behind his guard dogs, she settled into the chair, positioned so that Beck had a fine view of her long legs. He sank on to the bed, regretting he looked so scruffy.

'How'd ya know I was here?'

Justine pouted. 'I *am* a reporter. When I heard that Denver Beck is in the hunters' custody and that there is a search in progress for Master Blackthorne's daughter, I had to determine if it was all true.' She leaned closer. 'You wouldn't know where she is, would you?'

So this visit wasn't just a welfare check. Beck should have expected that, but his guy ego developed a new bruise.

'No, I don't know where she is or my ass wouldn't be sittin' in this room,' he growled. 'Riley could be anywhere. She knows a lot of places to hide.'

'Why do they want her? Is it because of the Fallen or something else?'

He stiffened. 'How do ya know about the Fallen?'

'One of the hunters told me.' She straightened her skirt. 'Why did Riley call you this morning?'

A nervous twitch crawled across Beck's back. *Too many questions*. 'That's private,' he said, crossing his arms over his chest. *End of conversation*.

Justine got the message. 'As you wish.' She rose, collecting her coat. 'I had hoped I could persuade Elias to release you, but he will need more information to justify that decision.'

Elias. Justine had a 'history' with the captain of the demon hunters and she wasn't above using that to get what she wanted. In this case, she was angling for inside information on Riley.

'I can't help him,' Beck insisted.

Justine gave him a sad smile, stepped forward and dropped a kiss on his cheek. Then she stepped back, adjusting her coat over an arm. 'For you,' she said, pointing at the newspaper on the nightstand.

He made no effort to pick it up, not about to reveal he could barely read.

'The next article will be longer,' she added.

'What?' he said, confused.

'You're an intriguing subject. One article will not do you justice.'

'I'm not good with—'

'Beck,' she said, softer now, immediately commanding his attention. 'The hunters will not give up until they have the girl. If you don't help them, they will hold you responsible.'

'I can't help them if I don't where she is.'

There was another kiss, longer this time and on the mouth. After the door closed behind her, a hint of her floral perfume lingered, reminding Beck of the time they'd spent together, of how good it'd been between them.

He opened the paper and began to hunt for the two words he knew best: his name. When he found the article, he worked through it at a tediously slow pace. Some words made sense, some did not. Nothing he read seemed too bad.

I'm too damn paranoid. It's her job to ask questions.

So why was he having second thoughts about Justine Armando?

To keep from losing his cool at being caged up, he'd

turned on the big-screen television. Tempting as it was to find a raunchy adult movie and charge it to the hunters' bill to piss them off, he opted for a show about the pyramids. He'd always wanted to travel around the world, but, other than the army and the Middle East, it'd been Georgia, Georgia and more Georgia. Just as the narrator was showing him the inside of one of the pharaoh's tombs, a demon hunter showed up at the door and handed him his phone.

'Beck.'

'It's Donovan.'

He sat up straighter. This was the county sheriff from where Beck grew up. He hadn't spoken to the man in over six months. More often than not he was usually on the wrong side of both Donovan and the law.

'What's up?' Beck asked neutrally.

'Things are starting to heat up down here. Questions being asked about what happened in the swamp all those years back. Those boys' parents are pushing me for answers. I thought you might like to know.'

Oh God. 'I told you I had nothin' to do with that.'

Silence.

Donovan wouldn't have called him just for that bad news. 'So what's really up?' Beck asked.

The sheriff cleared his throat. 'Your momma isn't well. You coming down to see her?'

Beck didn't like his tone, as if he was a misbehaving kid. 'When the time comes.'

'That wasn't what I wanted hear.'

Beck turned his back on the hunters at the door in an attempt to keep the conversation private. 'I'll be down there when I have time. Don't ya dare act like she wants to see me. Sadie's long past givin' a damn about me.'

There was lengthy silence. 'Do you know what's going on with her?'

'Last I heard she had pneumonia, but she was gettin' better.'

'Ah, damn,' the man said. 'She didn't tell you. Why can't that woman—'

'Tell me what?'

'She's got lung cancer. It's spread.'

Beck jammed his eyes shut as conflicting emotions churned within him. 'I didn't know, I swear,' he admitted.

'Well, now you do. I know things are bad up there, but she might not have that much time.'

Beck didn't bother to ask why Sadie hadn't told him. That was her way. It had nothing to do with being strong in the face of the illness, but everything to do with their toxic relationship.

He worked his jaw back and forth, trying to unclench it. 'I'll try to get down there as soon as I can.'

'That's all I ask. Thanks, Denver. Looking forward to seeing you again.'

Beck disconnected the call and stared at the display for a time. When he was growing up, Donovan had been like a big brother. Then he'd turned all law-man and run Beck out of Sadlersville when he was sixteen, driving him up to his uncle's house in Atlanta after Beck had got in a knife fight. Donovan laid it out in his simple way: Beck stayed out of town unless he wanted his next address to be a prison. Beck hadn't returned to Sadlersville until right before he went into the Army, in case his next trip home was in a body bag.

Beck tossed the phone back to the anxious hunter. 'Thanks.'

This time both of the Vatican's boys left the room. Perhaps they'd decided he wasn't going to try to make a break for it or hang himself in the shower. There was no way he could get back into the TV show, so he clicked it off. Of all the things in his world he feared, Hell and all its demons ran a slow second to Sadie Beck.

Now she's dyin'.

Sitting east of downtown Atlanta, Little Five Points' streets had its share of traffic, on foot or otherwise. Today was no different. As Riley headed towards the rendezvous point a mare pulling a cart rolled past, followed by a carriage and then a rusty Datsun with a do-it-yourself solar panel on its roof. Gas had grown so expensive that folks took mass transit, went horse-drawn or augmented their rides with the panels to offset the cost. Trappers had little choice in the matter – if they caught bigger demons, hauling them around in a wagon or on a city bus wasn't an option. They paid the going rate for the fuel and bitched a lot.

Despite the incredible disguise Mort had cooked up for

her, Riley's nerves jittered around like a ten-cup-a-day coffee addict. At any moment she expected sleek black demon hunter vans to screech to a halt and dudes in paramilitary garb to pour out on to the street. Then she'd be in a world of hurt.

What do they do to people who sleep with angels? She doubted if it was a slap on the wrist and a lecture about morality. *I'll just have to keep on the run until they go back to Rome.* She'd have to find a job that paid cash under the table. In short, her life was toast.

To short circuit her worrying, Riley strolled through one of the secondhand shops. If she was going to leave Atlanta, she needed some clothes.

A few people noticed her, but none of them posed a threat. One girl about her own age gave her a thumbs up and called out, 'Wicked!' Riley grinned. She'd never been one of the cool kids in school, not with both parents being teachers.

As she strolled down through the bins of used clothes, she spied a grey hoody with a cool winged design on the front. She checked the price – two dollars – and held it up against her to test the size. *That works.* A few bins later she found a black backpack. She loved her messenger bag, but it wasn't doing the trick as everything ended up in a jumble at the bottom of the thing. That was annoying if she was hunting for her lip gloss. It was dangerous when she was fumbling for a Holy Water sphere to lob at a demon, especially when every second counted. *Like I'll ever be able to trap again.* She pushed that gloomy thought aside.

Riley checked her wallet and bartered the price down to five bucks for both items. Once outside the shop there was no sign of Peter, so she moved her belongings from one pack to the other, including her father's research into the history of Holy Water. As she held the sheaf of papers, it made her smile. No matter if he was reanimate or not, Paul Blackthorne would always be an academic.

At the bottom of her messenger bag she found the chamois pouch her witch friend Ayden had given her. She'd forgotten about that. Ayden had said she should put items into it that mattered to her. Right now it only held a little dirt from her father's grave. Once everything was transferred to the new backpack, she folded up the messenger bag and crammed it inside. When she left Atlanta, she'd need both to carry her stuff.

Riley scanned the street again. There were no hunter vans, but now Peter King sat on a brick wall near a tattoo parlour, studying something on his cellphone. She crossed the street and sat about ten feet away from him. He shot her a quick look and went back to texting someone on his phone.

If her best friend didn't recognize her, this whole magic thing might work.

Peter looked different too, scruffier and less nerdy, though nothing as dramatic as her transformation, and he wasn't wearing his glasses, which suggested he'd finally got a pair of contacts. His brown hair was spikier now, something his mother never would have let him get away with. She'd moved out of the house and back to Illinois, leaving Peter's dad in charge, and that seemed to have been a catalyst for a few changes.

Though she was eager to talk to him, Riley scouted the area again. Once she was reasonably sure her friend hadn't been followed, she moved closer to him. Peter gave her a longer look this time and frowned. It had to be because of all her body jewellery.

'Hi,' she said, lowering her voice below what was normal for her. It made her sound like she had a cold.

'Hi,' he replied, then returned to his phone.

Score one for Mort.

'Peter?' she said in her usual voice. His eyes whipped back to her. 'What do you think of the new Riley?' she asked, teasingly.

His eyebrows shot up. 'Whoa! Get out of here. Have you seen yourself in a mirror?'

She stuck out her tongue, knowing what he'd do next.

'Oh, God,' he said, grimacing. 'You know I hate tongue studs. I can't believe you got one. And your hair is awful.'

Riley laughed and moved closer to him. 'It's all magic. I have this bracelet that does it. I take it off and I'm me again.'

'You're joking, right? No, you're not. So where have you been hiding?'

She leaned over and whispered the location in his ear.

'He's the necro who helped you with the magic?' She nodded. 'Well, it works.' Peter frowned. 'Is that a tattoo of a vampire bat on your neck?'

'Yup. Admit it – it's cool.'

'Yeah, it is,' he said grudgingly.

She did a quick look around. 'I found my dad. He's at Mort's.'

'Go you!' Peter said, and they executed a High Five. Then he quickly sobered at what that really meant. 'What's he like now?'

'He's sorta like when you've been up all night cramming for a test. There's moments of brilliance followed by long stretches of totally zoned.'

'That sucks.' Peter rose, stuffing his phone into a pocket, eager to be on the move. 'Remind me never to get reanimated.'

'That's two of us, dude.'

Chapter Five

Riley grinned at the role reversal. 'I could get used to this,' she said as Peter wove his car between two horse-drawn carriages. 'Usually I have to drive you around.'

Her friend looked over at her, made a face at her disguise and then returned his eyes to the road. 'Dad said I can borrow the car as long as I put gas in it. Which means I won't be taking it too often if I want a new computer this year.'

'Parents are devious like that,' Riley said. 'They give you something with one hand and then take it back with the other.'

'Why do the hunters want you?'

'I'll explain later.'

Peter gave her a worried look. 'You never stall unless it's something really bad.'

'That would be right.'

Belatedly, Riley realized the car was not heading towards her apartment. 'Hey, where are we going?'

'To the Holy Water plant we checked out the other day. We need to do a stakeout and see what's really going on in there.'

'What? I'm a fugitive from justice,' she replied. 'I *do not* have time to babysit some idiot building. I need to get out of this town.' *Before I lose my nerve.*

Peter shook his head. 'That's *exactly* what the hunters are counting on. They have to be watching every bus and train station. The airport too. And don't even think about going to your apartment.'

'I have to get my money. You know I can't keep it in the bank, not with the debt collectors swarming around.' Her mother's death had left behind a sizeable loan for her medical care and now that Riley's dad was dead she was the collectors' prime target. If she put money in a bank account, they just siphoned it off.

'If you run, they'll just hunt you down like a rabid dog. You need leverage with these guys, something to bargain with, and if we can bust that scam that will be your ticket to freedom.'

'But—'

'I'm dead serious, Riley,' he retorted, his voice rising. 'Since you're in my car, you'll just have to deal.'

She never heard Peter so intense before, and that told her he wasn't taking her anywhere he didn't want to go.

I shouldn't have called him. I should have just left town on my own.

'We'll do what we can at the plant,' Peter said, quieter now. 'If we're lucky, we'll get a break and then you can tell the hunters you busted the Holy Water scam.'

Which would be a big clue Riley wasn't on Hell's payroll.

The bogus Holy Water problem was a recent development.

Someone was substituting tap water for the consecrated liquid. Good Holy Water allowed the trappers to capture Hellspawn, at least some of the smaller varieties. Bad Holy Water = dead trappers.

'You're not giving me a choice in this, are you?'

Peter shook his head. 'Got to keep you off the streets.'

His friendship had always been rock solid. Would it survive once he knew about her and the angel?

It took time, but Peter eventually reached the recycling plant in East Point and parked the car in what looked to be as safe a location as any.

'If this ride gets trashed, I am so dead,' he said.

'We'll keep an eye on it somehow.'

Peter studied their surroundings. 'That building looks to be the place,' he said, pointing at a structure across the street from the recycling plant. It was abandoned, windows broken, the inside trashed. Perfect for their purposes.

'Let's check out the roof,' he suggested.

Claiming their gear, they trudged over to find the fire escape was missing. That wasn't unexpected: metal was worth money and, with so many out of work, scavenging a sizeable piece would be like finding a bag of cash on the street.

The sun was setting as they entered the building. The place reminded Riley of Master Harper's shop after the Geo-Fiend had trashed it. The roof was intact, but some of the interior walls had tumbled into heaps of broken bricks. Graffiti marked the ones that were still intact. As expected, the building stank of mould, dust and urine.

'Somebody needs to do some housekeeping,' Riley grumbled, nearly falling when a brick shifted under her foot. It seemed that every few feet there was another obstruction.

'On second thoughts, this could be a bad idea,' Peter said.'You saw all the needles and stuff, didn't you?'

Riley had seen those and tried to ignore them, though that meant the local druggies used the place to do their business. 'It's the best location to watch the plant.'

'Yeah, but it's not the safest,' he replied, no doubt trying to be the voice of reason. 'Maybe we can find another place.'

'No, it'll do.'

They'd had to work together to shift a large timber that blocked the stairway before they headed up to the roof. After they'd passed the first landing, Peter turned back. 'Hold on.' He began moving junk back in place. 'We don't want anyone to know we're up here.'

There were three flights and all were a gauntlet of debris. Finally, her friend shoved open the rickety wooden door to the roof. The floor underneath their feet felt solid, but they inched their way to the side closest to the plant with great care.

'Well, that's a good sign,' Peter said. 'No needles. That means the junkies don't come up here.'

'But the birds do,' Riley said, scooping away bird droppings with the toe of her tennis shoe.

'Birds I'm good with. Drugged-out crazies don't do it for me.'

It took Peter a few minutes to line up exactly where he

wanted to set up camp. From experience, Riley had learned to back off and let him do what he wanted. He had this organizational gene that had to be exercised every now and then. She'd never tell him, but she suspected it came from his mother's side of the family.

Peter announced he'd found the perfect location and began to unpack his backpack and large black bag. First out was a piece of heavy-grade plastic like you'd use for painting your house. He spread that on the asphalt roof, then placed a heavy blanket on top of it. Out came a camera and a tripod, followed by a notebook, bottles of water, beef jerky, power bars and his phone.

'You really are scaring me, dude,' Riley said, making sure to smile while she said it. 'Look at all this. You'd think you were sitting vigil in the graveyard or something.'

'I doubt any necros are going to be bothering us tonight.' He eyed her. 'So what did you bring? Lip gloss and a hairbrush?'

Smirking, she unpacked the sandwiches Mort's cook had made for her, along with an ample slice of chocolate cake. 'You owe me an apology.'

'Ohmigod, it's a feast! OK, you're forgiven.' He looked up from the food and grimaced. 'Your disguise is making my eyes bleed.'

The bracelet also sapped her energy. When she undid the snaps and set it aside, the relief was instant. *That's better.*

Once they were settled, they each ate a sandwich and divided up the slice of the cake. He shared his beef jerky.

Riley found she actually liked the stuff, and according to Peter there would be a side benefit – they wouldn't have to pee as often, not with all the salt.

As each truck rolled up to the plant, Riley recorded the times and licence plate numbers in her friend's notebook while Peter dutifully took pictures and video. Once the truck rumbled off, he would lean back against the short concrete wall and stuff his hands in his pockets to stay warm. After the third truck, Peter pinned his gaze on Riley.

'In case you haven't noticed, we are now on a stakeout across from the recycling plant. Time to tell me why the demon hunters have decided you're Public Enemy Number One.'

Riley wasn't sure how to start. 'They're after me . . .' she began.

Silence. He wasn't going to make this easy.

'Because of Ori. I met him at the market. He *said* he was a freelance demon hunter trying to kill the Five that murdered my dad. He saved my life at the Tabernacle so I believed everything he told me.'

'Is that the dude Simi was raving about?'

It appeared Riley's friends had been talking about her social life. That was a bit unnerving. 'Yeah, that's him. Last night he killed a Five at Harper's place and –' She paused.

Peter knew some of what she was talking about when it came to the different kinds of demons, but not all the details. Demon trappers ranked Hellspawn according to cunning and their ability to kill. Grade One demons were nuisances while

Grade Fives were so ferocious they could destroy whole cities It was important her friend understand exactly why she had come to trust Ori.

'A Five is really dangerous. It creates earthquakes and windstorms. The demon that attacked us flattened Harper's place. If Ori hadn't come to our rescue, we'd both be dead.'

Her companion frowned. 'Go on.'

She had to tell someone, and Peter was more like a brother than a friend.

Riley took a deep breath. 'I met Ori at the cemetery later and we . . .' Her voice hitched. 'We spent the night together.'

'Together like . . . *together*?' Peter asked, his voice rising along with both eyebrows.

She swallowed hard. 'Yes.'

'I thought you'd never. . . ' His voice trailed off.

'No, not until last night.' *Just tell him all of it.* 'There's something else. Ori's an angel, wings and all. Honest.'

Her friend stared at her. 'You went *horizontal* with an angel in a graveyard? Isn't that like blasphemy or something?' he spouted.

Riley's cheeks burned in acute embarrassment. 'Probably. After we . . . I found out he works for Lucifer. Ori's a *Fallen* angel and he's after my soul.'

Peter's mouth fell open in shock.

'Oh, and I got to talk to the Prince himself. He's one spooky guy, that's for sure.'

Peter's brain reengaged. 'You got hot and heavy with a fallen angel and then you chatted up the Prince of Hell?'

'Yeah. I owe Lucifer a favour so he doesn't let Ori kill everyone I love.' *Like you.*

'A favour,' Peter said flatly, then swiped a palm across his chin. 'What about the soul part?' he asked, quieter now.

'It's still mine.' She laughed bitterly. 'Lucifer didn't want it. He said I was better as a free agent, whatever that means. And I owe Heaven a favour too. That's why Hell came after me.'

Peter pushed off from the roof and stalked a few feet away, his back to her now. 'Please tell me this is all some kind of a sick joke.'

'It's the truth. All of it. That's why hunters are after me.'

'How did they find out?' Peter asked, swivelling towards her now.

'I think Beck ratted me out. I went to his house this morning and told him what had happened. He was furious, Peter. I've never seen anyone that angry.'

'Duh! Now *there's* a surprise,' her friend replied sarcastically. 'I saw the way he looked at you at your dad's funeral. Of course he'd be mad. You're about the only one on the planet who doesn't realize how he feels about you.'

'He never said anything,' she retorted.

'Hey, we guys don't blurt out that kind of stuff,' he replied. 'It's against the man code. Beck may never have said how he felt, but everything he did for you should have been a big clue. I mean, come on, how slow are you?'

She glowered at her friend. 'I figured he was doing it because of my dad.'

'Maybe, but the guy is really into you, Riley.'

'No way. If he'd liked me, he wouldn't have blown me off and—'

'Ancient history, girl!' he countered. 'You were, what, fifteen? Your dad would have torn him apart if he'd touched you. Beck had no other choice.'

'He didn't have to be so mean.'

'God, will you listen to yourself?' Peter retorted.

'You have no idea how much he hurt me.'

'Give it up, will you? You're my best friend, but you can be a real self-centred asshat sometimes.'

Ouch. That was the equivalent of a Peter backhand.

Riley blew out a long stream of air to gain control of her temper. Other than her parents, he was only other person who could get away with talking to her like that. Peter never lied to her, he never treated her like she was stupid, but he never cut her any slack, either.

Her friend returned to the blanket, so upset he kept popping his knuckles. When he ran out of fingers, he seemed to settle down.

'What will the hunters do to you?' he asked, quieter now.

'I don't know. Probably ask me a lot of questions.' *Or worse.*

'Beck wouldn't have called them. That's not his style.'

'He's never going to forgive me for what I did with the angel.'

'He'll still have your back.'

Riley doubted that. 'Are you mad at me for what I did?'

That was really important to her. She'd lost about everything else. To have her best friend turn his back on her would be a mortal wound.

'I'm not looking to date you,' Peter replied. 'How I feel about this is totally different.'

'That's not an answer.'

He tried to pop another knuckle, but failed. 'I'm not mad at you.'

God, I like this guy so much. It was a pity they'd never found each other dating material.

Peter peered down at the recycling plant, then back at her. 'I'm very worried about you,' he said, his eyes revealing that concern went heart deep. 'Too many things are going wrong in your life, Riley. I'm afraid I'm going lose you, one way or another.'

The tears came before she could stop them, surprising her. As she wept, Peter's arms went round her and she laid her head on his shoulder, tears coursing down her cheeks, wetting his jacket.

'I thought he loved me. I never would have . . .'

'I know.'

She snuffled. 'The deal I made with Heaven was for Simon's life. That's why he didn't die.'

Peter took in a sharp breath. 'Does he know that?' he asked coolly.

'No. He won't believe it anyway. He's sure I work for Hell.'

'Could he have told the hunters you were at Beck's?' Peter asked.

'No.' Only Backwoods Boy knew where she was this morning.

'Why does this feel like a bad episode of *Buffy the Vampire Slayer*?'

Riley smiled through tears. 'What would Buffy do now?'

Peter thought for a moment. 'She'd kick some ass, and look smoking hot doing it.'

'I'm worried you'll get caught up in all this, Peter. I don't want you hurt.'

'A little late for that. Ayden said I needed to be there for you, that what you were facing was off the scale scary, though she wasn't exactly sure what it was.' He gave a lengthy sigh. 'She doesn't exaggerate, does she?'

'No.' Riley blew her nose on a tissue. 'She's going to be totally pissed I was so stupid with the angel.'

'No comment,' he replied. Another truck pulled in at that moment and Peter let her go, turning his attention to the job at hand.

Now he knows it all. Well, most of it. It appeared that her best friend wasn't going to walk away and let her swing in the wind.

Please God, don't let him get hurt because of me.

Chapter Six

Peter needed to leave a little after ten, as late as he dared and not get busted by his dad. He tried to get her to come with him, arguing that it wasn't safe for her to be on the roof alone.

'It's not safe for me anywhere,' she'd replied. 'Not any more.'

Peter swore under his breath, then shot a look heavenward. 'Hey, you up there,' he called out, as if anyone was actually listening. 'If Riley is that important, then you keep an eye on her, you hear? Do not let her get hurt or you'll have me to deal with. Yes, that's Peter King in case you're taking notes.'

Any other time she would have found that hilarious, but Peter's tone told her not to laugh at him. She gave him the number of her new phone and after more fretting and fussing he finally he gave her hug, told her he'd be back at seven thirty in the morning, then took off. A few minutes later she heard the sound of a car starting, then there was silence.

'You're such a cool guy,' she whispered.

It was a typical Atlanta night in early February – cold and dark with stars in the clear night sky. The time passed much like it did in the graveyard when she'd been watching over her father – edging along like an arthritic turtle.

Peter's worried 'status check' calls finally tapered off after one a.m. From his hushed voice, it sounded like her confession had taken something out of him. She knew he'd never see her the same way. How could he? She'd hooked up with Hell and lived to tell the tale.

As the night passed, Riley see-sawed between two poles: first she chewed herself out for being so naïve, then cursed the angel for being a lying rat with wings.

I should have listened to Beck.

Weary from the mental self-flagellation, she dozed fitfully until a pair of addicts launched into a heated discussion about the fascist police state and how their individual freedom to get totally jacked on meth was being infringed upon. It involved a lot of shouting and 'f' words. Riley clutched a broken brick and waited for them to try to negotiate the stairs. They didn't bother, but eventually wandered off, leaving her in peace.

'Maybe Heaven does listen to Peter,' she said.

Riley would have slept through the next delivery if the twin slams of a truck's doors hadn't woken her. She groggily peered over the top of the low wall and found guys hurriedly unloading bottles into a huge wire basket on wheels. Once the basket was full, two men pulled it inside the plant. Another empty basket and even hastier unloading.

She tried to take a picture, then remembered the lens cap. After clicking a few shots, Riley fired up the video recorder and let it run. Nothing appeared out of the ordinary other than one of the men was extremely nervous, pacing around as he watched the street. As the last batch of bottles went into the building, she yawned. It was good her BFF was at home in bed: at least one of them would get a decent night's sleep.

To her surprise, the wire basket contraption appeared in the doorway again, this time loaded with bottles that were swiftly moved into the back of the truck.

'So what's this?' Maybe they were taking the processed bottles to the bottling plant in Doraville. It was open 24/7.

Though she felt it was a complete waste of time, Riley took video of the bottles being transferred into the truck. When it was full, the loaders drove away in a haze of exhaust fumes. She was too far away to make out the licence plate number. The whole operation had taken about twenty minutes.

Riley curled up in the blanket. As she fell asleep, she issued a silent prayer that she didn't have to stay on the run the rest of her life.

Riley . . .

The dream woke her again, this time near dawn. This time Ori's voice was clearer, more distinct. He was still at his post at the edge of the minefield, insistent that she trust him to save her. Someone else had taken Lucifer's place and that person's face was indistinct. Riley strained to identify the stranger, feeling it important somehow, but the dream ended abruptly. She woke to a cold and an aching body courtesy of the hard roof.

With difficulty, she sat up and leaned back against the wall, her eyes drifting closed again. In the faint reaches of her mind Ori's voice kept calling her name. Riley shook her head to clear it and the sound faded.

I'm going crazy.

Peter pulled up to the corner and helped her load the gear. Then he gave an exaggerated groan at her disguise. 'Tongue studs. I don't get it,' he said, shaking his head in dismay.

'I like it this way. All the effect, none of the pain,' she said.

'It's going to take me some time to go through the videos and the pictures. You should go stay at the necro's place until I find out if we've got something to work with.'

That wasn't in her plans, but maybe it was worth a few hours. 'How long will it take?'

'I have no idea since I don't know what I'm looking for.'

Maybe more than a few hours. 'If there is nothing we can use to bribe the hunters, then what?'

Peter sighed deeply. 'If there's nothing there, I'll help you get your stuff from your apartment and drive you to Chattanooga so you can catch a bus. I doubt the hunters are looking that far north.'

'Your dad will notice all the miles you'll put on the car.'

'I'll deal.'

He'd get grounded and then his crazy smothering mother would insist he move to Illinois and live with her. He would be screwing up his future just for Riley's sake.

I can't have him do this.

Peter was quiet after Riley gave him directions to Enchanter's Way. The silence was broken when her new cellphone rang, startling her. 'Hello?' she asked tentatively.

'If you're still in town, you need to come to my house right now,' Mort said without introduction.

'I am. My dad, is he—?'

'Your dad's fine. The hunters' have upped the stakes. You and I need to talk this out.'

That sounded bad. 'OK. We're headed to your place now.'

'See you soon.'

Peter looked over at her. 'What's up?'

'Don't know, but Mort sounded spooked. Something to do with the hunters.'

A short time later, Peter pulled into a parking place down from Mort's street, just like he owned it.

'How do you do that?' Riley complained. 'I have to circle the block for ages.'

Her friend shrugged. 'Always been lucky like that.'

After a moment's thought, Riley pulled a silver chain out from under her shirt. Tugging it over her head, she studied the pendant. The thick chain led to a three-inch black demon claw, the one the Guild's doctor had cut out of her leg after a solo trapping disaster. She handed the pendant over to her friend.

'Wow, look at this thing – it's sick,' Peter blurted. 'Where did you get this?'

'Beck had it made for me.'

Peter shook the claw at her. 'You still don't get this guy likes you? Wow.'

'Enough, already?' she said. 'Keep it safe for me. If I get arrested, I don't want the hunters to see it.' They'd never understand why she wore it, why it was like a badge of honour, a symbol of the normal life she'd left behind.

Right before she exited the car, she dropped a kiss on Peter's cheek.

'Hey, stay safe, you hear?' he said, his voice trembling. 'Let me know what's going down! I'll call you when I know something on my end.'

Riley waved and then walked away, not wanting him to see the tears forming in her eyes.

The instant she used the bracelet to open the rear door to Mort's home, the necromancer appeared in the hallway. He looked troubled.

'What's wrong?' she asked.

'Paul asked me to call Master Stewart. The news isn't good. If you haven't turned yourself in by nine this morning, the hunters will take Beck in front of the news cameras and charge him with aiding one of Lucifer's own.'

'What?' she blurted. 'He has nothing to do with this!'

'The hunters know that. They're just using him as bait.'

Riley slumped against the closed door, then immediately pushed away as magic as sharp as cat's claws scratched up her back. She might have issues with Beck, but he couldn't take the fall for her. 'I need to talk to my father.'

'He's in the garden.'

Paul Blackthorne sat on the stone bench in front of the fountain. He appeared to be running at quarter power.

When Riley settled next to him, he hugged her tightly. 'Oh, God, I thought you'd already gone.'

'Peter wouldn't let me leave town. Now with the hunters blaming Beck . . .'

She told her dad about the Holy Water recycling plant and what she'd been up to overnight with her friend.

'Something is wrong there. I couldn't figure it out. Maybe Peter can.'

'You'll work it out,' he said. 'You're both very smart. Just be careful.' He hesitated and then asked, 'What are you going to do about the hunters?'

'Beck can't take the fall for me.' *For so many reasons.*

She had to tell her father the truth. If not now, she might never have the chance.

'I . . . made a mistake with Ori. A big one. We . . .'

Her dad lightly touched her hair and that nearly pushed her over the edge.

He has to know why this is happening.

Leaning close, she whispered her dark secret, how she was no longer his little girl. It was the hardest confession she'd ever had to make.

Her father's response was to cup her head in his hands and kiss her forehead. His brown eyes searched deep into hers. 'It's all my fault,' he murmured.

'No. I listened to the angel.'

He touched her cheek with genuine fondness. 'You've been hurt so badly. I'm sorry . . . I should have let that demon kill me.' His eyes blinked like a sleepy toddler's. 'Trust Stewart. He'll help you. Tell him who . . . summoned me.'

'You sure?' A nod. Riley curled up with her head on his

shoulder, the scent of oranges tickling her nose. He was lukewarm, somewhere between dead and alive.

'I love you, Dad.'

Her father's eyes weren't moist, that was beyond him now, but she heard the emotion in his voice. 'I'll . . . always love you, Riley. No matter what.'

His eyes closed as he went dormant. She gave him one last fierce hug, then rose.

Her poor choices had put her on a collision course with the Guild and the demon hunters. It was time to pay the price for those mistakes, whatever that might be.

Instead of dropping Riley off in front of the Westin where the hunters had their headquarters, Mort found a spot five blocks away. In his own way he was giving her time to prepare for what she was about to face.

'It's probably best you not wear the bracelet,' he said, pointing at her wrist.

Riley peeled it off and handed it over, along with the cellphone he'd loaned her. She'd cleaned off most of the calls on her own cellphone so the hunters wouldn't know who'd been helping her.

'I'll contact Master Stewart as you asked,' Mort said.

That had been her other decision: to turn herself in before Stewart arrived on the scene. That way it looked like she'd stepped up to the plate, not been forced into it by the Atlanta Demon Trappers Guild. It was a stupid pride thing, but it was about all she had left.

Riley handed over Ayden's crinkled business card, the one she'd found at the bottom of her messenger bag. 'Please call her and tell her what's happened. I want Ayden to know.'

Mort studied the card with trepidation. 'You're asking a summoner to call a witch?' he said. At best, the magical relationship between the necros and 'those women' was an uneasy one.

'Ayden's OK. She won't turn you into a frog or anything.'

He raised an eyebrow as he tucked the card away.

'Just keep my dad safe. That's all I ask.'

'I promise I won't let the hunters get him,' he replied solemnly.

'Thanks, Mort. I mean it. You're awesome. You've been awesome since the first time we met.'

A faint blush appeared on his round cheeks. 'I do what I can.'

As the necro dialled Master Stewart's number, Riley crawled out of the car, not waiting to hear the conversation. Wending her way through the downtown crowd, she expected to be surrounded by hunters at any moment. Instead it was like any other day in Atlanta: people out shopping, going about their business.

She walked for a couple of blocks, checking out the shops along the way. They were located in parking spaces, the bankrupt city's idea of generating revenue any way it could. Tucked up against a place selling used clothes was a store that sold sacred items. *Holy Relics* the sign said. In between statues of the Virgin Mary, Jesus, Buddha and Kuan Yin, the Chinese

Goddess of Mercy, sat a pile of wooden crosses. They had a hole drilled in the wood and a long leather cord so you could wear them.

'Holy crosses made from the sacred Tabernacle,' the man called out from behind the counter. 'Blessed by angels.'

Somehow the enterprising shop owner had scavenged wood from the damaged building and fashioned it into crosses. If the wood even came from there.

Riley pushed through the crowd and confronted the guy. 'What do you think you're doing?' She pointed to the pile of crosses. 'Trappers died in that building. How could you do this?'

'Because my customers want them,' the man replied, nonplussed.

'No angels blessed these crosses. The only thing on them is trappers' blood.'

'Of course they did. I saw them on the television,' a customer retorted, then turned her attention to the shop owner. 'Do you have one about this size?' the woman asked as she indicated the required length with her fingers, 'but with the knotty wood in light brown?'

It was like she was picking out new living-room furniture.

'God, who do you think you are?' Riley said, balling her fists.

'It's not like it's hurting you personally,' the owner said.

'But I was there! I know what happened. I saw them die.'

'Sure, right.' The vendor said. 'Go someplace else and throw your hissy fit or I'll call a cop.' He went to help his customer find the 'perfect' cross.

A scream of rage rose in Riley's throat, but she swallowed it down. There was no fighting this. People believed what they wanted, even if it was a lie. If it made them feel safe, gave them a reason to ignore the truth, they were all over it.

Eyes blurring in tears, she turned to walk away. And stopped short. The captain of the demon hunters stood behind her, clad in his crisp uniform, his face pensive.

'Miss Blackthorne,' Salvatore said.

'How can they do that when so many died?' she said, trying to gain control over her emotions. They seemed all over the map now.

'The practice is centuries old. Did you know they used to make charms out of the bones of saints?'

'It's still not right.'

'No, it's not,' he said. 'Especially with what you've been through.'

She was instantly wary: this guy was too nice. Was this a ploy to gain her confidence, then spring some sort of trap?

'Shall we?' he said, gesturing down the street towards the hotel. They walked side by side. Why hadn't Salvatore summoned any of the other hunters? Slapped her in handcuffs and frog-marched her through the streets?

'How did you know I was here?' she asked.

'Stewart called me and said you were turning yourself in, that you should be at the hotel very shortly. I decided it was time to take a walk and see if I could find you before the others.'

'Why?' she asked, her suspicions increasing.

'I have my reasons,' he said.

'Who told you I was at Beck's house?'

'I'm not sure.' At her puzzled look, he explained, 'We have an anonymous tip line for demon spotting. The call came through there. We receive a lot of information that way, most of it totally bogus.'

'So it could have been Beck,' she said, her heart sinking.

The captain gave her a penetrating look. 'Why would he want us to raid his own home?'

He wouldn't. Beck was too much of a private person. He would have scooped her up and dumped her in this hunter's lap before allowing his personal space to be violated.

'Why did you threaten to charge him for something he didn't do?' she demanded.

'Father Rosetti has control of this investigation. It was his order.'

That still didn't explain why they'd done it.

The walk was quick and mostly silent. It was only when they reached the stairs leading to the Westin's front entrance that the captain paused. 'What do you think is going on in Simon Alder's head?' the hunter asked.

It wasn't a question she'd expected. Before the Tabernacle attack she and Simon had been dating and everything had gone just great. After he'd been seriously wounded, he'd come to believe that Riley or her dad had somehow conspired with Hell to destroy the Atlanta Guild. Simon's bizarre accusations had ended their relationship on a bitter note. In his own way, he'd sent Riley right into Ori's arms.

Instead of unloading her heartbreak, Riley shook her head, too weary to go there. 'Simon's changed. He was so nice and kind and now suddenly he's seeing Hellish conspiracies everywhere. He's nothing like he was before the fire.'

'Post traumatic stress disorder?' the captain asked. 'Or is someone playing with his mind?'

She looked up at the hunter, surprised by the latter suggestion. 'Maybe a little of both.' Lucifer had said something to that effect, but she didn't dare tell the hunter he was closer to the truth that he might imagine.

Salvatore nodded thoughtfully, as if she'd confirmed a suspicion. 'How do you like being a demon trapper?'

Another question she hadn't expected. 'I like it, when I get to do it. There's been too much . . . drama recently. That's not much fun.'

'I'll tell you a secret,' he said, looking around as if he was worried someone might overhear him. 'Being the captain of the demon hunters isn't as much fun as I thought, either.'

He's not playing nice. This is the real guy. She'd seen all the hunters as enemies, but maybe that was being shortsighted.

'What are you going to do with me?' she asked.

'Ask a lot of questions,' he responded.

'What if you guys like the answers?'

'You'll be set free.'

'And if you don't?'

No response.

'Got it,' Riley whispered.

Chapter Seven

After a night spent in fitful sleep, it came as a welcome relief when the guards returned to Beck's hotel room a little after nine. During all those hours he'd spent too much time dwelling on ancient history, most of which was littered with regrets, the kind that get a chokehold on you and never let go. Why hadn't the Guild bailed him out?

If they can't find Riley, will they let me take the fall?

The door opened. 'Come with us,' a hunter announced, beckoning to him.

Beck swung his feet over the side of the bed and pulled on his boots, lacing them with deliberate slowness while trying to read the situation. Was he free to go or was this the start of something worse?

'What's up?' he asked.

'Not my place to say,' his guard replied.

When he reached the hallway, Beck saw a grim-faced Captain Salvatore headed towards him.

'What's this all about?' Beck demanded.

Before the hunter could reply, he had his answer. At the end of the corridor, Lieutenant Amundson exited the elevator. The guy looked like he'd just won the lottery. Behind him, inside a cluster of four-heavily armed hunters, was a shorter figure.

Oh, God, they found her. No matter how angry he was at Riley, Beck had hoped she wouldn't have to face this. To her credit, she wasn't crying. In fact, her chin was up in defiance.

Amundson's booming voice echoed down the hall. 'Get that trapper out of here, now!'

'I'm not goin' anywhere,' Beck shot back. *No way I'm leavin' her on her own.*

Salvatore positioned himself between Beck and the approaching men, no doubt sensing the trapper's potential for violence. His hand was on his firearm.

'If you remain, it'll be harder on her. Grand Master Stewart is on his way,' he advised. 'We'll not question her until he's present.'

Beck eyed him. 'I got yer word on that, hunter?'

'Yes, you have my word.'

It was the best Beck could do. Grinding his teeth, he spun and then marched in the other direction. The hunter guarding the stairway moved out of his path in self-preservation.

The walk of shame.

Riley's fear translated into knocking knees and sweaty palms. She made sure to take deep, deliberate breaths to keep from spiralling into a panic attack. No need to look any guiltier.

The row of hunters positioned along the hallway was heavily armed, like they expected something bad to happen even in a downtown hotel. Beck had told her the guns used special ammunition that could take down a demon. She figured the same would happen with a human. Their eyes held no emotion, as if they'd seen all the evil in the world and it no longer registered.

Was this what Simon wanted to become? Maybe that was what it took to become a demon hunter – a close and brutal encounter with a fiend that forced you to see the world in only black and white, holy and hellish, with no room for shades of grey. If the job required selling out those you loved, her ex-boyfriend was all set.

A door opened further down the hallway and Beck exited, a dark scowl on his stubbled face. The front of his T-shirt was filthy, his jeans as well, like he'd been tossed into a pile of dirt. The look on his face was more than anger. Under it she read resentment and distrust, and all of it was aimed in her direction.

He and Salvatore traded words, none of which she caught, and then Beck erupted in a snarl and was gone, stomping away like he couldn't stand to share the same air as her. Her knees shook harder.

When she reached the room he'd had just vacated, one of the hunters beckoned for her to hand over her backpack. Salvatore had warned her they would do that, so she relinquished it without a struggle. Riley wasn't prepared for the other hunter insisting she lean against the wall so he could pat her down.

'It's not needed, Corsini,' the captain said. 'Secure her in the room. We'll wait until the Guild's representative arrives.'

'But, sir, Father Rosetti said he wanted to talk to her immediately,' the hunter replied.

'It will do no good. She isn't going to answer our questions until Stewart is here.'

Which was her clue to do exactly that. *Whose side is this guy on?*

'But, sir . . .' Corsini protested, no doubt realizing he was going to take the heat if the priest's orders weren't carried out properly.

'I'll talk to Rosetti. Make her comfortable. That's an order.' The captain turned towards Riley. 'If you need anything, let me know.'

Riley nodded. There seemed to be one decent guy in this shark tank. Unfortunately, he wasn't the one running the Inquisition.

As she entered the room, Riley let out the lungful of air she'd been holding tight inside her. After all the hunters and the weapons, the room seemed out of character. A sumptuous king bed, a royal blue couch and a large window overlooking the city. The morning sun filtered through the curtains. She noticed a tray on the desk, the remnants of the previous prisoner's breakfast. Next to it was a newspaper.

At least they didn't starve you.

Not knowing what else to do, she sat on the side of the bed. It was warm and the pillow had an indentation, suggesting that Beck had been here a few moments before. Ignoring the hunter sitting by the door, she stretched out, turning her back to the guy. The pillow smelt like Beck's aftershave.

I was so wrong. Even Peter thought Beck liked her, and he'd only met the guy once, at her father's funeral. Every time Beck tried to help her, she just pushed back, creating an increasingly unbreakable wall between them. Her way of paying him back for dissing her. Now she just felt like a stupid little kid.

I'm sorry. For all of it.

Maybe someday she'd get the chance to tell him that in person.

The raised voices outside Riley's door caught her attention because one of them had a familiar Scottish burr. *Yes!*

The master entered the room with a ruddier face than usual, like he'd been arguing. In his hand was her backpack. He didn't speak until he took a seat on a chair near the couch, then beckoned her over. Once she joined him, he gave her the pack. 'See if there's anythin' missin'.'

Riley dug through it, wondering what had caught the hunters' interest. No surprise, her father's Holy Water research papers were gone. Her cellphone was missing too.

She gave Stewart the news. 'They even went through my make-up kit.'

The master shot a glare at the hunter near the door. 'Ya can leave now.'

'Lieutenant Amundson said—' the man began.

'This lass has the right ta counsel, and that *must* be private.'

'Sir, I . . .'

'Out!' Stewart bellowed, and to Riley's astonishment the hunter complied. The door clicked shut. 'Sometimes ya just hafta shout,' the Scotsman complained.

Riley closed her eyes in an effort to calm herself. *He won't let them do anything bad to me.* If this had been Harper, she wouldn't be so sure.

'Riley?' She opened her eyes to find Stewart watching her intently. There were dark circles under his eyes, evidence that he hadn't had much sleep. 'Ya hafta trust me today.'

That didn't sound good.

He bent closer to her. 'We must talk very quietly now. We don't want ta be overheard. Ya ken?' She nodded. 'I wish ya'd come ta me first, but we'll work with what we have.' He leaned even closer now. 'Tell me what happened. Don't leave anythin' out. If ya lie ta me, I don't have a hope of savin' ya.'

Now she was really scared.

Riley took a deep breath and in the quietest voice possible she whispered all her secrets. About her dad and Ori and Lucifer and her deal with Heaven. With each confession tears began to build, stinging her eyes.

Stewart muttered something under his breath, shaking his head. 'I shoulda guessed Hell would come after ya.'

How would he have known that?

'Did ya give up yer soul?' he asked, his voice so low she almost couldn't hear it. Riley shook her head. 'Ya swear that on yer father's grave?'

'Yes.'

Relief lit the old master's face. He leaned away, tapping his fingers on a knee in thought. 'I knew somethin' was up, but I couldn't see it clear. Simon was dyin' that night at the Tabernacle, I was sure of it, but the next day he's on the mend. I wondered who had a hand in that.' Then he leaned towards her again. 'What does Heaven require of ya?'

He'll never believe me. 'I'm supposed to prevent Armageddon.' She waited for him to call her a liar, then leave her to deal with the hunters on her own.

Instead, the master sighed deeply.

'You believe me?' she said.

'Of course I do. Ya might not know it, but ya can't lie worth a damn. Besides, it all makes sense now.'

'It sure doesn't to me,' Riley grumbled.

'Anythin' else I should know?'

Riley filled him in on the Holy Water investigation and exactly what she had been up to overnight.

'My friend Peter has all the photographs and video. I can give you his number.'

Stewart pulled out his cellphone and stored the information as she dictated it. Then he leaned back and stared up at the plain white ceiling for a time, collecting his thoughts. She knew better than to interrupt though the tension was turning her stomach into tangled knots.

Finally he leaned close to her again. 'Tell them everythin' but that ya slept with a Fallen.'

'Even about Lucifer?' she asked, surprised.

'Aye.'

'They'll ask about Ori. They'll want to know what happened between us. There's no way I can talk about that.'

'I'm thinkin' they won't. Trust an old Scotsman's instincts,' Stewart replied.

'I hope you know what you're doing.'

The master gave her a wry grin. 'So do I, lass, so do I.'

Chapter Eight

They were kept waiting for another thirty minutes, as if punishing them for having defied the priest's command for a swift interview. If it hadn't been for Stewart, Riley would have totally lost it. To fill the time and keep her from worrying, the master had regaled her with tales about his childhood in Scotland.

'I started trappin' demons when I was ten,' he explained. 'My first solo trappin' was in a bakery in my hometown.'

'It went down perfectly, right?' she asked. *It always does for everyone else.*

'Nay, lass, the demon tore the place apart. I staggered out the front door, wee beastie in hand, covered in flour and bread dough. My poor father was stricken with horror.'

Riley laughed at the mental picture. 'At least my first trapping went better than that.'

The door opened and a hunter beckoned to them.

'It's time, lass,' the master said gently.

How many had heard those words over the centuries? How many had faced the certain knowledge that their mistakes might cost them everything?

Riley shot a frightened look at Stewart. 'I don't know

if I can do this. I'm so scared.'

He placed a reassuring hand on her shoulder. 'Yer a Blackthorne,' he murmured. 'Be strong and ya'll do just fine.'

He'd said exactly the right thing. Her father would expect her to be brave, to face this head on. *I'll do it for him.*

When Stewart moved at a deliberately slow pace, she matched his speed down the hallway, trailed by a pair of hunters. The room they entered was laid out like it had been designed for business meetings rather than a place to sleep. Three men sat round an oval conference table: Captain Salvatore, the brawny blond lieutenant who'd acted so mean to her and Father Rosetti, the Vatican's representative with his dark hair trimmed in silver. Riley took a seat and nestled her hands in her lap, trying hard to not look like a deer in the headlights of an oncoming truck. She wished her dad was here. Stewart settled in at her left. To her right was the captain. On the other side of the table were the dark-eyed priest and the glowering lieutenant.

'Miss Blackthorne,' Salvatore began, 'as you are an orphan and under age, will you allow Grand Master Stewart to serve as your legal guardian during these proceedings?'

Grand Master? 'Yes.'

'Then we shall begin with the paperwork that stipulates that agreement.'

Riley expected some long and complex legal form – instead it was one typewritten page that indicated that Stewart was the Designated Adult who would watch over her best interests during this and all future interactions with the Holy See.

She and Stewart signed on the dotted lines, then so did everyone else at the table, followed by the priest using an embossing stamp at the bottom of the page. He tucked it into a file with her name on it.

After a moment's pause, Father Rossini made the sign of the cross and intoned a prayer. Taking the hint from the others, she bowed her head. Riley didn't understand what the priest was saying so she made up her own plea in case God was actually listening.

You know I'm not evil. I made a stupid mistake. A little help here would be good. I really need it right now. And look out for my Dad, please? He needs your help too.

The instant the prayer ended, Rosetti pierced her with his cobalt eyes. 'Tell us of the fallen angel named Ori.'

That was the one person she didn't want to talk about.

'I met him at the Terminus market.' He'd been so ruggedly handsome, so kind and thoughtful it was impossible to ignore him. *I should have known he wasn't for real.*

'You do not seem surprised to hear he is a fallen angel.'

Riley took a deep breath and continued, 'Ori said he was a freelance demon hunter and that he knew my dad.' The moment the words were out, she realized that was a big mistake. She shouldn't have mentioned Paul Blackthorne and the angel in the same sentence.

'Was your father acquainted with the Fallen?' the priest asked, targeting her error.

If she admitted that Ori had been the one to claim her father's soul, this questioning would go bad in a hurry. She shrugged. 'Ori lied about a lot of stuff.'

'This Fallen, what else did he tell you?'

'That he was hunting the Five that killed my dad. That it was rogue and had to be destroyed.'

Amundson said something to Salvatore in Italian, but the lead hunter shook his head.

The priest continued. 'Why did the Fallen target you in particular?'

Riley didn't want to get into the whole *Hell is after me because of Heaven's deal* thing. 'I don't know. I'm just an apprentice trapper.'

'Yet you claim to have captured a Gastro-Fiend on your own.'

Rosetti's chiding hit a nerve. 'I don't *claim* anything. I caught it. I . . . got lucky,' she said. 'I should have been the thing's supper that night.'

More conversation in Italian. Did Stewart understand any of this? *He must be. He's not asking them to translate for him.*

The priest turned back towards her, his brows furrowed. 'Who destroyed the Geo-Fiend at your master's home?'

'The angel.'

'Why did you lie to Captain Salvatore and tell him it was Master Harper?' Rosetti pressed.

'Because Ori asked me not to tell anyone he'd done it.'

'Was Master Harper aware of this arrangement?'

'No. He was knocked out at the time.'

'Why would you do what the Fallen asked of you?' he asked.

'I'd found out he was an angel by then so I trusted him.'

Rosetti seemed taken aback. 'You *knew* he was a Fallen and yet you continued to have dealings with him?'

'No,' Riley retorted. 'I only knew he was an angel, not that he worked for Hell.' Her throat tightened and she struggled to take a breath. Sensing her distress, Stewart poured her a glass of water and placed it front of her. Murmuring her thanks, Riley picked it up in shaking hands. She took her time sipping the liquid, allowing her to think through what she would say next.

One wrong word and I'm history.

She set the glass down with a quaking hand. 'I was hanging with Ori in Centennial Park and someone bumped into me. It made me feel weird and next thing I know I can see Ori's got wings.' She shook her head at the memory. 'That pretty much told me he wasn't buying his clothes at Walmart.'

'Pardon?' Rosetti asked, puzzled.

The priest had no sense of humour. 'I didn't find out he worked for Hell until later.'

Amundson spoke up. 'Are you trappers so ignorant you don't recognize a Fallen when you see one?'

'Would you?' she shot back. 'It's not like there was a big X on his forehead or anything.'

'There are ways to tell who they serve,' the man replied.

'Well, nobody told me, and I'm certainly not a mind reader,' Riley replied. 'He was polite and didn't treat me like a child, unlike about every other person on this planet.'

A faint smile curved at the edges of Stewart's mouth.

'Apprentice trappers are not taught about the Fallen. It is assumed they will never encounter one until they reach master level. Clearly it's time ta revise that assumption.'

The priest nodded gravely. His eyes went back to Riley. 'Where is your father's corpse at this moment?'

Rosetti had unknowingly given her an out by specifying 'at this moment'. Her dad could be at Mort's or he might be somewhere else by now.

'I'm not sure.'

'Did you pledge your immortal soul to Hell?'

Though he frightened her more than any of the other hunters, she glared at Rosetti. 'No, I did not give up my soul,' she insisted.

Leaning forward, the priest rested his elbows on the table. 'You are the first female in the Atlanta Demon Trappers Guild. I understand that your apprenticeship has been turbulent, to say the least.' He paused for effect. 'Perhaps you were angry at how you've been treated by the other trappers and saw a means to seek your revenge.'

'I'm not getting you,' she said, wary.

'Was it you who let the demons inside the Holy Water ward at the Tabernacle?'

'What?' Riley replied. 'You're crazy. Simon almost died that night.'

'Ah, Mr Adler,' the priest said, shuffling papers until he reached the one with a picture of Simon and a lot of tiny writing. Like a dossier. The priest's attention rose from the document. 'We have spoken to him. He has serious concerns as to where your loyalties lie.'

That was an understatement.

'He was so concerned that he tested you with Holy Water.'

Stewart's attention swivelled her way, his brows knotted. 'Lass?'

Thanks for that, Simon. 'He wanted to see if I'd sprout horns. He seemed really upset when it didn't happen.'

'He tells us that you own a demon claw,' the priest said. 'Are you wearing it now?'

Riley shook her head, pleased she'd had the good sense to take it off. They'd probably just destroy it.

'Why do you possess a symbol of Hell? Does it make you feel closer to your master?'

'Harper?' Then it dawned on her who the priest meant. 'You mean Lucifer? Get real. I kept the claw because the thing almost killed me. I have the scars to prove it.' *Not that I'm going to show them to you.*

'You have to see this from our perspective, Miss Blackthorne,' the priest continued. 'You are in close contact with a Fallen and you often wear a symbol of Hell.' He paused for effect. 'You came out of the Tabernacle unscathed.'

'Unscathed? All these nightmares I have are nothing?'

'Compared to others, you are untouched.'

This guy's logic didn't track. 'Why would Hell try to kill me if I was one of theirs?'

'Perhaps it is to push you into giving your soul to the Fallen.'

That she hadn't considered. Had it all been a set-up so

Ori could save her and she'd feel so grateful she'd give him anything he wanted?

'Perhaps his seductions failed to convince you,' the priest added.

Oh God, they know. Or maybe Rosetti was trying to get her to admit what had really happened.

'What would that get him? I'm seventeen. I'm not the president of the United States or anyone important.'

'Hell corrupts one soul at a time. It is the Prince's plan.'

Then why didn't Lucifer want my soul?

'One last time – did you surrender yourself to Hell?' the priest demanded.

Riley's patience hit empty. 'No. No. And No. Are you, like, deaf?'

'Easy, lass,' Stewart murmured.

She pointed across the table at her accuser. 'He's not listening. I didn't sell my soul. I didn't get a bunch of trappers killed. My only mistake was to trust some guy with wings.'

'If you are unwilling to confess, then we shall be required to test you,' the priest concluded. Rosetti didn't seem very eager about that, like he'd hoped it wouldn't come down to this moment.

'Let me guess,' she said, her heart rate soaring in panic. 'This is the part when you put me on a dunking stool and see if I drown, right?'

Stewart shook his head in dismay. Riley knew she wasn't supposed to be this way, but contrite wasn't working for her.

She was frightened and tired and that gave her mouth a will of its own.

'We are not barbarians, Miss Blackthorne,' the priest replied coolly.

'Right. So that whole Inquisition thing was just a tea party?'

'Your attitude is not helping your case,' Salvatore cautioned.

She swung towards the hunters' captain. 'I've got attitude because you guys are *not* listening. I didn't give Ori my soul. That's the truth.'

I gave him enough as it was.

The cleric produced a small metal flask from a pocket. It looked like the kind you filled with liquor, but it had a cross emblazed in gold on the front of it. 'Put out your right hand.'

'No way. Not unless I know what you're doing.'

'Do you have something to hide?' Rosetti pressed.

Yes. 'No. I want to know what you going to do.'

'Please tell her what to expect,' the captain said. 'You're scaring her needlessly.' Salvatore's eyes radiated compassion, as if he knew what it was like to be on her side of the table. Did they test the hunters the same way?

Rosetti place his pen on the table. 'I apologize. I should have taken the time to explain the procedure.' It was the first indication that there was a beating heart underneath the churchman's cold, stony exterior.

The priest held up the flask for her inspection. 'This is

Holy Water and when it is applied to your skin, it will reveal if you are tainted by Hell.'

'It won't do a thing,' Riley argued. 'I handle that stuff every day. You're wasting your time.' At least she hoped that was the case.

'This is blessed by the Holy Father himself.'

Super strength Holy Water. Oh goodie. She looked over at Stewart. 'Do I have to do this?'

'If ya don't, they will assume yer guilty.'

'What would you do?'

'I would take the test.'

Perhaps the master had some plan in mind. With a sigh, Riley extended her right hand and tried not to twitch when the priest took hold of her arm. This was going to do nothing but make them look stupid.

A single drop of clear liquid descended from the lip of the flask and splashed on to her palm. Then Rosetti let go of her hand.

Yawn. I told you.

A second later a white-hot burst of heat rocketed throughout her body, causing her to cry out in shock. Stunned by the pain, Riley snatched her hand back. Embedded in the skin was something like a tattoo, but it didn't appear to be made of ink. About two inches in length and solid black, it was the image of a sword with flames rolling off the blade. It looked cool, but that probably wasn't a good thing given the grave expression on Rosetti's face.

'As I suspected,' the priest said mournfully. 'I do wish you had confessed when given the opportunity.' He appeared genuinely distressed at the discovery, like he'd hoped she was innocent.

'What is that thing?' Riley demanded, rubbing at it now that it'd stopped hurting. 'Where did that come from?' She'd never been into tattoos, couldn't legally have one in the state of Georgia because of her age.

'It is Hell's inscription, their brand,' Salvatore explained. 'Lucifer has claimed you as one of his own.'

Chapter Nine

Riley gave Stewart a panicked look, but the master didn't appear surprised at the mark on her palm. *He knew this would happen. Why do I keep trusting these guys?*

'Claiming her is not the same as owning her soul,' the master argued.

The priest readily nodded his agreement. 'The reaction would be profoundly more painful if that was the case. Still, she has Hell's mark upon her. They consider her one of their own.'

Stewart gestured. 'Show us yer left palm, Riley.'

'Why?' she hedged.

'Please, lass,' he said.

Riley turned over her left palm and gasped again. Embedded in the flesh was a delicately filigreed crown. 'Oh, great. Another one.' Desperate to get rid of it, she wet her finger and rubbed the mark but it didn't disappear.

Silence fell all round the table. The unsettling kind. When she looked up, Riley found the priest gaping at her, his mouth open in astonishment. He crossed himself and murmured something in Latin. The captain did the same. Lt Amundson's glare told her she was still on his enemies' list.

Stewart stirred in his chair, but didn't say a word.

'What is this? Am I, like, double damned or something?' Riley asked.

The silence continued.

'Someone tell me what this means. I have to know.'

It was Captain Salvatore who answered, and she swore she heard awe in his voice. 'The sword means you are in Hell's service, while the crown indicates you are in Heaven's. To have both . . .'

'Is seriously whacked, right?'

A soft smile came to the hunter's face. 'You could say that, yes. This is truly astounding.'

'This cannot be,' Amundson protested. 'This has to be Lucifer's trickery.'

'Is this because . . .' She trailed off. All eyes were on her in an instant. Riley shot Stewart a questioning look and he nodded in reply.

'Go on, it's time they knew.'

She took a deep breath. 'Simon was dying and so I made a deal with an angel. She said Heaven would heal him if I would owe them a favour.'

'What sort of favour?' Father Rosetti asked, dubious.

Riley opened her mouth with every intention of telling the truth, but something held her back. Whether that impulse came from the heavenly side of her heart, or the part Hell claimed, she wasn't sure. Her father had always said to trust her instincts, so she did.

'Just . . . a favour,' she replied.

Hopefully someone would give her a hint what to do when the time came. It wasn't like there was a book in the local library entitled *101 Creative Ways to Prevent Armageddon*.

'Does Mr Adler know this?'

She shook her head.

An intense conversation erupted between the hunters, all in Italian. Even though she didn't know what was being said, she got the notion that Salvatore was sticking up for her. Amundson certainly wasn't, not given the tone of his voice. In between them was the cleric. Which way would Rosetti rule?

Finally the argument ended.

Father Rosetti spoke to her in English. 'I am inclined to believe the lieutenant that this is Hell's trickery, however I do not wish to make an error on something of this grave importance. I must consult Rome on the matter.'

Rome? What if they summoned her to see the Pope? What if he didn't believe her? Would they lock her up in a musty dungeon forever?

Riley continued to worry the inside of her lip while inspecting the new additions to her palms. They weren't fading away, not like she'd hoped.

I'm going to look like a biker chick. That's so unfair.

As the hunters and their priest left the room, they were debating among themselves again.

Now what? Were they going to nominate her for sainthood or start chopping firewood like they did for Joan of Arc?

'Well done,' Stewart murmured, heaving himself out of his chair.

She frowned up at the master. 'You knew that would happen, didn't you?' she asked, pointing at Heaven's brand.

'I suspected it was there. It was worth the gamble.'

'Only because your butt wasn't on the line,' she shot back, then regretted it. She was mouthy today and Stewart had been there for her when it counted. 'Sorry. I'm a little spooked right now.'

'As ya have every right ta be. Worse case, they'll keep ya in custody until they feel yer no longer a threat.'

'How long will that be?' she asked dubiously.

'The way ya attract trouble, lass?' Stewart said. 'A very long time, I suspect.'

Grounded for life by the Vatican. Just my luck.

An aloof hunter dropped Beck off at his house, then drove away like it was no big deal. Maybe not to the hunter, but he could still see the imprint of his body in his own front yard and the black boot marks on the stairs leading to the front door. It was a safe bet every one of his neighbours had seen him out there, handcuffed like some punk-ass loser. For a long time he sat on his porch in the rocker, see-sawing back and forth in a fine fury. He was putting off the actual going inside part, because he knew it was going to piss him off even more.

How dare they bust into his place, even if they suspected Riley was there? Since when did they have the right to do whatever they pleased?

Ever since the mayor asked the hunters to come to Atlanta, that's when.

Beck dug out his phone and was about to dial Justine to let her know he was a free man when he stopped cold. Glaring at his cellphone, he tore the back off. Nothing appeared different inside, but the Vatican probably had technology that would make it look that way while recording every word he spoke.

As he reassembled the phone, he decided not to make the call. When he could no longer tolerate the suspense, Beck unlocked his door and went inside the house. The shattered drinking glass still lay on the floor in his kitchen. The chairs were moved around, the table scooted out of place. Someone had opened the door to his storage closet and rummaged among the trapping supplies.

Cursing under his breath, he went from room to room surveying the damage. More drawers open and stuff rearranged. Someone had thrown his Demon Trappers Manual on the floor. He picked it up, smoothed the wrinkled pages with reverence and swore some more.

None of this was needed if they were searching for a five-foot-seven-inch girl. They were messing with his head, letting him know how little they thought of demon trappers, and him, in particular. Since Amundson had been in charge of the actual raid, all this had happened with his blessing.

Beck tidied what was out of order, but it still didn't do anything for his sense of personal violation. When he finished cleaning up the glass in the kitchen, he broke out a beer. Then another. Eventually, he lined up a six pack of bottles and the opener on the floor next to the couch and began to work through them one by one. That would be more than he usually had in a week.

As he sucked on the brew, his mind conjured all sorts of plots. Had they bugged the place? Was his home phone safe to use? What about his computer? Had they seen his kiddie books and realized he couldn't read? Had they told Master Stewart that secret?

'Damn arrogant pricks,' he said.

All of this could be laid at Riley's doorstep. He'd done everything he could for the girl, trapped long past exhaustion to earn money to keep her fed and in her own place. She'd blown him off. Worse, she'd ignored every bit of advice he'd given her. Then she'd thrown herself at a fallen angel.

At least Simon wouldn't have gotten ya naked. He drained the fourth bottle and began on the fifth. His stomach protested at the abuse while his head buzzed like it was home to a hive of outraged wasps. Beck didn't care. He wanted to get so wasted he wouldn't feel any more. Couldn't think of Paul's daughter and that fiend together.

Another long swig. 'What's so special about that winged bastard?' he demanded of the empty room. 'Why couldn't ya have waited another year or so and then we . . .' The hand holding the beer bottle began to quake. 'My God, ya never gave us a chance.' Because, deep in his heart, he knew he didn't deserve her.

There was a noise outside his door, someone on the porch. Then a knock.

Beck ignored it. Another knock, louder this time. 'Go away,' he bellowed.

'Lad?' a voice called out in an unmistakable Scottish accent. 'We need ta talk.'

Stewart. 'Ah, dammit,' Beck said, rising. He stared at the empty bottles lying on the floor. He could hide them, but there was no way he'd disguise the level of alcohol in his system.

'Lad?' The voice was stronger now. 'Open this door!'

Beck cursed to himself and then let the man inside. Stewart headed to the living room and then sank on to the couch. His eyes took notice of bottles and nudged an empty one with his cane. 'Is that the first six pack or the second?' Stewart enquired.

'First.'

'Is the booze helpin?'

'Don't know yet.'

'Well, we'll get back ta that in a bit.' The older man looked around. 'First time I've been here. It's a nice place. Feels like a home.'

What the hell is he doin'? Instead of saying what he was really thinking, Beck muttered his thanks.

'Riley's still with the hunters. They're trying to figure out what ta do with her so they've asked Rome for guidance. It'll be a while before we hear their decision. In the meantime, they're treatin' her right.'

'Where'd they find her?'

'She came to them.'

'What? Why?' Beck demanded.

'If she hadn't, ya were gonna go down in her place.'

Ah, God . . . She turned herself in. It didn't mean anything. Stewart probably badgered her into it.

'Tell me about this Fallen,' the master ordered.

How much does he know? Did Riley tell him the truth?

Beck didn't care any more. 'Did she tell ya she slept with him?' he asked bitterly.

'Aye. I'm guessin' that's the problem ya called me about this mornin'.'

'Yeah. She came here and started wailin' about what he'd done to her. As I see it, she brought it on herself.'

One of Stewart's silver eyebrows ascended. 'Ours is not ta judge.'

'The hell it isn't,' Beck retorted, the booze boosting his anger. 'I figured she couldn't get into too much trouble with Simon, but I never thought she'd sleep with a damned demon.'

'A Fallen is *not* a demon. They were created by God himself, then took the wrong path. A lot of us are like that.'

'That doesn't matter. I never would have wasted my time with her if I'd known –'

Beck realized he'd gone too far, been too honest, but it was impossible to take back the words.

Stewart's face turned stony. 'This isn't just about the Fallen. This is about yer wounded pride. Did ya ever think ta tell Riley how ya felt about her?'

Beck shook his head. 'It doesn't matter.'

'Ya can lie to yerself, but not me. Paul told me how ya felt about the girl. I know all of it, so don't try ta pull the wool over my eyes.'

'Why do ya care?' Beck snarled.

'I have my own reasons,' Stewart replied testily.

Beck focused on the buzzing in his head. There was no reason for Riley to make a fool of him.

'I did what I thought was right. She should have listened to me about Ori. Instead she goes off with him. I'm not responsible for that.'

Stewart's eyes narrowed. 'As a master ya'll be responsible for every one of yer trappers, no matter what mistakes they make, and no matter how much of an idiot ya think they are.'

It was a rebuke and Beck felt it keenly. 'I'm not makin' master – we both know that.'

'I'll be the one making that decision, ya hear?' the Scotsman retorted. He took a deep breath to steady his temper. 'That reporter, the red-haired vixen. What is she ta ya? Are ya lovers?'

He meant Justine. 'Yeah, I've been seein' her for a spell. So?'

'Were ya with her when Riley called this morning?'

Beck groaned and nodded. This guy could read him like a book.

The frown on Stewart's face could have been chiselled in

stone. 'Did ya tell the reporter anythin' about the Fallen?'

'I asked Justine about Ori a while back. I wanted to see if she could find out something, since nobody around here knew him.'

'I see. Well, in the meantime, ya be careful what ya say around the woman, ya ken?'

Beck's temper grew. 'There's nothin' wrong with Justine. She's been straight with me all along.'

'That may be true, but watch yer tongue. That's an order.'

Beck heaved himself to his feet, his head still spinning. He'd had enough of the old master. 'Is that it?'

Stewart rose as well. 'Go talk ta Roscoe Clement,' he said. 'He tried ta purchase demons from Riley at a dear price, which meant he had a buyer all lined up, one that wasn't legal. No need ta be polite with him. We need answers.'

That sounded like a plan: Beck was in the mood to thump some skulls.

To his astonishment, Stewart clapped him on the shoulder. 'We'll make it out of this yet, lad. Now get sober. Stop tryin' ta drink away yer problems. I been there and it doesn't work.'

'Then why do ya carry that flask of whisky all the time?' Beck asked before he could catch himself.

The Scotsman smirked. 'Because it's better than drinkin' the whole damned bottle.'

Chapter Ten

Sitting on the kerb across from Roscoe's shop, Beck waited for the store to close. He'd expected the place to stay open until much later, but apparently Wednesday evenings weren't a big night for sales. As he waited he kept thinking of Riley, what it must be like for her to be with the hunters. Though Stewart had said they were treating her well, she had to be frightened. What if they found her guilty of some crime? What did they do to people like her?

Beck ran a hand through his hair. *No way I can handle all this.* He forced himself to focus on what Stewart required of him. That meant working over the guy who owned the shop across the street.

If a human could be lower than a cockroach, it'd be Roscoe Clement. It didn't trouble Beck that the perv owned a shop that sold adult videos: people had to make a living somehow. What bugged him was that the guy held a demon-trafficker's licence. Money had crossed palms for that travesty.

There was another reason the sleaze was on his radar: When Riley had come to sell him a few of the smaller demons, Roscoe had hit on her, tried to talk her into starring in one of his movies. No matter how angry Beck was at Paul's daughter, no one had a right to do that and keep breathing.

A pair of employees exited, talking back and forth as they headed down Peachtree Street. If Beck was lucky, that would leave their boss alone. He had thought of using his steel pipe to get what he wanted, but that was anger talking. The sleaze was a coward: All he had to do was get in the guy's face and Roscoe would squeal.

When his quarry didn't make an appearance, Beck put through a quick call to Master Stewart's house and received the same answer he'd received two hours earlier – Riley was still in the hunter's custody. That wasn't what he wanted to hear.

Beck had barely hung up when his phone began to oink like an agitated pig. He snarled – one of the hunters had erased his *Georgia on My Mind* ringtone and sent him another message in the process.

'Beck.'

'You sound upset. What is going on?' a soft voice enquired.

Justine. 'Nothin' much. I'm out gettin' some air,' Beck said, 'What're ya up to?'

'Missing you,' she said. He smiled at that. 'Did you like the article?'

Ah damn. He was afraid she'd ask about that and he'd only managed to get through a few paragraphs and that had taken him forever. 'Didn't get a chance to read it,' he fibbed. 'It's been kinda crazy.'

She didn't miss a beat. 'I heard the hunters don't know exactly what to do with Riley Blackthorne. Some think she is working for Hell, others aren't so sure.'

Stewart's warning replayed in his head. Justine was *too* plugged in for Beck's liking, though he shouldn't have been surprised.

'All I know is that they haven't set her free yet,' Beck replied.

'Will I see you later?' Her tone was more seductive now.

Beck knew he'd like that. A lot. 'Not keen to go to that hotel again,' he admitted.

'I make house calls,' she offered.

That was a no-go. He didn't have girls in his place. Well, Paul's daughter had been there, but that was different. 'I'll have to give ya a call.'

'I see.' Justine could execute a verbal pout with the best of them. 'Are you tired of me already?'

'No. Got somethin' goin' down.'

'May I join you? I'd love to watch you trapping.'

Before Beck could answer, a door opened and Roscoe stepped outside.

'Ah, not a good idea, sorry. I gotta go. Things are heatin' up here.'

'Hope to see you later,' Justine replied. 'I am missing you.' Then Beck was listening to a dial tone.

Missin' ya too, honey girl. Even if Stewart thinks yer not on the level.

Beck was across the street before Roscoe finished the locking up. He purposely didn't give the jerk a chance to turn around, but rammed him face first against the glass door.

Luckily the impact didn't set off the alarm.

'Evenin', Roscoe,' he said, loading his voice with unspoken threats.

'I don't have any money!' the man cried out, shaking. 'I already made the deposit.'

'I'm not here for money.'

'Beck? Is that you? Why did you scare me like that?'

If ya think that's scary . . .

Beck flipped the guy round and got in his face. His nose wrinkled in disgust: Roscoe smelt of pungent aftershave, like he was headed to a date.

'The Guild wants to know who yer sellin' the demons to.'

Roscoe blinked rapidly. 'It's . . . it's all in my records,' he stammered.

'Not those, dumbass. The ones ya sell under the table.'

Roscoe's florid face went ashen. 'I do everything legal.'

Beck gave Roscoe a shake that rattled the loser's teeth. 'Wrong answer, try again. And, so ya know, I'm way past bein' polite, Roscoe.'

'Can't say. Don't dare,' the man panted.

What now? In the past a little more pain therapy would have done the trick, but this time was different. Maybe it was better to work on Roscoe's mind instead of his bones.

Beck backed off. 'Well then, sorry it's come to this,' he said. 'I'll be sure to send flowers to yer funeral.' He turned and began to walk away, hoping his gamble would work.

'What do you mean? Hey! Stop!' Roscoe called out.

Beck paused and then took his time turning round. 'I'm

sayin' that I was yer only chance. It'll be up to the boys from Rome now. They don't give a damn about who ya've got watchin' yer back.'

'They can't touch me!' Roscoe shouted.

'They don't care, man,' Beck said, moving closer now. 'If yer lucky, they'll close yer little smut shop here. If they're really pissed, ya'll be six feet under and no one is gonna miss yer ass.'

Roscoe's face was sweaty now. 'For God's sake, don't do this,' he pleaded. 'Tell them I don't know anything.'

'Can't do that, Roscoe.'

The man's eyes darted left and right, looking for a way to escape.

'Ya run, it's gonna hurt, Roscoe. Talk to me. I can see yer in over yer head.'

The shop owner stared up at him. 'You know what's going on?'

'Some of it,' Beck said, trying to sound reassuring, though he really didn't have much of a clue what was really going down.

Roscoe sagged against the door like his bones had turned to jelly. 'This guy came to the shop and told me he'd pay a lot of money for demons. He wanted all he could get. Ones and up.'

'What'd he look like?'

'About your height with dark brown hair.'

'That's about every guy in this city. Ya gotta do better than that.'

'There was nothing special about him,' Roscoe complained. 'I'd drive to a different place each time. Empty parking lots, mostly. He'd show up in a truck, take the demons and give me cash.'

'Any idea where he went with them?' A shake of the head. 'How many did ya sell to him?'

'Why does it matter?' When Beck took a menacing step forward, Roscoe cowered. 'About thirty of the Threes, a dozen or so Twos and a few Ones. I've heard some of the other traffickers sold the same amounts.'

Beck whistled under his breath. 'That's a helluva lot of demons.'

The system was always straightforward: the trappers sold the fiends to the demon traffickers. Both sides of the deal received paperwork to show it was all legal. The trafficker then sold the demons to the Catholic Church, in bulk. But trying to sell fiends without the proper paperwork earned you jail time and a huge federal fine.

'Why would some guy pay way more than the goin' rate for a buttload of demons? What is he doin' with them?'

'Don't know. Don't care,' Roscoe said. 'I need the money. You think running this kind of business is cheap? There's lots of bribes to pay.'

Beck took a quick look around. Folks were going about their business, like they didn't care if Roscoe went down. 'What about the fake Holy Water? What do ya know about that?'

Roscoe frowned and shook his head. 'Fake Holy Water? Why would someone do that? That's dumb.'

The sleaze didn't know about the scam.

'One last thing –' In a heartbeat Roscoe was off his feet and rammed up against the door. The jarring impact set off the security alarm and drenched them in floodlights.

'If ya ever try to roll Paul Blackthorne's daughter again,' Beck bellowed inches from the man's ear, 'I will feed ya to a Three, a chunk at a time. Ya got that?'

Roscoe wilted. 'No, no, I won't do it again. I promise.'

The moment Beck released him, the loser went into a heap on the ground, quivering in terror.

Beck methodically wiped his hands on his jeans, like he'd touched something toxic. 'Thanks, Roscoe. The Guild appreciates yer help.'

'You'll square it with the hunters?' the man whined.

'Sure.'

If I remember to talk to 'em.

When voices woke Riley out of a tormented sleep, she pulled herself up in the bed, disorientated. The room was dark except for a glowing red light on the ceiling. For an instant she thought it was a demon preparing to attack and *eep*ed in startled surprise. Then felt foolish.

You dork. It's a smoke detector.

The mental fog parted like a stage curtain: she was still at the Westin with the demon hunters. A glance at the digital clock on the nightstand told her that it was nearly ten in the evening. She'd been their 'guest' for over twelve hours.

After a knock on the door, a young hunter stuck his head

in, his form outlined by the light from the hallway.

Riley clicked the lamp on next to the bed. 'What?' she mumbled.

'Come with me,' he said in a noticeable German accent. 'Now, please.'

The urgency in his voice made Riley scurry to lace up her shoes, then collect her coat and backpack. 'What's happening?' she asked, trying to finger comb her hair.

In lieu of a response the hunter herded her down the hall towards the fire exit. Another hunter followed behind them, moving with military precision. Voices crackled on their radio, echoing as they entered the stairwell.

'Where am I going?' No reply. What if they snuck her out of town without telling Stewart? Was this a one-way trip to Rome or somewhere else?

After a quick march down countless storeys, they exited on to the street behind the hotel. One of the hunters sheared off, leaving her alone with the German dude. His dark hair was cut short and his nose had a slight bump in it like it'd been broken and reset.

'Please, tell me what is going on.'

His attention never left the street as he answered. 'Near here there has been a report of an Archfiend.'

That explained why the hunter was so wired. Riley had never seen one, but from what she'd heard from Beck they were only a step below a fallen angel when it came to power. An Archfiend had cost her father his soul. It'd been that or his life.

That didn't explain why she was *outside* the hotel. As Riley was about to ask that question, Captain Salvatore exited the building, talking into his radio. When he reached their position, he gave a nod to the young hunter who promptly backed off.

'Is it really an Archfiend?' she asked.

Salvatore shook his head. 'Someone with a macabre sense of humour. The fool dressed up in a devil's costume and ran through the market in Centennial Park, setting off firecrackers and smoke bombs. People panicked. He's in custody now.'

'Wow. Fives are scary enough. I can't imagine an Archdemon.'

'Yet you stood up to a Fallen,' Salvatore replied.

'Ori didn't seem so scary, at least until I told him he wasn't getting my soul. He seemed . . . human, except for being too perfect, if you know what I mean.'

A nod. 'A decision has been made about your situation.'

Riley searched the captain's face for clues as to how this was going to go. He looked way grim. *Not good.*

'They don't believe me, do they?'

'Not completely, but the inscriptions on your palms pleaded your case to Rome more effectively than your testimony. We have received permission to release you from custody.'

What? 'You're letting me go?' she blurted. *Why would they do that?*

The captain smiled at her outburst. 'I'm as surprised as you. The decision came in record time: Galileo had to wait almost three hundred and sixty years for his reprieve.'

Did he just diss the Church? 'Then they've decided I'm not evil?' she asked, still not understanding the news.

'It's more of a wait-and-see attitude. Apparently the Holy Father knows something about these inscriptions that we don't. In the meantime, you are to be released to Grand Master Stewart's care.'

Riley cocked her head. 'What does that mean exactly?'

'Since he has agreed to act as your guardian in the eyes of the Church, you are the master's responsibility,' Salvatore replied. 'If you do anything that leads Rome to believe you are acting on Hell's behalf, you will be arrested and tried. So will Grand Master Stewart, which will create major diplomatic issues between the International Guild and the Holy See. If I were you, I'd try hard to stay out of trouble.'

'Stewart must have been crazy to make such a deal.'

Salvatore grunted in agreement.

Why did the Pope free me? Could Heaven have told him what I'm supposed to do? There was no way to know.

'So what does the priest think about this?'

'Father Rosetti initially believed you were at the centre of Atlanta's issues. After consulting Rome, he's unsure. Still, he fears you may eventually pose a threat.'

'What about the Nordic dude, the one with the attitude problem?'

'Lieutenant Amundson is very displeased.' Salvatore's smile grew as if he was enjoying that fact immensely. 'However, neither Rosetti nor the lieutenant dare contradict the Holy Father in such matters.'

What should she say now? *So long and thanks for not torturing me? You guys are awesome?*

Instead Riley went in another direction. 'Why do you think someone was messing with Simon's head?'

Salvatore studied her more closely now. 'It's been known to happen after a traumatic event. Hell seeks to exploit your doubts when you're most vulnerable. Just because someone is deeply religious doesn't keep the temptation at bay.'

'Heaven's the same way,' she murmured. 'They knew I wasn't going to let Simon die. They knew which button to push.'

'So it appears. We will be taking a closer look at Mr Adler. Perhaps we can learn who has been influencing him.'

'Why did you meet me outside the hotel?' she asked, curious.

'I wanted to judge you for myself before Rosetti put the fear of God into you. What I found was a young girl who was morally outraged that someone was making money at the expense of dead trappers. That told me your heart wasn't dark, or least not completely compromised.'

'So we could have skipped the whole anoint me with Holy Water episode?'

Salvatore shook his head. 'Besides, I wouldn't missed that for the world.'

Her cellphone was returned, followed by a business card. It was embossed with the seal of St George and the dragon and had his name written in Gothic script.

'Please check in with me every twenty-four hours so we know your whereabouts. I'll need a brief report of your activities to satisfy Rome.'

'I will. Thanks . . . Elias,' she said, hoping that wasn't a breach of protocol. The man had been decent to her and she wanted him to know she appreciated that.

'You're welcome, Riley. You will be taken to your apartment so you can gather what you need. From there Müller will drive you to Master Stewart's. You are to stay with him for the time being.'

Beats living on the streets.

Riley looked out into the darkness. 'You know, sometimes I wish I'd never seen a demon,' she conceded.

The captain sighed. 'Don't we all.'

Chapter Eleven

Riley's *I can't freakin' believe they let me go* euphoria continued during her ride in the tech-laden Demon Hunter van with Private Müller. The vehicle had more buttons and levers than a space shuttle and it was difficult to resist trying out a few of them.

'Are any of these rocket launchers?' she asked, waving a hand at a row of buttons on the console. Müller gave her a confused look, then realized she was joking.

'Sorry, no. Also, for all the money they spent, the stereo is third-rate.'

Riley laughed, liking this guy more by the minute. 'Guess it doesn't have to be good for all those Gregorian chants and stuff.'

He laughed too. 'You are not as I expected.'

I'm no longer the enemy. Whatever the orders the Pope had given the hunters had certainly made a difference to their behaviour.

Riley spied a thin band of silver on her escort's left hand. 'I didn't know hunters could marry,' she said, pointing at the ring. 'I thought you guys were all celibate or something.'

Müller shook his head. 'We are permitted to wed. It is

not encouraged, because of the danger we face. My wife understands.'

'How many of you are married?' she asked, curious.

'In this team there are two of us. Corsini is the other. His wife is expecting their first child.'

'You have any kids?'

The hunter's face lit up with pride, which told her she'd hit a soft spot. 'I have a son. His name is Ritter. He is two years old.'

'Too young to know what you're doing,' she mused.

'He will someday. Perhaps he will become a Demon Hunter as well.'

She studied him anew. 'That doesn't scare you?'

'If it's God's will, he shall follow in my path.'

'Like me and my dad, I guess,' she said. 'I just *knew* I had to be a trapper.'

Riley had always thought of the hunters as cold, calculating demon-killing machines. Now she realized they were like trappers: they had families and separate lives away from their work. They were so very human.

When they pulled up to the kerb in front of her apartment building, she expected her escort to follow her and wait while she packed for her stay at Stewart's. Instead Müller remained in the vehicle, talking to someone on his cellphone in German. From the gentle expression on his face it was mostly likely his wife. *What time is it in Germany?* It was probably like the military, the family answered the phone whenever the soldier had a chance to call, even if it was in the middle of the night.

Riley's home looked like it always did – worn around the edges. Once a hotel, now it was living its second life masquerading as an apartment complex. She checked the mailbox and was rewarded with a pile of bills and a notice that the rent was rising as of the first of April. If she was lucky, her dad's insurance check would be in by then. If not, she'd have to borrow money from Beck. That thought did not bring her any comfort.

He'll make my life a living hell. Which she so richly deserved considered all she'd put him through.

Riley held her breath as the door to her apartment swung open, sure the hunters had taken it apart. But they hadn't. Or if they had been inside they'd been respectful as nothing looked out of place.

The door across the hall squeaked open and her neighbour's wrinkled face appeared, crowned with a white head of hair. Mrs Litinsky was in a simple navy nightdress and wore a thick pink sweater. In the background a television droned on about the weather.

'Ah, you are home now,' the elderly woman said with a whisper of a Russian accent.

'Yeah. Sorry. A lot going on.' *How much does she know? Did the hunters say anything to her?*

'Mr Beck was looking for you. You know, the nice trapper.'

Sure wasn't nice the last time I saw him. 'He found me.'

As they talked, her neighbour's Maine Coon cat sauntered over to Riley then promptly rammed his shoulder into her calf, followed by a plaintive meow. Max always did that.

She knelt to scratch him and he leaned to her fingers as she worked the silky area under his chin. His purr engaged at full blast.

'Some men were here yesterday,' Mrs Litinsky added. 'Demon hunters. They were looking for you.'

'They found me. It's all done now.' At least Riley hoped that was the case.

Her first priority was to let her dad know she was safe, but she wasn't sure if she could trust any of her phones. She solved that problem by asking Mrs L if she could use hers. It was a weird request, but her neighbour didn't seem troubled by it. Sometimes Riley wondered if the old woman knew more than she was letting on.

Once the call to Mort was completed and the phone returned to its owner, Riley followed Max into the apartment, hoping her little demon roommate wasn't around. Trappers didn't usually have wee Hellspawn for roomies, but the Grade One Klepto-Fiend refused to leave. Since there seemed to be no way to get rid of the thing, short of putting Holy Water down at all the entrances, she let him come and go as he pleased.

The cat didn't go ballistic so apparently the demon was out ripping off sparkly stuff from her neighbours. Instead, Max investigated something white and rectangular just inside the door. With a flick of a paw he began to bat it across the floor. After distracting him, she picked it up.

Division of Family and Children Services (DFCS)

Riley knew it was only a matter of time before someone

in the state government took an interest in her living arrangements. She'd been too high profile, what with the Tabernacle massacre and the continuous coverage on CNN, for someone not to notice she was an orphan. Flipping over the card she found the lady had penciled a note. *Call me, please!*

Riley dropped the card into her backpack. Providing Armageddon didn't take out the world in the next week or so, she'd make the call. Until then, it could be safely ignored.

After a trip to the bathroom, she checked in with Peter on her cellphone. If the hunters wanted to trace it, that was fine.

'Hey, it's Riley. I'm home. It's all good.' Which was stretching the truth a bit, but that's what Peter would want to hear.

Her friend sighed in relief. 'I've been freaking, you know,' he admitted. 'So did they use the thumb screws on you?'

'No. They were scary and there were lots of questions, but they liked the answers. I have to stay at Master Stewart's for the time being.'

'Under house arrest?' he joked.

'Sorta. What did you find out about that *project* of yours?' she asked, hoping Peter would understand the need for discreet conversation.

He caught on immediately. 'Doing just fine. Master Stewart knows all the deets.'

'Got it,' she said, smiling now. 'I should go, Peter. Thanks for everything.'

'No sweat. Glad to hear you're not in a cell wearing

an iron mask or anything.'

That made her laugh. 'You're not the only one, dude.'

As the van pulled into the long driveway that led to Stewart's home, Riley recalled the last time she'd been here: Christmas Eve last year. Instead of spending the night alone in the apartment as her father trapped demons, they'd been invited to the master's home for supper. The house had been decorated for the holidays, including a huge Christmas tree in the entryway and evergreens laced through the banister leading to the second floor.

It'd been a magical evening. Stewart was witty and charming while the food was plentiful and really tasty. Even better, it was time spent with her dad, which was always precious. There were even presents; Stewart had given her father a gift card to a grocery store and Riley received one for a discount clothing shop. She'd used it for 'new' shirts and jeans. Never once had their host looked down on them as being poor, but had treated them both like they were family.

At the time, Riley had found it difficult to talk to Master Stewart as he seemed so much larger than life. Now, as she looked back, that evening had been special for a reason she'd not expected. It was the last Christmas with her father – three weeks later he would be dead.

After she thanked Müller for the ride, Riley ascended the steps to the broad wooden porch, her overstuffed backpack hanging off a shoulder. Painted in various shades of blue, Riley thought the Old Victorian structure looked like a giant dollhouse. When she pushed the doorbell, melodic chimes echoed inside the house. It took time for the door to open, mostly because Stewart didn't move that fast with his crippled leg.

'Lass,' he said, waving her in.

'Sir.' She gave a wave to the hunter and entered the house.

Inside there was the delicate scent of aromatic pipe smoke and the faint aroma of a previous meal. Roast beef, she thought. Now that she was here, she remembered the house with more clarity. Unlike Mort's home there were no pictures on the walls, only a long expanse of blue floral wallpaper with dark oak wainscoting underneath.

As Stewart stepped aside to let her in, the floor creaked underfoot. That was the other thing about the house – it had its own personality, much like its owner.

'Yer aware of what the Vatican requires of ya?' he asked.

'Yes. Keep out of trouble. Stay here until you tell me to leave.'

'That's pretty much it.'

Impatient, she blurted, 'What did Peter find out about the Holy Water?'

'All in due time, lass,' her host said, gesturing down the hallway. 'We've got other fish ta fry first. And that fish is named Harper.'

Here be dragons.

Master Harper had moved in with Stewart after his home had been destroyed, at least until he could find a new place to live. That meant he'd be here tonight.

'How much does he know?' she asked.

'Everythin' ya told me.'

'All of it?' she gulped. *Ori? Lucifer? Armageddon?*

'All of it.'

'Oh God. I am so screwed.'

'We'll get it sorted,' Stewart urged, waving her forward.

This was going to be just as bad as facing down the hunters. At least with Stewart present, Harper wouldn't leave bruises on her like he had in the past.

Her host led her to a room that was at least the size of Riley's entire apartment. She remembered it from last Christmas. There was a big fireplace with a Scottish flag above it, family pictures on the wall and comfortably padded chairs.

A cranky Master Harper sat in one of those chairs, glaring at her. He was probably in his early fifties. The lengthy scar along the side of his face was pulled taunt as if he was still in pain, but his colour was better than the last time she'd seen him. He'd been in considerable pain then, hobbling around the remains of the tyre shop that he'd converted into living quarters, trying to salvage his belongings after the Grade Five had completed its home-destruction project.

'Sit there,' Stewart said, pointing to a chair near the fireplace, which would put her in between the two masters. Riley sank into it, craving the warmth. The heat that had surged through her veins post Ori was gone now, replaced by a cold she could not tolerate. She wished she'd put on something heavier, like her new hoody.

Stewart poured her a glass of water from a pitcher and

handed it to her, without bothering to ask if she wanted one. Then he sat in his own chair, resting his leg on an ottoman.

Riley raised her eyes to Master Harper and found his were riveted on her. She braced herself for the coming onslaught.

'Talk,' he ordered.

His terse command set her off. 'You said I was twisted like my dad and you were right. Are you happy now?'

Harper's expression told her he wasn't.

'Yer not twisted, lass,' Stewart interjected. 'Yer . . . bendin'. Heaven doesn't take a stake in someone with a black heart.'

'Which is the only reason I'm talking to you right now,' Harper replied coldly. 'What makes you so damned special?'

Riley hitched a shoulder. 'I was an easy mark. Heaven knew I wasn't going to let Simon die.'

'I'm thinkin' that's why Rome let ya go,' Stewart said. 'The Pope and his people would know the signs of the comin' conflict.'

'Blackthorne's brat is going to save the world?' Harper chided. 'Then it's a helluva poor time for me to quit drinking.'

'Hey, I didn't ask for any of this!' Riley snapped.

'None of us did,' Stewart said.

'Tell me exactly what Lucifer said to you,' Harper ordered.

'It was more what he didn't say,' she began, recalling her surreal conversation with the Prince. 'Something's going on in Hell so he's testing his angels, trying to figure out who he could trust. Lucifer said there's another Fallen in Atlanta, besides Ori. I don't know his name, but I think he's been talking to Simon.'

Whispering lies her boyfriend had been *so* willing to accept.

'Oh ho,' Stewart hooted, nodding his head in understanding. 'I wondered why the lad had gone all paranoid on us.'

'I'll keep an eye on him,' Harper replied. His attention returned to Riley. 'Did your old man tell you he sold his soul to become a master?'

Riley gaped at him. 'How did you know that?'

Stewart muttered something under his breath.

'I didn't, until now,' Harper replied, smirking. 'I've always suspected it. Blackthorne changed after he killed that Archdemon. He became . . . invincible, and that's not the way it works. What did he sell it for? Sure as hell wasn't money.'

Riley's anger blazed anew. 'He bargained his soul to stay alive until I made master. That way I wouldn't starve.'

Harper shook his head. 'You're lying.'

'It's true,' Stewart said softly. 'Paul confessed ta me what had happened right after the incident.'

'Why the hell didn't you tell me?' Harper demanded, his voice rougher now.

'If I had, ya'd have pushed him out of the Guild. The only way he could support his bairn was by trappin'. If he wasn't doin' his job, Hell might have claimed him too soon.'

'You let him run around with Lucifer's brand on him? Are you crazy?'

Stewart glowered. 'I promised ta keep an eye on Paul's behaviour. If at any time he looked ta be favourin' Hell, that he'd gone dark and was usin' his master's knowledge for evil, I would have dealt with the problem. *Permanently.*'

Stewart wasn't talking about tossing her dad out of the Guild.

'You saying you would have killed him?' Harper asked.

'Aye,' Stewart replied simply. 'It would have brought me no joy.'

'There wouldn't have been any other way?' Riley asked, a chill threading up her spine.

'Nay. It's what a Grand Master must do, if needed,' the old Scotsman replied.

Oh. My. God. He might have killed my dad.

'Hell, I never knew that you guys did that kind of crap.' Harper shifted in his seat, clearly unsettled at the news. 'So why did that Five take out Blackthorne if he had a deal in place?'

'Ori said it was a rogue,' Riley explained.

The light dawned in Harper's eyes. 'Lucifer's losing control.'

'So it seems,' Stewart said. 'The demons at the Tabernacle were too coordinated. The Prince never wants his servants ta be that on the ball or they'd take over Hell.'

'Then who is commanding the rebel demons?' Riley asked.

Neither of the masters had a clue.

Chapter Twelve

Harper swore under his breath, obviously displeased with what he was about to say. 'If I kick you out now, everyone will blame the Guild for what's happening in the city. You're as dirty as they come, but I'll not take us down to get rid of you.' He cleared his throat. 'If the city's still standing once this is over, we'll have another talk, and you won't like what I'm going to say.'

That conversation will never happen. No way could she prevent Armageddon and both masters knew it.

Riley's phone rang deep inside her backpack. It was Peter.

'Hey, hi. Sorry. It's been sorta –' she looked over at the two masters – 'intense. I haven't talked to Stewart about the Holy Water yet.'

'Text me when you do. You *so* owe me.' He hung up.

'Yer friend Peter?' Riley nodded. 'He's a smart lad. While ya were at the hunters he sent over some photos and video that were really interestin'. The scam is pretty simple once ya see how it all works.' He shifted in his chair as his leg was bothering him.

'The recycling plant has a system: bottles are collected and then stored in bins until the labels and the tax stamps are stripped off and they're cleaned out. At that point they move to another set of bins in a different section of the plant,' he explained. 'Once there's a full load, they're taken ta the Celestial Suppliers plant in Doraville where they're refilled with fresh Holy Water, given a new label and a brand new tax stamp. Ya with me so far?'

'Yup.'

'Now the recyclin' plant inventories those bottles when they arrive and when they leave. So the only way ya can steal any is when they're inside the buildin'.'

'But if you take any of them, the count will be off.'

Stewart smiled. 'Not if ya replace them with new ones and put them in the bins with the cleaned bottles.'

Riley worked back through the logistics. Dirty bottles in, clean bottles out. Bad dudes steal some of the dirty bottles but leave behind new ones so the count is right.

'But wouldn't the guys who clean the bottles notice if some of them were missing?'

'Not if they're on the late shift and are bribed ta keep their mouths shut. Saves them work and they get some money on the side.'

'And as long as the count is right when the bottles leave. . .' she mused.

'Everybody is happy. The counterfeiters have bottles with legitimate tax stamps on them. All they need ta do is fill them with tap water and reprint the labels so the consecration dates are current. Then sell them and make a killin'.'

'Why not just steal the stamps from the city or Celestial Supplies?'

'A lot harder to do – the revenue types keep close control of them because they want every penny now that the city is bankrupt.'

'My dad was right all along. He knew something was wrong with the Holy Water.'

'Aye, he saw it before the rest of us,' Stewart replied. 'He just didn't know how it was done.'

'Someone is making a lot of money,' Harper said. 'These guys will silence anyone they see as a threat. Best to keep your mouth shut.'

Riley wondered if her friend realized that yet. 'I'll warn Peter.'

'I already did, lass,' the Scotsman replied.

'We need to find out where that truck takes the stolen bottles and where they're refilling them,' Harper said. 'That'll require another stakeout.'

'I'll get it organized,' Stewart offered.

Maybe not everything was going wrong after all.

'Can we do it? Can we really shut them down?' she asked eagerly.

'It's possible, lass.'

Master Harper sported a rare smile. 'The payback's gonna be a bitch.'

The bedroom that Stewart had pronounced as 'hers' for the duration was the kind of room you never wanted to leave: the bed was mind-numbingly comfortable and the thick down comforter was the stuff of legend. After yet another shower, Riley burrowed under the covers. Despite the snuggly warmth, she was annoyed to find that her mind refused to shut down.

Her father referred to it as *cataloguing the past.* He'd always said that a life was like a book, line by line written as each day passed. Once those lines were on the page, they couldn't be changed.

So much of what had happened in the last few days Riley would have gladly erased. It'd been a rollercoaster of emotions: her time with Ori in the mausoleum, her meeting with Lucifer, the brutally painful confrontation with Beck and the sickening realization that deep down he'd always hoped they had a future together.

Riley rolled over and stared at the ceiling. *Why can't I stop screwing things up?*

That wasn't being fair. She'd done OK with the demon hunters and she'd helped the masters with the Holy Water investigation. Not everything was bad. But the parts that were never stopped hurting.

It was times like this she wished her dad or mom were here, sitting by the bed, telling her a story like they did when she was a child. It always made her feel better. All she wanted was one tale with a happy ending. Even more, she wished it was hers.

What seemed only a few minutes later, Stewart roused her with a knock on the door. She moaned in response. *Go away!*

Another knock, more insistent this time.

'Duty calls, lass! It's stakeout time,' her host called out, then his footsteps retreated.

She hadn't been in bed that long. *When I'm old, I'm going to sleep all day.*

A few minutes later she trudged down the hallway, yawning widely, her mind foggy from the heavy slumber. As she descended the staircase, Riley spotted a figure by the front door clad in a familiar pair of worn work boots. Beck's trapping bag sat on the floor next to him.

She froze on the stairs. *What is he doing here?* Stewart wouldn't send her out with this guy, would he? He knew what had happened between them, at least the Ori part. Even he couldn't be that cruel.

The Scotsman appeared at the bottom of the stairs. 'Ah, there ya are.'

When she reached the last step, Beck glowered at her like a constipated gargoyle.

The master ignored him. 'I need the pair of ya ta watch the recyclin' plant. If a truck takes anythin' out in the middle of the night, follow it and find out where they've set up their business.' He shifted his eyes to Beck at this point. 'Then ya will call me, ya hear? Do *not* go after these bastards alone.'

'Yes, sir.' Beck angled his head towards Riley. 'Don't need her. Just tell me where I'm goin'.'

Riley winced at the acid in his voice.

'I say it's the two of ya on this job.'

Her protest came at the same time as Beck's.

'Silence, both of ya,' Stewart cut in. 'Ya'll do what a master tells ya or ya have no place in the Guild.' He gave each of them a stern look in turn. 'Since ya'll be tagether for a few hours, work on those *personal* problems. Get it sorted, ya hear?'

He stomped off, his cane thumping against the wood floor with every other step.

Oh, crap.

Beck shot her another glare, as if this was all her fault, then disappeared out through the front door. She could imagine Harper pulling this kind of stunt, but the Scotsman? Did he really hate her that much?

Riley returned to the bedroom and layered the hoody on top of her shirt and sweater, then put on her coat. No way would Beck be as prepared as Peter had been and she wasn't about to freeze her butt off all night.

She clomped out of the front door into the cold night air and then down the stairs.

I don't want to be here. Not with you. Not after . . .

The ominous expression on Beck's face proclaimed his head was in the exactly same place.

Riley climbed into his red pickup then gave him the directions. Turning away, she watched the streets roll past. There were a few people out and some were clearly drunk, weaving along the sidewalks. As the truck headed towards East Point, the silence felt so sharp it would have drawn blood if given physical form. The beginnings of a panic attack began to manifest – the tightening breaths, the swirl in her head. She rolled down the window and sucked in fresh air as deep as she could, trying to think of anything but spending hours with someone who hated her.

'Shut the damn window,' Beck growled. 'It's cold.'

The next breath tightened even further. He noticed. 'Ya OK?'

Riley shook her head, trying hard not to let her lungs constrict any further.

'Need me to pull over?'

She shook her head again focusing on Peter and how great he'd been with her when he'd learned the truth about Ori. *Why couldn't Beck have been like that?*

The tightness slowly dissipated and it became easier to breathe. Riley rolled up the truck window and leaned back against the seat.

'Ya OK now?' Beck asked.

'Yeah.'

'What the hell was that?'

'Panic attack,' she said. 'I'm getting them more often now.'

He grunted, then jammed a CD into the radio. He skipped past two songs to the third. It was low, mournful, the message clear: I gave you my heart and you destroyed it. I will never trust you again.

Guilt was one thing. Being bashed over the head with her sins was another. Riley pushed a button and jettisoned the CD, which immediately earned her Beck's furious glower.

'Don't like the music, get out,' he said.

'Can't. Stewart said I'm stuck with you so I have no choice.'

'Yeah, well, same thing on this side, girl.'

The question flew out of her before she could stop it. 'Why did you tell the hunters I was at your place?'

'I don't what yer talkin' about.'

'You were on the phone when you drove off. You called them, didn't you?'

'No, I called Stewart and he gave me hell for not bringin' ya to his place. By the time I turned round to pick ya up, the hunters were there.'

'I thought . . .' She'd been too quick to blame him.

'Ya thought wrong.' He pushed the CD back in and the music drowned out anything she might have said in apology.

After what seemed an eternity of depressing country music, they reached the warehouse. The neighbourhood was as gloomy as it had been the night before. Primarily an industrial district, it'd fallen on hard times and revealed its distress in shattered windows and vivid gang graffiti. One place had burned and now seemed to be the neighbourhood dump if the discarded sofa was any indication.

Beck quickly manoeuvred the vehicle around until it was backed up into an alley. Only then did he get out, duffel bag on his shoulder. Poking out of the top of the bag was his steel pipe.

'Where were ya when ya filmed them?' he demanded.

'On that roof,' she said, pointing. He studied the location and then grunted his approval with her choice. They crossed the street and edged into the building.

Beck halted after a few steps. 'Ya didn't say it was junkie heaven.'

'Watch where you walk and you'll be OK,' she said, pushing past him. He caught her arm and she shook herself free. 'I know the best way to the roof, so stop playing the hero and let me do this.'

'Then go for it, girl. Don't bitch at me when ya break yer leg.'

Riley didn't break a leg or anything else by the time she reached the roof. Once Beck joined her, she carefully rearranged the debris on the stairs like Peter had.

'That'll make it harder for us to get down if we have to go in a hurry,' he complained.

'Yes, but it keeps the scary people down below.' *Except you.*

This time there was no sleeping blanket, no friendly Peter and no yummy food, just the cold, hard asphalt of the roof grinding into her butt, and Beck's hostile presence.

Riley leaned against the wall that faced the plant, crossed her arms over her chest to conserve body heat and tuned him out. This was Stewart's payback. Couldn't be anything else. He really couldn't expect her to settle things with Backwoods Boy during this lifetime, let alone the few hours they had to be together.

Her companion's cellphone began oinking, causing him to swear. He muted it immediately, then rose and walked towards the centre of the roof to take the call, out of sight of the street below.

Probably his squeeze wondering why he's not knocking boots with her.

Sour jealousy rose inside her, which she didn't really understand. Beck wasn't anything to her, not any more, and yet she was angry that a perfect flirty chick was working him over. *Don't think about it. It's not your problem.* She turned her mind to math equations: anything but picturing Beck and Justine together.

The math solution failed miserably.

Beck returned a few minutes later and settled on the roof again without comment.

'That was *her*, wasn't it?'

'What?' he asked, confused.

'Justine. She missing her bed buddy?'

He eyed her. 'Yer jealous.' She shook her head. 'Yer lyin'. I can see it in yer eyes.'

'OK, maybe I am. I don't trust her.'

Beck looked away, his jaw tense. 'Yet ya'd trust that winged bastard?'

'Oh, now who's jealous, huh?' she taunted. 'Ori treated me like I was worth something, not some stupid kid. You wouldn't do a thing for me if it wasn't because of my dad.'

'What? Yer not –' Beck began, then went quiet. His *don't go there* face appeared and that was the end of it.

A few minutes later the phone vibrated on Beck's lap. He answered the call without moving this time, which told her it wasn't the stick chick.

'Yeah, I'll check it out. Thanks.' He flipped the phone closed.

Beck did a quick peek over the edge of the building towards the plant, then back at his boots as if he couldn't stand to look at her.

Riley gnawed on one fingernail, then another. Her gut churned like a witch's cauldron and her cramps would have dropped a horse in its tracks. That meant she wasn't pregnant, right? That meant Ori hadn't lied to her and if he hadn't fibbed about that, then maybe . . .

Stop it! All guys lie.

The agonizing silence stretched on.

When Beck finally spoke, it startled her. 'Yer daddy's insurance cheque came today,' he said. 'I'll have to slip ya the cash. No other way to do it. If we open a bank account, the loan dudes will take it all.'

'Do I get a weekly allowance?' she asked sarcastically.

Beck's hurt showed in an instant. 'No. It's all yers, girl. That's the way Paul would have wanted it.'

'Still does,' she said, before she could stop herself.

Beck turned, his eyes riveted on her. 'What do ya mean . . . still does?'

Good move there, Riley. Oh well, he might as well know. 'I found Dad. He's safe, with Mort.'

Beck double blinked. 'When were ya gonna tell me that?'

She shirted the question. 'He's . . . OK. Well, he's still dead. Sometimes he's like he used to be and then . . .'

Beck's flare of anger faded. 'Does he remember ya and all?'

'Yeah. His memory's good, but he's not quite himself.'

'Why did that damned necro think he had the right to summon Paul from his grave?' Beck asked, his tone chillier now.

'He didn't.'

After that he kept peppering her with questions about her father and about the angel, but she refused to answer any of them.

'Then I'll ask Paul myself,' Beck said defiant.

Go for it. You won't like the answer.

Riley turned away and curled up in a ball on the asphalt, trying to sleep. It was too cold. Her mind went to the angel and how cold it must be for him in the cemetery.

Ori had placed a stick of dynamite inside her heart and detonated it, and now there were pieces of her spread all over. Beck wasn't helping her pick them up. If anything, he was grinding them under the heel of his boot.

The truck arrived a little earlier than the night before, and for that Riley was grateful. Beck was instantly on the alert, but it took her longer to move into a crouched position with her cold-cramped muscles.

'That the same one?' he whispered.

'Looks like it.'

Two guys hopped out of the vehicle at the same time the door to the warehouse slid upward.

'That's them,' she said, remembering the man with the giant eagle emblazoned on the back of his denim jacket.

It was the same drill as the night before, but this time Beck zeroed in on the bottles with a pair of night-vision goggles.

'Yeah, they're the ones with the tax stamp,' he said. 'Stewart got it right.'

Actually Peter had got it right, but arguing with Backwoods Boy wasn't worth it.

'Time to go,' he said, carefully moving away from the side of the building so as not to be seen.

The junk on the stairs proved to be their undoing. Not only did it make a great obstacle course for any druggies keen to check out the roof, it made their hurried departure impossible.

Beck grew angry at the delay and would have tossed stuff in all directions if Riley hadn't warned him about the noise. By the time they made it to the ground floor, the recycling dudes had finished loading the bottles and fired up their truck.

'Move it!' Beck ordered, taking off across the debris field inside the building at a near run. Riley followed him, but with more caution. She wasn't wearing thick-soled boots. By the time they'd reach Beck's ride, the other truck was gone. He began to curse, every fourth word an expletive. Any other time it would have been impressive.

'Just drive. Maybe we'll see them,' Riley said.

'I warned ya about that shit on the stairway.'

'Just drive,' she repeated, refusing to buy into his anger.

They took the main street and after covering about a mile in either direction, it was obvious their quarry had escaped.

Chapter Thirteen

'Dammit,' Beck complained, slamming a palm down on the steering wheel as they waited for a garbage truck to clear an intersection. 'We should have stayed in the truck, not gone up on that freakin' roof.'

'No way. We did it right.'

Beck flipped on his turn signal. 'Stewart is not gonna see it that way.'

'Where are you going?'

'Before I call the Scotsman and tell him we effing blew it, I need food and coffee. There's an all-night burger joint a few blocks from here.'

He's given up. Riley would have driven all over trying to find that truck, but he'd backed off.

'I'll come back tomorrow night. *Alone,*' he added.

Like this was all her fault.

As he pulled up to a stop sign, Riley broke out in a smile. She pointed at the truck chugging through the intersection – it was the one from the recycling place.

'Well, I'll be damned,' Beck muttered. 'Sometimes ya do get lucky.'

As the vehicle moved away, the licence plate became

visible. Riley scrambled to find a piece of paper and a pen in her backpack. 'Was that an eight or a nine after the one?' she asked.

'Eight.' Which told her Beck may not be able to read words very well, but numbers weren't a problem for him.

'Don't crowd them,' she warned. 'They'll see us.'

'I know what I'm doin', girl.'

They didn't have to follow the truck for long when it turned into a side street and eventually lumbered to a halt in front of a run-down warehouse in yet another industrial district. As if on cue, the building's overhead door began to rise at a crawl. To avoid being spotted, Beck pulled over and parked on the street a half block away from the structure, then turned off the truck.

Beck called Stewart with the news. 'Understood,' he said, then put the phone in his pocket.

'What are we going to do?' Riley asked, nerves taut. They were so close now.

'Nothin' until Stewart gets here,' he said.

This was a new side to Beck. She'd expected him to single-handedly charge into the place like a rampaging action hero, but instead he was taking orders like a good soldier. *He respects Stewart so he listens to him.* That wasn't a bad thing. The old Scotsman would keep him out of trouble, like her father had.

Once the bottles were inside the plant, the overhead door went down.

Beck shot her a look. 'Just tell me who summoned Paul, will ya? I gotta know. Was it that bastard Ozymandias?'

Riley couldn't go there. If she did, Beck would realize her father had sold his soul and that would crush him. He didn't have many men he looked up to.

She shook her head. 'Talk to Dad.'

'Why don't ya just tell me? This have somethin' to do with that damned angel?'

'Yes.'

He went back to his coffee.

When the trappers arrived, Riley and Beck walked to the end of the street to meet them. It was a small team: Masters Stewart and Harper, along with Journeymen Trappers Remmers and Jackson. The last member of the team was a surprise: her ex-boyfriend Simon. That had to be their master's doing, probably Harper's way of getting 'Saint' back in action after his horrific injury at the Tabernacle.

Beck did all the talking, bringing the trappers up to speed. While she listened, Riley couldn't help but notice that Simon kept watching her. She ignored him as best she could, but it wasn't easy. Their history wasn't the best, though it'd started out really good – they'd been dating, maybe even falling in love – and then he'd almost died at the hands of a demon. From that moment on he'd changed into a bitter, paranoid guy.

Stop staring at me!

Riley shuffled her feet to deal with the cold, her breath and that of her companions clouding white in the night air. As the trappers talked among themselves, a man wandered up to the group, one of the countless homeless dudes in the city. He was clad in numerous layers of second-hand clothes with a ragged red-and-black checked blanket on the top. His stocking cap proclaimed he was an Iowa Hawkeyes fan, or at least a fan of warm outerwear. Riley didn't want to imagine what it was like to live on the streets when it was this cold.

'You folks got any spare change?' the man asked, his eyes a piercing blue despite his unshaven face. The guy wasn't as smelly as most of the transients and that suggested he found a spot at a shelter every now and then.

Simon dug in his pocket and handed over a few dollars. Jackson added a five to the donation. Riley had a dollar in her pocket and she gave it to him. Then Beck waved the man over.

'Hang around here a lot?' Beck asked, and got a nod in return. 'That buildin',' he said, pointing down the street. 'Any idea of how many work there?'

'Five or six.'

'What happens in there?'

The fellow cocked his head in thought. 'Bottles in and bottles out. I ask them to help me out, but they don't pay any attention to me. I'm just another street ghost to them.'

Beck extracted a ten from his billfold and put in the dude's hand. 'Thanks. Have breakfast on me.'

'God bless you,' the fellow replied. Then he smiled, his teeth surprisingly healthy. 'Keep looking up, man. That's where the truth is. *Always* look up.' He shuffled off.

'Another crazy,' Remmers said, shaking his head. 'They're everywhere now.'

'Probably a vet. There's a lot of them on the streets now,' Jackson said. 'But then you'd know about that, wouldn't you Den?'

'Yeah. Just the thanks of a grateful nation . . .' Beck muttered.

Beck waved Riley to the side and dropped his keys in her hands. 'Wait in the truck with the doors locked,' he ordered. 'If this goes down wrong, call the cops and get out of here fast.'

'You be careful,' she cautioned.

'I will,' was the curt reply.

In the past Riley would have been pissed Beck was treating her like a fragile flower, but not tonight. She was bone tired and the cramps were still torturing her. Once she'd settled into the pickup, she dug out her bottle of water. After downing a couple of Advil, she leaned back in the seat to watch the action.

The trappers quickly made their way to the plant, then fanned out. Beck tried the service door and it swung open. He gave a thumbs up and the trappers entered the building.

Wish you were here to see this, Dad. In his own methodical, teacher sort of way, he'd laid out the groundwork for this raid. By morning the Holy Water scam would be history, and, if they were lucky, no one would have got hurt.

The first room the trappers entered was nearly empty, only a few wooden pallets and someone's motorcycle parked in a corner. The soda machine along one wall seemed on its last legs, its lights blinking erratically.

Beck cautiously crossed the open area, following the sound of voices from the next room. Flattening himself against the wall near the door, he took a quick check of the space beyond. He shouldn't have been surprised, but he was: it was almost all bottles, rows and rows of them. A rudimentary assembly line was in force where two guys traded off filling the jugs with water from a garden hose and then another poured something white into the liquid. Salt.

That's smart. If the liquid touched an open wound it would sting, making the user believe it was real stuff. A fourth man capped the bottle then set it near a card table where a guy with blond dreadlocks printed the new label. Once the label was in place, the bogus Holy Water went on to a pallet, ready to be sold to the clueless public.

Beck had to admire the operation: simple, efficient and dirt cheap to run.

He slipped back to the other trappers. 'Five guys,' he whispered. 'No weapons that I can see. Looks doable.'

'Then let's take it down,' Harper ordered.

Beck went first, quietly entering the work room then moving to the right, Jackson behind him. Harper, Stewart and Remmers went left, leaving Simon to guard the door.

One of the workers glanced up and froze. A second fell on his knees, babbling in a language Beck had never heard before. *We must look badass.*

The dreadlocked man at the desk rose. 'Who the hell are you? How did you get in here?'

'Demon Trappers Guild,' Harper said, slapping his steel pipe into his palm. The master was grinning now, and with the tortuous scar on his face it wasn't the kind of sight you wanted to see a second time. 'You shouldn't leave your front door open, you know?'

Then there was a brief scuffle as Dreadlocks made a break for it. Instead of running towards freedom, he fled into a nearby restroom, locking himself in.

'Ah, hell, I'll get him,' Beck said, aggravated at the hassle. He pounded on the door. 'Get yer ass out here!' No reply.

'Kick it in,' Harper ordered.

That's more like it. Beck put all his frustration in the kick and the door flew open and landed on the floor in a shriek of mangled hinges and the groan of abused wood. The guy inside the restroom gasped in shock, then ditched his cellphone into the toilet. With a quick flush it vanished into the sewer system.

Beck manhandled him back to Harper and reported what had happened.

'Who the hell were you calling?' the master asked.

'I don't know,' the fellow replied, shaking in terror, his face as pale as his braids. 'I was to call if something went wrong.'

'What did you say?'

'That trappers were here. The guy said that everything would be good, that we should stay here until he showed up.'

'Why ya toss the phone in the can?' Beck asked.

'He told me to.'

'Sounds like someone's going to pull some strings and make this problem go away,' Harper replied, frowning.

'Can't make it all go away if we have the evidence,' Stewart said, but he was frowning too.

A twitch rolled across Beck's shoulders. They were missing something.

'This doesn't feel right.' He gestured at the endless rows of plastic containers. 'Look at all these damned bottles. There's at least, what, eighty or ninety thousand dollars worth of fake Holy Water here, and no one's guardin' the place but one dude with a cellphone?'

Harper nodded his agreement. 'Beck's got a point. Let's clear out until we know what's up. Jackson? Get photos of this on that fancy phone of yours, will you?'

'Sure,' was the swift reply.

While the journeyman clicked away, Beck studied the layout. Why hadn't they used the whole warehouse? Sure, it was the portion that had the overhead door, but why crowd it all in this one section?

Another twitch skittered across his shoulders. He'd learned to trust it when he was in the Army, especially when he was on patrol.

Always look up. That's where the truth is.

The homeless dude's voice was so strong Beck swore he was standing next to him. So he did look up, feeling like a total fool for doing it. Nothing stared back, only the roof and the wooden beams. *What's that?* He stepped a few paces to the left, his attention caught by the junction between one of the beams and the roof supports. There was something up there. His eyes danced to the next beam. Nothing. There was something attached to the second beam over and two more over from that.

Beck kept inching sideways until he could see the main beam more clearly. Now that he had time to study it closely, he realized that a dark green electrical cord snaked down from the rafters and plugged into another cord that led to a small item nestled inside a bundle taped in place. The bundle contained a cellphone. The last time he'd seen something like that was in the war. He and his team had been patrolling near a village market and . . .

'Bomb!' he shouted. 'Get out of here!' The other trappers gaped at him in disbelief. 'Go!' he bellowed, waving them away.

The message got through and they took off at a run. Jackson clicked one last picture, and then sprinted for the door that led into the other part of the building. He skidded to a halt when he realized Beck wasn't with him.

'Come on, man!' he shouted.

Beck waved him off. If he was right, they needed more evidence than a few cellphone pictures. He hammered his palm against the button on the wall that opened the overhead door, then hurried to the desk. Grabbing files and sheets of paper, he jammed them under his jacket.

Behind him the door continued its painfully slow ascent.

The computer. He ripped the cords out of the laptop, and slid it down the front of his jacket, zipping the garment tight to keep it in place. Glancing up, he zeroed in on the dial of the cellphone in the rafters. It was dark. As long as it stayed that way, it was all good. Once the dial lit up and the phone rang, the detonator would trigger the package of explosives, then the other packages on the nearby beams.

If he was still inside . . .

'Come on, ya damned slow piece of crap!' Beck complained, pacing back and forth as the door's chain drive rattled like dried bones. Still not high enough. His eyes flicked back to the cellphone and froze in place. The dial lit up, bright orange as the call came through.

'Oh, sweet Jesus.'

Chapter Fourteen

Beck didn't dare roll under the door, not with the computer, so he ducked and scrambled out into the night. Feet pumping, breath coming in short bursts, he sprinted across the open ground as fast as his feet could move. In the distance was a knot of trappers. Some were laughing, pointing at him, thinking this was a joke.

'Down!' he shouted, waving. 'Get down!'

The first explosion's shock wave lifted him into the air until gravity kicked in. He twisted at the last moment to protect the laptop and that meant his left shoulder took the full impact on the concrete, driving the air out of him and sending a searing stab of agony coursing through his side. A second explosion rent the air. He covered his head and tried to make love to the concrete.

There were shouts and the sound of someone running towards him. Beck pulled himself up, crying out in pain. He looked up into terrified blue eyes.

'Beck?' Riley called out. 'Oh my God, are you OK?'

He nodded, though it was a lie. When he gingerly moved his left arm, something popped in the joint. The pain was so intense he had to bite back a scream. Then the agony eased.

Not broken. That was good news.

'Beck?' Riley said, gently touching his face. 'Are you OK?'

She really cares. Or maybe it was because if he died she wouldn't get her father's money. How could he tell with her?

His head kept spinning and it took Jackson and Riley to help him to his feet. After he'd staggered to a kerb and hunkered down, a low rumble brought his attention back to the building. The rumble was the roof collapsing, crushing everything underneath. Spot fires danced where electrical wires had been severed. With all that plastic and wood as fuel, there would nothing worth salvaging.

That homeless guy saved my butt. If he'd still be around, Beck would have given him every dollar in his wallet.

His eyes drifted to the other trappers. They all wore grim expressions, glaring at the guys from inside the building. The workers were too scared to move, fearing retaliation. One of them was crying.

'What the hell was that?' Jackson asked, his brows furrowed.

'An IED,' Beck said, cautiously moving his injured shoulder. It was stiffening already. 'They wire a cellphone to explosives, then they call the number and. . . .' *Soldiers die.* Or in this case it would have been trappers. 'Probably been there since the first day they opened for business, knowin' they could take it down any time.' *No witnesses. No evidence.* Whoever was behind this was a cold-blooded bastard.

Remmers snarled and grabbed the dreadlocked dude. 'You almost got us killed.' The man frantically shook his head, clawing at the thickly muscled arm encircling his neck.

'Ease up, Remmers. Let him talk,' Harper said. With an oath, the trapper reluctantly complied.

'I swear to God I didn't know it was up there!' Dreads squeaked. 'I would have bought it too!'

'Talk,' Harper ordered. 'We want to hear it all.'

'OK, OK,' the man said, raising his hands in surrender. 'I've only met the dude who runs this gig a few times. He's really creepy. Gave me the shakes being around him.'

'What did this asshole look like?'

'He wore a suit.'

'Hair colour? Height?'

If someone could be totally lost, it was Dreadlocks. He opened and closed his mouth a couple times. 'I really can't remember him that well.'

'How were you paid?'

'Cash. Every Friday.'

'How did you get in touch with the guy?'

'I didn't. He came to us. Every morning a truck picks up the bottles and delivers them . . . wherever,' he said, vaguely waving a hand.

Stewart looked over at the other men they'd rousted from the building. 'What about the rest of ya?'

'Just some suit,' one man said.

'That's all ya can remember?' Nods all around.

'We've got six guys who know diddle shit and a burning building full of evidence. The Guild is going to take the blame for this,' Harper complained.

Beck tugged on Riley's coat and when she leaned closer he whispered into her ear. He watched as she processed what he'd told her.

'You're full of awesome, you know that?' she said, grinning.

For a second, he believed her.

Riley crossed to Stewart and passed on the message in a whisper. Then she did the same with Harper. The two masters traded looks. With a quick order from Harper, the workers were herded down the street and made to sit on the kerb in a tidy row, guarded by Remmers and Jackson.

'Go on, Saint, earn your keep,' Harper said.

As he passed Riley, Simon murmured to her something to her that Beck didn't catch. A second later, she was in her ex's face, shoving the apprentice away in fury.

'Don't you dare say that,' she hissed. 'I had nothing to do with it.'

'Then why is Hell always one step ahead of us?' he countered.

'Stand down, the pair of you,' Harper bellowed. Riley jerked away, her chest heaving in anger, fists clenched.

The young apprentice gave Riley a final scathing glare, then headed up the street to watch over their prisoners.

With Riley's help, Beck made it to his ride. Leaning against the passenger side door, out of sight of the plant workers and the other trappers, he had her unzip his jacket. She carefully tugged out the computer and the paperwork, then displayed them to the two older men.

Stewart's eyes lit up like fireworks. 'That's why ya stayed in there so long.'

'Hell, boy, you might have saved our asses,' Harper said, grinning.

Sirens wailed in the distance.

Stewart pointed at the evidence. 'Take this stuff to my place. I'll have Jackson come over later and go through the computer. We'll need back-ups of everythin'. Same with the paperwork. I want copies. Spread them around.'

'You think we're going to get stonewalled, Angus?' Harper asked.

Stewart nodded. 'I'm countin' on it.'

It took considerable effort on Riley's part to help Beck into his pickup. He was so sore she had to buckle his seatbelt for him, ignoring how close that put them and how she had to reach across him to get the thing latched.

'Ya have anythin' to drink?' he asked.

Riley dug out a bottle of water from her backpack and handed it over. It was beyond him to get the cap off one-handed. When she remedied the situation, he drained half the liquid in a few gulps.

Adjusting the seat so she could reach the pedals elicited a hiss of pain from her passenger.

'Sorry.'

'Don't ya wreck my truck,' he warned.

'I won't.' At least she hoped she wouldn't: she'd never driven anything this big before. Riley edged away from the kerb, trying to get a feel for the steering and the brakes. As she crossed the first intersection on her way to Stewart's house, two police cars went flying by them, headed towards the collapsed building. A fire truck followed a short distance behind.

Seeing Beck running for his life, then blown into the air like a bird with no wings had been the stuff of nightmares. Riley had been sure he was dead. Convinced she'd never have a chance to apologize.

Her fears took a voice. 'What the hell were you thinking?' she shouted, startling her passenger. 'Why did you stay in that building when you knew there was a bomb? Are you totally crazy?'

Beck turned towards her, his face still sweaty from the pain. 'We had to have proof or they'll move their operation and start over and more folks will die.'

'But you nearly died, you moron!'

He smirked. 'Ya keep it up, girl, and I'll think yer care for me.'

'I *do* care, Beck. I keep telling you that. We just don't get along.'

'Whose fault is that?' he retorted.

'Mine,' she said without hesitation. 'And yours. We're both to blame.'

He took a deep breath and then nodded in agreement. 'Always been harder talkin' to ya than other girls. Don't know why.'

Riley knew how that was. She could chat all day with

Peter and never step on one emotional landmine. Beck? He was riddled with them, and she managed to hit every one of them without trying.

'What did Simon say to ya that made ya so mad?'

Riley kept her eyes on the road. 'He thinks I'm working for Hell and that I'm sabotaging everything we trappers do.'

Beck huffed in disgust. 'Shows what a dumbass he is.'

Riley shot him a quick glance. His face was less pale now. 'How are you doing?'

'Hurts like hell, but I'll live.' He looked out of the window at the passing scenery. 'That call I got on the roof,' he said. 'The first one. It wasn't from Justine.'

'Then why didn't you tell me that?'

'I just wanted to piss ya off.' He cleared his throat. 'The call was from a doc down in Sadlersville. Sadie's worse. He says she'll be goin' to the hospital soon.'

'Your mom? What's wrong with her?'

Beck took another long drink of water before he answered. 'She's got . . . cancer. She's dyin',' he said, his voice quavering.

Oh God, I'm a complete asshat. 'I'm so sorry, Beck. I mean it. I had no idea.' Even apologizing didn't make her feel any better. *I totally blew it.*

He stared out of the side window, his face indistinct in the dashboard lights.

'Sadie and I have never been on good terms. I remind her too much of my daddy, whoever the hell he was. I'm the next best thing to hate since he's not around.'

He really thinks his mother hates him. Could that be for

real? 'You're going down to see her, aren't you? I mean . . . before . . .'

'Don't know yet. We need to get things straightened out up here first.'

If this had been anyone else, she would have jumped all over them for not leaving town immediately, but this was Beck and his life was complicated. Apparently his relationship with his mother was no different.

For a moment, Riley remembered how it had felt when she'd learned about her mom's cancer, how there was no medicine in the world that would keep Miriam Blackthorne alive. How helpless Riley had felt. She'd only made it through that hell because Peter and her dad had been there for her.

'Let me know if you need anything, OK?' she said. 'I'm serious. I'm there for you.'

When he turned towards her, there was a sheen of tears in his eyes. He looked away immediately, as if he'd realized he was showing weakness.

'Thanks,' he whispered, barely audible over the truck's engine.

The Guild's physician, Carmela Wilson, was waiting for them at Stewart's house. Beck didn't take that well.

'I don't need a doctor,' he growled.

'Get your butt inside or I'll strip you down and do the exam in the driveway,' Carmela replied.

Beck didn't argue, as if his protest was all that was needed to preserve his macho trapper ego. Or he knew that Carmela wasn't bluffing.

He insisted on making his own way into the kitchen without any help. The exertion cost him and he dropped into a chair with a prolonged groan, his face ashen.

Carmela rolled her eyes at the sight. 'Must be something in these guys' DNA,' she grumbled.

When they finally removed his jacket and T-shirt, his entire left shoulder was red and swollen.

'Oh yeah, you're going to be one sore sucker in the morning,' the doctor said.

'Already am,' Beck muttered.

'He needs an ice pack,' Carmela added, then began her examination.

Riley raided the kitchen drawers to locate a sturdy plastic bag and then filled it with ice from the freezer. From Beck's occasional exclamations, he was in considerable discomfort.

'Not broken,' Carmela announced. 'I'm guessing it popped back in place.' The trapper's moan acknowledged the fact. 'You'll need to keep it iced overnight. I'll give you something for the pain. Give it a day or two and then start moving it around, but be careful, OK? No trapping.'

Beck didn't argue with her, which meant one of two things: he was hurting bad enough he'd actually do what the doc wanted or he was tuning her out. Riley was betting on the latter.

After Carmela departed, he insisted on getting into his truck and driving home before he took the pain pills.

'You should stay here. I can help you—' she began.

'No, I'm goin' home. If the Scotsman doesn't like it, to hell with him.'

'Then call me when you get home. You hear me?'

Riley buckled his seatbelt (again) and then watched in horror as he managed to get the truck out of the drive and on to the street one-handed, the ice pack still perched on his damaged shoulder like a frozen parrot.

'You are such a masochist, dude,' she said, shaking her head. How he was going to unlatch the seatbelt once he got home? *Not my problem.*

Riley left the computer and paperwork on Stewart's desk, raided the kitchen for a banana, then trucked upstairs to her bedroom. She'd begun to strip for a shower when her cellphone rang.

'I'm home. Ya happy now?' Beck's gravelly voice demanded.

'Yes, I am.'

'Yer treatin' me like I'm some idiot kid,' he complained.

'Gee, I wonder where I learned that?'

He hung up on her.

Chapter Fifteen

At first it was faint, a whisper in the back of Riley's mind. Then it grew progressively stronger. Always her name, over and over. Ori was at it again.

'No way, you jerk,' she said, rolling over on her side. He probably thought he could turn on the charm and she'd be all apologetic and hand over her soul. *Not happening*. He had to know that, so why was he calling to her? Why at the same time each morning?

Because he loved the dawn. Ori had claimed it reminded him of Heaven. He'd said the same thing about her.

The voice wouldn't stop, not matter how she tried to block it out. The more she fought, the more it rose in intensity, almost like a psychic scream. If it didn't end soon, it would become incapacitating. *Like Mom's migraines*.

After Riley had dressed and laced on her tennis shoes, she had second thoughts. What would the masters say if they saw her leave? A quick check proved Stewart's car wasn't in the driveway. They were busy with the Holy Water issue, so she could slip out without them knowing. As long as Ori remained a statue, he wasn't a threat. If she did his bidding this once, maybe that would shut him up and she could sleep in.

Riley crept out of the house. The moment she turned her car south, the pressure in her head eased and it continued to throttle down the closer she came to Oakland Cemetery. The journey went quickly – there wasn't much traffic on the road – and this time she drove into the graveyard itself. That way she could take off in a hurry if this was a trap.

Even though Ori had lied to her, seduced her and then tried to claim her soul, he had saved her life. More than once. He could have allowed Beck's soul to be taken that night at the Armageddon Lounge when two Mezmers had targeted the trapper. But he hadn't. Ori had said he stepped in because she'd lost too much already. If anything, she would have thought he'd want Beck out of the way.

She parked near the Bell Tower, ensuring the car was pointed in the right direction for a swift escape. There was blessed silence inside her mind now, as if Ori had got exactly what he wanted. With the sun barely edging above the eastern horizon, the morning frost hadn't burned off yet. In the distance she heard the whine of a MARTA train headed into King Memorial station.

The moment after she shut the car door, Riley froze. She could see Ori's statue now. Both fists were still raised in the air as if challenging Heaven, white wings spread. Clad in jeans, his chest and feet were bare. A fine layer of frost covered his body. What would it be like to be trapped in a statue? Did he know what was going on around him, or was it like being asleep?

It took a lot to force herself to the base of the statue.

Staring upward, it seemed to shimmer in the morning light. 'Do you even know I'm here?' she mused.

'Of course he does.'

Riley whirled round in fright. To her relief, it wasn't Lucifer this time but a solemn old lady in a long black dress and orthopedic shoes. Or, if you knew her real form, Martha, the angel of Oakland Cemetery, the one who'd made the deal for Simon's life that had left Riley on the hook to prevent Armageddon.

'How are you, child?' the angel asked, her eyes kind.

Riley could think of a dozen different snarky replies. She decided not to go there. 'I've been better.'

A sage nod. 'You came to see the entombed one. Why?'

'I keep hearing him in my mind. I know that's crazy.'

'Not really. You've been touched by a Fallen. That does not fade quickly.'

'If you knew what he was, why didn't you warn me?'

'It was your choice if you trusted him. Free will, you see,' Martha explained.

That means . . . 'You know what happened between us?'

'Of course,' was the swift reply. Martha tidied a leaf off a headstone like it was somehow responsible for all the chaos in the world. 'I made sure to be at the *far* end of the cemetery that night when you were with him.'

'I thought he . . . loved me,' Riley said, her cheeks flaming in embarrassment.

'You mortals always do.'

Riley's eyes rose to the marble figure. 'What keeps the

cemetery people from seeing him? I mean, they'd have to notice a new statue.'

'They won't see him. Only a few of us realize he's here.'

Since it seemed to be a good time to ask, Riley thrust her palms towards the angel. 'What are these inscription things on my hands? You know, they got me in a bunch of trouble with the Vatican.'

'Heaven's seal appeared when you agreed to help us,' the angel replied. 'And the other mark was inscribed when you agreed to work for the Prince.'

'What does that make me? Good or evil?'

'It makes you human, dear.'

Riley dropped her hands. 'Did you know Simon would turn on me like that?'

'No,' Martha replied. 'I'm truly sorry that happened. That young man has a lot to answer for.'

Riley opened her mouth to fire off the next question, the one about how she should stop Armageddon, but the angel shook her head. She was reading Riley's mind again.

OK . . . next question. 'He,' she said, jabbing a finger upward at the statue, 'is messing with my mind. Why is he doing that?'

'You shall have to ask him that question. He's one of the most honest of the Fallen so you might even get a straight answer. Of course, that's not saying much, is it?' Martha promptly vanished into the morning air.

Cold even with her gloves on, Riley slotted her hands inside her pockets as she gazed up at the stone angel. *Oh well, what can it hurt?* She could always go back to bed later.

'I'm here and now you're all quiet. So what do you want?' she muttered, annoyed.

If there was a reply, it was inaudible. To the east, the sunlight sifted through the bare trees, rosy gold. There was the occasional twitter of a bird in a nearby magnolia tree. Riley's eyes roamed to her parents' graves. Then to the mausoleum. Her memories sparked to life: the myriad candles that had awaited them when Ori had opened the doors that night. His warm wings, his seductive words.

His lies.

When she regarded the statue again, the sunlight had reached the top of the angel's head, crowning him in silky light, almost like a halo. The glow did not remain stationary, but continued to spread downward, caressing his face, then his neck and then touching his chest like a lover might. Each muscle was outlined, each feather glistened like a prism, bending the light into an iridescent rainbow.

She recalled the velvety softness of those feathers and how Ori had brought her to a new awareness, gently tutoring her in what it meant to be a woman.

Riley shivered at the memories, running her hands up and down her arms to warm herself. She was about to turn away when the glow halted at the top of the angel's jeans. With a flash of light, the golden marble turned soft, and then it became skin.

'Hey, what's going on here?' Riley manoeuvred around a headstone until she had a clear path to run, just in case Ori escaped his marble prison.

The angel shook out his wings, dropped his arms to his sides and gazed downward, his eyes pinning her in place.

'Oh my God,' she whispered. His dark hair hung around his face, framing it. His black eyes seemed as endlessly deep as that night he'd held her, made love to her.

'Come to gloat, have you?' he said, his voice harsher than she recalled.

'No! You were the one who called me here.'

'You know why Lucifer only allows me to see the dawn? It's revenge. He knows I crave the Light, and so he torments me with it every morning.'

No. If she'd been on that pedestal, watching the sunrise would have given her hope that someday Lucifer might turn her loose. But the angel wasn't seeing that, too caught up in his imprisonment and the shame at having failed his master.

Ori struggled against the remaining marble, but it held. Swearing in Hellspeak, he roared his fury into the morning sky. Though she was frightened, Riley held her ground. As long as she remembered what he'd done to her, what he really wanted, the angel had no hold over her.

'Why did you want me here?'

'So that you could see what you've done to me. You are to blame for my imprisonment, Riley Anora Blackthorne.'

'Wait a minute. I'm supposed to feel sorry for you?' she gasped. 'You seduced me you asshat! You stole my—'

'No!' he shouted, his voice echoing off the stillness. 'I didn't *steal* your virginity. I *accepted* it.'

She felt her cheeks warm. 'You stole my dad's soul. You can't deny that.'

The angel shook his head. 'If I hadn't stepped in, that Archfiend would have killed Paul Blackthorne and fed on his corpse. Instead, I gave your father chance to live, to spend more time with his beloved child.'

'He died anyway. You broke your part of the deal!'

Ori's dark eyes went flinty. 'If I had known the rogue would go after Paul, I would have stopped it. By the time I realized what was happening, your father was dead. That proved . . .'

'Inconvenient?' she chided, her fists clenched.

'An ill omen,' he replied. 'The death of Master Blackthorne sent a message that the Prince is incapable of protecting his own. That weakens His position.'

'Why would us mere mortals care if Lucifer isn't top dog? It'd still be all Hell and damnation no matter who was in charge.'

'There are worse who would take his place.' Ori frowned in thought. 'Perhaps it is time that they did. Perhaps we have been too merciful.'

His gaze drifted down to meet hers again.

She heard other words now, in her mind, telling her how it would be so easy to set the angel loose from his prison. How grateful he would be. All it took was her to touch her blood to the stone and they could be together forever.

'No!' she said, shaking her head to dislodge the treacherous thoughts. 'It's not happening, you lying bastard. We've done this dance and I'm not going to get hurt again.'

'You are a vain, selfish child,' the prisoner retorted. 'Do you not see the bigger picture? Of the war that comes our way?'

'I know what's coming,' Riley replied, her voice calmer now. She'd resisted his best efforts and that gave her courage. 'I'm supposed to stop that war, or did you forget that?'

'I will continue to hammer at your mind until you free me. Or you will go insane.'

'You can try, Fallen.'

Ori's rage abruptly vanished as quickly as it had appeared. He fell silent and shook his head in deep despair: the golden glow was climbing up his torso now, then sped upward across his chest. The angel saw it too.

'So soon,' he said sadly. Ori flexed his wings, as if desperate to absorb the sunbeams even as his body swiftly returned to stone.

The last of the glow melted away, leaving alabaster marble in its absence. Water droplets fled down Ori's face, much like tears. This time the Fallen's hands were not raised in anger, but at his sides in resignation, wings partially folded against his back. His dark eyes were closed, head bowed, as if it was too painful to see the world and not be part of it.

Worried that the masters would wonder where she was, Riley returned to Stewart's place as quickly as possible. Unfortunately, her host's car was in the driveway, which meant both of them had returned from the warehouse. She parked behind Stewart's vehicle, turned off the car and just sat there.

Ori's mental pull had been so strong she hadn't even thought of the consequences or what exactly might happen to her and to Stewart if the Vatican found out she was hanging with a Fallen.

To give her time to calm down so the masters wouldn't know something was wrong, she called Peter to bring him up to date on what had happened with the Holy Water scam. He didn't answer his phone – probably in the shower – so she left him a lengthy message and promised to work on her homework assignments for class.

When she couldn't put it off any longer, Riley headed for the back door. The moment it opened she was greeted by the enticing scent of freshly baked cinnamon rolls. After hanging her coat on the rack, she headed towards the kitchen, putting on a neutral expression. At least one she hoped didn't say *Ask Me Where I've Been. You Will Really Love the Answer.*

She found the Scotsman and Harper at the large kitchen table, eating their breakfast. A woman – ample of bosom, rosy-cheeked and with silver streaks in her dark hair – stood in front of the stove. She wore black slacks, a red shirt and an apron that proclaimed *Dinner is Ready When the Smoke Alarm Goes Off.*

That wasn't encouraging. Still, the cinnamon rolls were causing Riley's stomach to growl in anticipation.

'Good mornin', lass, yer just in time for breakfast,' Stewart said more cheerfully than she thought humanly possible.

'Brat,' Harper added, which was about as cheery as he got, but better than she'd expected.

'Sirs,' she said. She chose a chair opposite the two masters. Neither of them seemed to be in a bad mood, so maybe they had good news. More importantly, they didn't seem worried about where she'd been.

'Mrs Ayers, how's about we feed up this lass?' Stewart said after a sip of coffee. 'She's too thin for my likin'.'

'My pleasure. What do you usually eat, Riley?' Mrs Ayers asked, her words overlaid with a lilting British accent.

'Ah, usually cereal. Sometimes oatmeal.'

'That's all you eat?' When Riley nodded, Mrs Ayers shook her head in dismay. 'Oh, no, not in this house, luv. We eat a *proper* breakfast here.'

Five minutes later Riley learned what a proper English breakfast entailed. It could have fed at least two other Rileys. There was a cooked egg, fat sausages, grilled mushrooms, a tomato and baked beans, all jostling for space on one plate. To top it off a massive cinnamon roll sat on a napkin near a tall glass of orange juice.

Who eats beans and tomatoes for breakfast?

Riley made a brave effort anyway and soon came to realize that the hunters had done her a huge favour by requiring her to stay at Stewart's house, even in the short term. The food immediately calmed her nervous stomach and she could feel her energy level rising though she hadn't had much sleep overnight.

'Everyone fine?' Mrs Ayers asked. There were nods all around. 'Then I'll leave you to it,' she said, and headed into the main part of the house. Apparently she doubled as Stewart's housekeeper as well.

As Riley ate, the two masters talked back and forth, analysing the raid and what they'd netted out of the warehouse.

'The paperwork Beck salvaged is mostly an inventory of the bottles,' Harper explained for her benefit. 'Nothing that tells us where they were selling the fake stuff.'

'What about the computer?' Riley asked.

'That's where we got lucky. There wasn't much on the thing itself, only the files for the labels. But it was registered to the city.'

'What?' Riley said, fumbling one of the sausages in surprise.

'We don't know which department yet, but I've got a cop buddy of mine working on it.'

She pondered that as she scooped up a forkful of beans. 'How about the department that hands out the tax stickers?'

Stewart shook his head. 'No. Someone higher up. I'll swear it.'

'The building's owner is raising holy hell,' Harper said. 'He claims *we* planted the explosives.'

'We need ta get our side of the story in front of the public,' Stewart said. 'I'll put a call in to CNN.'

'Have Beck talk to that woman reporter,' Harper suggested.

Riley halted mid-chew. *That woman reporter* would be Justine. Like Beck needed an excuse to spend time with her.

'He'll be with her anyway,' Harper added. 'He might as well be talking up the party line when they're not screwing.'

Riley nearly choked.

'Something wrong, lass?' Stewart asked, studying her.

'No. Just getting full,' she fibbed.

Harper set down his fork, extracted a pill from his shirt pocket, then washed it with a sip of coffee. It didn't look like the pain medication he'd been toting around since he'd been injured at the Tabernacle.

He noticed she was watching him. 'What?'

'Nothing.' He was so different now. Get him off the booze and he was almost human.

'Did the doctor check out Beck?' Stewart quizzed.

'Yeah. She said he'd live. He insisted on driving himself home,' she said, rolling her eyes. 'He's such a moron sometimes.'

Stewart snorted. 'Comes with being twenty-two and invincible. Give the lad a few more years and he'll learn ta listen ta those aches.'

'God, that's the truth,' Harper said.

Her master left the kitchen a short time later and Riley waited until he was out of earshot. 'Is he sick?' she asked. 'Those were different pills than he usually takes.'

'The medicine keeps him from drinkin',' Stewart replied. 'He'll get hellishly ill if he takes any alcohol when he's on those things.'

That's why. 'He's better this way. Less . . . volatile.' Less likely to leave bruises on her like he had in the past.

'Aye. This is the way he used ta be before his son died.'

Son? 'He said he'd lost his dad, but . . .'

Her host lowered his voice, though there was no way Harper could hear them.

'His eldest lad was a trapper in Detroit. He was killed about three years back. Donald found the best way ta cope was the alcohol.'

Donald. She hadn't even known her master's first name.

'Losin' two family members ta Archdemons makes it very hard for him. Especially since yer father survived his battle with one.'

Now she knew why Harper had hated her from the moment they'd met. In his shoes, she might have felt the same way.

Chapter Sixteen

About four in the afternoon Riley joined her dad in Mort's garden. His eyes were closed, breathing slowed, like he was meditating. A bottle of the orange stabilizer sat at his elbow and a book lay on his lap. When she took it from him and laid it aside, she wasn't surprised to see it was about the Civil War.

Her dad stirred to life, smiling when he recognized her.

'Pumpkin!'

Riley grinned at the nickname: she was beginning to like it more every day. The embrace came next. He didn't rush it and Riley felt no reason to either.

When it finally ended, he took a long sip of his drink. That was her clue to talk.

'The hunters say I have to stay at Stewart's,' she reported.

'There are worse fates,' her father said, smiling.

Riley thought of all the yummy food. 'So I found out. If I behave, the hunters will leave me be.'

'It's never that simple with the Church. Just be careful with them, OK?'

She nodded. 'We kicked butt last night.' Then she told him how Beck had been the total hero of the raid.

'Is he OK?' The concern was as strong as it would have been if he'd been asking about her.

'He was bitching up a storm when I last saw him so that's always a good sign.'

Her father laughed. It reminded Riley of what it'd been like before her father had died. How much they'd enjoyed talking to each other, even about stupid stuff like how many cat hairs constituted a hairball.

'I told Beck you were here. I hope that was OK.'

'Good. I want to see him again. I miss him.'

That meeting would be wicked hard for both of them. Beck would have to go through the same 'Ohmigod, this is creepy' adjustment as she had. All the grief would come back again. Not that it had ever gone away.

'He wants to know who reanimated you,' she warned.

'I'm sure he does,' was the swift reply. 'Do the masters know where I am?'

'Yeah.'

Her father stared at the fountain and the stylishly nude nymph cavorting in the centre of it. 'I wish now I'd refused to let you become a demon trapper,' he said.

'Why? I'm doing OK,' she said. 'Really, I'm getting better. I haven't trashed a library this week.'

He chuckled. 'It's not about you being a good trapper, because you are. It's what the job does to you. When I look at you, you're still my beautiful daughter, but your eyes tell me you've aged so much. Seen too much, too soon.'

'Like Beck?' He nodded. 'If you hadn't gotten me my

licence, you would have been in trouble with Hell, broken your deal with them. They want me in the business.'

'True, but I had the option to blow them off.'

'They would have killed you.'

'They did anyway. At least I would have had the satisfaction of knowing you'd grow up in an easier life.'

'What, in Fargo with Auntie Nasty?' she said. 'Or as a foster kid? Those don't sound easier to me.'

Her father placed his hand on her shoulder and gave a gentle squeeze. 'So how's school going?'

'It goes. We're still slogging through the Civil War and my grades are OK.'

'Just OK?' her dad asked.

'A's and B's. I'm good. Oh, and Allan is in my class now.'

Frowning, her father muttered something under his breath she couldn't catch. 'If he's bothering you, tell the teacher. If that doesn't work, let Beck now. Do not let him hurt you again.'

'I'm not giving him a second chance.'

He sighed in relief. 'How are you and Beck doing by the way?'

'It's really bad right now. He's angry at me because of Ori and I'm . . . mad at him about Justine.'

'Who?'

Riley brought him up to speed on the stick chick and why she was sure that Ms Perfect was going to hurt Beck in the long run.

'Beck's such a hard guy to talk to,' she said. 'You get too close and he clams up.'

'Keep trying. He's worth . . . the effort. He has so much potential.' Her father's eyes began to blink. Apparently they were closing in on his nap time.

She leaned over and kissed him on the cheek. 'I'll come tomorrow. I promise.'

'Listen to Beck and Stewart. They'll . . . watch out . . . for you.'

Then he shut down.

It's like he's a really old guy. Awake for a while, then asleep.

Riley watched him rest for a few minutes, not eager to leave her remaining parent behind. Carefully placing the book next to him on the bench so he could find it when he woke, she left her father dozing in the garden.

Each separation grew harder. One day there will be no more talk, no more time together. Her father's body would be laid to rest, but his soul would be Lucifer's for eternity.

There has to be a way to set him free.

A text reached her as she drove back towards Stewart's. It was from Peter.

Hot chocolate. Homework. You game?

Riley pulled over into a grocery-store parking lot and replied.

Buy me lemon cake & I'm yours.

The reply came instantly. *You're so easy! See you there.*

Laughing, she turned the car round and headed downtown. As it was, she beat him to the coffee shop by only a few minutes.

'Hey, you awake?' Peter said, placing his computer bag on the table near the back of the shop. He shucked off his coat.

Riley peeled open her eyes to stare at her friend across the table. 'Barely. It was a rough night.'

'Well, pull it together. I doubt Mrs Haggerty will accept "I've been taking down bad guys" as an excuse for not finishing your homework.'

Riley glowered up at him. 'You promised me hot chocolate. And lemon cake.'

'And I hang with you because . . .?' Peter gestured for her to fill in the blank.

'I'm charming and I could drop a demon inside your computer that would turn it to expensive mush.'

'Got it.' He trotted off to buy the promised goodies.

Homework seemed pointless in a non-apocalyptic sort of way. What if the world did end? Would it matter if her grades were As, Bs or Cs?

The world might not care, but her father the teacher sure would. If the world didn't blow up and he remained in Mort's care, he might be around for another year or so. It was a safe bet Dead Dad would want to see her report cards. If her grades weren't up to par . . .

It's not like he can ground me any more.

Still, she needed to get back into the normal flow of things. Not everything in the world was about demons and angels.

It took two servings of hot chocolate before Riley's brain began to click at full speed. Hopped up on the caffeine and the sugar from the yummy lemon cake, she dug into her maths homework. It was lucky she was good at quadratic equations because she had a whole page of them to do.

Peter was working on his sociology assignment about a tribe in New Guinea that sent their young boys into the rainforest to kill a monkey as a rite of passage. He seemed fairly bored with the topic, but perked up when someone plopped into the seat next to him. That someone was a girl.

Simi's multicoloured hair was more monochrome at the moment, varying shades of blue ranging from navy to turquoise. It wasn't as eye-blinding as some of her colour schemes.

'Hey. I thought it was your day off. What are you doing here?' Riley said.

'Coffee. I get it free,' Simi replied, hefting a large paper cup as evidence. She popped the top off, added three packets of sugar, then covered it again. No wonder she was wired all the time.

'Good to see you again,' Peter said. 'Your hair totally rocks.'

Simi unabashedly checked Peter over, then nodded her approval. 'Yours too. I like the brown tips.'

He shrugged like it was no big deal, but Riley could tell he was pleased she'd noticed.

'I bought those tickets for the Gnarly Scalenes' concert,' Simi added. 'Consider it an early birthday present.'

Way early since Riley's birthday wasn't for a few months.

'I have money to pay for them.'

'So do I,' Simi replied. 'How's the smoking-hot dude? You

know, the one I met on the street. Ori?'

Peter choked on his ice tea.

The one time she actually remembers a guy's name. 'Ah, well . . .'

'I told you to go wild, but you didn't listen to me, did you?' Simi asked.

Her friend would not back down until she'd got all the deets. 'Ah, I did go wild.'

Simi blinked. 'For real? You let him kiss you?' she gushed. At Riley's nod, Simi pressed on. 'What was it like? Awesome. Brain melting?'

'Totally soul stealing,' Peter said with a smirk.

Riley kicked him under the table. 'It was OK,' she said.

'So you two going to hook up?'

Been there. Got the mark to prove it. 'No,' Riley retorted. 'No way.'

'Ah, damn,' Simi muttered. 'That sucks. So who are you going out with?'

'Why do I have to be dating someone?'

Simi rolled her eyes in mock despair and turned her attention to Peter. 'What about you? You seeing anyone?'

His mouth locked up for a second, then he got it in gear. 'No. Not at the moment.'

'God, you guys are like . . . dull.'

Before Riley had the chance to explain why that was a good thing, someone called out her name. It was Beck, his trapping bag on his shoulder. For once she welcomed the interruption.

Simi jumped up and offered him her seat. 'I'm outta here.

You guys can talk demons and –' she pointed a figure at Riley's homework – 'stuff. I'll catch up with you later, girlfriend.'

Beck waited until Simi was out of the way and then asked, 'Mind if I join ya?'

When Riley shook her head, he settled into the chair opposite her, dropping his Braves cap on the table. At least Backwoods Boy wouldn't be talking about Ori.

'Peter, right? I saw ya at Paul's funeral,' he said, offering his hand.

'That's right.' They shook. 'How goes it?' her friend asked.

'Not bad, how about you?'

As the two males traded harmless chit chat, Riley tried to work out exactly why Beck was at the coffee shop. He wasn't the social type unless there was a pool table involved, so there had to be something behind his sudden appearance.

She finally interrupted, unable to help herself. 'Why are you here?' It was Peter's turn to kick her under the table. She glowered at him in response.

Beck ignored their drama. 'Ya didn't answer yer phone, so I figured ya might be here.'

What? Riley dug out the offending piece of technology. The battery was dead and the charging cord was in her bedroom at Stewart's. 'Sorry.'

'No big. I'm going trappin' tonight,' he said. 'Thought ya might like come along.'

'What about your shoulder?'

'It's better. The pain pills are helpin'.' Beck paused and

added, 'We'd need to leave about eight. That work for ya?'

No, it does not work for me. Riley did not want to go trapping. She wanted to stay here in the coffee shop, do her homework and talk to Peter. Then maybe she'd go back to Stewart's, catch some TV.

'Do I have to go?' she asked, trying to determine if this was an order issued by one of the masters.

'Ya don't want to?' Beck asked, confused. Then he nodded in resignation as if something had suddenly become clear. 'Ya don't want to go with me, is that it?'

Peter sprang up from his seat. 'OK . . . I think I need . . . to refill on my iced tea. I'll be back.' He was headed towards the counter before she could respond, though his glass was still three-quarters full.

Coward. He knew this might spiral down into a shouting match.

'Just tell me if I'm the problem, OK?' Beck pushed. 'I need to know where we stand on this.'

'It's not you, Beck. It's the whole trapping thing. All the crazy hours, the crazy people, the demons. I'm so tired of it.'

His expression softened. 'I hear ya, girl. Hell, I'd love nothin' more than to jump in my truck and go fishin' for a week, away from everythin'. It's gettin' too much to handle.'

Riley had never expected to hear Beck admit he felt he was in over his head.

'It's not only me, then,' she said.

He picked up a straw and folded it into a square so the two

ends nested together. 'No, it's all of us. Even the masters.'

'If I don't go, will you be out there alone?' she asked.

'No, Jackson will be with me. Harper says we work two-man teams from now on. It's no longer a choice.'

As long as he has back-up, he'll be OK. 'Then I'm staying here and doing my homework.'

'Fair enough.' He rose and placed the cap on his head. 'See ya later, girl.'

As Beck cleared the front door, Peter slid back into the booth, setting his full ice tea glass in front of him. 'No fireworks. I'm impressed. I figured you two would go thermonuclear in a heartbeat.'

'No. We're both too tired to go there. Too much has happened between us.'

'Hey, he's still talking to you, even after the guy with the wings. That means something, even if you don't want to go there.'

It did mean something.

Riley turned her mind back to the maths questions – those were always a safe subject – but her mind remained restless. Part of her wanted a normal life, the other part craved the excitement, the danger that demon trapping amply provided.

I'm so messed up.

*

Peter packed it in about seven, having promised his dad he'd be home for a late dinner. The moment he left, Simi took his place.

'Is the dude dating anyone?'

'Who? You mean Peter?' Riley asked, confused. Simi was known for changing subjects at whim. 'Not that I know of. Why?'

'I like him – he's cool.'

'He told me you blew him off when he asked you out.'

Simi hitched a shoulder, pushing her multicolour braids in all directions. 'I do that sometimes, to figure out of the guy's worth the hassle. He has to meet certain criteria before I go out with him. Good hair is tops. A little weird is good. Some smarts, though that isn't always required. Did you know some of the best kissers are nerds?'

Riley thought of Simon. 'Yeah, I did.'

'So name your poison – you want to talk about this Ori guy or about the hunky trapper?'

Her friend was blunt to a fault. 'Neither.'

'Choose one or I will,' Simi shot back.

Ah crap. 'Beck.'

'Good choice,' her friend replied, nodding her approval. 'Why are you two dancing around each other?'

Simi didn't know their history: she and Riley had met *after* the Beck debacle. Riley gave her a short version of the Princess vs Backwoods Boy saga and their current battle over Ori. Without mentioning her overnight romp with the angel, or the demon hunters.

'Be right back,' Simi said, popping up and motoring towards the counter for a refill of her coffee.

She's like an overactive chihuahua. But underneath that

flakiness was a working brain, one of the reasons Riley liked her so much.

Simi surged back in her seat, her cup full again. 'So let's recap: you like him. He likes you. Agreed?'

Riley had to grant her that assessment.

'OK, first thing, apologize for hanging with this Ori guy. Then he can stammer an apology for being a jerk. Then you two can hook up.'

It was not that simple. 'Beck is . . .'

'A total pain in the butt,' Simi retorted. 'But I know the signs: there's a really cool guy under that skin, who'll be totally worth all the hassles. You're an idiot if you let this one slide, girlfriend.'

Riley's father had said almost the same thing. 'But . . .'

'You're talking to the hand now,' Simi said, raising the appropriate body part. Up she popped again, her braids swinging. 'Let's go somewhere fun. I want dessert.'

Hurricane Simi propelled Riley out of the coffee shop and into the street before she could protest. Then her friend suddenly gave her a big hug.

'What's that all about?' Riley said, smiling at the unexpected gesture.

'It felt right,' Simi replied. She sobered for a fraction of a second. 'I meant it about Beck. Make it right between you. Trapping is way scary stuff and he might not be around someday. You'll hate yourself forever if he gets hurt and you never got things fixed between you.'

'I'll try.'

'Excellent! Now let's go find some ice cream.'

'You're not going to mix the four flavours again, are you?' Riley moaned.

'Of course. What is life without a little danger?'

Chapter Seventeen

Though Simi had pleaded with unbridled passion over large helpings of ice cream, Riley had passed on the opportunity to go to a club to hear some new band. Instead, she'd gone to her apartment to charge her phone and to collect fresh underwear. Two pairs of panties left and those were the ones with the frilly lace on them. *Oh well, at least no one sees them.* She loaded up on pills for her cramps. They'd ratcheted down a notch, but they were still there.

As she waited for the spare charger to bring her cellphone back to the land of the living, she used the landline to call Captain Elias Salvatore for her daily check-in. Riley thought of it as her 'I'm still in Atlanta, I'm staying out of trouble and I'm not partying down with Lucifer and his buds' status report. As she gave him a sanitized version of her activities there were background noises that sounded a lot like gunshots. She made sure to keep the conversation brief.

Riley had barely reached her car for the trip back to Stewart's when her phone rang. It was the master himself.

'Lass? Where are ya?' he demanded.

'On the way to your place.'

'No, get ta Beck's house as fast as ya can. The lad's been hurt.'

Riley didn't hesitate. 'I'm there.'

Tossing her phone in the backpack, she peeled out of the parking lot.

Riley rolled into Beck's driveway at high speed, slammed on the brakes and bailed out of the car. She needn't have bothered – his truck wasn't there and knocking on the front door received no response.

Oh, God. He's really bad. They took him to the hospital.

Before she could dial Stewart to find out what was going on, Beck's pickup pulled in behind her car. Jackson was driving. He climbed out and then went to the passenger side door and opened it.

When Riley joined him, she gasped in shock. Beck had a thin line of blood curling down his face and into his collar. His eyes were pinched shut and his expression reminded her of how her mother looked when she was fighting one of her killer headaches.

'What happened?'

'Fell . . .' Beck said. 'Hit . . . the ground.'

Riley gave the other trapper a withering look.

'He refused to go to the hospital,' Jackson explained. 'Carmela will be by to check him out.'

'Let's get inside,' Riley muttered.

It took all their efforts to move the wounded trapper on to his porch. Riley dug his keys out of his jeans pocket and fumbled with the lock. The moment the door opened, the alarm started to beep. Riley tapped in the numbers she'd used the last time she'd been here. The alarm kept ticking down the time.

'What's the code?' she called out. Beck stared at her blankly, leaning heavily on Jackson. 'Beck! Help me here.'

The injured trapper closed his eyes in an effort to concentrate. '17 . . . 88.'

That'd be my first guess. She typed it in and the alarm went silent.

With Jackson's help, the trapper made his way to the couch and flopped down with a deep groan. Then bent over and held his head like it was exploding from within.

Probably is. Riley had a headache of her own and she hadn't collided with the pavement. As Jackson retrieved Beck's duffel bag, she made up an ice pack.

'I gotta go. I need to get back to Demon Central,' Jackson. 'Remmers has a lead on those two guys who stole your demon last month. We're hoping we can find them and figure out who is buying the fiends illegally.'

Riley nodded, juggling the ice pack in her hands to keep her fingers from freezing. 'Thanks, Jackson.'

'No sweat. Call if you need me.' The door shut behind him.

Remembering a lesson learned from her mother's headaches, Riley found the biggest bowl in the cupboard in case Beck's stomach decided to weigh in.

Though the bathroom was clean, the medicine cabinet was nearly empty: a box of aspirin and spare razors. No bandages or peroxide. It took her a moment to remember where she'd seen them during one of her other visits. The hall closet had everything she needed. She selected the supplies and hurried back to the front room.

Beck hadn't moved. She knelt next to him and asked quietly, 'How are you doing?'

His brown eyes met hers. 'Hurts like hell.'

'Worse than a hangover?'

'Yeah.'

That's not good.

'I'd kill for some aspirin,' he admitted.

Somehow she didn't think that was a good idea.

Riley had just begun to clean the wound when there was a knock at the front door, then the Guild's doctor ploughed inside without waiting for an invitation.

Carmela sat next to Beck on the couch, her medical bag on the floor at her feet. 'My life would be perfect if it weren't for stubborn, macho trappers,' she complained. 'Oh look, here's another one.' She pulled out a small flashlight and took hold of his chin. 'Try not to blink, OK?'

The doctor took her time checking out both his pupils. 'No dilation. That's a good thing.' Then she felt around his head and asked him a bunch of questions, like the day of the week, how old he was and the name of the governor. Then she had him grip her hands. Finally she examined the head wound. 'OK, the cut is not that bad, which is the only reason you're not bleeding all over the place. You can stay here unless something changes. If you get worse, you're in the hospital, no argument.'

Beck sagged against the couch. 'Thanks. I'll call ya both in the mornin' if I need anything.'

Riley and the doctor traded looks.

'Nice try,' Riley said. 'I'm not going anywhere.'

'Ya don't need –' Seconds later Beck needed the big bowl, his body quaking violently. Once he'd stopped heaving, he leaned back. 'OK, y'all win,' he said weakly. 'Ya can stay.'

'That was too easy,' Carmela replied. Drawing Riley aside, she explained: 'Every two hours I need you to do neurological checks. These will determine if something's going wrong inside his skull. If the test results change, or he gets drowsy or you think something's not right, get him to the hospital immediately, then call me.'

'OK . . .' The doctor gave her the instructions, but they were so involved she had to take notes on a grocery receipt she found on the table.

'You got all that?' Carmela asked. 'If not, we'll woman-handle him into my car and take him to ER.'

'I got this.'

The doc knelt next to Beck. 'No pain pills until I'm sure you don't have a concussion. It's going to be a rough night, for both of you. I'll be back in the morning unless I get a call before then.'

'Thanks,' Beck said.

'You owe me a beer when you're better. And Thai food.' The doctor paused. 'This is the second injury this week, Den. You're pushing too hard. Back off and give yourself time to heal.' She rose. 'And next time, don't take a civilian on a trapping run. That was damned dumb, no matter what National says.'

Having delivered her broadside, Carmela sailed out of the door, medical bag in hand, off to treat the next casualty.

Civilian? Trappers didn't take regular folks on the runs. It was too dangerous. Who would want to be where they could get clawed up or eaten? Who would be that crazy . . .

A reporter. Maybe like the one Backwoods Boy was dating.

Now it all made sense: Justine had been on the run. Beck was naturally protective of women; it was hardwired into him. He was that way with Riley and he'd be doubly so with someone he was hooking up with. Something had gone wrong and he'd been the one to get hurt.

Riley knelt next to Beck to ask the question, then changed her mind. He was in too much pain.

If this is the stick chick's fault, she is so dead.

To keep herself out of ranting mode, she hurried to the restroom with the bowl and dumped it into the toilet, wrinkling her nose at the smell. After rinsing it out, she wet a facecloth with cold water: it'd feel good on his forehead.

As she wrung out the cloth, her hands shook. *He could have died tonight.* Simi had warned her – maybe she didn't have that much time to make things right with Beck.

She replaced the bowl at his feet, then began to clean the blood off his face with gentle strokes.

Beck roused. 'Is the doc gone?'

'Yes.' *Unless you go really bad on me, which you better not do, mister.*

'I need ya to do somethin'.' There was a long pause and then he sighed. 'Lock the door.'

That was a weird request, but she did as he asked.

'Ya can't tell anyone about this,' he said. 'It won't look right.'

'Got that. What can I do for you?' she asked, her exasperation rising.

'In the small bedroom. Ya'll know what I mean.'

As she moved down the hallway, Riley chose the first door she came to, hoping it was the right one. She cautiously pushed it open, then felt around for a light switch, unsure of what she'd find. Who knew with a guy like Beck? The light came on, illuminating a big poster on the far wall. A beautiful blonde woman, totally clothed, beamed a wholesome smile in Riley's direction. It was Taylor Swift, Beck's favourite country western singer.

'You're such a fanboy,' Riley said, shaking her head. She half expected a shrine underneath the poster, but instead there was a desk with a laptop computer, a chequebook and a stack of what looked like bills. As she studied the space, movement in the corner of the room caught her notice. She stared, the sight taking a few seconds to register.

Something small and furry sat inside a huge cage on the floor, something that was really cute.

'Oh, wow!' Riley said, breaking out in a wide smile. She knelt in front of a rabbit cage so big it could have housed at least three bunnies. The metal alone would have been way expensive, and the resident even had a special floor mat.

Beck has a rabbit? Riley would have expected a dog, a poisonous snake or maybe a tarantula to go with his tough-guy image, not something fluffy and adorable.

It was a small bunny, maybe all of two pounds, with gorgeous fawn-coloured fur and expressive dark eyes. The critter studied her, nose twitching.

'You want to come out?'

The bunny executed an energetic bounce, which Riley took as a *yes*. She bent over the enclosure and removed the occupant as carefully as possible. When she was a kid, she'd played with the one at school, though its teeth and claws had always scared her. Not now. Not after tangling with a Three.

When she returned to the living room, she found Beck sitting up, the icepack on the back of his neck. He looked a bit better, which gave her hope that maybe nothing was going wrong in that brain of his.

After she set the rabbit on the couch, it promptly hopped over and settled next to him like it knew exactly what he wanted. Beck scratched it, then looked up at her, eyes wary.

'Don't start,' he warned.

'What?' she said, grinning. 'I'm sure all the big, bad trappers have a bun-bun in their house.'

His cheeks spotted crimson. 'She's not mine, not really.'

'Then why is she here?'

He sighed. 'I was hookin' up with this girl . . . and she was movin' away and she asked me to turn Rennie loose in one of the parks.' He sucked in a deep breath. 'I thought that wouldn't be right because somethin' would eat her so I . . . never got around to it.'

In Beck's world, the longer the explanation the more he was embarrassed.

'Ya can't tell any of the trappers,' he said, genuinely worried now. 'None of them.'

That was the truth: the others would give him tons of grief over this little bundle of cuddly fur. Wouldn't be *guy* enough for them.

'Did the hunters see her?'

'No. She was at the neighbour's that mornin'. Mrs Merton watches over her sometimes.'

That's why he was so hot to get home last night. He was worried about his rabbit.

'Did Dad know?' Beck slowly nodded, a tremendous effort given his injury. 'Don't worry, we'll keep it our secret,' she said.

He sagged in relief. This really did mean a lot to him.

'Why name her Rennie?'

'It's Renwick,' he said. 'I shortened it.'

Renwick? Now there's a name. 'Why keep a bunny?'

'She's real quiet and doesn't nag at me. I like that.'

Riley took the hint and stopped asking questions. The rabbit was still sitting next to Beck, absolutely content as he petted it. His eyes drifted closed and for the moment her patient seemed at peace, despite what had to be a raging headache.

Even Superman had his kryptonite.

*

Later, after she'd fed his furry companion and played with her, she tucked Rennie back into her cage. Beck gave her a long list of detailed instructions to make sure the rabbit was comfortable, including running a line of Holy Water around the floor and dabbing some on the cage wires in case they got a visit from a hungry demon. Clearly he adored the critter.

Backwoods Boy had surprised her. *Again.*

As Riley rose from the cage, something caught her notice on the desk: a box of text-to-speech software. *Oops.* She was supposed to ask Peter about that but she'd forgotten. Somehow Beck had found it on his own. Curious, Riley jiggled the mouse and an article from the local newspaper came up on the computer screen. He'd been reading along as the voice spoke the words.

If he kept this up, he'd be able to read anything he wanted.

'You're amazing,' Riley whispered. Not that she was going to tell him that or anything.

Beck objected to her help, but needed it to make it to his bed. More griping as she unlaced his boots and helped him out of his shirt. He'd made her turn round as he stripped off his blue jeans.

'I'm not going to faint at the sight of your butt,' she said.

'Ya might, and I don't want that on my conscience,' he said, tossing the jeans aside.

He was in the bed when she turned round. She'd seen him without a shirt before, but this time he seemed different. His arms were muscled and his chest well defined, evidence of a regular weight-lifting regime. He had the classic six-pack abs, now visible just above the bedcovers. Beck might drink beer, but it certainly didn't show.

'That's one wicked bruise,' she said, pointing at his left shoulder.

'It'll heal.'

After a fresh icepack on his forehead, he was good to go.

Once Beck was settled, she headed towards the front of the house and dialled Stewart's number to deliver an update.

'How's he doin'?' the master asked.

Riley gave him a rundown, minus the rabbit.

'He's got the hardest head I've ever seen,' was the reply. 'Do ya need any help watchin' over the lad?'

'Ah, no. It'll be OK.' Riley ran a bluff. 'What was Justine doing on the run?'

Stewart didn't miss a beat. 'The red-haired vixen wheedled the National Guild into allowin' her ta be embedded with a trappin' team. Harper and I had no choice in the matter. She insisted on joinin' up with Beck and Jackson tonight.'

Riley's hunch had been right. 'How'd he get hurt?' she asked, pacing from wall to wall in the front room in agitation.

'Jackson said the reporter snapped a photo and the camera's flash made the Three go mad. It charged towards her and Beck got in the way.'

Of course he did. 'Is the stick chick still alive?' Riley asked.

'Aye. And unharmed.'

'Then why isn't she here watching over Beck? She got him hurt. It's her responsibility to help him out. No, let me guess, Justine's too busy filing her nails.'

'Lord, lass, that's a load of jealousy I'm hearin'.'

'Yeah, it is,' she said as her insides boiled with righteous anger. 'He's hurting bad and she's nowhere to be seen. That sucks.'

'I agree. Yer there instead of her because Beck refused to allow the woman in his house. Said he'd only let Paul's daughter take care of him.'

Riley stumbled in mid-pace. 'You're just saying that.'

'Ya wouldn't be callin' me a liar, now would ya?'

Oh crap. Not good. 'Ah, no. Sorry.'

'I swear, the pair of ya are gonna be the death of me yet,' Stewart grumbled. 'Like two pissed-off cats in a barrel clawin' at each other.'

'I'll watch over him, don't worry.'

'Good. That's what I wanted ta hear. Call if ya need me.'

'Yes, sir.'

Riley ended the call, wondering what had come over her. Calling a Grand Master a liar was a dumb move, even on her worst day. She tapped the phone against her cheek. Beck had specifically asked for her, not Justine or anyone else. He'd told the woman he was hooking up with that he didn't want her to care for him, *or* be in his house. Was he that mad at the reporter for screwing things up? Or was it something else?

When Riley returned to the bedroom, her patient seemed to be sleeping, but it wasn't deep and restful. She took up her post in the chair near the bed, caught by how roles had reversed. Usually it was him watching over her after she'd done some blazingly stupid stunt.

For a time she monitored every breath, in and out. When Beck paused for a moment, she panicked, then he issued a light snore and resumed his natural rhythm.

What if he got really bad when she was asleep and she didn't know it? Then when she went to wake him he'd have gone into a deep coma . . .

Will you quit already? She was psyching herself out. *Just keep an eye on him. It'll be OK.*

In an effort to remain awake, Riley checked out his bedroom by the light from the hallway. It was a guy room. Navy blue comforter, curtains and sheets, like he'd bought one of those bed-in-a-bag kits. It suited him – tidy in a manly sort of way. No fuss needed.

Like Beck.

Not wanting to drift off to sleep, she snagged up the book laying on the night stand. Unable to read it in the dim room, she moved into the hallway, curious about what Beck was reading. It was a kid's book and the back cover said it was a story about a wolf cub named Runt who really wanted to prove himself to his father. The choice of the reading material was telling: Beck had tried to prove himself to Riley's father ever since he'd returned from the army. Now he was doing the same with Stewart.

Inside the book was a paper, a vocabulary list written in her dad's sprawling handwriting. After every word was its pronunciation and what it meant.

Riley knew guys who admitted they were uneducated – they usually said 'dumb' – but they wouldn't do anything about it. Like their fate was set in stone. Beck wasn't accepting his fate, but fighting back, trying to make the best of a new life after a crappy childhood.

Go for it. As long as he felt he was worth all the effort, he'd make it. The moment Beck's confidence began to crack, and his drive faltered, he'd be like the others: another loser who felt he deserved all the evil life had thrown at him.

Returning to the chair, Riley replaced the book where it had been so its owner wouldn't know she'd looked at it: he could be touchy that way. Though it seemed impossible, she dozed for a time, then woke Beck for his first two-hour check. Groggy, he answered the questions she put to him. *So far so good.*

'Ya sleepin' in the chair?' he asked, then yawned.

'Trying. It's not real comfortable.'

He gave her a grave look. 'There's a sleepin' bag in the storage closet. It's clean. It'll keep ya warm.'

Riley nodded her thanks and watched him drift back to sleep. After a time, her butt grew tired so she wandered out into the front room. Bored and desperate to do anything to stay awake, she checked out the shelves on the wall to the right of the front window. She'd seen the pictures, but never had the opportunity to look at them close up.

Riley was taken aback to find a photo of her father posed in front of the high school where he'd taught history classes. She guessed it to be from about five years earlier. Her guess was confirmed when she found a photo of her mom and a twelve-year-old Riley.

Boy, was I that ugly? On the other hand, her mother was

as pretty as she remembered. The camera had caught them laughing about something, the love between them so strong Riley could still feel it today. *I really miss you. You'd know what to do, what I should say to Beck to make it right again.*

There were more photographs, all of them either of her patient or members of the Blackthorne family. None were of his people. His mother sure wasn't up on that mantel.

Riley picked up one of the frames. 'Look at you two,' she said, smiling now. The photo was of her dad standing next to a beaming Private Beck decked out in a crisp uniform, fresh out of boot camp. He was one hot-looking dude. *Still is.*

As Riley set the photograph aside, her hand brushed against a plain wooden box. Though she knew it was rude, she opened the lid. And gasped. Inside were Beck's war medals: a Silver Star and two Purple Hearts. She picked up the five-pointed star – it was gold instead of silver like she'd expected, and the back was engraved *FOR GALLANTRY IN ACTION*. She didn't know much about medals, but guessed they didn't give this to just anyone. In the bottom of the box were photographs of Beck receiving the three awards from some seriously uptight senior officers. The picture with the Silver Star showed him on crutches, proud, but in obvious discomfort from a leg wound.

Why don't you have these out where people can see them? It was like he was ashamed of them or something.

'I really don't understand you sometimes,' she murmured.

After putting the pictures and the medals back where she found them, Riley retrieved the sleeping bag from the storage closet and then made herself a bed on the floor in Beck's room. She was about to fall asleep when she remembered to set her phone alarm or there wouldn't be another check up. Above her she could hear Beck mumbling about demons and butt-kicking.

Some things never change.

Chapter Eighteen

By the time Riley hit the five a.m. 'check Beck's brain' she was running on empty. The stress of worrying about him took a greater toll than the lack of sleep.

'Dammit, can't ya leave me be?' he grumbled, glaring at her as she nudged him awake.

That's the old Beck. Her worry level dropped by half.

'How's the headache?' she quizzed.

'Better. Like a hangover now.'

'When's your birthday?' He told her the date – it was coming up really soon. 'How old are you going to be?'

'Ya know that.'

'If you won't answer the question, I'll start asking ones about Justine.'

A groan. 'I'll be twenty-three.'

Riley did the flashlight trick, ensuring his pupils were equal in size. She hadn't realized that the brown irises had pale flecks of gold in them. *Nice.*

'What? Is something wrong with them?' Beck asked.

Flustered that she'd been caught, she said, 'No, they look fine. Just being . . . thorough.' Much to her relief, he accepted that explanation.

Once the hand-grip test was completed without any obvious weakness, Riley sighed in profound relief. According to the doc, if any of the tests hadn't turned out right his brain was doing really bad things, like bleeding. That didn't seem to be the case.

'I'd say you lucked out, Backwoods Boy. That hard head of yours came in handy for once.'

He gave a slow nod, but didn't release her hands right away. It made her uneasy, so she slid them out of his grasp.

'Riley . . .' he began.

'You should get some rest,' she replied, rising.

'No, talk to me for a while. Ya wake me up and it's hard to go back to sleep.'

She reluctantly returned to the side of the bed. 'Why aren't there any pictures of your family on the mantel?'

'Only have one of my grandparents, but haven't got it framed yet. Never did get any of my uncle. Wish I did now.'

She noted that regret didn't extend to his mother. *They really must not get along.* 'Is your uncle dead?'

'Yeah. He moved to Vegas when I went into the army and died in a car accident. I was in the hospital when it happened so I couldn't get back for the funeral.'

'Sorry.'

He wasn't looking at her now, still fussing with the sheet on his lap. That meant something was troubling him.

'What's up, dude?' she asked.

Beck finally met her gaze. 'That mornin', before the hunters came here, I said some stuff.'

He hadn't said it, he'd shouted it, furious that she'd allowed Ori to touch her. It was the first time she'd realized Beck saw her as potential girlfriend material.

'It doesn't matter,' Riley said, opting for a safe answer. She was unwilling to examine how much happiness she might have lost by believing Ori's lies.

'It *does* matter.' Beck was frowning now. 'I can't help it – I'm still angry at ya for goin' with him.'

That rankled. 'Oh, really? So you can hook with the stick chick or one of those girls at the pool hall, but I'm supposed to be all pure and virginal until you finally get around to noticing me? How does *that* work?'

Beck's frown deepened. 'Ya owed me respect. After all I've done and then ya go and let him . . .'

What? 'Because you paid the rent you thought that gave you dibs on me? Like buying a girl supper and then expecting her to put out?'

He jolted in surprise, then winced in pain. 'What? Hell no! That's not what I was thinkin'.'

'You sure?'

'Yes, I'm sure,' he said emphatically. 'All I wanted was respect.'

He sounded for real so she met that head on. 'Respect goes both ways, Beck,' she argued. 'You treat me like a kid all the time. If nothing more, Ori treated me like a woman.'

Riley waited for a lurid comment in retaliation, but instead he opened his mouth then closed it again, unable to come up with a response.

She rose, wanting a timeout from the guy on the bed. 'I'll be back in two hours. Get some rest.'

'Yer nothin' like Justine,' he blurted. 'Never will be. She's . . . nice and all that, but . . .' He paused, then took a long breath as if to prepare himself for what he was about to reveal. 'Ya mean more to me than she ever will.'

Riley sank into the chair, astounded at the longing in his voice. 'You never told me that. All you did was give me lectures and bitch me out when I didn't follow your every command.'

'I know I did it all wrong. I'm sorry. I couldn't . . . tell ya how I felt.'

'Why not?' she pushed.

His eyes were focused on the sheets again. 'Because of what I am. Where I come from.'

A warning bell went off in her head, urging her to tread carefully. Or, better yet, not go there at all.

'You go to sleep. I'll be back in a little while to bug you again.' Riley tucked the sheet around him, her eyes never leaving his careworn face.

'Ya didn't have to take care of me,' he said. 'Ya could have walked away tonight.'

'And leave you alone? No way.'

'I owe ya for this,' he said simply.

'No, we're even.' *Let's keep it that way.*

Beck's eyes were closed by the time she reached the doorway. Slowly his breath evened out and then he was asleep. There was something so peaceful about watching him.

Though he'd let her have a quick peek inside his industrial-strength armour, Riley knew better than to read too much into that. By morning he'd be sure to put distance between them. That was just his way.

Maybe someday he won't have to.

Just as Riley had predicted, Beck crawled out of his sick bed a short time before dawn and then terse announcements came fast and furious: he had a tolerable headache and she didn't need to ask him a bunch of questions because he wasn't going to die today. And he really needed a shower.

'Ya can go home now,' he said, shutting the bathroom door behind him like she'd served her purpose and was now an embarrassing annoyance.

Jerk. Then she sighed. In the past Riley would have been furious at him, but she'd begun to anticipate this complex man's emotional swings.

Two steps forward, one step back.

The bathroom door opened and Beck poked his head out, blond hair sticking up in all directions like a punk rocker. It looked kinda cute. 'Call me when ya get to Stewart's, OK?'

He was playing big brother again. Riley shook her head.

'No.'

Beck opened his mouth to argue, then changed his mind. 'OK,' he said. 'Yer not a kid any more. No reason I should be treatin' ya like one.' The door closed again and an electric razor hummed to life.

Maybe I should have hit him on the head a long time ago.

*

Though she'd told Beck she was heading to Stewart's, the moment Riley turned the key in the ignition Ori's voice called out to her. Right on time – it was nearly dawn.

'Go away, angel. If you're bored, talk to another statue. Just leave me alone.'

She'd backed on to the street when the full blast of Ori's will hit her. Riley rocked in her seat, tears streaming from her eyes. Her head felt like an overripe watermelon the second it hits the pavement.

'Stop it!' she called, cradling her head. The pain abruptly vanished. Behind the sudden respite was the unspoken threat: come to me or the pain will be back. Three-fold.

Swearing loudly, Riley headed towards the cemetery. At least Beck was in the shower. If he knew she was having morning séances with Lucifer's Number One Seducer, he'd go ballistic.

Since it appeared that Ori couldn't break free of his prison, Riley parked at the west entrance and hiked in. As she hoped, the chilly morning air did the trick, clearing her mental cobwebs while the exercise eased aches in her back and legs. The discomfort would pass; what was important was that Beck would be OK. She'd been there for him, like he'd always been for her. That felt really good.

Martha the angel was sitting on the steps to the Watch House, like she'd been waiting for Riley to appear. Her knitting needles moved at warp speed, generating what appeared to be a stocking cap in bright purple yarn.

'Oh, good, you've come. The Fallen has been making such an unholy racket,' the angel said disapprovingly. 'He's disturbing the peace of this place.'

'Wouldn't that be what a spawn of Hell would do?'

Martha pondered on that and then shrugged. The needles kept moving.

Laying her backpack down, Riley sat on the stone wall in front of the small brick building.

'Can you get him out of my head?' she asked. 'Do an exorcism or something?'

'He's there because of your free will. You'll just have to deal.'

Tough love from an angel. That bites.

'He thinks I'm going to set him free,' Riley said. 'His ego is the size of a planet or something.'

'That's not uncommon with us angel types,' Martha replied, her eyes twinkling now.

Riley scuffed the toe of her tennis shoe against a paving stone. 'Why didn't Lucifer want my soul?'

Martha gave her a sidelong glance. 'You say his name so casually.'

'So what do you guys call him?'

'We have a number of names for the Morning Star,' the angel replied tartly. 'Many of them are not polite.'

Then Riley understood. 'Lucifer tests angels too, not just us mortals.' A nod came her way. 'What happens when you fail one of those pop quizzes? Do you all become statues?'

'That's not for you to know.'

Frustration set in. Heaven's messenger never seemed that helpful except when it suited her boss. 'What *can* you tell me?'

'Ask the Fallen about another of his kind. One named Sartael. Listen carefully how he answers and you will learn a great deal. Enough to make it worth your time on this cold morning.'

'But who is—'

Martha cut her off. 'Go talk to the traitor, dear, or he'll start shouting again. It makes the squirrels nervous.' She rose and tucked her knitting away into her bag, walked a few paces and then vanished. She'd never bothered to answer Riley's question about Lucifer.

All I want to know is the truth.

Riley took her time walking to the statue, savouring the morning. From what she could tell, the statue hadn't changed since yesterday morning, other than bird droppings on one of his wings. *I bet that bugs him.* She positioned herself at the base of the marble angel, waiting impatiently for the sun to rise. Rather than stare like some gawking tourist, she closed her eyes and listened to the birdsong, the whine of a MARTA train pulling into the station, and the occasional skitter of something in the trees around her. That was probably those nervous squirrels.

Riley sensed more than saw when Ori became alive. Heat poured through her, as if she was reawakening along with him. When she opened her eyes, he was staring down at her. What would it be today? More wrath? More seductive lies?

The angel shook out his wings. 'Back again?' he said.

'You keep calling me, remember? I have better things to do than hanging around watching you go from stone to creep to stone again.'

'You can ignore my call if you're strong enough,' he replied.

That she doubted. 'Then what? You send the flying monkeys after me?'

Ori frowned, confused. 'I do not command primates. I only command mortals,' he said loftily.

Apparently the angel wasn't a fan of *The Wizard of Oz*.

'Wow, that's an oversized ego for a stupid statue. I know it's all bluff – you can't order me to free you, or you would have already.'

Ori didn't appear pleased that she'd worked that out on her own.

'Right before Lucifer turned you into a pigeon roost, you were about to tell me why it was so important that I give you my soul. What were you going to say?'

Ori's dark eyes bore into hers. 'Free me and that knowledge is yours.'

'Will you give it a rest? It's not happening.'

'Someday you'll have no choice,' he shot back.

'Answer my question or I'm outta here.'

Ori cocked his head. 'You've changed. You're harder now, less . . .'

'Innocent. Trusting? That would be your doing, angel.' Riley's patience was history. 'Who is this Fallen you guys call Sartael?'

Ori went totally still, as if he had instantly become a statue again. 'How do you know of him?'

She decided to turn the tables and not answer the question. 'Did he turn Simon against me? Is he the one who gave you bad advice and set you up to take the fall?'

'Yes.' The single word came out as a venomous hiss. 'Sartael lied to me, told me our Prince wished me to do something that he did not.'

That something was bedding Riley.

'He was the reason I arrived late at Master Harper's that night you were attacked by the Five. He was the Five's demi-lord. That was why Astaring was so difficult to kill.'

The demons have names? Oh goodie.

'Why is he doing this?' Riley quizzed.

'Power. He seeks the Prince's throne.'

Riley leaned against a headstone, which was probably disrespectful; but she was tired.

'Why does everyone want to rule Hell?' she grumbled. 'It looks a sucky job to me. You're up to your eyes in demons and you have to test mortals and angels, who all hate you.'

Ori carefully tidied the wing that had been sullied by a bird. After brushing it off, his dark eyes met hers again. 'Sartael will not test anyone. He will destroy. He will start a war with Heaven.'

The one I'm supposed to prevent.

'Indeed,' Ori replied.

She'd forgotten he could read her mind. 'Why doesn't Lucifer take him down? I mean, he's the Prince of

Darkness. That can't only be a job title.'

Ori scrutinized her, puzzled. 'You carry my master's mark, but your soul is your own.'

'He said he didn't want it. I owe him a favour instead. It got me in a ton of trouble with the Church.'

'Yet it has kept you alive,' Ori said, nodding now as if he understood. 'Only the most foolish among us would cross the Prince and destroy his pet.'

'Pet?' she spat. She was done with this jerk. 'Don't call me again. We have nothing to talk about.'

'You'll be here, at the last,' Ori said. 'Then you will listen to me, Riley Anora Blackthorne. You will have no choice.'

'We'll see about that, angel.'

Riley spun on her heel and marched away, her temper pushing her along. It wasn't until she reached the Bell Tower that she looked over her shoulder. Ori was stone again, his eyes open, gazing at the dawn. His arms were at his sides, hands palm up as if in supplication.

It *had* been a productive sunrise: she knew the name of the angel who'd been pulling everyone's strings, the Fallen who had brought chaos to both the blessed and the damned.

After a big breakfast and a long nap, Riley reluctantly dragged herself to Stewart's library. With a few hours to burn until class, this would be the quietest place to do her homework. Hopefully the library's owner wouldn't mind.

The moment Riley turned on the overhead light, she sighed in envy. This wasn't a crowded nook, but a full-size room that told her that Stewart was serious about his scholarship. Floor-to-ceiling bookshelves greeted her, along with a round wood table, two padded chairs and a Tiffany-style desk lamp. It appeared as if this library had magically been transported from another century.

Wonder if my dad ever saw this? Probably not. If he had, he'd never have left.

Riley placed her notebook, phone and pen on the tabletop and then began her search through the shelves. She quickly realized there was a system in place: paperback fiction all in one bookcase – the Scotsman seemed to prefer military fiction and mysteries set in Victorian and Edwardian England – then non-fiction by topic. She moved from shelf to shelf, trailing her fingers over the books' spines in nearly religious awe.

In a corner were two bookcases stocked with tomes about angels, demons, Heaven and Hell. Riley had no idea which to pick, so she let her fingers do the choosing.

Rebellious Angels: Lucifer's Descent from Heaven

That sounded promising. When she removed the book from the shelf, she found that it was bound in brown leather and creaked softly when she opened it. The ink was muted with age. It'd been published in 1898.

She was holding a book that was one hundred and twenty years old.

Riley reverently carried it to the table and placed it on the book stand. After removing the thick green afghan from the chair, she settled in. The blanket went round her legs: the library may be truly awesome, but it was chilly.

The book's first chapter began with the creation of man (Adam) and the ire that stirred within the ranks of the angels. It was written in awkward, hard-to-read prose, but Riley worked through it nonetheless. Her dad had read some pretty dense books in his time and always insisted on quoting passages to her. In his own way, he'd prepared her for this research.

'Many argued against the creation of the clay creature, as they called Adam. That God would spare His love for such a lowly being did not sit well with the angelic host, chief among them being the Morning Star. When God ordered that all bow their knee to Adam and his descendents, a rebellion arose among the angels and they did depart Heaven.'

After four more pages about that departure – these types of books never got to the good part quickly – there was a multi-page list of angels who'd sided with Lucifer against the Almighty. Riley traced down it until she found the one who'd tried to steal her soul

Ori: an angel of the higher realm known for charm and seduction.

'Tell me about it.'

It went to say that once Ori had taken residence in Hell he served as an agent of retribution, executing those who challenged Lucifer's authority. That tallied with his claim of why he was in Atlanta. Maybe not everything Ori told her was a lie.

Further down on the page she found:

Sartael (also known as Satarel): a devious archangel who works

hidden deceits. Said to be one of the prime movers behind the Fall of Lucifer. Is known for corrupting the minds of mortals and bending them to his will.

Tucking the afghan tighter round her legs, Riley dug into the text to learn more about the angel who had done his best to destroy her life.

The next morning brought thick Scottish oatmeal, bacon, more mushrooms, tomatoes and hot scones. *If I stay here much longer, I'll have to buy larger jeans.*

Master Stewart was eyeing the newspaper, muttering under his breath every now and then. When he looked up at Riley, the frown was so deep she figured she'd done something wrong.

'What?' she asked, lowering her spoon.

'How's yer classes goin'?'

'Fine. I got an A on my maths homework and aced a test on the Civil War.'

A grunt. 'Did ya talk ta the red-haired reporter?'

What? He'd done it again – changing topics midstream. 'No, I did not talk to *that* skank.'

'Ah, well, she's gettin' creative then.' He shoved the newspaper across the table. When Riley saw the headline, her spoon dropped on her plate with a clatter. The photograph made her heart clench: an injured Beck hunched over in a street that had to be in Demon Central. She checked out the headline.

Trapper Injured During Run – Is the Guild Jinxed?

The article recounted Justine's version of how Beck and Jackson had found themselves 'outmatched' by a Three. At no time did she indicate she'd been at the root of the problem.

'This is total crap. Beck wouldn't have got hurt if she hadn't been there. He was playing hero. He always does that.'

Stewart nodded thoughtfully. 'Third paragraph down.'

Riley hunted for the text and felt her jaw clench. There was a quote from an unnamed source that the Guild was cursed because they'd allowed a female in their ranks. Riley jerked her head up, her blood boiling. 'Do they really think that?' she demanded.

'Some. Like havin' a woman on a ship. Same thing.'

Riley shoved the paper away in disgust.

'It's only gonna get worse,' the master warned. 'Prepare yerself for that.'

She nodded grimly and went back to her oatmeal. If she ever saw Justine Armando again, it wasn't going to be pretty.

Somewhere in the house a cellphone rang and then footsteps approached as Harper returned to the kitchen.

'We can do that,' he said into the phone, a hint of unease in his voice. 'How many will you need?' A pause. 'OK, I'll send two trappers over.' He ended the call and placed the phone on the table.

'Trouble?' Stewart asked.

'Not sure. The hunters got a tip there's demons inside that abandoned building on Forsyth, the big one that used to be an insurance company.'

'The hunters asked for our aid?' Stewart asked.

Harper grinned. 'Yeah. Suddenly we're useful, at least when it comes to Demon Central. It seems Rome wants us to play together like good boys and –' he looked over at Riley – 'girls.'

'Who ya sendin'?'

'Beck, if he's up for it. He's the best choice since he's trapped in that building a number of times. Most of the others wouldn't go near it.'

'He'll not turn ya down, even if he's hurtin',' Stewart advised. 'That's not his way.'

'Then he needs to learn his limits,' Harper replied. His eyes moved to Riley. 'You'll go with him, Brat.'

'What?' she yelped, dropping what remained of her scone.

'Good learning experience,' Harper replied with a sneering grin. 'You'll have three hunters and a journeyman watching your back. What could go wrong?'

'This is me, remember?' she protested, wiping her hands on a napkin. 'I take a breath and something goes wrong.' *I shouldn't be anywhere near the hunters. In case they change their mind about me.*

'I'm not buying that. You need to learn how to do a building search and this way you'll get to see the big boys in action.'

She would have continued to argue, but Stewart hadn't disagreed with the assignment. That meant she really should be going on this run.

'I'll go change my clothes.'

Chapter Nineteen

Beck swung by and picked Riley up at Stewart's house, and then drove towards downtown.

'What the hell is Harper thinkin'?' he asked, giving her a stern look. 'Ya shouldn't be on this run. I've been inside this buildin' before and it's brutal.' *It's no damned place for a girl.*

'According to my master I need the experience,' she replied. 'Speaking of which, how's your head *and* your shoulder?'

'They're OK,' he lied. *Better she not know I'm hurtin'.* 'Doc says I can take the pain pills again so that's helped a lot.'

Riley scowled at him and that told him she wasn't buying his lie. 'Carmela also said no trapping.'

'One out of two isn't bad,' he conceded.

Beck found the demon hunter's van on Forsyth Street and slotted his truck right behind it. Three of the Vatican's team waited for them: Captain Salvatore along with Müller and the one named Corsini. They stood alongside their vehicle, staring up at the dilapidated building across the street. The structure was five storeys of brick and faded marble with faded gang graffiti decorating the upper sections and windows covered in warped plywood. The ones that weren't covered sported sooty scorch marks. There was no front door now – that entrance was walled off in concrete blocks as were all the windows on street level. Which meant they'd have to go in through one of the first-storey windows or come in through the back of the building.

'A friend of mine used to live here,' Beck remarked.

'Here?' Riley asked, incredulous. 'Before it was like this, you mean?'

'No. Ike's homeless so anythin' out of the weather works for him. Right now he's at one of the shelters, but sometimes he isn't so lucky.'

'That has to be scary,' she said. 'Never knowing where you're going to be from one day to the next.'

'He takes it in his stride. He was in the army, like me. Ya learn to deal.'

'You served together?' She actually sounded interested.

'No. He was in the First Gulf War, back in the nineties. I wasn't even born yet.' He zipped the duffel bag shut. 'Ike said he saw ya that night ya trapped the Three down here.'

Riley thought for a bit. 'The old black guy who walks funny?'

'That's him. I'll introduce ya someday.'

'I think I'd like that,' she replied.

Was she being polite or did she really mean it? Why did he care? Why did it matter what Paul's daughter thought of him?

Beck pushed that thought away as he climbed out of the truck. Riley joined him, shouldering her backpack. As they approached the team, the captain greeted them.

'Captain Salvatore,' Beck replied. 'What's the news here?'

'We've been told there's increased demon activity in this area, particularly around this building. We thought we'd work the location and see what we could flush out. Do you know the place?'

'Paul and I trapped Pyro-Fiends in there. More often than not it's a good place to find a Three.'

'You armed?' the hunter asked.

'Yup,' Beck said, tapping the end of the steel pipe sticking out of the bag.

'I meant a firearm.'

'I prefer this kind of cold steel,' Beck replied.

'Your choice.' Then he looked over at Riley. 'What about you?'

'I've got Holy Water. The real stuff,' she replied. 'And I run fast.'

The captain gave a half-smile. 'Well, with talents like that, how can we fail?'

'Are we it or is the rest of the team on the way?' Beck asked.

'They're handling a call up near a university north of town. It's a full sweep so takes more men. If we encounter too much resistance, we'll fall back and call for reinforcements.'

'Sounds like a plan.' Beck pointed. 'There's a way in at the back. Saves havin' to climb up to one of the upper windows.' *So my shoulder doesn't kill me.*

'You will need this.' A black baseball cap came his way,

one with a logo of St George and the dragon on the front of it. 'It's got lights built in. Keeps your hands free.'

Beck checked it out. There was one main light in the brim and two under the bill. He clicked them on and off, and nodded his approval. Stripping off his Braves cap, he stashed it in the duffel bag, then put on the new one. He found it amusing when Riley got one of her own.

'Y'all do have really fine toys,' he admitted.

Salvatore smiled in response. 'One of the perks of working for the Holy See.'

'I'd never make it with you guys. I swear too much.'

A twinkle appeared in the captain's eyes. 'So do we when nobody important is listening.'

Beck took them down the sidewalk to the west side of the building, ignoring the curious stares of passers-by. There was a covered entrance on that side, though it was blocked off. Above it was a window, which was the best way in.

Out of habit, Beck did a one-eighty to check their surroundings. A few noisy people. He gritted his teeth as he hefted his bag and then himself on to the overhang above the entrance. His shoulder told him this was a stupid idea, sending slicing pain down to his fingertips and numbing them. He shook feeling back into them. At least the pain meds were doing some good.

The canopy shifted under his weight. 'Be careful,' he cautioned. 'This thing is on its last legs.'

The hunters pulled themselves up one by one. That left Riley. He could tell she was re-evaluating this adventure.

'Well?' he said, keeping his voice neutral. He wanted her to make the decision, not feel she had to do this to prove something to him or the others.

With a determined expression, Riley reached up and took his right hand. He lifted her up, but he noticed she made it as easy as possible for him to keep his left shoulder from complaining. It took her a moment to regain her footing.

'You sure this thing's going to hold us?' she said, concerned.

'We'll know soon enough.'

After carefully edging across the overhang, Beck pushed aside the remaining chunks of weather-stained plywood from the window. This is the way he and Paul had entered the last two times and, from the looks of it, it remained the local favourite.

'I'll take point,' he said, mostly because he knew the place and that would put Riley in the middle of the hunters. If something bad went down, he'd have to trust them to keep her safe. If that asshat Amundson had been on the team, she'd be in the truck right now.

Beck stepped through the hole into the murky room. He knew from experience it was littered with junk and contained a million places for a demon to hide, even a fiend the size of a Three. Remembering the cap, he clicked it on. The light on the brim shot forward like a searchlight.

'Sweeeeet,' he said. *Gotta get me one of these.*

By turning right, then left, Beck was pleased to see the cap did a fair job of illuminating the area. Not as bright as a

flashlight, but it kept his hands free for the pipe, and that's what counted.

He waited until the others crawled through the window behind him.

'Whoa, it smells in here,' Riley said, waving a hand in front of her nose. 'Does everyone in Atlanta use this place as a toilet?'

Beck moved forward with deliberate slowness, careful where he was putting his feet. Broken glass littered the floor.

'Watch where ya walk, girl,' he warned.

Dirty streams of light crept round the seams in the boarded-up windows, barely enough to do any good as the cap lights danced around the room like erratic fireflies.

Riley let loose a barely stifled shriek as something swooped down from the busted ceiling tile right over the top of her; a bird, heading for the nearest patch of sunlight. A moment later a second joined it. This time she merely ducked.

'Sorry,' she said. He didn't have to look to know her face would be red with embarrassment. 'Why is all this stuff in here?'

'A Three went on a rampage in the buildin'. Killed a bunch of folks. The buildin's owners couldn't get anyone to clean the place out, so they walked away.'

'I can see why.'

About forty feet in Beck found a mound of dirty bedding, someone's nest in this hellhole. 'Home sweet home,' he murmured.

Further on from the makeshift bed was a rickety table

made of discarded boxes and a plastic lawn chair. It never failed to amaze him how people tried so hard to make the best of what they had. He'd seen that when he was overseas. A woman might live in a dirt hut, but she'd be sweeping it out, trying to keep it clean. From the looks of it, the tenant hadn't been here for a while.

Riley picked up a newspaper that sat on the table. 'January. This year,' she said. 'The want ads.'

Beck's cap light caught on a pile of something curiously white. He stepped closer. *No need for that job now.*

He clicked off his light and turned towards the others. 'We got a body here.' Then he looked directly at Riley. 'This isn't pretty. Ya sure ya want to see this?'

Her furrowed brows told him she was wrestling with the question.

'If you want to back out of this, we won't think less of you,' the captain said quietly.

That earned him points in Beck's book. 'What he said.'

Riley swallowed hard. 'It's what a trapper does,' she replied. 'I'll deal.'

She's Paul's daughter all right.

Beck manoeuvred back to the corpse, clicked on his cap and knelt next to the disjointed pile of bones. Strings of dried flesh hung from a few of them, but for the most part they'd been stripped clean. The skull lay about four feet to the left, the empty eye sockets staring into eternity.

The captain knelt by the bone pile then shifted one with the tip of his service revolver. 'Gnaw marks. Large ones.

Probably a Three.' The hunter rose, shifted his gun to his left hand and then crossed himself.

'I'll call the city and they'll send someone up to take care of him.'

'Is there any way the cops can tell who he was?' Riley asked, her voice fainter. 'Let his family know?'

'His clothes are gone so there's no I.D. He'll be a John Doe,' Beck said. Harsh but true. 'The cops won't bother. They got enough live people causin' trouble to worry about one dead one.'

Riley sucked in a breath. 'That's so . . . sad.'

That's the way of it, girl. Ya make a mistake and ya die. If yer lucky, someone will be there to weep over yer grave.

Once past the corpse, Beck led the team deeper into the building where it was darker and the floor increasingly cluttered with debris. Portions of the ceiling had fallen into jumbled heaps, and broken furniture lay strewn around from when the former occupants had run for their lives. He intended to walk the length of the room, but paused by the stairs. His light picked up marks in the dust leading to the third floor, and not the kind a human made.

Beck held up his hand and the others halted. Then he pointed. 'Best if we keep quiet from now on,' he said for Riley's benefit.

She nodded her understanding, clutching a Holy Water sphere tightly in one hand.

Beck began his ascent, trying not to make any noise. It was nearly impossible. Though the stairs themselves were solid, the debris on them crunched loudly underfoot.

As he emerged on the third floor, his nose picked up the stench of fresh demon crap. He didn't bother to tell the others: they would notice it just as well as he had. A check of the stairs leading upward showed no paw marks. It was darker up here, all the windows covered by plywood: a perfect place for a Three to hide.

'Which way?' the captain asked in a lowered voice.

'Left,' Beck replied, more on gut instinct than anything. That would take them towards the front of the building. If they didn't encounter a demon along the way, they'd head back towards the exit.

The terrain didn't look any different than the floor below: piles of broken furniture. A desk calendar. A photo of someone's family. A smashed coffee cup.

Riley stuck close to him instead of the others. That he hadn't expected: Beck figured she'd feel safer with the hunters and their guns. When she stepped on something and nearly lost her balance, he caught her arm and she righted herself. There was a murmured thank you. Despite the cold, he could see a thin trickle of sweat thread its way down the side of her face.

Harper is pushin' her too hard. She's not ready for this. But when was any trapper truly ready to go out on their own? What if she faced this kind of situation down the line and didn't know how to handle it?

At a faint sound, Beck halted, raising his hand to signal to the others to hold their places. Snuffling. Growls. The sound of something moving around in the next room. He tapped his ear a couple of times and then pointed. The captain nodded.

Cautiously they inched forward, working around the rubble. They had fanned out as well, Müller and Corsini on his left, the captain on his right.

He was missing someone. Looking over his shoulder he found Riley with her back to him, staring at the far door.

'Girl?' he whispered.

She mimicked his hand signals perfectly – tapping her ear and then pointing to the other room.

Ah, hell.

One demon ahead, one behind. They were caught in the middle.

Chapter Twenty

Riley wiped away the sweat on her forehead with a sleeve, panic percolating through her veins. There weren't that many demons and she had four guys with her, all pros. The hunters had guns with special bullets so this wasn't at all like the Tabernacle.

Riley gasped instinctively as the doorway in front of her filled with a hairy slavering demon. It was one of the mature Grade Threes with a double row of teeth. Its muscles rippled under rank black fur, eyes glowing like two high-intensity lasers.

Demon voices rose, howling like Hell's wolves.

'We got more than two of these things,' Beck said.

'Agreed,' Salvatore replied. 'Retreat to the stairs. We're in close quarters, so be careful with your fire, gentlemen.' The captain cued his radio. 'Team Angelus, this is Team Gabriel. We have made contact with multiple Hellspawn and need immediate back-up.' He sounded so in control, as if they weren't boxed in by ravenous demons.

Amundson's voice came back immediately. 'Roger, Team Gabriel. Where are you in the structure?'

'Third floor. We'll be moving down one floor and then towards the west exit.'

There were more laser eyes now, glinting in the semi-darkness.

'Roger,' Amundson replied crisply. 'Team Angelus estimates arrival in ten minutes.'

An eternity when you were in a building full of hungry demons.

'Push the junk in front of ya, slow 'em down,' Beck suggested. Riley nodded and carefully replaced the Holy Water sphere in her backpack, then began to retreat, each step in slow motion as she kept her attention on the threats in front of her. Any debris in her way she shoved between her and the fiends: busted plywood, broken chairs and Lord knows what. Müller was at her side now, covering her with his weapon.

Thanks, Harper. I so needed this experience.

The two groups made the stairs at the same time. Beck headed down to the second floor, but had gone only a few steps before he thundered back up. 'We got more below us.'

A howling chorus sprang up, like an ancient demonic battle cry, as a solid mass of furry bodies surged forward out of the darkness. Muzzle flashes lit the room. Riley cringed at the noise of gunfire, her nose rebelling at the sickening odour of demon. A few feet to her left a Three took a bullet in the chest, pitching forward on to the floor. Another joined it a moment later. Then another.

It was slow going on the stairs: the handrails were gone and Riley had to feel her way up using the dusty wall as support. Her heart beat so rapidly she felt dizzy: a panic attack would be fatal now.

She issued a warning cry as a Three launched itself down the stairs towards them, its teeth glistening in the cap lights. Beck married his steel pipe with its skull and it tumbled by them, sending up a cloud of choking dust.

'Keep movin'!' he urged.

The captain's radio spewed words. 'Nine minutes ETA for the back-up team,' he called out, jettisoning a magazine from the gun and then ramming a full one home. 'We need to find a defensive position, buy ourselves some time.'

'The roof,' Beck said. 'It's the best chance we got.'

Despite the snarling pack on their heels, there were no more demons as they climbed. Right before they reached the fifth floor, Müller asked permission to try to hold the things at bay while the others made their way to the roof.

'We stay together,' was the curt reply from his superior.

'But, sir—'

'No! We will not repeat Barcelona's mistakes,' Salvatore countered.

Barcelona? Maybe the hunters weren't as infallible as Riley had thought.

When they reached the top floor, Beck hunted for the door to the roof. He shoved furniture around, his cap light swinging wildly as he searched.

What if he can't find it?

'Got it!' he called out. Riley nearly wept with relief.

From there on the stairs became narrower, then curved

to the right. A door stood in their way at the very top. Beck looked back over his shoulder, his face glistening with sweat and his breathing ragged. She knew what he was thinking: what was on that roof? More Threes? Or something worse lying in wait?

Corsini pushed past her and joined Beck. 'We go up together,' he said. 'Captain's orders.' He offered her fellow trapper a pistol. This time Beck didn't refuse the offer.

'Here,' he said, handing her the steel pipe. 'Ya know how to take 'em down.'

She did. She'd killed a Three with a folding chair at the Tabernacle and the pipe was a much better weapon.

Beck clicked off the safety, chambered a round and then used his steel-toed boot to kick open the door. It swung on rusty hinges, screeching like a cat caught under a truck tyre.

He went through first, then Corsini.

Riley took a step up, but Müller caught her arm. 'Wait please.'

She forced herself to stay put. Her mind began to conjure up the screams, the sound of Beck and Corsini being torn apart. Nothing. Silence behind them as well. The demons had backed off for the moment.

Why is it so quiet? 'Beck?' No reply. 'Beck!' she shouted.

'It's clear!' he called down.

Thank God. Riley made sure to hustle. Müller was next. The captain was last, toting a piece of lumber. Once the door was closed, he used the wood to wedge it tight.

'That's not going to hold them very long,' he admitted.

'How many did ya see?' Beck asked, scouting along the side of the rooftop.

'I counted eighteen and I know there were more,' the captain replied.

'Why are they like this?' Corsini demanded. He appeared the most jittery of the hunters, but then he had an unborn child to think of. 'I thought the trappers were just –' He caught Beck's sudden glare and closed his mouth.

'Makin' up stories about all those demons workin' together because we couldn't cut it? Well, now ya know the truth, hunter.'

And the truth will set you free. That'd been one of Paul Blackthorne's favourite sayings. In this case the truth had them on a roof five storeys up with no way of getting down unless they wanted to wade through a sea of ravenous Hellspawn. Somehow she doubted the Threes would take note of Hell's mark on her palm before they ate her.

Salvatore addressed his radio. 'Team Angelus, what is your ETA?'

'Seven minutes,' came the prompt reply.

'We are on the roof. Do you copy?'

'Roger.'

There was a pronounced thump as something threw itself against the door.

'Here's as good as any,' Beck advised from a position near the front of the building. 'Gives us a clear shot at the door.'

Salvatore agreed. 'When the teams arrive, they'll clear out the demons and we'll make our way down.'

These guys have a plan. There's more coming to help us. It'll work out.

They made a defensive position in a corner, where front and side walls met. On the captain's suggestion Riley placed a line of Holy Water in a large semi-circle approximately fifteen feet from their position. When she ran out part way through the ward, she cannibalized the sphere in her backpack and finished the job. By the time she'd finished, the men were in position, the hunters' backpacks on the ground in front of them, their extra ammunition laid out, ready to go.

The door took another solid blow.

Beck pulled out his phone and punched in a number. 'Jackson? We need help here.' He relayed the situation. 'Don't come into the buildin'. It's ass deep in demons.' Their fellow trapper must have asked about the hunters. 'About five minutes out. If ya can give us back-up on the street, that'd be good . . . Yeah . . . Later.'

He never says goodbye. This might be the one time he wished he had.

Beck had just ended the call when the phone lit up. 'Hello? . . . Oh, hi there.' He listened intently, his eyes riveted on the door. 'Thanks for the tip, dude. I owe ya. What am I doin'? I'm on top of a buildin' full of Threes. How's yer day goin'?'

How can you be so calm? Her knees were knocking so badly she could hardly stand.

Something made her turn, instinct perhaps. A furry muzzle peered over the top of the wall as its owner's claws dug into the bricks for leverage. *How had the thing got up here?* With immense effort, it heaved itself up right behind Beck. He was still yapping away, no clue he was about to become lunch.

Before it could crawl on to the roof, Riley whacked it with the steel pipe. Teeth flew in all directions, pelting her, then the demon slid out of sight, claws scraping as it lost its hold. There were shouts from below as gravity did its job. When she checked, the body lay sprawled in the street. Bystanders pointed at it, while some took pictures with their cellphones.

Beck said his goodbyes and ended the call. Once he was paying attention again, she pointed downward with the pipe. Peering over the edge of the building, he blinked at the sight, then grinned and gave her a thumbs up. 'Good job. Remind me not to piss ya off. Ya might think of usin' that on me sometime.'

'So tempting,' she said, shaking her head. *Except I'd aim for your knees. Your head's too hard.*

The wedge on the door cracked and then burst into pieces as it flew open. Demons poured on to the roof. Four, five, more. The hunters opened fire in a volley and their attackers fell. One large demon took a hit between its eyes and crumpled only a few feet from the ward. It twitched, then stop moving, dead.

We'll be OK. They'll shoot them and then we'll get out of here.

The demon corpse twitched again, rising up on its haunches, black blood flowing down its hideous face. Reddish yellow eyes flickered, then grew brighter. Howling in rage, it waved its clawed arms above its head.

'But you shot it!' Riley exclaimed. The bullets had papal Holy Water in them. No demon could withstand that. 'It should be dead.'

Salvatore put another three rounds into the thing. It jerked, but didn't fall. It couldn't die because it was already a corpse.

'Ah, hell. Zombie demons? Give me a freakin' break!' Beck yelled.

More of the dead Threes rose now, all with that strange yellow flickering in their eyes.

'Hold your fire unless they cross the ward,' Salvatore ordered. 'Don't waste the ammunition.'

'This is an epic fail,' Beck said, casting a worried glance over the side of the building.

If he's scared, we're in big trouble.

Heaven wouldn't let her die. She couldn't stop Armageddon if that was the case. *Now I sound like Simon.* He'd been so sure his faith would keep him safe that he'd never thought the angels might have other plans.

'Have ya ever seen somethin' like this before?' Beck asked.

Salvatore shook his head. 'This is a new evil.'

Riley frowned in thought. The demons were all wrong. There'd been no chorus of 'Blackthorne's daughter' that she'd come to expect whenever she encountered a fiend. Didn't matter if it was the small ones or a Five, they all did it. These hadn't.

'Their eyes are different. They're yellow,' she said.

Beck huffed in agreement. 'Didn't figure Lucifer would go this far.'

The demons growled, but there was no cringing and wails of 'Name not he!' like they usually did. It appeared that the wounds had stopped bleeding and Riley swore she could smell the stench of decay.

'Lucifer is a wimp,' she shouted. No reaction whatsoever. 'I don't think these guys are his.'

'They have to be the Prince's,' Salvatore argued.

'Then why don't they fear his name?' Riley asked.

Before the captain could answer, his radio came to life. 'The other team is closing in,' he announced.

The fiends continued to hold their positions outside the Holy Water ward.

'What are they doing?' Riley asked. 'They could break through if they wanted. What are they waiting for?'

Beck swore under his breath. 'Ah, hell, don't ya see? They're usin' us to draw the others in. We're the damned bait!'

The captain whirled towards him. 'You think this is a trap for the back-up team?'

'Why not? They could have shattered that ward any time, so why are they standin' there?'

'Sir, I think the trapper is correct,' Müller said.

The captain muttered under his breath, then cued the radio. 'This is Team Gabriel. Do not enter the structure. I repeat, *do not* enter the building. Set up a five-man team by the west entrance to keep the Hellspawn confined. Use Holy Water grenades only. Ammunition is ineffective.'

There was a pause on the other end as Amundson digested that troubling news. 'We copy you, Team Gabriel. Local fire department's hook and ladder truck is five out.'

Salvatore peered over the edge of the building. 'We'll need to move sooner than that. Send up ropes and we will rappel down.'

What? 'Ah.' Riley raised her hand like she was in class. 'Rappelling is not in my skill set, guys.'

Salvatore didn't miss a beat. 'Cancel the ropes. Employ tarp extraction.'

Tarp extraction? What did that mean?

The low growls from their watchers grew more intense, like the demons had figured out that their prey wasn't going to be there for much longer.

Riley's breath became tighter with each inhalation.

Can't panic. Just breathe in. Breathe out. We're not going to die.

Beck moved closer to her, touching her arm. 'Hang in there, girl – we're almost outta here,' he said quietly. His strong voice reassured her, and she loosened her death grip on the steel pipe.

When shouts came from below, Riley took a quick peek over the side of the building. The demon corpse was gone. She doubted it was because someone had toted it home as a souvenir.

A screech of tyres announced the arrival of four black

vans. The doors flew open and men bolted out of the vehicles at top speed. Riley caught sight of Jackson and Remmers running up the street. Then Simon's bright blond hair. They joined the hunters and set about preventing Atlanta's clueless citizens from wandering into the middle of a war zone.

The growls behind Riley escalated in volume and she turned in time to see the demons begin to move forward.

'Steady,' Salvatore advised. 'It'll take time for them to get through the ward.'

Beginning to panic, she looked down again and found that something large and white was being unfolded in the middle of the street, gradually becoming a giant square. A huge tarp. Hunters shuttled around the edge of it, getting a strong grip on the fabric. Then, one by one, they looked up expectantly.

The captain's radio crackled. 'The tarp is in place, Team Gabriel,' Amundson reported. 'Whenever you're ready.'

'Excellent. Begin evacuation,' the captain replied.

If they thought she was going to jump off the roof . . .

'No, no way,' Riley said, backing up.

Beck was next to her in an instant. Over her protests, he pulled her cap off, tossed it aside, then peeled the pipe out of her fingers. It fell near his duffel bag.

'Riley?' She didn't answer him, too afraid of what would happen if she did. Shivers raced across her body and each breath grew ominously tighter.

'Come on, girl,' he urged. 'Link yer arms round the

backpack and hold it tight to yer chest. Then jump. It'll be fine.'

'I can't do it,' she insisted.

The demons were at the circle now. A lone howl went, then amplified as each fiend added its voice to the unholy chorus. The first Three bounced off the ward, cringing and crying as the Holy Water scorched it. Then another struck the barrier, and another. Eventually the line would break and they'd all die.

'Ya have to go, now!' Beck said, scooping her up his arms. There was a hiss of pain in her ear as his shoulder reacted to the increased weight.

'Oh God, don't do this!' she cried.

Beck must have seen how frightened she was because his expression softened. He leaned close and whispered. 'Do ya trust me, Riley?'

Tears built in her eyes. *Do I?*

'Yes,' she whispered, trembling in fear. *Always.*

Beck gently placed a kiss on her forehead. 'Then it'll be all right,' he replied.

Then he tossed her over the side of the five-storey building.

Chapter Twenty-One

Riley would have screamed all the way down, but there wasn't time. She bounced once, twice, then slid off the edge of the tarp and on to the ground, assisted by a pair of hunters. Her head spun and it took one of them to help her to the kerb. She sank on to the concrete, shaking, her arms in a death grip round her backpack. Finally she loosened her grip and it slid to the ground.

Her eyes rose at the sound of multiple gunshots. Beck leaped off the building, his duffel bag cradled to his chest.

'Oh my God,' she whispered, then held her breath as he plummeted towards the ground.

Beck landed, slid off and took a few steps away from the tarp, grimacing in pain. Müller and Corsini were next. Captain Salvatore didn't wait for the last hunter to clear the tarp, but dove over the edge, hastily tucking into a ball. Above him, demons lined the roof, bellowing in rage.

Beck joined her, sinking down on the kerb, cradling his shoulder. He hissed when something popped in his back, then straightened up.

'You OK?' she asked.

'Yeah. I just gotta stop doin' this stupid shit. Makes the

shoulder hurt like hell.' He looked over at her, concerned. 'Sorry about the roof, but there was no other way.'

'I know.' She never would have jumped on her own, at least not until a demon was about to eat her. And he'd kissed her, well sort of. That had been . . . interesting. Maybe he wasn't holding on to his grudge as hard as she thought.

Extracting a pint of water from her pack, Riley took a lengthy drink, trying to prevent her hands from shaking. She failed. Then she handed the water to Beck. As she'd hoped, he dug around the inside of his duffel bag and produced a bottle of pain pills. He dropped one on to his palm and gulped it down with the rest of the liquid. The hunter cap she'd been wearing came her way.

'Thought ya might want to keep this as a souvenir,' he said.

A roof full of demons and he'd taken time to pick up the cap.

'Thanks.'

Her eyes went to the top of the building again: the demons were no longer visible, probably regrouping, waiting for another chance to catch their prey unawares.

'The hunters aren't going inside there again, are they?'

'By the time they do the Threes will be gone.' Beck wiped sweat off his brow with his uninjured arm. 'There's a series of tunnels throughout this part of the city. They'll just move to a new location.'

Jackson squatted next to Riley and winked at her. 'You fly real well for a trapper.'

'Yeah, one of my many mad skills.'

'I'll teach you how to rappel if ya want,' Beck offered.

She gave him a sidelong look. 'You're serious?'

'Sure. Ya have to build up some upper-body strength, but it's doable.'

Riley filed that away for future reference.

'We need to get ya boots, though,' he added. 'Those high tops are not cuttin' it.'

That she wasn't so sure about: she liked her Converse.

'What happened in there?' Jackson asked.

Beck shook his head immediately. 'I'll tell ya somewhere less . . . public.'

'Got it,' the other trapper replied, frowning now. 'Stewart and Harper will be here soon. They're making a condolence call.'

Beck looked up. 'Who did we lose?'

'Tom Ashton. A couple Threes got him.'

'Sweet Jesus,' Beck murmured.

'Which one was he?' Riley asked.

'The guy with the big handlebar moustache,' Jackson replied.

Oh. She remembered him. He'd been nice.

Riley rose, the urge to be somewhere else so strong she thought it might strangle her. She needed to see her dad, feel him hug her and have him tell her the world wasn't such a horrible place. She wouldn't believe him, but at least she could try to delude herself that he was right.

'I'm going,' she said. When Beck protested that she should

wait until Stewart arrived to catch a ride back to the master's house, she waved him off. 'I'm good. I'll catch the bus.'

'Suit yerself.'

Staring down at him, Riley tried to think of how to let him know she was grateful for saving her. Despite all that had fallen between them, he'd watched out for her.

'Thank you,' she said simply.

'Yer welcome,' he replied.

As Riley wove her way around the barricades, there was the click of camera shutters. The press was all over the place. Someone called her name – it was Justine pushing her way through the rubber-necking bystanders.

Riley turned her back and kept walking. If the reporter got in her face, there would be big trouble, the kind that would most certainly rate another article in the newspaper.

Another nemesis waited for her at the next street corner: Simon. His usually bright blue eyes were dull and his expression said he couldn't make up his mind if he was pleased she was alive or not.

As Riley drew closer, he moved into her path. 'Can't you see that Hell is using you as its tool?' he asked, so quietly she barely heard him.

'Go away, Simon,' she said. 'I'm not in the mood.'

He caught her arm, pulling her to a halt. 'Why do you keep luring the demons to you? If the hunters hadn't come in time, all those men would be dead.'

'So would I, Simon. You seem to have missed that little detail.'

'I doubt Hell would do that to one of its own.'

She glowered up at him. 'Who was the guy who visited you at the hospital and at your house? The one your brother said made you so weird?'

'No one came to see me at the hospital except my family and Father Harrison,' Simon retorted. He sounded so certain, like someone had drilled that into his brain.

'Really? I came to see you, so did Beck. Did you forget that?'

He blinked. 'You're trying to confuse me,' he replied, his hand retreating from her arm.

'Ask your mom. She won't lie to you. Then tell me who Hell is playing for a fool, Simon Adler.'

Riley pushed past him, feeling his contempt follow her up the street. She only slowed her pace a block away because her body ached from the tarp landing and the seemingly never-ending cramps. As she hiked towards the bus stop, all she could think of was Beck holding her in his arms. How he'd given her such a gentle smile like he'd forgotten all about Ori. He'd even kissed her forehead. When she'd been fifteen that would have sent her into ecstasy. Not now. She'd seen how quickly joy could turn to heartbreak.

'Do ya trust me?' he'd asked.

I do. That didn't mean her trust wouldn't end in tears.

The bus trip to her apartment complex was tolerable, except for a scruffy teen and his mp3 player. It was one of the really nice ones and he was seriously rocking to the tunes. So was

Riley, six rows back. When she'd boarded the bus, she noticed a wet line at the bottom step and a jug of Holy Water stashed near the driver's seat. When she'd asked about it, the guy said it was a city by-law now. All buses and trains had to be warded against demons.

Oh, crap. That meant sneaking small fiends on public transport had come to an end. Hellspawn on the buses and trains had always been illegal, but trappers usually ignored the rules and no one complained, at least for the small Grade One fiends. No one would dare haul a Three on to a MARTA train and not expect some blowback.

Once she reached home, Riley went through the motions: retrieving the bills from the mailbox, looking at the notices posted on the corkboard near the entrance. Sometimes you could score cheap furniture that way when someone was moving out. The newest note was from Mrs Ivey on the fourth floor who was missing her hearing-aid battery (again). Being a cranky old woman, she was convinced someone had stolen it.

She might be right. If the battery had any shininess to it, it was a good bet it'd been thieved by the fiend that shared Riley's apartment. If the demon showed his face, maybe she could convince him to give it back.

The apartment smelt stale, but Riley wasn't staying there often enough for it to be any other way. Despite the chilly air she popped open a window then cycled through her voicemails. The most important message was from Fireman Jack, a demon trafficker who doubled as the Guild's lawyer. It was bad news: the Consolidated Debt Collection people had set their sights on Riley's car. However, if she was willing to give up her father, they'd be happy to leave the vehicle in her possession.

Blackmail? After all the hell she'd been through in the last few days the car problem was barely a flicker on her problem meter. Jack would sort it out. He was good with that kind of thing.

After her shower and clean clothes, Riley dropped on to her couch. For some reason Mrs Ivey's problem resurfaced in her mind. It had to be awful not being able to hear.

Was the little demon in residence?

'Hello? Are you here?' There was a flash on one of the bookshelves and there he was, all of three inches of light brown fiend with a forked tail and tiny red eyes. His ears were peaked and he dressed like a ninja. He even had the little tabi shoes ninja assassins wore. Except this guy was a thief, not a killer. Sitting next to him was a bag of loot, prizes he'd liberated from other people's apartments. She often wondered if Lucifer regretted creating such a stealthy kleptomaniac.

'Did you take someone's hearing-aid battery?' She got a shrug in reply. Maybe the demon had no idea what she was talking about. 'Can you check? Please? Mrs Ivey needs it back. She can't hear without it and she's a grouchy old lady on good days.' Riley had learned that when she'd left her clothes in the communal dryer a few seconds longer than was necessary.

The fiend dug in his little bag and began to haul out pieces of loot, each one shiny or sparkly. That was a Magpie's weakness – they were all about the bling. The pile of loot kept growing and included earrings, a small toe ring, gold tone paperclips, tie clip, *I LUV Las Vegas* key ring. There had to be demon magic involved as his loot bag wasn't large enough to hold all the goodies inside. He pulled out a battery, held it up and squeaked at her. The demon equivalent of: 'Is this it?'

'Yes, I think it is. Can I have it, please?'

The demon issued another squeak. 'In return for what?' she guessed.

Riley dug around in her backpack and came up with a slightly dented chocolate kiss from the coffee shop. How it'd survived in one piece, she had no idea.

'How's about this?' she said, turning it so he could see the shiny tinfoil.

The trade happened even before she could blink her eyes, the battery lying on her palm, the silver-wrapped kiss in the demon's hands.

'Thanks.' She pulled on her coat and dropped the battery into a pocket. Then froze. Something was inside. Something sticky. Riley carefully removed the object and held it up, then nearly gagged: it was a three-inch-long bloody demon tooth, probably from the monster she'd batted off the roof.

'Yuck,' she said, 'that's gross.'

There was a sharp hiss of fright from the small demon on the bookshelf.

'It's OK. The thing's dead. Well, mostly dead I guess.'

The demon kept hissing and pointing at the tooth. 'It's not going to hurt you.' She placed it on her palm and held it out to him. 'See?'

The fiend was frantic now, backed into a corner near an old dictionary. The loot bag was on the other side of the shelf. His eyes darted to it and then back, growing more agitated with each passing second.

Klepto-Fiends never let their loot out of arm's reach.

'Is it because a Grade Three will eat you little guys?'

The demon shook his head, eyes bright red saucers.

Riley closed her fist round the tooth, confused. 'Then why would this scare you? All you guys work for Lucifer,' she said.

The demon cringed and cried out at the name of his master. Like they always did. *Except for the ones on the roof.*

'OK, I'll put it away,' she said, dropping it back into her coat pocket. 'Better?'

It must have been because the Magpie flew to its bag and clutched it to his chest, rocking back and forth in profound relief.

'I'm sorry,' she said. 'I didn't know it would scare you.'

Reality check. You just apologized to a demon.

The Magpie finally ceased shivering and hoisted its bag over a shoulder.

'You never call me Blackthorne's daughter like the others. Why?'

There were more high-pitched noises and then the fiend was a blur of nothing.

'You did, huh. Somehow I missed that.' Why didn't the

demons in the old building? *Why are those so different from the rest?*

Now that the Magpie was gone, Riley pulled out the tooth, letting it rest on her palm. A tingling sensation tickled her skin, skittering down her fingers.

Magic.

Riley decided to take the problem to a supernatural expert, in this case Mort. At the same time she could reassure her father that she was in one piece.

But first there was the matter of returning Mrs Ivey's missing battery. She wondered just how long it would be before the Magpie stole it again.

Chapter Twenty-Two

Little Five Points was as full of humanity as usual, but Enchanter's Way, the street where Mort lived, was unusually empty. Riley had a quick look in the café – there was only a bored waitress sitting at a table reading a magazine. Further down the street at Bell, Book and Broomstick, the witch store, her friend Ayden busied herself sweeping the front steps of the establishment. She was dressed in a long black shirt and a low-cut white blouse overlaid with an embroidered red vest. When you added in her curly russet hair, she looked like she'd escaped from a Renaissance Faire. Ayden was probably in her late forties, but it was hard to tell. Once again, she'd used her magic to alter the huge tattoo on her neck and chest – this time it was a line of grim-faced fairies marching across a field in full battle gear.

As Riley approached, Ayden stopped sweeping and leaned against the broom. They studied each other for a time as if neither had any idea what to say.

Riley tried for something benign. 'You're not at the market today.'

'No. We rotate. I'll be at the market stall tomorrow.'

More awkward silence. Apparently Mort had let the witch

know about Riley's time with the demon hunters.

'Ah, look, if it's not good for you to be seen with me, I understand,' Riley said.

'That's not it.' Another pause. 'Thank you for having –' Ayden angled her head down the road towards Mort's home – 'let me know what was going on. I was really worried about you.'

'Me too.' Riley waved her friend away from the front door, in case there was someone inside who might overhear them. Then she flipped over her palms. She couldn't see the inscriptions any more, but she was wondering if Ayden would.

The witch stared, then a lone eyebrow rose in surprise. 'I understand why you have the one from Heaven. What did you do to earn the one from Hell?' her friend asked.

Can't hide much from a witch. 'I owe Lucifer a promise. And I slept with a fallen angel.'

The eyebrow went stratospheric. 'Goddess, girl, are you insane?'

'I thought he worked for Heaven.' *I thought I was in love.*

Ayden blew out a long stream of air as she mulled over that reply. 'Was it Lucifer who raised Paul?' Riley nodded. 'Where is your dad now?'

'At Mort's. He knows the Prince is my father's summoner.'

'Can it possibly get any more bizarre?' Ayden grumbled.

'Oh yeah. Someone is raising demons from the dead now and the hunters can't kill them.'

The witch's eyebrow reversed direction, joined the

other and formed an impressive frown. 'What damned fool necromancer thought that was a good idea?' Ayden retorted. 'Why do they think the next life is their personal playground?'

Whoa. Riley knew there was little love lost between the witches and the necros, but Ayden's bitterness seemed pretty harsh.

She removed the demon tooth from her pocket. 'This is from one of the weird demons. Can you –'

Ayden waved it away. 'Go talk to the summoners' advocate,' the witch said. 'I do not want to get into the middle of it.'

Riley dropped the tooth back into the safety of her jacket pocket.

'Do the hunters know about those inscriptions on your palms?' Ayden asked.

'Yes. Apparently it took the Pope to figure out I wasn't a threat.'

'Riiiight.' Ayden's frown lessened. 'No matter what, be careful. Something's going down, something nasty. Watch your back, OK?'

'I will.'

'No more messing around with Hell. They play for keeps.'

'So does Heaven.'

As Riley crossed the threshold into the summoner's house, she felt her nerves slowly unwind. She'd come to think of it as Mort Magic because she always felt better here. She found her dad in the summoner's office with his bottle of jazzed-up orange drink, much brighter than the last time she'd seen him.

His eyes lit up the moment he spied her. 'Riley!' he called out.

'Hey, Dad,' she said, hurrying into his arms. The hug was off the scale. She knew he'd been concerned about her, but the embrace told her it was more than that.

'Beck was here this morning,' he announced.

Backwoods Boy hadn't said a word to her about his visit. 'Did you tell him about your deal with Hell?'

'No. It's not time for him to know that yet.'

There was a slight whooshing sound a second before Mort walked through the illusionary magical wall that led to the back of the house. Their host had pulled that stunt the first time she'd visited, so this time she wasn't surprised.

'Riley. Good to see you're finally free from the Vatican's clutches,' Mort said. He settled on the bench seat opposite her and her dad, a smile filling his face.

She was about to ruin his good mood. Removing the tooth from her pocket, Riley set it on the picnic table in front of their host. The summoner's attention went to it immediately. The frown came next.

'Where did you get that?' he asked.

'From a Grade Three demon. It thought it was going to eat Beck, so I hit it with a steel pipe.' Like every girl her age thumped Hellspawn on the head for a living.

'Is Beck OK?' her father asked, concerned.

'He's good.'

Mort went to reach for the tooth and then snatched his hand back like it had encountered a blow torch. His eyes rose to hers. 'This is riddled with necromantic magic.'

Riley beamed. 'I knew it. I didn't think Lucifer was *that* crazy.'

'What are you talking about?'

Riley ran down the events at the abandoned building, skipping most of the 'here's where we could have been eaten' parts so as to not upset her father. She stressed the 'demons that wouldn't stay dead' portions instead.

'That's . . . that's *so* against the rules,' Mort stammered in shock.

In contrast, her father was silent. In fact, he didn't seem surprised at all.

'Dad?'

'Yes,' he said solemnly.

'Did you know this was going to happen, the undead demons thing?'

No reply.

'Come on, stop dodging my questions. We need to figure this out. Does Ozy have something to do with this?'

Her father's hand touched hers and then he suddenly embraced her, catching her off guard. He whispered, 'I love you. No matter how this plays out, that will never change. Always remember that.'

His seriousness frightened her. 'Dad, what's wrong?'

When the sound began, a barely noticeable low frequency hum, Mort surged to his feet, knocking the bench seat over in his haste to rise.

'No!' he said. 'You wouldn't dare!'

The hum grew in intensity, higher in pitch, causing the china cups on the picnic table to rattle. It built, stronger and louder, until Riley's whole body vibrated along with it. The tea pot jostled off the table, smashing on to the wood floor, followed by the cups and Mort's books. Riley scrambled to move the old volumes away from the flowing liquid.

'What is happening?' she called out.

In lieu of an answer, the summoner raised his hands at chest level, palms out. Blue waves of magic swept around him, arcing to the ceiling and deep into the floor. If it hadn't been so eerie it would have been pretty.

Mort chanted in Latin, his face beet red. The hum became unbearable, then exploded in sharp fragments, like musical shrapnel. Riley covered her ears, but it did no good. The power drove into her skull, into her bones. Glass shattered somewhere in the house.

Then nothing – magic on, magic off – like someone had flipped a switch.

Had one of Mort's magical spells gone wrong?

Riley's father rose and walked a few paces away, seemingly unconcerned with the chaos.

'Dad?'

He shook his head, indicating she should stay where she was.

What's going on here?

Fresh air poured into the room. As Riley's vision cleared,

she realized the magical wall was gone and there was a clear path to the back door and the alley beyond. Mort crumpled on to the floor like a tired doll. His entire body quaked.

'Mort! Do something!' she pleaded.

'Can't,' he moaned. 'Too strong.' He pressed his hand against his nose and it came away bloody.

There was movement in the hallway as a figure strode towards them out of the late afternoon sunlight. Something flowed behind it, like a cloak. *Or a duster.* Ori had worn one of those.

Were the Fallen free of Lucifer's bondage? Was he here to exact his revenge?

The figure that entered the room wasn't the least angelic. Lord Ozymandias's flowing cloak was the empty black of midnight and his silver hair set off the stark and pulsating green sigil in the centre of his forehead.

'Ah, Summoner Alexander. Good day,' he said in a jovial tone, obviously pleased his efforts had been a success. 'Sorry about this. Your magical wards were better than I anticipated.'

'What are you doing?' Riley demanded.

Those bizarre eyes turned to her and ceased being amused. 'I would think that was obvious.' His attention moved to her father. 'Time to go, Paul Blackthorne. I'll skip the threats. You know what I'm capable of.'

'You can't take him,' Riley protested. 'He's not yours.'

'Of course I can. Mortimer is out of the fight and you were never in it.'

Riley lunged forward and impacted a solid wall of . . .

nothing. Careening backwards, she tried again and bounced off something invisible, but impenetrable. Magic scratched against her skin like razor blades.

'Dad! Don't go with him!'

'It'll be OK, Riley,' her father said. 'Trust me.'

Her panic mounting, she rammed her fists against the invisible barrier, but it wouldn't yield. 'Dad, no!'

Ignoring her attempts to escape, Lord Ozymandias clapped a hand round her father's shoulders and led him towards the back of the house. 'Tell me, master trapper,' he said, 'who summoned you from your grave?'

'Lucifer, the Prince of Hell,' her father replied, not missing a beat.

The necromancer's deep laugh echoed throughout the building. 'I was so hoping you'd say that.'

The moment after Ozy and her father vanished through the back door, the magical barrier fell and its disappearance caught Riley unawares. She sprawled to the floor in a heap. Crying out in despair, she curled up into a heap, but this time the scalding tears wouldn't come. Instead they burned deep inside her, trapped by a grief that she couldn't possibly exorcise. She'd lost her father, over and over. There was no peace for Paul Blackthorne, not in this life or the next.

Mort hadn't moved. Pushing her grief aside, Riley hurried to the summoner. As she reached out to him, he shook his head, flinging blood in all directions.

'Don't touch me!' he said. 'Wards broken. Inside me.'

'What can I do?' she asked, panicking.

'Too weak . . . to ground magic.' His face was alabaster now, his breathing hoarse. Mort wasn't going to survive this if she didn't get help quickly. Maybe one of the other summoners might know what to do. *But how do I let them know?*

'Riley?' a voice called out

Ayden. 'Back here!' Riley cried.

A few seconds later Riley's witch friend stormed in. Her eyes swept the scene.

'Oh my Goddess, it's as bad as I thought.' She shooed Riley away and knelt in front of Mort. 'Summoner? Can you ground yourself?'

Mort shook his head. 'Can't focus. Can't see the spell.'

The witch sucked in a deep breath. 'Riley, go get an ice pack.'

'But what about him?'

'Go!' her friend commanded.

Riley took off, suspecting that Ayden was about to do something she didn't want her to see. In the front hall, Tereyza, Mort's dead housekeeper, cowered near the open door. Mort's reanimate cook was in the same pitiful state, hiding under the table. Riley had to rummage through the drawers to find a plastic bag. After scooping up heaps of ice from the freezer, she wet a kitchen towel and ran back towards Mort's office. She was almost there when the world lurched underneath her feet, flinging her into a wall. Riley clutched the ice pack to her chest and waited for the quaking to cease, then took off again at a sprint.

When she skidded into Mort's office, the room felt

different now. Less . . . volatile. Ayden stood behind the summoner, a hand on each shoulder, her eyes closed. Her eyes snapped open at the same time as the summoner sat upright. They were brilliant blue. She blinked a few times and they returned to their usual brown.

Whoa . . .

'You can touch him now,' Ayden said, then shook her head like she had a hive of bees trapped inside her skull. Her fingers still pulsed with magic. When she noticed, she leaned back against the wall. Brilliant spiky green halos formed round her body then embedded themselves into the individual bricks.

'What are you doing?' Riley asked.

'Grounding the magic.'

Riley gave the summoner the ice pack and he pressed it against his forehead. She knelt and delicately began to clean his face with the wet towel.

There was a lot of blood on his shirt. 'Are you going to be OK?' she asked.

There was a nod. The ice pack lowered, revealing two bloodshot eyes.

'Help me up, will you?'

Riley righted one of the bench seats and helped the necromancer rise. He tottered to the seat and sank on to it with a weary sigh.

'I'll have to file a formal complaint with the Society,' the necromancer said.

Ayden snorted. 'You know that won't do a damned thing.'

'I have no other recourse,' Mort replied. 'Do you have any idea what it's like to have your wards torn away, have your house violated by some . . .'

'Don't get pissed at me, summoner,' the witch snapped. 'I wasn't the one who did this.'

Mort's shoulders sagged. 'I know. It's just . . .' He took a deep breath and slowly let it out. His bloodshot eyes rose and fixed on Riley. 'I can't help you with the demon tooth, even if we can find it in this . . . mess. Everything is drenched in Ozymandias's magic now, so I won't be able to pinpoint who is enchanting the demons.'

'So that's it? The bad guy gets my dad and nobody will do anything?' Riley demanded, her voice rising.

'I'll do what I can, Riley, but I think we're out of options.'

You might be . . .

Riley had a wish on hold with Lucifer. She'd planned on using it for her dad's soul, but getting him back from Ozymandias was almost as good.

How do I find the Prince of Hell? It wasn't like he was on speed dial.

'I know that look,' Ayden said. 'Promise me you won't go after your father.'

Riley shook her head. 'I won't make that promise.'

'Come on, think it through,' the witch urged. 'If it was so important that Paul remain free, why didn't the Prince protect your father when the necro came for him? Has it occurred to you that Lucifer might want your father with Ozymandias?'

Riley hadn't considered that. It made sense, though. Her dad hadn't looked the least surprised at Ozymandias's sudden arrival. In fact, he'd appeared resigned to his fate.

You knew he was coming for you. That's why you said goodbye.

The feeling of helplessness that poured through her at that moment was nearly overwhelming. Knowing if she remained here any longer she'd be on the floor, sobbing, broken beyond repair, Riley picked up her backpack and fled. As she ran down the alley that led to the street, she swore she heard Ozymandias's mocking laughter.

Chapter Twenty-Three

Beck finished off his supper of steak and eggs in record time. He actually felt pretty good for all the abuse his body had taken over the last few days. For once he'd actually followed most of the doctor's advice and it had worked. The dull throb in his shoulder told him it was about time for more pain pills, but he'd wait until his meeting with Justine was at an end. He needed a clear head for that.

He glanced at his phone, checking the time: the reporter was late. That wasn't like her, but then Justine had said she had a meeting with the mayor right before this.

As he sipped his coffee, he recalled his visit with Paul this morning. It'd been rough for both of them and not only because he felt so much guilt for not saving his friend. The master was hiding the truth from him.

Why won't ya tell me who summoned ya? Why is it such a damned big deal? Beck had even promised not to kill the necro who did it, but Paul wouldn't budge.

'Not the right time,' his friend had said. So that's the way they'd left it.

Beck hadn't mentioned his visit to Riley because he saw no point. Paul would the next time she saw him.

After another long sip of coffee, and considerable thought, he talked himself into making a call he'd been avoiding since the moment Paul had died in Demon Central. It was time Riley's aunt in Fargo knew the girl was on her own. As far as he could tell, Esther Henley was Riley closest relation, the sister to the girl's mom. He also knew some of the family history: Esther had disliked Paul from the start, beginning the night he'd started dating her sister. Once Miriam died, Esther had pretty much ignored the remaining Blackthornes.

No choice. The woman needed to know of Riley's situation. What Aunt Esther did after that was on her head. Beck knew it'd been a low stunt digging through Riley's cellphone to find the phone number, especially when she hadn't given him permission, but she'd never make the call. Or so he kept telling himself.

Just get it done. He dialled the number and waited as the waitress refilled his coffee.

'The number you have dialled is no longer in service,' an automated voice announced.

Oh, hell, ya gotta be jokin'. He disconnected the call, then tried it again in case he'd dialled wrong. Same message. All that hassle and the girl's aunt was AWOL? To cover all his bases, he dialled directory assistance and learned there was no listing for Esther Henley in snow-bound Fargo. Apparently the woman had found a warmer place to live and not bothered to tell either her brother-in-law or her niece.

Though Beck wasn't sure why, part of him was pleased at the news.

There was a swish of fabric as Justine slid into the bench seat opposite him. The reporter was dressed in a pale cream pantsuit that set off her brilliant red hair and deep emerald eyes. As usual, she looked perfect. As she settled her belongings on the table, her perfume drifted across to him.

The waitress poured her coffee and then left them alone after Justine refused the menu.

'Sorry I'm late,' she said.

Beck glanced at the newspaper on the table, the one with his photo. He jabbed a finger at it. 'Who told ya Riley's a jinx?'

Justine shook her head. 'I do not reveal my sources.'

'Well, it's a lie. She's a damned good trapper.'

'Then why did the hunter's mission go wrong today?' Justine asked. 'Why didn't they kill the demons? What really happened in that building?'

Apparently the hunters had closed ranks and Justine wasn't getting her usual flow of info; she was hoping Beck would fill in the missing pieces.

'No comment,' he said.

A slight frown creased her forehead. 'Perhaps I should ask questions you will answer.'

'Not gonna be many of those now,' he said coldly.

Her eyes flared. 'Why didn't you tell me your mother was dying?'

Beck nearly dropped his coffee. 'What?'

'Your mother. She is gravely ill and you never said a thing to me.'

'How do ya know that?' he demanded.

'I have been researching you for the next article,' Justine replied. 'I spoke with her on the telephone. She is quite . . . bitter. No wonder your life has been so hard.'

Beck didn't need her pity. He needed her to back off.

'Ya had no right diggin' into my life,' he said, trying to keep his voice down. How dare the woman do this to him? Sure, she was a reporter and it was her job, but there were lines you didn't cross, not with people you cared about. 'Besides, Sadie's on pain killers. Ya can't believe half of what she says.'

'She is not my only source.' Justine picked up her coffee cup, the expression on her face much like a child who'd found a secret stash of candy bars. 'I spoke on the telephone with a few of your neighbours in Sadlersville. You appear to have quite a reputation, Beck.'

Oh, sweet Jesus. What had they told her? *Was this what Donovan was warnin' me about?* He dropped his voice to a low growl. 'I *do not* want my personal life in the papers.'

'Grow up,' Justine shot back. 'People want to read a story like yours. A trapper from a broken home with a dying mother who has no notion of who his father is? That's award-winning material. It sells papers. It helps pay my bills.'

Beck's muscles bunched. 'Ya forget, it's *my* life.'

'You are a public figure now. It's a great story, Beck – the small-town boy who pulls himself out of poverty and becomes a war hero. Will he succeed or drown in alcohol like his prostitute mother?' She leaned forward, eager. 'Why haven't you visited her? I would if my mother was dying.'

'I'm warnin' ya, Justine, back the hell off!' he said through gritted teeth. *If she keeps diggin'* . . .

Her eyes narrowed. 'I do not respond to threats, Beck.'

'I thought we had somethin' goin' here.'

'We do, but it goes both ways. You receive information about the hunters from me and I get an award-winning story from you. *Quid pro quo.*'

He had no idea what that meant, but he suspected he was the one who would come out of it on the short end of the stick.

Riley was right. She's just usin' me.

'I'm askin' ya all polite. Don't listen to those old gossips down south.'

'Then tell me your side of the story,' Justine urged. 'Have your say for a change.'

I trusted you. I should have known better. Beck shook his head. 'We're done here.'

'There is no reason to be this way.'

'We. Are. Done,' he repeated. 'In bed and every other way.'

'I see,' Justine said, glowering at him. 'I thought you'd be more professional about this.' When she rose, he didn't bother to do the same. This wasn't a lady – this was a predator in expensive clothes.

'Have no fear, Beck – soon I will know everything about you and then I will tell your story to the world,' she retorted. 'I will make you famous, whether you want it or not.'

That was his worst nightmare.

*

Beck took his outrage to his house, away from anyone who might see him. The way he felt wasn't healthy. It wanted him to go to the closest bar and get hammered and then beat the hell out of someone. Anyone. That wouldn't do a thing for his Justine problem. If anything, it'd reinforce her pack of lies.

Since the day Paul had challenged him to become something better, Beck had done his damndest to do just that. He'd gone into the Army, learned some discipline. Learned that life is precious in a world where death came calling without any warning. When he'd returned to Atlanta, Paul had been there to take the reins, teach him how to trap, how to respect himself as someone more than the illegitimate son of a drunk. Even Paul didn't know all his secrets.

There was already talk at the National Guild about restricting who could become a master. It wouldn't be enough that you took down one of the higher level fiends and completed the tests. They were discussing intensive background checks, interviews with family members and the like. Beck's past could ruin his future.

What could he do? Go to Stewart? Lay all his sins on the table?

'No, he'll boot me out before the Guild does.' The events from that summer when he was fifteen wouldn't leave Stewart any other choice.

When his phone began to buzz, he answered it immediately. It was the Scotsman.

'One of the necromancers came for Paul this afternoon,'

Stewart announced. 'Mort had no choice but ta let him go.'

'Which necromancer?' Beck asked coldly.

'Their High Lord Ozymandias. Yer not goin' after him, lad. If ya try, I'll personally throw ya out the Guild, providin' yer still alive. Ya ken?'

Beck knew a direct order when he heard it, even though it chafed him.

'Yes, sir.' *I'll get that bastard someday.* 'How's Riley takin' it?'

'Poorly. She was there when it went down.'

'Oh, God. Does she need me to come over?'

'No need. She's gone ta bed early and that's the best place for her. One other thing – that article in the paper? From this point on yer ta have no contact with Miss Armando. She's trouble.'

Amen to that. 'Already done, sir.'

'Good. We've got a meetin' with the Summoners' Society tomorrow evenin'. Ya need ta be there.'

'I can't wait,' Beck said, clenching and unclenching his free fist.

The moment the master hung up, Beck slammed that fist into the closest wall. Once for Justine. Once for Paul. All it did was make his hand hurt and put a dent in the wallboard.

Stupid.

Slinging his trapping bag on to his shoulder, Beck headed out of the door. It was time to do his job, at least until they took it away from him.

*

Ori was strangely silent at dawn. That creeped Riley out more than him shouting at her. Unable to sleep any longer – it'd been a fitful night – she slogged downstairs to the library and began her homework. The maths, the history, the sociology seemed useless now, but at least it kept her mind off her kidnapped dad.

Riley was rousted out of her studies at nine by the housekeeper who insisted on feeding her up. She had no appetite, but she did what she could to the meal or the woman would have fretted about her health. After showering, she returned to the library and went back to work. After she'd finished the basic research on Sartael and his role in Hell, Riley found a book about the history of demon trapping written by one of Stewart's ancestors in the early nineteen century.

The history of demons and their role in the history of mankind made for lengthy but interesting reading. The consensus was that the demons had first appeared when Adam and Eve were shown the door out of Eden. As mankind grew more sophisticated, so did the Hellspawn. As humans built city states, the demons were right there with them, exploiting every weakness. As technology evolved, so did the Hellspawn. The invention of computers led to the appearance of the Techno-Fiends and so forth. As humans grew in number, so did the role of Lucifer's minions, back and forth across the ages.

When the chapter ended, Riley stretched and then glanced at the cellphone to check the time and froze. *Oh crap! I can't be late for class.*

The last thing she needed was detention.

*

Her teacher, Mrs Haggerty, had already summoned the students into the defunct Starbucks that served as their classroom. Riley hurried in and dropped her backpack near the small table that was her desk. There was a frown of disapproval from her teacher, but no public humiliation or detention.

As Riley settled into her chair, she inhaled deeply to savour the lingering aroma of fresh-ground coffee. There was none, of course, but the building would always retain that smell. She wasn't complaining: with the budget cuts she could be back in an abandoned grocery that had smelt way worse.

Peter sat to her right. He mouthed a greeting and she nodded back. The girl in front of her, Brandy, wasn't actually a friend, but not an enemy either. Just someone who tolerated Riley as long as she seemed useful.

Her long brown hair kept swishing across Riley's desk and her notebook. Tempting as it was to tie something to it and see if Brandy ever noticed, Riley decided not to go there. That would only make the offending party consider retaliation.

Riley scooted her desk back with a noticeable squeak.

'Mute or turn off those phones, people,' Mrs Haggerty warned.

The moment Riley turned hers to silent, it vibrated, as if taunting her. She surreptitiously checked the incoming text, her actions partially hidden by her notebook. Then swore under her breath. The text was from Allan, her ex-boyfriend, who sat only a few desks away.

Hang with me after class?

Riley deleted the text with extreme prejudice, then forced herself not to look in his direction. She'd dated Allan a couple years before and had accumulated a lifetime of experiences, all in one punch.

How did he get my number?

Peter wouldn't have given it up, even under extreme torture. That left Brandy or one of her girl pack. The phone vibrated again, but this time Riley ignored it, dropping it into her backpack. When Peter shot her a questioning look, she frowned in response.

Once the maths homework had been corrected, Mrs Haggerty moved on to another lengthy lecture about the Civil War. It would have been interesting if Riley hadn't grown up with a dad devoted to the subject. Some of her earliest memories were of her teacher father surrounded by books and campaign maps, muttering about General McClellan's tactics or the Battle of Kennesaw.

Only one more week of this. Then the class would move on to some other dark period of American history.

As class dragged on, she came to realize that Allan had spent most of his time staring at her. That couldn't be good news.

He won't try anything, not in front of anyone. She just had to make sure she wasn't on her own around him.

After school, as she and Peter filed out into the parking lot, Brandy and her friends were chattering about some music video.

Peter shot her a glance. 'You're acting weird. You OK?' he asked.

'No. Life sucks. One of the necros stole Dad away from Mort.'

He stopped dead in his tracks. 'God, I'm sorry. Any chance you can get him back?'

'Don't know. I'm meeting with the necros in an hour. Maybe they'll take pity on a poor orphan and do the right thing.'

'I wouldn't count on it.' His hand dived into his jacket pocket and extracted the demon-claw pendant. He held it out. 'Figured you'd want this back.'

'Thanks for keeping it safe.' Riley hid it underneath her shirt. Then she tugged her friend away from the other students so nobody would hear what she was about to ask. She already had a reputation for being odd.

'How do you kill a zombie?' she asked.

Peter stared at her for a second, then smirked. 'Oh come on, everybody knows how to kill a revenant.'

'Not me. I'm the one who doesn't like scary movies, remember?'

'You won't watch a horror flick, but you'll live in one. Go figure.'

'Peter,' she warned. 'Out with it.'

'The best way is to cut off its head,' he said solemnly.

'I'll need a sword for that,' Riley mused. Fortunately, Stewart had a wall full of them in his office.

'Adding zombie hunter to your skills?' Peter asked,

smirking. He had no idea that's exactly what was about to happen.

She looked around to ensure no one was close. 'There are undead demons out there now. Bullets won't kill them. That's why I want to know.'

For a second Peter must have thought she was joking, then his smile eroded away.

'You know, I hear Illinois is really pretty this time of year. I could go visit my wacked-out mom, hang with the little bros. Get out of town, if you know what I mean.'

'I'd do just that if you can, Peter.'

'For once I wish you were lying.' He sighed. 'If it was me, I'd use a chainsaw on the things,' he said, warming to the subject of zombie decimation. 'Or a machete. You don't need gasoline for that. Maybe a guillotine might work.'

Riley was beginning to regret her question, given Peter's gory enthusiasm.

'What are you talking about?' Brandy asked, inserting herself into the conversation as if it was all about her. For once, Riley actually appreciated Brandy and her entourage butting in. They were all in black this afternoon – shirts, skirts and boots. She could imagine the flurry of text messages that had flown back and forth to coordinate that fashion statement.

'We're discussing zombies and how to kill them,' Peter replied matter-of-factly. 'Got any suggestions?'

'Yuck,' the girl replied, shuddering. 'Too messy.'

Time to change the subject. 'Why did you give Allan my number?' Riley demanded. 'Are you like stupid or something?'

Brandy looked confused. 'He said you guys used to date so I didn't think it was any big deal.'

'The key words there are "used to".'

'He seems OK to me. Maybe a little creepy, but not too bad.'

At least Brandy didn't know where she lived. The last thing she needed was for Allan to stake out her place. Or Stewart's, for that matter.

'Incoming lurker,' Peter announced, shooting a glance over Riley's shoulder.

'Hey, Riley, I sent you a couple texts,' her ex said. He made sure to stand too close for comfort, but she refused to retreat. His brown hair was pretty much like it'd been when they'd dated, but he'd grown taller and more muscular over the last two years, bulk he didn't need because he already knew how to bully people.

'I saw them. And deleted them.'

'Why?'

'You know why. Don't text me. Don't call me. Don't act as if I exist.'

'I told you I was sorry.'

Like I believe you.

Brandy was frowning now. 'What's going on?'

'Nothing important,' Allan replied. 'Riley's just got an attitude problem.'

Incensed, Peter glowered up at a guy who outweighed him by at least sixty pounds. 'You want to know the short history of Riley and this Neanderthal?' He didn't wait for Brandy to reply, but ploughed on, his voice bristling with anger. 'He got her to steal stuff for him. When she wouldn't rip off a computer, he punched her in the face. Even loosened one of her teeth.'

The muscles tensed in Allan's neck and he glowered at Riley's best friend.

She knew that look – he was planning payback in some seriously painful way. If there was a fight, Peter would get creamed and then he'd get tossed out of school.

To her surprise Brandy stepped in. 'Hey, who's the guy in the truck?' she called out, louder than needed. 'He's definitely hunky.' Her gaggle of girls turned as one and a couple murmured appreciatively.

The hunk in question was Beck, who had just pulled into the parking lot. He took one look and was out of the truck, leaning on the door, watching the situation closely.

Your timing is awesome. Even though she had no idea why he was here. If Allan went physical, he'd find himself up against a seasoned fighter with a steel pipe rather than a guy half his size.

'That would be one of the trappers,' Riley replied.

'Niiiiice . . .' Brandy said. 'Can you introduce us?'

Beck and Brandy? That would be a match made in Hell. *Time to shut the girl down.* 'Do you like country music?'

'Ew, no!' she retorted, as if Riley had suggested she eat live frogs for breakfast.

'That's all he listens to.'

'Boo,' Brandy said. 'Should have known he was too cute to be for real.'

As she walked Peter to his car, Riley shot him an exasperated look. 'What were you doing? You're lucky Allan didn't nail you.'

'Time someone stood up that jerk,' Peter said, dumping his computer bag into the car.

'Just watch yourself. You made him look bad and he won't forget it.'

'He hits me he goes to jail. Simple as that.'

'Not so simple if your jaw is wired shut and you're in a coma.'

He paled. 'Yeah, that would be a bummer.'

'I'd better go see what Backwoods Boy wants,' she said, looking over at Beck again.

'Call me later, will you?' Peter said, climbing into his car.

'Sure.' As she walked away, she heard the door locks engage. He was driving away by the time she reached Beck's truck.

'What's happening?' she asked.

'Stewart wants me to take ya to the summoner's meetin',' he replied, his eyes tracking Allan across the parking lot as her ex headed towards his ride.

'You know, I have a car. I even have a licence. I'm capable of driving there on my own,' she replied.

'The order was that ya come with me. Ya gotta problem, call the Scotsman.'

Which he knew she wouldn't do. It wasn't fair to rag on the messenger, so she climbed into Beck's ride. His truck was less cramped as he'd somehow scrounged up a backpack –

camo of course – and it took up a lot less space than his duffel bag on the front seat. It was worn and had tears and rusty brown spots on it, which made her wonder if it was the one he'd used in the army.

'How's the head?' she asked.

'Better.' He turned on to Peachtree Street and joined the flow of traffic. 'Jackson and Remmers picked up those two guys who ripped off your demon a few weeks back. They're bein' real helpful.' He smirked at the thought. 'They gave me the name of the dude who's buyin' the Hellspawn under the table. I'll be settin' up a meetin' with him. I'm lookin' to bust that racket wide open.'

'Cool. Just be careful,' she cautioned.

'Don't worry, Jackson's comin' along as back-up. We'll get it done.'

Beck manoeuvred them through a crowded intersection with a minimum of horn honking. 'I know it's probably none of my business, but that big guy who was standin' next to ya in the parkin' lot? I'm thinkin' he's got issues. The violent kind.'

Riley looked over at him, intrigued that he'd figured out Allan so quickly. 'Why do you think that?'

'He feels . . . bad. He thinks he owns the world. The way he was lookin' at ya made the hair on my neck stand up.' Beck executed a turn, then added, 'That doesn't mean ya should go out of yer way to date the dude because I don't like him. I made that mistake with that angel.'

Riley grinned, savouring the irony. 'Too late. Already been

there. That's Allan, the psycho-ex. Well, the first psycho-ex, if you count Simon.'

'The one that hit ya?'

'Yup. He's in my class now. Isn't that special?'

'If he . . .' Beck took a deep breath and swallowed whatever he had planned to say. 'I figure ya can handle him. If not, let me know. I'll be happy to pound his ass into the ground for ya.'

Who are you and what have you done with Backwoods Boy?

'Thank you,' she said, not sure what had just happened.

Like Peter, if anything happened to her she'd head for the cops. That had been their mistake the last time: rather than earn Allan a police record her dad had talked to his parents, hoping to get the creep some professional help. Instead her ex had gone on to terrorize other girlfriends.

'Ya be careful,' Beck said. 'I've seen the type before. They beat ya and then apologize. Then they hit ya again because they can get away with it. No matter what, yer always to blame.'

There was too much emotion overlaying his words for this to just be a warning.

'Did that happen you?' she asked, fearing the answer.

Beck nodded.

How many monsters are hiding in your closet of horrors?

Chapter Twenty-Four

The Summoners' Society was housed in a grand three-storey building where ivy clung to the weathered grey stones and ran riot over mullioned windows. There was a portico at the front of the building, but Beck ignored that and parked in a lot on the south side near Stewart's car. When he climbed out, he whistled his appreciation of the structure.

'I'm thinkin' I should have been a grave robber.'

'I think they do their chants in Latin, Beck.'

He scowled. 'Yeah, well, then I'd be screwed.'

They were met at the entrance by a portly butler who looked like he'd been an extra in an old British movie. After he ensured their names were on the official guest list, they were led down a panelled hallway to a set of double doors.

Beyond those doors was a ballroom littered with summoners. Riley guessed there were at least fifty of them, each in coloured robes befitting their status within the Society. Clusters of them gossiped away in a room that would have been fashionable during the Civil War. Two massive fireplaces sat at either end of the room, both giving off generous heat, which promptly headed for the ceiling at least fifteen feet above them. Weighty, blood-red damask drapes hung at the windows, sealing out the night's chill, while a string quartet played something by Bach.

It's like something out of a Victorian novel.

They found Master Stewart near one of the fireplaces. He steered them away from the closest summoners.

'No matter what,' he said in a lowered voice, 'do not mention the undead beasties we've been seein'. If that becomes public knowledge, there will be panic. Ya ken?'

They both nodded.

'Do you think they'll give us Dad back?' Riley asked.

'I don't know, lass. We'll give it our best.'

A few minutes later, the meeting was called to order. Riley, Beck and the master were shown to chairs near the front of the room as the final strains of J. S. Bach melted away. Behind them, summoners found their own seats, as if this was a performance. Maybe to them it was.

The man running the meeting, Lord Barnes, laid out the complaint in excruciating detail. Then it was Stewart's turn. The master spoke of her father's death, how Beck had valiantly tried to save his friend's life. Riley's eyes burned, on the verge of crying as she dug her fingernails into her palms to keep the tears away. Beck's face was stony now, no doubt reliving that night in vivid memories.

The master movingly described the many nights she'd spent in the graveyard protecting her father's corpse, and the summoners' attempts to buy his body. He took particular care in describing Lord Ozymandias's heinous magical tricks. There were murmurs behind her and they weren't happy ones. Apparently some of the necros thought the dark lord's behaviour had been over the top, at least by their standards.

Where is he? Did the jerk not even bother to show up?

The question was answered a moment later when the rear doors opened. Heads turned.

Lord Ozymandias was in his customary black cloak and toting his staff, the sigil on his forehead pulsing like a star.

'Really, Master Stewart,' he said, sweeping dramatically down the aisle, 'you make me sound like a predator.'

'That's because ya are. Weavin' magic against a young lass ta steal her father's body is dishonourable. It's not what bein' a summoner is all about, and ya know it.'

'Oh dear, I have been chastised,' Ozymandias laughed, touching his chest in mock horror. Then his tone went icy cold. 'I do what any summoner does – I reanimate the dead. If that corpse happens to be a master trapper, one known for his skills, I will do anything I can to achieve my goal. Even if it frightens a little girl.'

Little girl? Riley would have risen, but Beck's fingers closed round her arm.

'Stay put. Let Stewart handle it,' he whispered. She gritted her teeth and remained seated.

'On behalf of the Atlanta Demon Trappers Guild and the National Guild,' the master began, 'we *require* the return Master Paul Blackthorne so he may go ta his final rest.'

'Require?' Ozymandias took a position near the front of the room. 'That's a bold statement.'

'Ya don't want ta make enemies of us.'

'Oh, you're talking about the *International* Guild now. It may come as a surprise, but I have no awe for you *Grand Masters*. You're just jumped-up rat catchers.'

Riley gasped at the insult.

'Ya son of a . . .' Beck murmured.

Stewart held himself in check, his eyes flinty. 'Return Paul Blackthorne and we'll back away from this like gentlemen.'

'I need a better argument than that, trapper,' Ozymandias replied, toying with the master.

Mort shot up from among the pack. 'Lord Barnes, I would like to speak, if I may?'

'The chair recognizes Summoner Alexander.'

The necromancer trudged to the front of the room, then turned towards his fellow summoners. There was a sheen of sweat on his face, which told Riley he was about to do something risky.

'Section Four, Item Thirteen of the Summoners' Code allows for the transference of ownership should the original summoner no longer be able to conduct his or her duties in regard to the reanimate.' He placed a document on the podium in front of Barnes. 'Paul Blackthorne has designated me his summoner of record. Therefore, in conjunction with the Trappers Guild, I request that his body be returned immediately to my care.'

Go, Mort!

Ozymandias glared at him. 'You challenge me, Summoner Alexander?'

'No, Lord Ozymandias, I will not challenge you to a duel of magic, though I have adequate cause.' Mort drew himself up. 'You shattered the wards on my house, you *stole* Paul Blackthorne without my permission. Those are heinous crimes within our Society.'

The summoners began to whisper amongst themselves. If Ozy could do that to Mort, he'd do it to one of them. Suddenly this whole stolen-corpse problem had become personal.

'Order!' Barnes shouted, waving his hands. It seemed odd that he didn't do something magical to get their attention.

It was Stewart's turn. 'The proper paperwork has been issued and Summoner Alexander has requested that this Society do what is right in this matter.' He shifted weight on his cane. 'Paul Blackthorne was a good man and he deserves ta be returned ta his daughter's care.'

Ozymandias thoughtfully adjusted a cloak sleeve. 'I somehow doubt that a *good* man would be summoned from his grave by the Prince of Hell himself.'

A collective gasp ran through the room.

Oh, great. Now the whole world knows.

Beck grabbed her arm again, eyes wide. 'For God's sake,' he said in a tense whisper, 'tell me he's lyin'.'

'No,' she replied. 'He's not.' *Which is why Dad never told you the truth.*

Riley dislodged his fingers and rose. She fidgeted while she waited for the confusion to die down.

'Miss Blackthorne,' Barnes said. 'You wish to add something?'

Since it was out in the open, why not use it to her advantage?

She turned so that all the summoners could hear her. 'It's true – Lucifer did summon my dad,' she said. 'He did it for one reason: to keep my father out of Ozymandias's control.'

'*Lord* Ozymandias,' her nemesis replied.

'Whatever,' Riley snarked back, ignoring Ozy's glare. 'All I want is my dad. I don't care about the rest of this. Just give him back.'

Her nemesis delivered a cunning smile. 'How eloquent,' Ozymandias said. 'However, as a token of my appreciation for Paul's assistance in my . . . studies, I've cleared your outstanding loan.'

The necromancer produced a single sheet of paper from nowhere and sent it sailing to the podium. It landed in front of Barnes with a rustle. 'There is the paperwork. The debt you owe for your dead mother's medical care is no more.'

He's trying to buy me off. 'I don't care about the damned money,' Riley declared. 'I want my dad. How hard is it for you to get that? You want me to beg? OK, I'll do it. *Please* return my father, O High Lord of All Dark Things!'

'Careful, lass,' Stewart warned.

Nervous whispers erupted around them. Instead of a blast of magic, Ozymandias seemed amused by her outburst.

'The child did say "please",' he replied, chuckling. 'How can I resist such courtesy?' With a theatrical wave of one hand, the necromancer vanished in a swirl of blinding light. In his place was a bewildered Paul Blackthorne.

'Dad?' Riley cried. She rushed forward, trying to wriggle through the crush of chairs and bodies. When she reached where he'd been standing, her father was gone.

'Dad?' she called out. 'Where are you?' *If this was all a trick . . .*

When a summoner pointed towards the double doors, Riley took off at a run, barrelling past the startled butler and down the long expanse of hall. She found her father cowering behind an azalea bush near the far end of the building. He would have been weeping if that was possible. Instead, he trembled from head to toe, his face tormented by horrors only he could see.

'Dad?'

His pale brown eyes tracked up to hers. 'Demons, demons everywhere,' he said, rocking back and forth like a toddler awakened from a horrific nightmare.

'Dad? It's Riley.' When she touched his arm, he jerked away in fear, like she was a stranger.

Mort knelt near them. 'Paul? You remember me? I'm Mortimer.' The summoner's calm voice made her dad look up at him. He seemed less freaked by Mort than anyone else. *Even his own daughter.*

It took a quarter of an hour of the summoner's patient coaxing until Riley's father would rise from the ground. The curious crowd of necromancers who'd gathered around hadn't helped the man's skittishness. Once Paul was mobile, Mort steered him towards the parking lot.

'We'll take him to my house,' he said, his attention

never leaving the frightened man.

'I want to come with you,' Riley replied.

'No, you'll only confuse him more. Right now he needs to rest. I'll let you know how he's doing.'

Mort was right: her father was in his own little hell-filled world and the compassionate summoner was the best person to help him.

As her dad and Mort prepared to leave, Riley touched the car window that stood between her and her parent.

What if he never remembers me again?

Chapter Twenty-Five

Numb from shock, Riley went on auto-pilot. She climbed into Beck's truck, clicked the seatbelt, then stared out of the side window. She didn't ask where they were going. It didn't matter. If she went home, she'd be alone in the apartment, surrounded by echoes of her dead father: the refrigerator that still held his favourite soda, his clothes in the closet and his toothbrush in the bathroom.

Riley choked up, jamming a fist to her mouth.

'Hang on, girl. I'm takin' you somewhere quiet,' Beck said softly. 'We'll talk it out, just the two of us. I won't leave ya alone, not until ya want me gone.'

'I don't want to be alone.'

'I know. Me neither. Not right now.'

In time he parked behind a multi-story apartment complex, one designed for older people. It was probably built in the seventies, but it was well maintained and offered a decent view of Centennial Park.

'What is this?' she asked, puzzled. 'Why are we here?'

'Ya'll see,' Beck said. He retrieved a pair of blankets from behind the seat and got out of the car. 'This way,' he said, gesturing to a side door in the building.

Beck produced a key and ushered her into a hallway, then a service elevator that went to the top floor. Despite everything that had happened, Riley's curiosity began to grow.

At her quizzical expression, Beck explained. 'I trap here every now and then, mostly Magpies. The supervisor made it so I can come and go without troublin' him.'

When they reached the top of the building and stepped outside, Riley shivered in the brisk breeze. 'Can't say I like roofs that much, not after the last one.'

'It's safe. No demons on this one.' Beck laid the first blanket on the far side of a stack of air-conditioning equipment, which provided shelter from the wind 'Have a seat. The show will start in a little bit,' he said.

Show? Still confused, she did as he asked, tugging her coat closer for warmth. When he joined her, he dutifully tucked the second blanket round them, which put her in close proximity to him, close enough to smell his aftershave and see the short blond stubble on his chin.

'What am I supposed to be doing?' she asked.

'It'll be a while. Just wait,' he said. Below them cars and people went by, but up here was another world. Quieter. Like they were looking down from Heaven and watching all the little people scramble around. As if the world wasn't bent on destroying everyone she loved.

The silence split open her grief. Riley closed her eyes, trying to seal it shut, but it broke through in a choked sob. At the sound, Beck's arms went round her, pulling her close.

'Go on, ya've earned the right,' he said. 'Hell, I'd do the same if I could.'

The tears came in unrelenting torrents. Riley wept until there was no more to give. When she finally looked up, Beck's eyes were moist. She offered him a tissue, but he shook his head.

'Guys don't use those,' he said, trying hard to sound tough.

'I won't tell anyone.'

He took one from her, but didn't wipe his eyes.

Nestled against him, Riley blew her nose. 'Talk to me, Beck. Talk to me about anything but necromancers, dead fathers and weird demons. I want some normal for a change. I want to stop hurting inside.'

He sighed in her ear. 'So do I, girl.'

Beck thought for a time, as if he had to struggle for a topic that was safe. 'Did . . . you see that computer program I got? It was on my desk.'

Riley nodded, though she had no idea why he'd thought of that subject. 'Is it helping you?'

'Yeah,' he said. 'I'm readin' better. I listen to it when I have time.' The corners of his mouth tugged into a smile. 'Would ya . . . you be willin' to help me?'

It would be her way of honouring her father's legacy. 'Sure, I'd be happy to, Beck.' Riley blinked – something was wrong with what he'd said. '"*You*"? What happened to "ya"?'

Beck took a slow and deliberate breath. 'I've been workin' on how I talk.'

'Why?'

'I'm proud to be a Georgia boy and that's never gonna change. But . . .' He swiped a hand through his hair, always a sign he was agitated. 'Stewart says he wants to take me over to Scotland and have me meet the masters in the International Guild.'

'Wow!' said Riley, shifting so suddenly the blanket slid off her shoulders. 'That's a big deal, Beck. He wouldn't do that if he didn't think you were amazing.'

'I don't know about that,' he hedged, 'but I want to do the man proud. I don't want to sound like a hick.'

'It's just the way you speak.'

'Yeah, well, people judge ya . . . you just the same.' He paused, clearly planning out the next sentence. 'You call me Backwoods Boy. That's not because I sound . . . educated.' The Southern drawl was still there, but smoother now, like sinfully rich chocolate.

'Backwoods Boy is just a nickname,' Riley replied. 'You call me Princess and I don't live in a castle.'

'I know. It's just I've been listenin' to the tapes and I find myself changin' how I talk. I don't think that's a bad thing.'

There was more here than Stewart and his plans for Beck's future with the Guild. 'Did Justine say something to you about this?'

He nodded. 'She thinks I sound *quaint*. I don't want that. I want folks to take me seriously.'

Who does the stick chick think she is? Then again, if he was willing to make this big a change, maybe he was more serious about the reporter than Riley realized.

What do you see in her?

Someone had to be on Beck's side. 'Don't let anyone tell you how you should talk or act or any of that. Be yourself. That's cool enough.'

'Thanks, I will,' he said. 'I've seen how it works. I dated this girl in the Army. Her name was Caitlin. She was from North Carolina, but I never knew it until she told me. We were . . . close.'

The way he spoke, it was more than just a hook-up kind of thing. From his melancholy expression, she decided she'd best not ask for any details.

'How about changing that drawl to a British accent?' Riley suggested. 'Or a Scottish one like Stewart's?' she said, waggling her eyebrows. 'That'd be sexy cool.'

'Don't start with me, girl,' he said.

A siren blared into existence somewhere nearby, then faded into the distance.

The oppressive sadness began to lift. Beck was helping her find her way through the darkness. For a brief moment, she wished they could be this close all the time.

When Riley nestled up next to him again, he thoughtfully rearranged the blanket to keep her warm.

'Can I ask you something?' she said. He nodded. Unwilling to admit she'd snooped in Beck's personal possessions, she framed the question carefully. 'Dad said you got some medals in the Army. Why don't you have them out where people can see them?'

He was shaking his head before she finished the question.

'I know some folks believe they're real important, but all I can think of is the guys who didn't make it back. Whenever I look at those things, I see their faces and what kind of lives they might have had if I'd saved them. I didn't do enough to make that happen, so I can't act like the medals make up for that.'

That's why he sounds so old sometimes. 'You can't be responsible for everyone in this world,' she said.

His arm tightened round her possessively. 'I know.' He peered out at the building beyond. 'Look! It's show time,' he said. 'See?'

What am I looking at?

The only difference was that the building across from them had a row of lights now, a single floor among the countless levels. Then another floor lit up and another, like a Christmas tree coming to life one bulb at a time. Other lights flicked on as the twilight gained supremacy. Some were bright white, others golden yellow – the battered city transitioning from day to night.

'Watch the top of the Bank of America buildin',' Beck said, full of anticipation. She turned in that direction, studying the structure. It had a unique point at the top that made it look like a huge mechanical pencil.

'Any time now. Throw that switch!' Beck coaxed.

His enthusiasm was catching. 'Come on! You know you want to!'

As if Beck had done the deed himself, the top of the structure began to glow like the filaments in a massive light bulb.

'Ohhh, that's so cool,' Riley said, captivated by the beacon of light she'd always taken for granted. 'I've never seen it come on before.'

'That's why I climb up here whenever things are botherin' me. I watch the lights come on, and sometimes, if I'm up here at dawn, I watch them go off. It helps me remember I'm part of somethin' bigger, that all those folks down there need my help and that I can't let them down.'

There are so many layers to this guy. You could spend forever with him and never uncover them all.

'Thanks for bringing me up here. It's really neat.'

'Did it help?'

She nodded. 'I don't feel so alone any more.' It was more him than the lights, but he didn't need to know that.

Beck cleared his throat. 'Can I ask you somethin' too?'

It was only fair. 'Sure, as long as it's not about the lying angel.'

Beck grunted his agreement. 'Paul sold his soul for you, didn't he?'

Riley turned towards him, astonished. 'How did you know?'

Beck adjusted the blanket again. 'I just figured it out. That's what a man should do for his daughter. Or his woman.' He looked her straight in the eyes. 'I'd do it for you if it kept ya safe,' he said tenderly.

He'd go to Hell for me. In that instant, Riley knew she'd do the same for him.

Suddenly uncomfortable by how intimate they'd become,

she disentangled herself and went to lean against the railing. The chill wind pushed past her, on its way to wherever. Beck joined her at the rail, wrapping the blanket round her.

Riley owed him so much, but most of all she owed him an apology.

'I'm really sorry about Ori,' she said. 'I hurt you and I feel bad about that. It wasn't right, not after everything you did for me. I was just . . . lonely.'

Beck moved closer and touched her cheek with his fingers. They were rough with callouses, but surprisingly gentle. 'I was too. That's why I went with Justine. I'm sorry.'

Am I dreaming? Pinching herself would mean she'd have to move and that wasn't on the cards.

Inevitably they had drifted towards each other, drawn by something stronger than either one of them could voice. The closer they came, the stronger the pull. Like this moment had been destined.

He's going to kiss me. Her heart began to beat faster. She'd dreamed of this moment, fantasized about how wonderful it would be. Now it was happening.

Let it be awesome.

Beck was so close all she could see was his eyes. In a fleeting moment she thought she could peer deep into his unguarded soul.

His hand shook where it touched her cheek. *He's nervous.* She was too. Trying to let him know this was all right, Riley put her hand over his. Closing her own eyes, she waiting for their lips to touch.

On the street below, a cop car flew by, siren wailing.

Riley could feel his breath in her hair now, smell his aftershave. She inhaled deeply, memorizing his scent. The faint touch of his lips came a second before the sharp blast of an air horn. Startled, they jumped apart, the tender interlude ruined.

From the shocked expression on Beck's face, she saw he knew it too, and he stepped further away as if she presented too much temptation. Shaking his head, he murmured. 'Sorry, I shouldn't have done that. I had no right.'

Before she could tell him that he had every right, his cellphone rang. As he took the call, Riley glowered down at the city that seemed determined to screw up her life.

Damn! One little kiss? What would it have hurt?

A pair of black vans sped round the corner, then a third. All had the demon hunter insignia.

Beck was facing west now, towards Centennial Park. 'We'll be there.'

Before she could ask what was going on, he'd snatched up the blankets and headed towards the exit. He had his trapper face on now, no hint of the nervous young man who'd almost kissed her.

'What's happening?' she called out as he wrenched the door open.

'There's demons in the market,' he replied. 'They're tearin' everythin' to hell.'

Chapter Twenty-Six

When they reached his truck, Beck tossed the blankets on the seat, then turned towards her. 'Yer not gonna stay out of this, are ya?' he asked, frowning.

'Would you?' she said, adjusting the backpack on her shoulders.

'No.' He dug around behind the seat and came up with his spare steel pipe. 'Use it wisely.'

'Thanks, Yoda.'

He frowned and took off towards the market. For such a solidly built guy, he could move fast. As she jogged, the backpack kept thumping into her kidneys, but there was no time to adjust it. Streams of people fled towards them. Some had obvious wounds and others were hysterical. One man doused himself with a bottle of water to extinguish his smouldering clothes.

The market itself was a sea of colourful tents and campers, all strung with lights to allow sales to continue late into the night. Now only chaos was shopping here. Gunfire echoed off nearby buildings, either from the hunters or vendors who were armed.

Beck spied a Three near a barbecue tent, gnawing on a

roasted goat hanging from the spit. The shop's owner kept trying to shoo it away with a tablecloth, yelling in agitated Spanish.

'Get away from it!' Beck shouted at the man. The demon turned at the sound of his voice and howled. Leaving its meal behind, it careened towards the trapper, forcing him to take to his heels. As he ran, Beck kept calling out to the thing, leading it away from Riley and the others.

You're going to get yourself killed.

Another Three scrambled across an open area, then leaped a table to take a man down. His buddy hit the fiend hard on the head with a tent pole, dazing it, then dragged his wounded friend out of reach. When he returned with a revolver, he put a single shot into the demon's head. Pleased, he turned his back on it.

'Look out!' Riley shouted, but it was too late. The demon rose and cut him down with its razor-sharp claws.

Bullets were useless today. These Hellspawn weren't the dying kind.

Peter's litany of zombie-killing techniques tumbled through her mind. It took a while for her to orient herself; the scene was so disjointed it was hard to remember where the sword vendor had his tent. Riley kept moving at a jog, dodging panicky people and demons on the prowl. One of the Hellspawn had a huge patch of bleached white fur on its neck. She knew that one personally – it was the Three that had nearly killed her at Demon Central.

Riley hurried past a shop with toppled bookshelves. Past

the Deader tent. All of the reanimates were gone, the sides of the canvas slashed. She jogged by a burning tent and the soft *pop, pop, pop* of custom-designed candles crackling in the flames.

It was dark enough for the shadows to play tricks on her, looking like demons where there were none. Riley finally found the one she wanted. It was a popular location as the owner was handing out swords to anyone who would take them, not expecting payment. With a 'thanks', she grabbed one that looked like it might do the job, then headed out to find Beck.

Müller and the captain of the hunters ran past her, the leader shouting orders into his radio as he coordinated the attack. Salvatore frowned at her, but kept moving.

No matter how hard she tried, she couldn't stay out of trouble.

Riley finally found Beck hemmed in by a Three near a small travel trailer that had seen better days. He was guarding the door, a woman and two small children huddling inside the camper.

Not a hero, huh?

'Beck!' she called, holding up the sword. He didn't hear her, too focused on the teeth and claws in front of him. 'Hey, Backwoods Boy!' That got his attention. Cautiously moving closer, she tossed the blade so it landed near his feet, barely missing one of his boots. In one swift movement he threw the pipe at the Three to distract it, picked up the sword and was back in a fighting stance in an instant. When the demon lunged, he struck at it, cutting a slice from its shoulder. When the second cut did more damage, the demon howled in rage.

'Cut off its head!' she shouted, slicing a thumb across her throat for emphasis.

With a nod to say he'd got the message, the third sweeping slice delivered the death blow as the demon's skull ceased to be part of its body. Both portions tumbled on to the Georgia clay . . . and stayed down.

Peter had been right.

'Yes!' Beck crowed, pumping his fist into the air. 'That rocks!' Then he charged off in search of another Three to decapitate.

Riley sighed to herself. 'I've created a monster.'

Knowing she really wasn't a match for a demon right now, she went from tent to tent telling those inside how to stop the slaughter. Some thought she was crazy, but a few of the merchants took her seriously.

Riley watched in fascinated horror as the bookshop owner bashed a Three over the head with a shovel. When it hit the ground, another stall owner joined in, and between the two of them they savagely decapitated the fiend. When it didn't rise from the dead, the men shouted their victory and hurried after another demon.

The tide slowly began to turn in favour of the humans. Some of the shop owners had died from claws or teeth, but the rest of them weren't giving up.

As Riley made her way through the tent city and the damaged trailers, she stopped to help the injured. There wasn't much she could do but offer sympathy, or hold down a compress to slow the bleeding. Most of the injured had claw marks and those would be infected very soon if not treated properly.

As she held a young boy's hand, she instructed his father to pour Holy Water on to the child's leg wound. The boy cried out in pain the moment the liquid hit it.

'It's supposed to do that. You'll be OK,' she said.

'How do you know?' he demanded, fat tears rolling down his face.

'Because I'm a demon trapper,' she said, feeling pride at being able to say that.

'Where the hell were you? Why didn't you stop them?' the child's father demanded, his worry shifting to anger now that he had a viable target.

Riley's pride faded. 'We're trying.' She pointed at the bottle of the sacred liquid. 'That's the good stuff. Keep using it on his leg every two hours. It'll heal him.'

She moved on down the line, testing every bottle of Holy Water she found. Running a wet finger over the label told her if it was fake or real. She was tempted to use the demon claw to test the liquid, but given the mood of the survivors that might not have been a smart idea. If the Holy Water proved to be fake, she poured the liquid on to the ground and explained why. Not everyone believed her.

'What the hell are you doin'?' one man complained. 'I need that for my buddy. The stuff's supposed to cure him.'

His buddy had a gaping stomach wound and wasn't going to be around for long if his friend kept treating him with tap water. 'Take him to the hospital. They'll have real Holy Water there. This stuff is fake. It will kill him.'

'You're lying.'

'No,' Riley said, shoving the empty quart bottle into the guy's hands. 'I'm not. Get him out of here! Now!'

The guy actually backed off. 'OK, don't go psycho on me, girl.'

'Sorry.'

When a team of paramedics trotted by, followed by a policeman, Riley realized the battle was over. Looking back into the heart of the market was like seeing an open wound. There were cries and shouts and the sound of a fire engine in the distance.

Riley aimed for the one place that might offer sanctuary. To her relief the witches' tent was intact. Three of the practitioners were fanned out in a semi-circle. They all had some weapon in hand, including her friend Ayden, who held a sword like she knew what to do with it. Then Riley saw a body near the tent. It was a witch, an older one, and she was cradled in the arms of a weeping girl.

Not even the magic users were safe.

'I figured you had to be in this hell somewhere,' Ayden said solemnly.

Riley's eyes were still caught by the dead woman. 'I sorry. I didn't think . . .'

'That witches don't get hurt and die? We're as mortal as you trappers. At least Elspeth went quick. She's in the Summerlands now and . . .' Ayden blinked away tears. 'Come on, let's see what we can do for the living.' She tossed her sword to one of the others and headed out into the market.

Riley lost track of time as she and the witch made the rounds. A few people wouldn't let her friend near them. Harsh words came their way, but Ayden held her tongue.

'They need a scapegoat,' she explained as they moved on after a man called them names. 'Soon it'll be all over the city that we summoned the demons in the first place.'

The witch veered towards where one of the fiends lay sprawled in the dirt. It was in multiple pieces, evidence of the crowd's fury. Ayden knelt and then hovered her hand in the air above the thing's severed head. She closed her eyes, murmuring something. A frown came next. Then she went totally still. Riley gasped.

The point of a sword rested against the back of Ayden's neck.

'Don't you think it killed enough folks today, witch?' a man growled. His shirt was scorched and he had a wicked burn on his cheek. He appeared to be one of the vendors, a money bag tied round his waist. 'You trying to raise it from the dead again?'

'Why would I want to do that?' Ayden replied evenly.

His sword arm shook in rage. 'Because you're one of Hell's own.'

Beck came out of nowhere, his face sweaty and jacket smeared in demon blood. 'Ya know, it's been a bitch of a day,' he said. 'Let's not make it any worse, OK?'

'Why the hell do you care?' the man asked, glaring at the trapper.

'Because yer about to make a mistake that's gonna cost ya yer life,' Beck said, casually wiping the blade clean on his jeans. 'This lady is not a threat.'

'I don't see any of their kind bleeding.'

'I'm sure the dead witch at their tent might disagree,' Riley retorted.

The guy hesitated. 'You trappers are as bad as these damned witches. I should kill both of you right here and now.'

It might have got uglier if Captain Salvatore and two of his men hadn't pushed through the crowd and joined them.

The leader hunter assessed the situation immediately. 'Why do you have this woman at sword point?' He was using the *don't screw me, I've had a really bad night* kind of voice.

'This witch was trying to call the demon back to life. I saw it myself,' the man reported. 'I want you to arrest her or something. Burn her, maybe.'

Ayden's mouth flattened in a thin line.

'The Church is long past that horror,' Salvatore scolded. 'Step back and put the sword down.'

'But she—'

'Is not your problem,' Salvatore replied. He snapped his fingers and his escort flanked their captain in one step, hands on their weapons.

The vendor shook his head in disgust, but the sword fell from his fingers. 'The trappers and the witches are fooling all of you.' Then he marched away in disgust.

Ayden rose and dusted off her skirt. 'Thank you,' she said.

'You're welcome.' Salvatore rubbed his neck pensively as

he keyed his radio. 'This is Team Gabriel. I need four men to spread out through the market to keep an eye out for trouble.' The order was acknowledged immediately.

The captain addressed his escort. 'Müller, you and Tamson take a prominent position near the pagans' tent, in case somebody decides to get creative.' After two 'yes, sir's', the hunters hiked off at a brisk pace.

'Again, thank you,' Ayden said.

Salvatore gestured towards a set of wooden benches. 'Let's have a talk, over here, where it's quiet.' As they walked, the captain eyed Riley.

'I know, I was supposed to say out of the middle of things,' she said. 'It's not working out that way.'

'Apparently not.' He moved his attention to Ayden as she sank on to a bench. 'What were you doing with the demon corpse?'

'I was hoping to sense the magical signature, get an idea of who is behind all this. What I felt was part necromancer, part something else. The something else was very old, no pagan or summoner magic.' Her eyes were on Riley now, trying to send her a message.

'Come to the Westin. We can talk about it there,' the captain offered.

'No. Somewhere neutral,' she replied, voice strained. 'If I come to your headquarters, that implies guilt. One mistake and the pagans in this town are going to be paying for something they didn't do.'

Salvatore considered her observation. 'What about Master

Stewart's house? You have good relations with the trappers, don't you? That would be neutral ground.'

'If it is OK with Master Stewart, I'm good with it. Give me time . . . to get things taken care of.'

'I understand. I'm truly sorry about your loss.'

The witch seemed caught off guard by the compassion. 'As I am for yours,' she said, then swept away.

'Who'd ya lose?' Beck asked as he mopped off his forehead with the cleanest coat sleeve. It still left a smear of black on his skin.

'One of our newer hunters,' the captain replied. Salvatore's gaze drifted back towards the centre of the market. Vendors were trying to retrieve their goods from the wreckage. A line of bodies lay near one of the tents, covered by whatever was at hand.

'Why didn't y'all have swords?' Beck asked. 'Ya knew bullets are useless.'

Salvatore's eyes flared at Beck's dressing down. 'The Vatican is weighing the issue,' he said tersely. 'They're not known for making decisions lightly. Or with any speed.'

'So more folks are gonna die while they're talkin' it out?' Beck snarled.

'Isn't that always the way?'

Chapter Twenty-Seven

It was Jackson who took Riley to collect her car. He wasn't his usual jovial self, too caught up in what had gone down at the market. Riley was grateful for the silence.

Should I tell the hunters about Sartael? No, better not. It would open up questions as to how she knew about the Fallen and that would lead right back to the talking statue in the cemetery. Consorting with the minions of Lucifer is what they'd call it and she'd be back in custody in a heartbeat.

To her annoyance Riley found a note stuck under her windshield wiper – it was from Allan. It had his phone number and e-mail address and his usual terse commands: *Call me! Tonight!*

She crumpled it up, dropped it on the ground and then pulverized it into the cracked concrete with the toe of her tennis shoe.

By the time she'd made it to Stewart's house and taken a shower, the blowback from the market's attack had heated up. The phones wouldn't stop ringing. Riley heard only one side of the conversations with the mayor, the governor and the National Guild. All had the same order: put the demons back in the bottle. **Now.** No doubt Captain Salvatore was receiving the same butt-chewing from his superiors in Rome.

No one needed to tell them that. If the trappers and hunters failed, the city would turn into a feeding ground for every ravenous demon in the area. For some reason, the higher-ups always felt the need to state the obvious.

It was nearing eleven when the phone calls finally tapered off. Stewart decided that dessert was the solution to all their problems. Harper begged off and headed for bed, which left Riley alone with the Scotsman and a hefty piece of peach pie with a scoop of vanilla ice cream on the side.

Stewart pushed his plate away first. 'I talked ta Mort earlier this evenin'. Yer father has settled down a bit, but he's still . . . out there. I wish I had better news for ya.'

Riley hadn't expected any. 'What's so important that Ozymandias would do that to my dad?'

'Masters know a fair amount of demonic knowledge, but I'm not sure exactly what the necro was hopin' for. We may never know.'

'What about Grand Masters?'

'Ah, well, we are taught a lot more about demons and angels and all that.'

'You really would have killed my dad?'

'Aye,' he said quietly. 'I've had another friend who went dark. His face still haunts me.'

Riley pushed her plate away, her appetite gone.

Stewart sighed, then brightened. 'Ya play chess, lass?'

'Sometimes. I'm not very good at it.' Actually, her father

beat her every time. That didn't bother her at all – it was Dad face time.

Stewart pushed back his chair. 'Come along. I've got somethin' ta show ya.'

Though this really was the last thing Riley wanted to do, she followed him anyway. He'd taken her side against the hunters, given her a place to live and treated her with respect. A chess game wasn't going to kill her.

Stewart retrieved a plain black box from his office and carried it into the library where he set it in the centre of the table. The set was old, ancient even, carved out of wood, each piece hand painted. The white pieces wore kilts.

'The Scots versus the Sassenach,' Stewart said, laying out the pieces. At her bewildered expression, he added, 'The Scots versus the English.'

'Oh,' Riley said, picking up a kilt-clad knight who held a honking huge sword. 'How old is this set?'

'About three hundred years. It's been passed down through the family.'

'1718?' she said, astounded. 'I can't even imagine what it was like then.'

'People don't change that much, lass. We just think we do. Since yer a Blackthorne, ya can represent the English side.'

She lined up her pieces and prepared to be slaughtered.

'Have ya ever seen yer namesake? The tree, I mean?' Stewart questioned as he moved a pawn forward. Riley shook her head. 'Wicked thorns on the thing, but it has delicate little flowers and the sweetest berries, but only after a hard frost of course.'

She wondered where he was going with his arboreal lecture. 'Ah, that means what?'

He smiled patiently. 'Trials and setbacks. Strife often leads ta a sweeter life. That's the lesson of the blackthorn.'

'I'm due for some of the sweet, I think.'

'Aye. We all are, lass.'

He fell silent after that as they played. It was hard to concentrate, but she tried, not wanting to look like a complete dork in front of the master. Riley suspected he had another reason for spending time with an amateur chess player when the world was melting down around them. Stewart would get to the point when he was ready.

The old master won handily. Left on the board were only a few pieces, the majority of which were his. He picked up one of her pawns, twisting it between his thumb and middle finger as he examined it. 'I'm guessin' this is how ya see yerself right now.'

Riley nodded.

'Ya've been doin' research in the library. Ya left the books out.'

'Oh, I'm sorry,' she said. 'I won't do it again.'

'It's nay a problem, lass,' he said, and set the chess piece down. 'After all that readin' about fallen angels, tell me what ya think is goin' on.'

Riley marshalled her thoughts, since the old master was too savvy to allow her to throw just anything at him.

'Ozymandias has found a way to mess with the demons. Someone, who isn't a necro, is helping him.' It seemed the right time to reveal her secret. 'I'm thinking that's Sartael. He's the fallen angel who lied to Ori, told him that Lucifer wanted my soul.' She took a deep breath. 'He turned Simon against me and he set the Five on my dad.'

One of Stewart's silver eyebrows arched. 'How do ya know this Fallen's name?'

She told Stewart about Ori and his status as a statue, courtesy of Lucifer. Then she related her conversation with the two Divines in the cemetery.

The master leaned back in the chair, pensive. 'Why did ya think it was wise ta go to the cemetery?'

'No choice. He kept shouting at me and it was driving me crazy. I thought my head would explode.'

'Ya do know that move put both of our lives in peril?' he asked, sterner now.

'I know, but Martha wanted me to talk to him. She gave me Sartael's name so I could use it against Ori.'

'Really?' He scratched his chin in thought.

'Do you have to tell the hunters about this?'

Stewart groaned. 'By God, I should. I won't, because we need ta work as a team and we can't do that if we're in the Vatican's custody awaitin' trial.'

'Thanks,' she murmured. 'What do *you* think is going on?'

The Scotsman sat forward in his chair. 'At best, Lucifer keeps a tentative hold on Hell's denizens. Many of those have been eager for a final battle. Sartael is one of the chief among them. If he's been whisperin' in a certain necromancer's ear, the result would be undead demons in our midst.'

'Why hasn't Lucifer taken out the dude?'

'The prince is a strategist. If there's going to be a war in Hell, he needs ta know exactly who he can trust. Sometimes the best way ta flush out yer enemies is by playin' them against each other.'

'Like Ori and Sartael,' she murmured.

Stewart's tired face crinkled in thought. 'Yer a Blackthorne. Heaven doesn't choose their champion without a lot of thought. Neither does Hell, for that matter.'

'But what do I do?' Riley asked, frustrated. 'No one will tell me, at least not the angel Martha. She clams up when I ask. Lucifer won't say a word. Neither will Ori.'

'As best as I remember, ya will be forced ta make a decision. If ya decide correctly, then ya'll plead humanity's case in front of the angels.'

'You mean when I'm dead?' she asked, not liking where this was headed.

'No, the angels will be massed for war,' he responded. 'Ya'll be standin' between the two armies.'

Ohmigod. 'What can I say to keep them from toasting us all?'

'I have no idea. All I can suggest is that ya speak from yer heart.'

In the distance a clock began to toll midnight. 'Get some rest. Come back down at nine for breakfast. Harper and I are havin' a meetin' of interested parties. Ya need ta be there for the last part of it.'

'Is it a council of war?'

'Aye, lass. It's time to put an end to this misery, one way or another.'

Later, as she drifted to sleep, Riley thought of Beck and the lost kiss. What would it have been like?

Amazing? Just OK? Disappointing? No, never disappointing. Beck wasn't that kind of guy.

'Probably awesome.' The demons had screwed up her life again.

It's time to return the favour.

Chapter Twenty-Eight

As instructed, Riley tromped down the stairs at nine in the morning. The kitchen table was full of coffee cake and people. Father Rosetti and Captain Salvatore were there for the hunters, Ayden and Mort for the magical folks, then the two masters and Beck. Riley pulled out a chair and eyed the plate mounded with coffee cake and doughnuts.

'I can try to break the enchantment that binds the demons,' Mort said, 'but I need a focus for that spell.'

'Ya heard Salvatore, they destroyed all the bodies,' Beck replied, shorter than usual. He looked totally wiped, like he hadn't slept in days. 'There has to be another way.'

'There is – I try to break the spell and fail. Get me one of those demons and I'll have a lot better chance.'

'That'll take too much time,' Beck muttered.

'What about that demon tooth I brought you?'

Mort shook his head. 'It's too magically charged to be of use. I destroyed it.'

Oh . . . Riley had another option, one the Vatican already knew about.

'How about a demon claw?' she said, pulling the talon out from under her sweater. 'It belongs to one of the weird ones.

I saw the thing at the market last night.'

'How can you be sure?' Mort asked. 'Don't they all look the same?'

'It's the one with the big white splotch on the back of its neck. It tried to eat me in Demon Central, so I remember it *really* well.'

'We didn't burn that one's corpse, so it's still alive,' Salvatore said.

'Then you can use it for whatever it is Mort wants to do,' Riley said.

'There's a red flag on that play,' Ayden replied. 'The claw was once physically part of you, soaked in your blood. That changes things.'

'Why would it matter?'

Ayden and Mort exchanged looks. It was the necromancer who explained.

'You have a direct connection with that demon now.' He let out a heavy breath. 'That means you're going to have to cast the spell.'

'What? I don't do magic.'

'Don't worry, I'll help you with the Latin,' Mort replied.

'It doesn't matter if it's in Latin or whatever. I don't cast spells. I'm a trapper. That's enough hassle.' Especially when Rome's grand inquisitor was taking notes on her every move.

'I'm sorry, Riley, but you're the strongest candidate,' Mort replied.

'You should not pressure the child into evil,' Father Rosetti retorted.

'I'm not. I'm being honest,' Mort shot back. 'If we want to destroy these demons, our best chance is to have Riley perform the spell. She has a direct connection with one of them.'

'You will be taking your soul one step closer to Hell,' Rosetti said, speaking to her now. 'Rome *will* make note of that.'

How do I get into this mess? 'If it destroys the demons, I'll do it,' she said.

'Your soul . . .' Rosetti began.

'Is mine. Why do people keep telling me what to do with the thing? If I choose to barter it away to save people's lives, it will be my choice,' Riley said, flushing with anger.

'Then you will bear consequences,' the priest warned. 'The terms of our agreement with Master Stewart precluded you from participating in any activity that put your soul in jeopardy.'

'I got that,' she said. 'I don't see any other option. Do you, Father Rosetti?'

Riley expected a lecture, maybe even handcuffs. Instead, the priest shook his head in dismay.

'I fear you are correct,' he replied. 'As is often the case, the road to Hell is paved with good intentions.'

Stewart snorted. 'So is the one ta Heaven, I've heard.'

It took another half hour of haggling over the details, but when all the talking was done they'd agreed it should go down at dawn the next day. The location shouldn't have been a surprise: Oakland Cemetery. There'd be a strategy meeting tonight, but Riley wasn't going to be there because she'd be learning rudimentary Latin pronunciation.

'Come over to the house about at three thirty,' Mort said as she walked him to the front door. 'We'll work for a few hours, you can rest, then we'll do more.'

'How hard is it? I mean, is the spell really difficult?'

'It's not the hardest, but it's certainly not the easiest.'

Which in Mort-speak meant it was a big deal, but he was trying not to scare her.

She changed subjects. 'How's my dad?'

'Not much better,' the summoner admitted. 'He keeps raving about the demons. His mind is lost, Riley. I'm not sure if it's ever coming back.'

'Ozy will pay for that, right? He has to,' she insisted.

'I wouldn't count on it.' The summoner let himself out.

Confused as to what the future might bring, how bad it might become, Riley took the stairs up to her room, trailing her hand along the smooth wooden banister. There was no sunlight in her life now. Instead it grew darker by degrees, like approaching nightfall. Maybe that was the way it was supposed to be for the one who would stand between the eternal armies of Heaven and Hell.

There was only one consolation.

Her father wouldn't notice that the world had ended.

If Riley had ever made a list of what she would do on her last day on earth, it wouldn't include watching her clothes tumble dry in a dryer that squeaked with every turn. Still, she refused to leave dirty underwear behind, or a grubby refrigerator or a messy apartment. Even if the rest of humanity wasn't going to be around to appreciate her tidiness.

Once that task was complete, Riley returned to her apartment and stuffed money into envelopes to pay for various bills. The world might survive, but if she didn't she wanted her slate clean. With the Consolidated Debt creeps out of her hair now – they'd even left a snarky 'thank you for paying off your loan even though we had to hound you to the ends of the earth' message on her answering machine – that left the everyday bills. In the background, the television news ran special reports about the citywide Holy Water distribution plan. With Rome's assistance, the local diocese had figured out a way to bless entire tanker-loads of water and distribute the sacred liquid around the city, *for free.*

That should keep people from freaking out.

Her cellphone pinged a new message from Peter. NO SCHOOL TODAY!!!

Riley sent back her THANKS for the update, but didn't bother to tell him she'd have cut class anyway. No way she could become a Latin scholar and take a pop quiz on Sherman's military tactics at the same time.

Her ears caught the faint sound of little feet pattering across the kitchen counter. Funny how her demon roomie could choose to be stealthy or not. She waited until he came into sight.

'Hey, guy.' The wee fiend observed her for a moment, then leaped on to the table, his bag in hand.

How does he do that? It would have been the equivalent of a human jumping the Grand Canyon. The Magpie dropped the bag of loot in front of him and began to root around inside. Out came all sorts of items, including a steady stream of multicoloured glitter. Finally he found what he was hunting for and came forward toting her silver seashell earring. The one he'd taken from her dresser. Standing on his tiptoes, he offered it up to her. If this hadn't been one of Lucifer's minions, it would have been way cute.

'Thanks,' she said, but she didn't take it from him. 'You keep it. I'll need the good luck.'

The demon smiled, revealing pointed teeth, then gave her a nod. She didn't have to tell him twice: the earring was back inside the bag in an instant. Then he zipped out of sight.

Riley sighed. 'I'll miss you. Even if you work for . . . *him*.'

When she looked down at her list of bills to see who was next, the paper had glitter all over it. Right before she was about to brush it off, Riley realized the sparkles formed words in bright reds and golds.

Free the angel.

'What? You mean Ori?' Riley called out, feeling stupid she was talking to what appeared to be an empty kitchen. A squeak came from the top of the refrigerator. The fiend equivalent of a 'you betcha, sister'.

'I don't know if I can trust him.'

Another squeak. She guessed it was: 'That's your problem.'

Once freed, Ori might try to gain his revenge against the Prince who'd imprisoned him. Maybe side with Sartael. *But*

Lucifer would know that. He's playing with my head again.

Unable to decide the best course, Riley dumped the glitter into the trashcan and continued to pay her bills. Bills made sense.

The rest of my life? Not so much.

Peter's face lit up in surprise when he found Riley on his doorstep.

'Hey!' Then his joy faded. 'What's up? You've never come to my place before.'

'Can we go for a walk?' she asked, trying not to sound all gloomy and totally failing. He grabbed his coat and they headed down the sidewalk in a suburban neighbourhood stocked with small kids on bikes and barking dogs. The kind of neighbourhood Riley had never known.

'Did you get any of the Holy Water they're giving out downtown?' she asked.

'We're OK. The stuff we have is good. I checked it.'

'I've got a couple gallons in the car for you. Use it anywhere you think a demon can get in.'

Peter stopped in the middle of the sidewalk. 'What's going on, Riley?'

She gave him the latest, except for the End of the World part. Sometimes it was best not to be that honest. Peter's eyes widened when she admitted that she was going to be spell casting.

'The hunters went for that?' he asked, dubious.

'Not really, but they're cornered like the rest of us. The

attack at the market means the demons are going after everyone now, not just the pros. If the spells work, everything will be good again.'

'If it doesn't?'

Atlanta will become a killing ground.

'You'll need the Holy Water,' she urged. 'And swords. That's what kills them, just like you said.'

'Oh my God, you're serious.' Peter looked away for moment, trying to master his growing panic. 'At least Mom and the twins are in Illinois. It'd be really bad if they were here.'

'I wouldn't tell your dad,' Riley advised. 'He'll freak. You know what to do. You're really good at taking care of your peeps.'

Her friend wasn't listening. 'I can sneak out early in the morning, be there with you. Maybe I can help.'

He would do it too. *But I won't let you.* If this battle led to Armageddon, Peter should be home in those last moments. Home with the people he loved, not being savaged by a demon in a graveyard.

'No. You *have* to guard your family. The trappers will watch out for me.'

Peter shook his head in resignation. 'You're right. What can I do? Throw a hard drive at the things? Beck will watch your back.'

Until he's dead like all the others.

They circumnavigated the block, talking about subjects that weren't so final, like homework assignments and if Peter would get a chance to visit his mom this summer. Things that had little chance of coming true. Like Peter's love life.

'You should talk to Simi. I think she'd like to go out with you.'

Peter gave her a sidelong look. 'Seriously?'

'Yeah. She thinks you're cute.'

'Cool. Consider it done.'

By the time they'd made it back to his house, it was nearly three.

'You call me when this is over, OK?' Peter urged. 'Please let me know what's going on.'

'I will,' she replied, hoping she could keep that promise. 'You stay inside, keep the Holy Water wards up. We'll do the rest.' She felt like she was delivering lines in some film. *Don't worry, we're the good guys and we always defeat evil.* But life wasn't like a movie.

They embraced right in front of his house. It was a friend type of hug, but the emotion was there. When they broke apart, she began to turn away, but he caught her elbow.

'If anyone can pull this off, it's you. You're really amazing, Riley. Remember that.'

She had Peter and Heaven pulling for her. *Maybe that would be enough.*

Chapter Twenty-Nine

She found her father huddled against the wall in Mort's circular office. He sat on a fat pillow, a blanket over his shoulders. A bottle of the orange stabilizer was within reach. The only thing her father didn't have was his brilliant mind.

'He's under a confusion spell,' Mort said quietly. 'I can't break it. I don't understand why Ozymandias felt the need to cast it.'

'So we wouldn't know what he did when Ozy had him?' Riley suggested.

Mort nodded his agreement. 'Approach him slowly. He's easily frightened.'

Riley did as the summoner advised. It took time, but eventually she sat on the floor next to her dad. He looked over at her then went back to studying nothing. At least he wasn't raving at the demons any longer.

'Dad,' she said. No reaction. She'd known this was going to be hard, but this was awful. So she began to talk to him about everyday things, like how she'd paid the bills, that her grades were good and how she'd visited Peter's house. She talked until her throat went dry.

'Schoooool?' her father asked.

Leave it to a teacher to know when she was skipping class.

'They cancelled it because . . . just because.'

He didn't seem to realize that made no sense.

When Riley handed her father the bottle of orange liquid, he drank from it. That was progress.

'I'm here to learn Latin from Mort,' she explained, figuring he might like to know that.

Her father murmured something.

'What?' He repeated it, but she didn't understand what it meant.

When he finally fell asleep, she tucked the blanket around him and sought out the summoner. Mort had chosen the garden as their study location. It was fairly warm in the afternoon sun and birds were trying to drive a squirrel away from the feeder in a frenzy of wings.

'We'll start with the simplest words,' the summoner said. 'You repeat them after me and I'll correct your pronunciation. We'll do that over and over until your brain seizes up.'

She couldn't hide the smile. 'Is there any chance this will work?'

He shrugged. 'Only way to find out.'

It was only at the very end, after three hours of work that she figured out what her father said.

'What does *alea iacta est* mean?'

'The die has been cast,' Mort replied. 'It means that events have reached a point of no return.'

Her father knew what she was going to do and that

her chances of surviving were nil.

After her brain could hold no more Latin, Riley said her final goodbye to Paul Blackthorne. As she stumbled through her farewell, he stared at an invisible horizon, a slight frown in place like the world wasn't playing fair. When the time came, she kissed him, straightened his hair and then left him behind. Instead of crying, she kept whispering Latin words.

I'll do what I have to do to save the world. Then she would try to save her dad. Because what was the point of a sacrifice if it wasn't meant for the ones you loved?

Though it was nearly midnight, Riley couldn't sleep. She took her Latin and stress-induced headache to the back stairs of Stewart's old house. The grass was beginning to green and the porch light cast shadows on the daffodil leaves poking up through the soil. In a few weeks those flowers would be blooming. *Maybe.*

Stifling a yawn, Riley's brain began to catalogue trouble. What if there were more demons than they thought? What if she screwed up the spell? What if she wasn't alive when The End came? Would someone else prevent Armageddon or was she the only one this time round?

To her relief, the door behind her creaked open, then Beck joined her on the stairs. In his one hand was a napkin topped by a huge cookie while his other held a bottle of water.

He passed the cookie over, then set the bottle near her leg. 'Figured you needed fuel about now.'

'Thanks,' she said. He had a broad smile on his face,

something she wouldn't have expected to see given the way things were going.

'What's up?'

'Jackson and me, we caught the guy buyin' the demons,' he said, the smile growing wider. 'The dude rolled over on the one who was running the operation, some suit in Mayor Montgomery's office.'

'That's great news.' The *mayor* part caught up with her. 'It was that high up?' she asked, astounded.

'It was Montgomery's assistant and it was a Mezmer,' he said, shaking his head. 'It went down perfect: we cracked open a Babel sphere and the thing turned into a Four just like that,' Beck said, snapping his fingers for emphasis. 'Damn, it was righteous.'

'Wow. Wish I'd been there.' *That would have been so cool.*

'It was the two masters, Salvatore and me. It was great,' he replied, still jazzed. 'Shoulda seen the mayor's face. I thought he was goin' to hurl.'

'But don't they ward the city offices?'

'The demon was in charge of buyin' the Holy Water, so it made sure it wasn't the real deal.'

'In charge of the Holy Water . . .' Her mind whirled. 'Could it have been behind—'

'It's all tied together. The fake Holy Water paid for buyin' the demons. The mayor had no clue what was goin' on but he couldn't deny it – the laptop I lifted out of that warehouse came from his assistant's office.'

No wonder he was sporting a ten megawatt smile. Riley

raised her hand and they did a high five. 'You guys rock.'

'The mayor's *very* helpful now. Seems he doesn't want the voters to know there was a Hellspawn in city government.'

'Makes you wonder how many of them there really are.' *This has to be Sartael's plan.* But how could she prove it? 'Any chance the Four will tell us who's behind all this?'

'No. Won't say a word.' Beck pointed at the cookie that lay ignored in her lap. 'It's chocolate chip. Pretty good too.' He lowered his voice. 'Not as good as yer momma's oatmeal cookies she sent me in the army. Those were the best.'

He'd summoned a positive memory. Her and her mom spending a full afternoon baking dozens of cookies, packing them up and shipping them overseas.

'The guys loved them,' Beck continued. 'Yer momma kept havin' to send more and more each time because I'd pass 'em around.'

'I used to help her make them.'

'I know. That made them more special,' he replied.

Riley felt warmth blossom in her cheeks. To keep from blurting something she'd regret, she turned her attention to the cookie. *Oh man, I have it bad.*

'I sent Rennie to the neighbour's house,' he said. 'If I'm not around when this is over, I told Mrs Merton that she should go to you.'

The guy was bequeathing her the one thing he adored more than anything else in the world. 'Ohhhhkay. I'll watch over her. I promise.'

'Good. Oh, and I put yer daddy's cheque in my bank and

rewrote my will,' he added. 'Ya get it all if somethin' happens to me. Stewart can help ya open a bank account of your own.'

That she didn't want to think about. Still . . . 'What if neither of us are around?'

'It goes to the trappers' fund to help out their families. I figured ya wouldn't mind that.'

It's exactly what she would have done.

Beck fussed with a shoelace, though it was double-knotted like always. Something else was on his mind. 'Maybe, when this is all over, will ya . . . you make me some of yer momma's cookies?' he asked.

There was much more to it than that. He was hoping that when all the fighting was done she'd be there to bake him cookies, and he'd be alive to eat them.

'Sure,' she said, smiling over at him. 'How many you want?'

'A couple dozen will do it. I'm sure the other trappers will want some.'

No way could she tell him about Heaven's job assignment now. He needed that glimmer of hope. They all did.

'Riley, I . . .' Beck looked deeply into her eyes. 'If this doesn't go right . . .'

You're not going to have to worry anyone will find out about your rabbit or the fact you can't read or write. You won't have to worry about anything for eternity.

'No matter what, you be careful,' he said.

'Of course I will,' she replied, wondering what else he

might have said if he'd had the courage. 'I've got a baking assignment.'

Beck smiled at that. He brushed a cookie crumb off her face. For a second, she thought he might try to kiss her, but he didn't.

'It goes both ways,' she urged. 'You *have* to stop playing the hero.' *I don't want to watch you die.*

'No worries about that.'

We're lying and we both know it.

Beck rose and dusted off his jeans, though they didn't need it. 'I should go. Stewart's waitin' for me. Says he wants to teach me how to use a sword *properly*.'

Riley hooted. 'Can I watch? This should be totally hilarious.'

'Ya've got no respect, woman,' Beck retorted. After the door closed behind him she realized what he'd said.

'Woman?' He wasn't calling her *girl* any longer.

If that wasn't a sign the world was ending, what other proof did she need?

Chapter Thirty

At six in the morning they gathered their forces at the west entrance to Oakland Cemetery. They'd chosen the graveyard because holy ground was the ultimate weapon against Hellspawn. For Riley, this hour seemed symbolic – the light pushing back against the dark as the sun rose for a new day.

The weather was like most days in February, with frost lacing the brickwork above the cemetery's arched entrance. Their mingled breaths clouding the air, twenty hunters stood in two rigid lines outside the entrance gate. They were dressed in combat gear, their red ears and noses the only hint that the cold was having any effect. Each had a sword lying on the ground in front of them. They were currently on their knees, heads bowed, as Father Rosetti intoned a prayer.

'That's not changed much over the centuries,' Stewart said quietly as he joined her, angling his head towards the hunters and their priest. 'We always seek divine assistance right before a battle.'

'Did you?' she asked, looking up at the man who felt more like a grandfather to her than a master.

'Aye, I said a few words ta the Almighty. Whether He listened, I have no notion.'

'I did too,' she admitted. 'I keep wondering if there was something I could have done to prevent this.'

Stewart heaved a sigh, his face lined with worry. 'I doubt it, lass. Once yer caught in a whirlpool, there is no way out.'

Off to the side, the trappers stood in their own group well away from their rivals, a motley bunch compared to the Vatican's spit-shined team. Some wore leather coats, other denim. There was an assortment of weapons, including swords, steel pipes and baseball bats. They talked among themselves and every now and then she heard her name mentioned. Simon was with them. Riley should have expected he'd be here, but it troubled her nonetheless. She really didn't want to see him hurt again. He looked over at her from time to time, no warmth in his eyes.

Probably blaming me for this whole thing.

Beck was chatting with Jackson and McGuire. She wanted to talk to him, possibly for the last time ever, but the crowd around him didn't allow for that. Instead, she smiled in his direction. Hopefully he could read something in that smile that told him how she really felt about him.

Turning away, Riley reluctantly joined the magic users. Mort was clad in his cloak and fedora, though the hat seemed oddly out of place. He stomped his feet to stay warm. Ayden wore sleek leather gloves and a thick emerald cloak, the hood up. Peeking out from under the garment was a scabbard.

They both had large tapestry bags at their feet. Who knew it took so much stuff to do a little hocus pocus? Riley only had her backpack filled with objects that meant something to her – the locket containing the photo of her parents, an envelope with a tiny braid of her mom's hair, a picture of her and Peter. The demon claw hung round her neck.

The plan, as she understood it, was for her and the magical folks to lure the demons to the cemetery while the hunters and the trappers lay in wait on hallowed ground. Once the Hellspawn clustered around the edge of the graveyard, the men would attack them and hopefully kill them all.

Too many things can go wrong.

When Ayden and Mort headed into the cemetery, Riley didn't budge. She couldn't make herself take another step. Surely they could do this without her.

Ayden turned. 'Riley? You OK?'

She shook her head, shivering. 'No.'

'Scared?' the witch asked gently.

'Yeah. Out-of-my-mind scared. I don't know if I can do this.'

'If you think I want to be here, you're a lunatic,' Mort said.

'Same with me, but it's the job,' Ayden replied. 'You can step up and face your fears or let them rule you. It's your choice. No one else can tell you what to do next.'

Riley looked back over her shoulder at the hunters. They were gearing up for what was to come. The trappers were doing the same. She found herself watching Beck again as he joked around with Jackson, trying to master his own fears.

You're as frightened as I am. All of them are.

Beck turned towards her, gave a faint smile and excused

himself from the other trapper. He joined her just inside the cemetery gate.

'Riley . . .' he began, then halted, like he wasn't sure what to say.

This was what she'd really wanted, a chance to say goodbye, but now it was way awkward. Too many eyes were on them and that made Riley nervous. Beck noticed and drew her away from the entrance and down a side path, out of sight of most of the others.

The witch took the hint. 'You can catch up with us,' Ayden said, and walked away, Mort at her side.

Riley gazed up into Beck's deep brown eyes. *What do I say to this guy? What if this is the last time we ever see each other alive?*

Beck took a deep breath. 'Stewart told me what yer up against, what Heaven expects ya to do.'

That jarred her. 'Why did he tell you that?'

'So I wouldn't be an idiot.'

She had no idea what he was talking about.

'Beck, I . . .'

He gently caressed her hair, studying her face with near reverence.

'I've been a damned fool, Riley. I pushed you when I should have backed off. I wasn't there for you when I shoulda been.'

'No, you were always there for me.'

'Not like I'd wanted. I wish . . . we'd had a chance.' He looked away for a moment, then back at her. He placed his forehead against hers. His breath was ragged and uneven. 'Do what ya have to do to pay off yer debt with Heaven,' he said, his concern for proper speech abandoned. 'But ya do not die on me, ya understand? I can't live without ya. Yer all I got, woman.'

Her breath caught in her lungs. 'I don't want to be here if you're not.'

Beck's hands slipped round her waist, pulling her closer. She could feel each of his breaths, so close they were almost one. Their lips touched, hesitantly, and to her relief the skies didn't rain demons or the earth boil under the feet. Emboldened, he deepened the kiss, pulling her body tight against his. Her hands slipped through his hair as the passion built between them. She felt the heat roar through her body, singeing her, marking her as his. It was the kiss of a man who had waited years for the moment, and feared that it would never come again.

When it ended, Beck pulled her into a bone-crushing embrace. It was hard to breathe, but she didn't want it to end. Riley rested her head on his shoulder and felt their world change.

Someone called out his name and he swore under his breath.

'I have to go,' he whispered, then stepped away, suddenly all business. There was dampness in his eyes, evidence he'd felt the power between them. Riley straightened his collar and though it proved nearly impossible she pasted on a fake smile.

'Go kick some demon butt, Backwoods Boy,' she said, trying to sound brave.

'You do the same, Princess.' He caressed her cheek. 'I'll see you soon, wherever that might be.'

By walking away first, Beck proved he was stronger than she was. When he joined Stewart outside the gate, the master asked him a question and Beck nodded. He looked back her for a second, wistful, then turned away.

Why did we wait until now? Why were we so blind?

She took the time to catalogue Beck in detail. His unruly blond hair, his deep brown eyes, his broad shoulders. She memorized how he held himself, that boyish smile, how he felt in her arms. She wished it had been him who'd been her first lover rather than the angel.

Reluctantly, Riley turned and hiked into the cemetery, each step away from Beck agony. She finally caught up with the witch and necromancer near the Watch House.

'That was a kiss for the record books,' Ayden said, arching an eyebrow.

Riley couldn't muster a blush. 'Saw that, huh?' A nod returned. 'Totally earthshaking.'

'Then remember every second of it and what it means. It'll give you a reason to stay alive.'

That she could do.

They continued on in silence, each caught in their own thoughts. Past the stark white Bell Tower, Riley could see the roof of her family's mausoleum and those creepy gargoyles. Her eyes strayed to Ori's statue. Melancholy still clung to his body like the frost.

When Mort asked her what location felt right to cast the spell, Riley chose the exact spot where she'd sat vigil for her father. Knowing she had little to contribute until the other two were done unloading magical paraphernalia and grouching at each other, Riley stayed out of their way. Snippets of conversation reached her ears: where to place the candles, cones of power, why witch magic was less powerful than necro magic and why the witch thought that was total BS.

In an effort to shut them out, Riley walked to the base of Ori's statue. Would he come to life at dawn like always? Would she still be alive to talk to him one last time?

Riley gazed up at the tortured eyes. 'I don't think you were lying to me. That makes it even harder, angel.'

When she returned to her companions, they had constructed a complicated pattern of coloured marks on the ground. Those looked to be Mort's doing as they were similar to those she'd seen in his house. The candles and the crystal spheres were Ayden's contribution.

'Do summoner and witch magic mix?' Riley asked, realizing that's exactly what they'd be doing in a few minutes.

Ayden gave her a raised eyebrow. 'A lot like a stick of dynamite and a match.'

'So if the demons don't kill us we might blow ourselves into itty bitty pieces?'

'Being blown into bits would be a good outcome,' Mort replied.

'What if Ozy shows up?'

'Then we're in deep trouble. I'm not strong enough to out-magic him.'

'Neither am I,' the witch admitted. 'But together? We'll have to find out, won't we, summoner?'

'You wouldn't sound that bold if you knew what he's capable of,' Mort argued.

'You forget, I know exactly what he's capable of,' Ayden retorted. 'I saw what he did to your wards.'

'Ah, guys, let's keep it cool here,' Riley said. 'It won't matter who's right if there is no tomorrow, you know?'

That seemed to shut down the magical kindergarten. It wasn't like they hated each other – it's just that there was no trust between them.

Riley's butt instantly complained about the cold ground the moment the two connected. For some reason she'd not packed anything for this do-or-die scenario. What would you pack for Armageddon? Sunscreen and shades? Flame-proof underwear? Maybe a travel guide to the Underworld?

There *was* a sleeping bag in the mausoleum. As she unlocked the twin bronze doors, she was immediately surrounded by all the memories of this place: the day they'd buried her mother, the many hours she'd been here watching over her father, the night she'd shared the wine with Ayden and got totally ripped, the time she'd spent here with Beck after the Tabernacle burned. How he'd held her close though he was injured. Then *that night* with Ori. The mausoleum was more to her than a resting place for departed relatives – it was an integral part of her personal history, both good and bad.

A red rose lay on the storage box in the rear of the structure, the one Ori had given her the night they'd made love. Though it had been over a week, the petals were only just beginning to wilt. *Angel magic.* Riley set it aside, then raised the heavy marble lid of the storage box. As she reached in, she found a white envelope lying on top of the sleeping bag. It was addressed to her in her father's handwriting.

It hadn't been there the last time she'd opened the box so apparently he'd put it here sometime after he'd been reanimated.

Dearest Riley,

Everything hangs in the balance now. No matter your choice, no matter what happens, you will always be in my heart, for you are my beloved child. Forgive me for what I have done and for what I will do. It was all meant for you.

With all my love,

Dad

A tear trickled down her cheek. 'There is nothing to forgive, Dad. You did what you thought was right. I'll try to do the same.'

Riley kissed the note, then carefully returned it to the envelope. On a whim, though it wouldn't be comfortable, she tucked it inside her shirt next to her heart. If her father couldn't be with her, his love would be.

Chapter Thirty-One

'Looks like we're ready,' Mort announced.

'What do I need to do?' Riley asked. Luckily the circle was big enough to accommodate her sleeping bag without trashing all their complex preparations.

'You can tell the hunters we're about to begin and then turn down the radio.'

With considerable nervousness, Riley clicked the communication device they'd given her. 'Ah, hello?'

Captain Salvatore immediately responded. 'Go ahead Team Demon.'

At least that was better than Team Hellbound.

She relayed the news and Captain Salvatore acknowledged it. 'Teams Gabriel and Angelus are in place. May God grant us victory,' he said.

'Go us,' she said, then lowered the volume on the radio.

'Turn off your phone too,' Mort advised. 'We don't need any distractions.'

Right before she did as he asked, she sent a last text message to Peter.

It's about to go down. Wish us luck. Prayers are good too. Love you!

Once the electronics were tamed, it was a matter of watching the others work their magic. All the woo-woo reminded Riley that she really was an outsider to their world of spells and charms.

'Magic is a lot like trying to work around high power lines,' Ayden cautioned, adjusting a candle and the corresponding crystal next to it. 'You've got to stay focused or you'll get fried. We'll help you through this as much as possible. Just keep your mind focused on the task at hand.'

It was the witch who built the cone of power, weaving the potent spell that would hopefully protect them from Ozymandias, should he decide to retaliate. As Ayden patiently constructed the spell, Riley felt spiky magic crab-walk across her skin. There were sparkles in the air around them now, like inside one of those holiday globes you find in the stores at Christmas. Ayden finished calling the corners and invoked the circle to life. Immediately there was a sharp spark and a pop. Riley grimaced as her ears slowly adapted to the air pressure change. This was a protective circle on steroids.

The magic swirled around and above them, peaking about ten feet in the air as iridescent patches glimmered in the pre-dawn light. Everything beyond the circle – the gravestones, the Bell Tower, even the trees looked gauzy and indistinct, like she was viewing them from inside a soap bubble.

Mort nodded his approval, his equivalent of a standing ovation.

Maybe this will work.

Riley's palms began to itch. *Oh boy.* The inscriptions were pulsating, clearly visible. Somehow the magic had triggered them. She resisted the urge to scratch them.

'Do I want to know what those mean?' Mort asked, staring down at her palms. She shook her head.

'Ignorance does have its good points,' Ayden replied. 'Especially in this case.'

Once the circle had been secured, the summoner sat next to Riley and methodically arranged his supplies. The main object was a leather spell book engraved with a complex symbol on the front cover, probably the necromantic equivalent of a skull and crossbones.

'This is my book of spells,' Mort explained, caressing the aged cover with genuine fondness. 'It's been passed down through my master's line for hundreds of years.'

Like Stewart's chess set. 'They gave you that when you first started?' That certainly wasn't the way the trappers handled things; they dribbled out information to keep apprentices from dying a quick death at the hands of a senior demon.

'I didn't receive this until my master passed away. Then I was ready.'

Riley was tempted to ask how that death had happened, then decided against it. She doubted the guy had died of boredom.

Mort opened the spell book to a page dense with Latin. It wasn't typeset, but in calligraphy. The letters literally *glowed.* It reminded her of one of those texts the monks used to create in their little stone cells.

Riley gulped as her heart rate rose. 'This is really hard to read,' she said, hoping that might give her a pass.

'I know. That's why we have this,' he said, handing her a typed sheet of paper. 'It's the same incantation with the pronunciations underneath each word.'

OK, that's better. Sort of.

Riley had *never* wanted to do magic, but here she was. If she succeeded, she bet the Vatican would reopen her investigation even if the spell saved every one of the hunters' lives.

The summoner flicked his fingers and a miniature ball of light hovered over the top of the printed page. At least she could see the words now. It also revealed there was a fine sheen of sweat on Mort's forehead, which showed he was worried. That didn't help Riley's confidence.

Damn! She'd been pushed into this corner by Lucifer, by Ori and by her own foolish choices. There was a crackle under her shirt, her father's letter. *It'll be OK.* That's what he always said. *Maybe this time you're right.*

'We'll need the demon claw,' Mort said. 'Place it in the centre of the book.' Riley did as he asked, the silver chain coiling round the black talon. It reminded her of Beck, of the day he'd given it to her and how concerned he'd been she might not like it. Even then he was telling her how much he cared for her.

He's out there somewhere. He and Simon and all the rest of them. They'll die if I don't get this right.

'We'll start by summoning this particular fiend,' Mort explained. 'If that works, we'll do the unbinding spell. Take your time. We are not in any hurry.'

Not yet. As soon as she started this first incantation, Ozymandias would know. He'd probably send his Hellspawn and the battle would begin.

'Do not let anything distract you. That is vital,' Mort cautioned.

Riley nodded, her heart racing so hard it was difficult to breathe. *What if I get a panic attack in the middle of the spell? What if –*

Ayden touched her arm, gaining her attention, then traced something in the air between them. She'd done that before at the market, and claimed she was waving away a mosquito.

'What *is* that?' Riley demanded.

'A grounding spell. It'll help.'

And it did, though Riley had no idea why. Her breathing gradually eased and her muscles loosened. She could even see through the protective circle.

'Sometimes the strongest among us are those who seem just the opposite,' Ayden said, her eyes on the summoner now. 'The courage is there. You just have to find it deep inside you.'

Mort began to chant. Whatever he was saying sounded way serious, but then anything in Latin did. When the incantation was complete, he handed her a piece of paper. 'Read this.'

Riley did as he instructed, taking it slow. There were only two lines to the spell and it went quickly. When she finished, he took the sheet and tossed it into the air where it ignited in blue flames. As it was consumed, it filtered to the ground in a fine blue ash.

'That wasn't so bad.' Better than she'd figured. *I got myself all worked up over this?*

'No, that's rather a simple spell. Now we wait and see if our demon friend shows up,' Mort replied. 'The claw will begin to move when the creature gets close. Then we'll do the unbinding spell. That one is infinitely more complex.'

Time passed. Riley tried not to fidget, but she failed. She wanted to reread her dad's letter, but not in front of the others. That was just between the two of them. Then the fine hairs on the back of her neck began to twitch, a primitive response to an unseen threat. A second later the demon claw began to rock back and forth on the page.

There was a snuffling sound from far behind them, followed by a long, wailing howl. The demon was on the other side of the north cemetery wall – it knew better than to cross on to sacred ground and risk being destroyed.

'I did it,' Riley said, grinning. 'Wow!'

'You did. Now we'll begin the unbinding incantation and –' Mort began, then lost his ability to speak.

A pair of reddish-yellow eyes glared at them from outside the circle. The demon was on holy ground.

Chapter Thirty-Two

'That's not right! It can't be here,' Riley exclaimed. 'It should be a French fry.'

Mort took a long and deep breath to steady himself. Then he pointed at the Three. 'See the faint red aura round it? That's part of Ozymandias's reanimation spell. That's what's allowing it to be on sanctified ground.'

'Oh God, no,' Riley whispered.

'You'd better tell the hunters. They won't be expecting this,' Ayden said. 'I certainly wasn't.'

With a trembling voice, Riley delivered the bad news. She'd counted up to five before the reply came through.

'Roger, Team Demon.' Salvatore's response was clipped now, stressed. All the captain's careful planning had just been trashed.

There was a clicking sound and then Salvatore began to issue orders, moving his men into new positions, along with the warning that Hell was not playing by the rules.

Riley had seen what happened to one of Lucifer's demons when it'd stepped on cemetery soil – instant death. This was definitely an Ozymandias special-Hellspawn upgrade.

They can go into churches now. They can anywhere they want.

As her mind catalogued the horrors the city would face, the Three remained outside the circle, treading up and down, looking for a weak spot in the barrier. When it touched the circle, the magic sparked, causing it to whimper and back off.

'Goddess, it's ugly,' Ayden said, wrinkling her face in disgust. That earned her a hiss from the fiend. 'Hey, I call them as I see them, demon.'

The creature kept staring at Riley and then at the claw, which had finally stopped moving.

Yeah, it's yours. Shouldn't have left it behind in my leg.

'It doesn't look like it's dead . . . yet,' she observed. Not that she could tell by smell. They all stank.

'It's not,' Mort said. 'The spell has been continually altered and each new incantation demanded greater changes to the demon's natural behaviour. It's a very impressive bit of magic even if it is totally evil.'

Riley frowned. 'But how did he know we were going to be in the cemetery?'

'It might not have anything to do with us,' Mort replied. 'Ozy might have intended it as another breach in the city's defences. With this alteration, there is no place to find sanctuary.'

'Goddess, that's evil,' Ayden said.

'Ozymandias is cold and ruthless,' Mort said, 'but even this is beyond what I thought him capable of. The magical signature feels like Lucifer's, but it's not. I don't get that.'

Because it's another Fallen. She'd been right – Sartael was behind all this. If Hellspawn violated sanctified ground it was a good bet that Heaven would retaliate.

'Well, we have a demon. Let's unbind it.' Another sheet of paper came Riley's way. There were a lot more words this time, a whole pageful, which told her this one wasn't going to be a snap.

'Take hold of the claw and recite the spell, slowly and with great care,' the summoner said. 'If you get a word wrong, we'll have to start over. If we're still alive.'

No pressure there.

Riley took the claw in her left hand, the one with Heaven's inscription. Big mistake. The flesh reacted like she'd dipped it in acid. She hastily switched hands and it was fine. Hell's claw on Hell's side of Riley. Spell on Heaven's side. She wondered what the Vatican would think of that.

She took the paper into her left hand and eyed the page: she knew these words, though not in this order, no doubt Mort's way of keeping her from involuntarily conjuring the spell before they were safely inside a circle.

After a deep, cleansing breath, she began to read the Latin. In reaction, the demon's pacing increased while it made short, barking sounds. Never having heard that from a Three before, it distracted her and Riley stumbled on a word.

Mort sighed, then said something in Latin. 'I've nullified the spell. Begin again.'

Meum pactum dictum . . .

As Riley started over, a pounding ache formed behind her eyes. The further into the spell she went the more magic warmed her, as if she was standing nude in a desert at midday and each of the sun's rays was an insanely sharp needle.

She screwed up the fifteenth word in. Mort nullified the spell . . . again.

'Give me a couple minutes,' Riley said, her head thumping so hard it made her eyeballs feel like they were about to explode.

'Not an option,' Ayden said, her eyes riveted on the stretch of ground behind them. 'There are more demons coming over the wall now.'

Riley carefully glanced over her shoulder – the movement did nothing good for her headache – and spied the dark figures clamouring over the brick wall. Once they hit the ground, they moved at amazing speed. All had those weird yellow-red eyes.

The radio crackled at her side and she jumped in response. The hunters had spied their enemies and the teams were moving forward.

The demons were at the circle almost before she could take another breath. Instead of howling and launching themselves against it, trying to break it, they shied away when the magic stung their noses.

One of them lifted its muzzle, staring right at Riley. It was a mature Three with the second row of spiky, discoloured teeth. It was still alive so drool cascaded from its mouth. It set up a howl and the others picked it up, like a chorus of rabid wolves.

Riley jammed her hands against her ears, trying to block the sound, shaking from terror that knew no bounds. They'd kill her, Mort and Ayden, and then tear Beck apart and . . .

Someone shook her arm, but she ignored it. Then again it came, harder this time.

'Riley!' It was the necromancer. When she uncovered her ears, the howling had ceased.

'I know you're frightened, but we have to get this done,' Mort urged. 'Go slow and ignore them.'

That was impossible. *They* kept staring at her, slobbering and grunting, waving their claws. Guttural voices echoed in her mind, whispering that she was too weak to break their bondage, that they would rip her apart the moment she failed. That it would be better if she gave in and then they'd be merciful.

Like I believe that.

Riley closed her eyes and thought of fluffy bunnies. Rennie, in particular. How Beck truly loved that little rabbit. They'd sit and eat oatmeal cookies while Rennie hopped around them. Maybe then they'd kiss. But the only way that was going to happen was if she completed the spell.

Opening her eyes, Riley concentrated on the words, ignoring everything else around her. There was the sound of claws being honed on headstones, the howls, the constant whispering in her mind. She ignored it all. There was only the Latin, the spell and the talon.

The sentences grew more difficult to pronounce as her mouth grew dry. She didn't dare pause. *Only a few more*. Then a few more after that.

Riley finally ran out of words, the sheet quaking so

badly she could barely keep hold of it.

'Toss the paper in the air,' Mort ordered. Up it went and then it burst into pretty blue flames almost like fireworks. Outside the circle the demons watched it burn, then they backed away, grunting.

Did I do it?

Before she could ask, something struck the exterior of the circle like a sledge hammer pummelling an egg. The ground vibrated and nearby headstones shattered, slinging aged spears of stone in all directions. The witch cried out and threw her hands up, pushing back, golden magic arcing against the interior of the sphere.

'Help her!' Riley cried.

Mort was already on his feet, adding his own power. The gold and the blue turned to a incandescent green as the magics converged and built up against each other.

It was over as quickly as it had come. When Riley could see through the sphere again, the demons were gone.

'We did it?' she said. 'Oh my God, we did it!'

In the distance there were shouts, then screams of agony. The demons weren't dead. They'd just gone after weaker prey.

Chapter Thirty-Three

As the teams moved forward, Beck kept at Stewart's side. He'd like to think it was because he was trying to protect the old guy, but in truth it was more the other way round. Stewart looked impressive in his kilt and he even had a knife tucked into one of his socks. His bum knee was in a brace, which made his movements awkward, but that way he didn't need a cane. Instead, he had a two-handed sword. A big one. The way he handled it told Beck he'd probably been using the thing since he was a kid.

Harper stood next to them, a steel pipe in one hand and a short blade in the other. He wasn't moving that fast, not with all the injuries he'd taken over the last few weeks, but he was there and that's what counted. So were Remmers and McGuire, Jackson and a number of the other trappers. All the hunters were present, even their priest.

'How many are there?' Salvatore asked into the radio as he peered up at the sentry positioned in the Bell Tower.

'At least five dozen or more, sir. They're still coming.'

'Sixty plus Hellspawn. I copy.'

'Sixty? No way in hell we can take that many of them,' Harper said.

'No choice,' the captain replied. 'We issued the invitation; we have to dance.'

When fireworks erupted into the air near the mausoleum, Beck's heart clenched in worry.

'Looks like we've got a magical duel on our hands, gents,' Stewart said.

'So what do we do?' Beck asked. He didn't like this standing around. He'd never liked that before a battle.

'We keep the beasties busy until they can break the spell.'

'If they don't?' Beck asked.

'Then we're out of luck.'

'Here they come!' the captain shouted. 'Work in pairs. Get them down and get them dead.'

As the first wave of demons roared towards them, Beck was stunned by the sight of so many furry bodies intent on carnage. It reminded him of this old movie he'd seen about a bunch of warriors surrounded by all kinds of evil creatures. The fighters had known they were going to die and yet they held their ground. In the end, they'd won because some guy had thrown a magical ring into a volcano. But there was no dude with ring, only a bunch of humans against a legion of Hellspawn.

Today is not a good day to die.

The first Three reared up in front of Stewart. The master shouted something and with a blurring sweep of the mighty blade, the demon's head flew in one direction and the bleeding trunk in the other.

'Sweeeet!' Beck said. He gave a Southern yell of defiance

and went for the next demon in line. It took him two hacks, but the thing was finally dead.

'Sloppy, but ya got potential,' the Scotsman said. Then he sobered, staring out into the darkness. 'Ah, dear God, look at all of them.'

Amber-red eyes poured out of the night, moving at incredible speed. Behind there were taller Grade Four fiends. The wave quickly overran the men, slashing at any who got in their way. Screams erupted and there was spotty gunfire, though that wasn't going to stop the onslaught.

Beck and Stewart put their backs to each other, killing as swiftly as their arms and their swords would allow.

'There's no end to them!' Jackson called out, his face bleeding from a claw slash.

'Keep fighting!' Harper shouted, caving in the skull of a Three before it had a chance to gut him.

As Beck struggled to gain his breath, the ground beneath him began to shake.

'Five!' someone shouted.

'Oh my god,' another called out. 'There's more of them!'

Demons swarmed the landscape like locusts, crawling across the headstones and climbing into trees to drop down on those below. Remmers went down, clutching his thigh. Beck struck the nearest demon hard across the neck and it fell. Three steps later, he encountered another one. That one went down too. By the time he'd made Remmers' position, the wounded man was surrounded by his fellow trappers. Just beyond them were the hunters. They were like

Stewart – they knew blades. The captain was fighting two demons at once and holding his own.

Stewart began to sing something under his breath as his sword met flesh and mastered it. A death song? Whatever it was, it stirred Beck's blood. His soldier's instincts made him duck as a black sword swept over the top of his head and embedded itself blade deep in the tree behind him. Beck found himself staring up at a Four, desperately trying to extricate its sword out of the bark.

'Well, aren't you a beauty?' he said. The thing began to whisper to him, but he shut it up by introducing the fiend to his steel. It didn't go down easy, but eventually it joined its comrades on the blood-soaked ground.

Come on, God, we need some help here.

'But I did the spell correctly!' Riley protested. 'Why didn't it work?'

'Ozymandias reversed it. If the witch hadn't set such a solid protective shield, we'd be dead,' Mort replied, his expression troubled.

'A compliment, necromancer?' Ayden replied, her face sweaty from all the exertion. 'Next you'll be asking me out on a date.'

'What do we do?' Riley said, so rattled she couldn't get a handle on what was happening.

'We'll have to do it the old-fashioned way,' Ayden explained. She let the cape drop to reveal a leather jerkin layered over a white shirt. Black jeans tucked into knee-high boots. She positioned the flat edge of her sword on her shoulder, looking more like a warrior than a witch. 'You know how to fight, summoner?'

'Not with a blade.' Mort delicately removed his hat, rose to his feet and seconds later his hands went blue from the wrists to the tips of his fingers as magic surged around them like writhing electric eels.

'Show off.' Ayden carefully touched a finger to the edge of her blade, blooding it. It ignited and brilliant gold ran down the length of the steel.

'Look who's talking,' the necro chided.

'Riley, there's a knife in my bag,' Ayden said. 'You'll be OK inside the circle unless I'm . . . disabled. I think you should arm yourself in case that happens.'

That's a good idea. Riley found the blade tucked inside a sheath marked with runes. It dawned on her what they were about to do. 'You can't go out there! They'll kill you.'

'Maybe, maybe not,' Mort said. 'We need to find Ozymandias. He's here somewhere. I can feel him.'

Riley certainly hadn't, not with all the magic flying around.

'There,' Ayden said, pointing. 'See the shimmering near the statue of Niobe? That's a protective circle. Bet he's inside.'

Mort murmured something in Latin, then shot a bolt of blue out from the ends of his fingers. The distant shimmer turned transparent revealing their enemy. Though his eyes were closed as he worked his spell, Ozymandias's sigil glowed brilliantly in the early morning light.

'How'd he get here without us seeing him?' Riley asked, rising to her feet.

'He's got a lot of power and loves to use it.' Mort loosened up his shoulders. 'Well, witch, are you up for a visit to the dark lord's lair?'

'Why not?' Ayden said. 'I'm getting damned tired of being stuck inside this bubble. Let's go hack stuff up.'

Mort turned and looked out at the mass of demons. 'By heaven, there are so many of them,' he murmured.

Riley followed his gaze. Threes were everywhere. Pyro-Fiends were leaping around the headstones, setting fire to leaves as they passed, creating an effective smoke screen. There were taller figures as well – Grade Four demons – but these didn't look like the 'whisper in your ear, soul stealing type'. These had blades and armour.

'Demons don't use swords,' Riley complained. 'Doesn't anyone follow the rules any more?'

'It's total war,' Ayden replied. 'Remember the big one you're supposed to stop?'

Don't remind me.

'Shall we?' the witch asked, gesturing towards the magical boundary that separated being safe from being dead.

'Ladies first,' Mort replied.

Ayden laughed and crossed the circle, followed by her magical counterpart. The protective barrier quickly reformed behind them. Once they were outside, Threes immediately targeted them. One leaped at the summoner and a second later it squealed and turned into a bright blue flame and then a black ash cloud. Ayden dispatched one with her sword, which seemed to burn demon flesh like acid.

There would be no way for them to bust open Ozymandias's protective circle. He was too powerful.

They're throwing their lives away.

Through the smoke and haze she saw something tall rise above the other Hellspawn. The Geo-Fiend was nearly seven feet tall and its head resembled a bull's. When it opened its mouth, ruby red flames roared inside its maw. Another joined it, causing the lesser demons to scatter like frightened puppies. These had to be traitors from Hell, come to aid Sartael in his quest for Lucifer's throne.

Her heart nearly stopped when the Geo-Fiends stepped aside, bowing. There were only two beings that would frighten a Five: an Archfiend or a Fallen.

This wasn't an angel, more the love child of a demented goblin and an ancient vampire. Unrelenting evil, her father had said as he described such a creature. He hadn't exaggerated.

Riley never could stand the burning red eyes of the lesser demons, but these gleamed like they reflected the centre of Hell itself. Shorter than the Geo-Fiends, the Archfiend stood about six and a half feet, its body a blend of rigid muscles, sinews and claws. There were no feathers on its wings and you could clearly see the veins. Its four fangs were like a vampire's, long and white. The domed skull housed three pairs of eyes set deep into the bone. Nearly nude except for a loincloth, it toted a sword that blazed ebony fire.

Riley clicked on the radio. 'There's an Archfiend!' she called out. No response. Panicking, she cried, 'Did you hear me?'

'Where?' Salvatore came back, along with the sound of clashing steel.

'Near the Bell Tower.' *Not just one*. 'There's *three* of them!'

The lead Archfiend gestured upward and one of its companions took to the air with a clap of wings. It veered towards the top of the Bell Tower. The sentry didn't see it coming and though Riley screamed to warn him, he couldn't hear her over the sounds of battle. The fiend clutched at the soldier with its talons, dragging him away from his perch. As his body plummeted to the ground, the demon gave a shriek of triumph.

'Why isn't Heaven helping us?' she cried out. Even if it meant Armageddon, they couldn't let all these people die.

'Team Demon. What can you see?' Salvatore called out.

'You lost the guy in the Bell Tower. And something's in the air. Something . . . Ohmigod . . .'

The figure descending from the clouds had grey wings and was clothed in a black robe with a simple rope belt tied at its middle, like a monk might wear.

'There's a Fallen here now,' she said.

'Is it the Prince?' the hunter demanded.

'No.' As the newcomer's feet touched the ground, the demons raised their voices in adulation. In the midst of the cacophony was a name: Sartael.

This was Lucifer's enemy.

And mine. 'How do you kill a Fallen?' she asked, her fingers cramped round the knife's hilt, feeling an anger that transcended everything else.

'You can't,' was the curt reply, and then the radio went silent.

Sartael raised his flaming sword into the air and cried out in a hellish tongue. Riley didn't need to know the language – it was a call to war.

Chapter Thirty-Four

The Fallen took the field and his first target was Corsini. The hunter's body flew through the smoke-stained air until it hit a tombstone and crumpled. Sartael stalked forward and stood over the wounded man, laughing at his feeble attempts to crawl away.

With a cry of rage, Captain Salvatore charged forward, mowing down a Three with his blade. Other hunters joined him, as did some of the trappers. Stewart's sword sang through the air as they tried to carve a path to the fallen man.

Sartael raised his sword and plunged it into Corsini's chest, pinning the dying man to the soil. The body erupted into flames and burned like a funeral pyre.

'Oh God, oh God no!' Riley cried, doubling over, her stomach churning.

'War! War! War!' the demons shrieked.

By impaling the hunter on holy ground Sartael had issued a challenge, one that Heaven could not ignore. The Hellspawn knew it too. The earth beneath her rocked as their cries rose.

An Archfiend jumped one of the trappers and the man was dead before he reached the ground. Beck swung wildly at a Three, trying to cut off one of its arms. The instant before he made the sweeping cut, the ground quaked and he fell.

Riley screamed in horror. The Three dove in for the kill, but was beheaded by Müller's stroke. Next to him was Father Rosetti, his cassock swinging with each thrust of his blade.

Release me or they will all die.

Riley jumped in shock. It was Ori's voice deep within her mind, though the statue was completely encased in marble. The sun was above the horizon now, bringing him to life in the midst of death.

'Talk to me angel.' *Make me believe today isn't the day we all die.*

Pledge your soul to me and I will stop Sartael.

Was this the decision her father spoke of? If Ori was able to destroy the rogue Fallen, would that prevent the war?

If Riley didn't do something, everyone she cared for would be slain and the world would face endless slaughter until Heaven put an end to Sartael's unholy reign. How many would die before that happened?

Countless millions. Ori's voice was stronger in her mind now.

Riley closed her eyes, the stench of blood and the acrid smoke scorching each breath. Across the field, another man cried out as he died.

Sometimes she wished the big questions in life were multiple choice.

Riley gazed up at the statue of her first and only lover, at the angel who had said he'd never lied to her. The same angel that Martha had said was the most honest of the Fallen.

'What keeps you from siding with Sartael and taking over Hell?'

Nothing.

Was this exactly what Sartael wanted?

'Where the hell are you, Lucifer?' she cried. No reply. No way she could use her one wish now. It was up to her.

Riley nearly choked on the irony. Her father had given up his soul to save her. Now she was giving up hers to save others. She glared up at the angel and set out her terms.

Here's the deal: my soul will be yours, but only yours. You will not give it away to anyone, not even Lucifer himself. Riley sucked in a hasty breath, her mind reeling with the enormity of what she was about to do. *You will not sell it or trade it. If you die, it returns to me.* Another breath, this one thick with the stench of smoke.

And what we did in the mausoleum? It will never happen again. That's the deal – if you want my soul, you swear on it. You swear a vow on the Light you were created from. You swear on the Hellish master that you serve. You swear on everything you hold dear.

Silence.

Take it or leave it, angel. I'm not going down easy. Her hands shook so violently she nearly dropped the knife.

Still no reply. Apparently Ori had just expected her to say 'yes'.

'Ah, screw this,' Riley said, taking a step towards the circle's boundary, fully intending to join the others. If the angel wasn't going to help her, she'd do what she could with the knife until something killed her.

I agree to your terms, Riley Anora Blackthorne. I shall hold your soul until the day I am no more, and vow I shall not give it to another. Now free me.

She jolted to a stop. He'd actually agreed. *How do I . . . ?*

Your blood will release me from my prison.

Riley stepped through the circle with surprising ease, then ran across the road towards the statue. The tip of Ori's head glowed gold now as it reacted to the sunrise.

Hurry!

At first no one paid any attention to her. That ended when Sartael took note of where she was headed.

'Bring her to me!' he cried. Instantly a Three swerved towards her, but Riley evaded its claws and kept moving. Behind her, it cried out and fell to the ground, writhing.

For an instant she thought it had been one of the hunters helping her out, but when she glanced over her shoulder she freaked. It was an Archfiend, eager to claim her as its own prize. Riley sprinted now, tripping as she fled across the uneven bricks. If she died before reaching the statue, Ori would remain entombed and there would be no chance to stop Sartael.

A clawed wing grabbed at her, nicking her shoulder. She whirled, chest heaving as the demon closed in, clicking its teeth in anticipation. Like the others, a weird aura cloaked it from head to toe, allowing the monster to stand on hallowed ground. Up close it was truly hideous, its seething red eyes slitted like a goat's. It stank of death and mortal blood.

If only her spell had worked, this thing would be a mound of ashes.

'Does Lucifer know you're cheating on him?' she asked, hoping to distract it as she edged closer to Ori's statue.

The demon roared in fury. 'Name not that weakling!' it cried, its voice like sharp nails on a blackboard. 'Long have we sought our revenge. Sartael will give us the flesh we crave.' When it reached out a clawed hand, she threatened it with the blade. It was like waving a penknife at a T-rex.

'Delicious,' it said, licking its lips. 'I shall make you my servant. The last one endured two hundred years of torture before I broke it.'

Riley shuddered at what that might mean when her butt bumped into Ori's statue. As she moved the knife to jab her palm, the Archfiend leaped forward with astounding speed, snaring her in its wings. The knife tumbled to the ground.

Riley kicked and shouted and fought the abomination until she landed at Sartael's feet. As she rose, the Fallen's flaming blade rose with her, level with her face. Even from five feet away she could feel the stinging heat.

Now that she was up close, the angel did look familiar: It was the guy in the hallway at the hospital, the one who'd been visiting Simon. Probably the same one who'd been visiting him at home. She'd seen him around the city as well, near the market and in the crowd outside the Tabernacle the night it had been destroyed. Sartael had been at the heart of this since the beginning.

Desperate to look at anything but that flaming sword, she

hunted for Beck. Was he still alive? She sighed her relief when she spied him hemmed in by a ring of demons, along with the rest of the fighters. Stewart, Harper and Jackson were with him as they stood guard over the wounded. Simon was alive, as well. His stricken face stared at her. No, not at her. His eyes were only for Sartael. Now he knew who'd been whispering in his ear, telling him lies about his girlfriend.

Welcome to my hell, Simon Adler.

A demonic snarl drew her attention towards Ozymandias's circle. The witch and the summoner were in no better position, hemmed in by at least a dozen Hellspawn. Both appeared exhausted, and the magical glow on Mort's fingertips flickered weakly like an anaemic firefly.

'Do you hear that?' Sartael gazed upward, his brilliant blue eyes reflecting a timeless lunacy. 'The Archangel Michael comes with his cohort. But I ask, where is Lucifer?' He laughed and cried out, 'Why is the Great Prince not here?'

Because he's not suicidal?

It dawned on her that the angel wasn't hearing her thoughts. Was that something Ori did or was it Ayden's calming spell?

The blade drew closer now, making Riley's eyes water and her throat burn. She could hear Beck shouting something, but there was no way he could get to her. Her time was running out.

'Why did you have my dad killed?' she demanded.

'He stood in the way,' was the simple answer. 'As do you. That is why I wanted your soul in my hands.'

'Ori wouldn't have given it to you.'

'He would not have had a choice. No one denies me. I should have been chosen as the Prince, not Lucifer. Now I will rectify that error and rid Heaven of my enemies.'

This one was totally insane. *Must come from breathing too much brimstone.*

'I thought you Fallen were all powerful,' she chided, even as her will felt the strength of the Fallen's mind against it. 'Guess that's not the case if you had to use a summoner to get the job done.'

The angel didn't flinch at her jibe. 'The necromancer was hungry for power and I was happy to feed his delusions.'

'Without the spell, you'd be kissing Lucifer's boots,' she said, knowing that would goad him. Maybe he'd make a mistake and she could get free, run to Ori. Or he'd just kill her quicker.

Twin claws clamped into her shoulders, pinning her place. Behind her, the Archfiend laughed in derision. The sword was only a foot away from her throat now, heating her face and her chest. Beck was bellowing curses. She didn't have to look to know he was trying to reach her, that the others were preventing him from throwing his life away.

Sorry, guy. You don't get to play hero this time.

'Give me your soul and I will grant you your life,' Sartael offered.

Riley felt the letter hidden under her shirt. *Forgive me for what I'm about to do.*

'Your soul, pledge it to me, now!'

Then she raised her eyes to the angel's, facing the power behind crazed blue orbs.

'Go back to hell, you Fallen bastard.'

With a vicious snarl, Sartael pulled the sword backwards for the thrust that would kill her, burn her like it had Corsini.

With a resounding pop, a familiar figure appeared out of nowhere.

'Dad?' she exclaimed, blinking in astonishment. 'What are you doing here?'

This Paul Blackthorne wasn't the broken man she'd last seen in Mort's house. In fact, he looked like he did before he'd died, with those curious, intelligent eyes and determined expression.

'Pumpkin,' he said, placing a hand on her shoulder. Where he touched her the skin tingled. 'I'm sorry for all this. I shall miss you.'

Before she could reply, he dropped a kiss on her cheek and walked away.

'Dad?'

Sartael gestured and one of the Fours moved to seize her father. When it touched him, it flamed in a fireball, wailing and shrieking as it died.

What's up with that? Her father wasn't at all magical.

'Hold, Paul Blackthorne, or I will kill your child,' the Fallen warned.

'If you do, Heaven will win,' was the swift reply.

Her father was playing Russian roulette with her life. He must have something up his sleeve. At least she hoped he did.

Her dad kept walking, pausing only when he reached the edge of the necromancer's circle. After a polite nod at Ayden and Mort, he stuck his hand through the protective magic that shielded Ozymandias. She'd expected his arm to melt or something gruesome to happen, instead the summoner's hand grasped her father's and they traded places: Dad inside the circle, Ozy out.

'What are you doing?' Riley muttered.

'Summoner?' Sartael barked. 'Return to your circle and protect the spell. I have not called you forth.'

Ozymandias calmly dusted off his cloak, his strange eyes riveted on the archangel. 'One tiny mistake and I summoned you instead of a demon. Teaches me there's a price for arrogance,' he muttered, shaking his head.

'Return to your task!' the archangel bellowed, causing many of the lesser demons to cower in terror.

'Another has taken my place. He will manage the spell, for a little while at least.'

'He is not a sorcerer. He does not have your power,' Sartael argued.

'No, he doesn't,' Ozymandias admitted, 'which is the point. The spell is burning through him even as we speak. In a short period of time, Paul Blackthorne will be no more and, when he goes, so goes the enchantment and your accursed demons.' The necro's attention shifted to Riley. 'I'm sorry – there was no other way. It's what he wanted.'

Then Ozymandias vanished, leaving behind an infuriated archangel and her father slowly withering inside the circle.

Chapter Thirty-Five

'Dad!'

Riley took only a few steps before the Archfiend blocked her way. 'Move!' she shouted, but it refused to allow her to pass.

The snarl that came from Sartael was more bestial than divine. 'Kill them all! Pile their corpses to the heavens. Michael shall see what has become of his mighty demon hunters.'

'But, Lord, what of the summoner's spell?' one of Fives cried.

'Once they are dead, we have no need of it.'

'But, my Lord Sartael –'

It was the distraction she needed. Riley bolted, ducking round the Archfiend's wing and dashing along the road towards Ori's statue. Behind her there were shouts as the battle began anew.

If I free him, he'll kill Sartael. Maybe that way her dad won't be destroyed.

It was like an obstacle course in a role-playing game: ravenous demons, headstones looking to trip her, then more demons. Sartael kept shouting orders, and when none of the fiends came close to catching her the ground erupted beneath her feet. Leaping sideways, she avoided being roasted by a tower of blood-red flames that poured out of the earth. Hail began to rain down, slicking the asphalt under her feet as wind hurtled through the trees.

It felt like the end of the world. Probably because it was.

Hurry! Ori urged.

Riley skidded to a halt in front of his statue, panting. She retrieved the knife and pressed it against her left palm. With no time to spare, she made the slice and felt the warm blood begin to drip. She slammed her hand down on Ori's cold foot, her palm throbbing as her life's essence trickled on to the marble.

'Come on!' she shouted. 'Do it now!'

The Archfiend was in front of her again, sniffing the air, leering at her. 'Your blood is soooo sweet. Soon it will be mine.'

Riley steadied the knife in her right hand. 'Sorry, but I'm already spoken for.'

The chilly toes under her left hand flexed, followed by a cracking sound, like lake ice breaking up in early spring. Small pieces of marble rained down, making the Archfiend veer backwards in surprise.

With a shout, Ori unfurled his wings and shot into the sky to near treetop level.

'Freedom!' he crowed. 'How I've longed for this moment!' Below him, the battle was momentarily suspended as demons and mortals stared up in wonder.

Sartael's uneasy laugh echoed across the cemetery. 'Ori! Welcome! We have missed you.'

'Have you, *old friend*?'

'Join us. Take your revenge. Begin with Blackthorne's child if you wish. She was the cause of your imprisonment after all.'

As he sank closer to the ground, Ori's dark eyes sought her out. 'Tempting, but I think there's another that deserves my sword first.' His focus moved to a figure sprinting across the graveyard. *Beck.* The trapper vaulted one of the gravestones, closing in at a run.

'No!' she cried. *This wasn't our deal!*

Everyone dies, Ori murmured in her mind. *Some sooner than others.*

Beck skidded to a stop and squared off with the Archfiend, though he wasn't a match for the thing. But there he was with a sword and a totally ferocious glower on his face.

The demon laughed in delight. 'Denver Beck,' it cried. 'Your mother's soul calls to us. It will be ours soon. Come join her!'

'Oh, shut the hell up,' Beck said, aiming a blow at the demon's chest. He was slung back by a wing, his shoulder bleeding where the slicing edge caught it.

The Archdemon was in the air before Riley could draw a breath and it dived at Beck like an owl does a wounded squirrel. The trapper delivered a deep cut to one its wings, earning him a string of hellish obscenities. Steaming black blood drained from the wound, and when it touched the ground it burned in a bright fire.

'No wonder Lucifer doesn't want ya . . .' Beck taunted.

The demon roared its fury and slashed at its opponent, flattening the trapper to the ground with a clawed foot. It stood over him, sword poised for the kill as Beck struggled to free himself.

Without thinking, Riley threw herself at the monster, aiming the knife at the leg pinning the trapper. The flap of a wing deflected the thrust and instead of hitting its thigh, she nailed the fiend in a rock-hard butt cheek. Bellowing, it reared round and batted at her, dislodging the knife. To avoid having her throat slit by its claws, Riley threw herself to the ground and rolled out of reach. When she pulled herself up, spitting dirt, the fiend was motionless, its mouth open as a strange gurgling noise came from its throat. As it slowly turned, a fiery sword came into view, buried to the hilt inside its chest.

Ori deftly extracted the blade and the demon crumpled.

'That's twice I've saved your life, trapper,' he observed. 'I really don't know why I bother.'

Beck swore, scrambled to his feet, sword ready. A feral light filled his eyes. 'No way ya touch her again.'

The angel looked Riley over, his face an unreadable mask. 'So she told me.'

Then Ori abruptly spun on his heels and strode across the battlefield towards the other Fallen. 'What is all this chaos, Sartael?' he said, gesturing expansively.

'I have challenged Heaven. Today the war begins,' the other Fallen replied. He gazed upward. 'Can you not hear them scurrying around like rats in an attic? They're frantic. They did not see this coming.'

'Of course they did,' Ori replied, drawing closer. 'Surely Lucifer has not given you permission for such a campaign.'

'He is in hiding, fearing my wrath,' Sartael boasted. 'He was always a coward.'

Ori halted about fifteen feet from the other angel. Whenever his eyes swept over a demon, it retreated, even the Archfiends.

'I expected you to be smarter than that, Sartael. Our Prince was testing you, as he did me. I failed, but now I have paid my penance. As has Blackthorne's daughter.'

Sartael's expression went from insane to cunning. 'Then let us form a truce,' he said, his eyes straying to Riley.

You promised, Ori. You cannot give up my soul.

But what if he did? Is that what Ori had intended all along, his way of re-establishing his status in Hell?

You have so little trust, Riley.

Ori raised his sword in a fighting stance. 'I name you traitor, Sartael. You have renounced the Eternal One and turned against our master. My commission is to destroy those who would threaten the Eternal Balance. That would include you.'

'You would side with our enemies?'

'With pleasure, *old friend.*'

With twin cries of rage, the angels soared high into the air like exploding stars. Slashing at each other, wings snapping, they began a battle for supremacy that had festered for countless millennia.

Chapter Thirty-Six

With a barked order, Salvatore and the hunters pushed forward, leaving only a few behind to guard the wounded. Sensing an advantage, the trappers joined the fray, attacking demons without mercy.

A tremor shook the ground, tossing men and Hellspawn in all directions. A few feet away from Riley, a hole broke open and tree roots twisted out of the soil, seeking anything they could ensnare and drag deep into the earth.

A coarse cry came from above. Splashes of blue blood fell like a morning drizzle. Ori wasn't moving as fast now, only reacting a few seconds before each strike, his wounds slowing him. Sartael wasn't much better. A blow went wide, opening him to Ori's counterthrust. Ori rammed his blade deep into one of Sartael's wings, and the rogue angel spiralled to the ground, trailing blood and feathers.

The moment the archangel struck the ground, a bolt of lightning sheared out of the sky, following immediately by a deafening clap of thunder. As it faded away, an armour-clad figure marched across the battlefield, stepping over the dead as if they didn't exist.

Sartael crawled to his feet, one wing hanging awkwardly.

He scowled up at the Prince of Hell.

'Traitor,' Lucifer said simply.

'You *dare* to call me that?' Sartael retorted, spitting blue blood on to the grass at his former master's feet.

'I have that right,' the Prince replied. 'I have borne the weight of that word and know how it devours you over the ages. I, of all creation, know the price it demands. Now you will as well.' He gestured and something began to slither across the prisoner's body, loop after thick loop. The chains seemed impossibly heavy, forged of an alloy Riley had never seen before. No doubt it had to be strong to hold a Fallen in bondage.

Sartael sagged under the weight as the coils shifted like a python seeking to strangle its prey, tightening, re-forming, always on the move. The chains did not rest, which meant their prisoner would not either.

'Those are yours for eternity. Do not think I am as merciful as the One who created us.'

The Prince swept his gaze over the demons, the abominations that were no longer his servants. Then his eyes rested on the circle that held her father.

'Make an end to it, Paul Arthur Blackthorne,' he commanded.

In the split second after the order was given, the shell round Riley's father began to disintegrate. Cracks appeared and through the gaps the magic began to buckle. Her father seemed at peace, tears on his cheeks, though he shouldn't have been able to weep. As he smiled at Riley one last time, the light in his eyes died.

'Dad!' Riley called out, stumbling forward in a futile effort to reach him. It was too late. The bubble collapsed in on itself, folding and bending, and in its wake left only a bald patch of earth behind.

'No!' *No. No.* She fell to her knees. The paper underneath her shirt crinkled. Now his note made sense: he'd known he was going to destroy himself to save them all. He'd known it from the very beginning.

'Hellspawn,' Lucifer called out. 'This is a holy place. Die as you were meant to.'

A great cry rose around them as the fiends suddenly came in contact with the ground. Gouts of flame rose from each as the sacred soil cleansed itself of the unholy taint.

Sartael began to rave and fight his chains. Then he fell quiet, though his lips kept moving.

'Silence is indeed golden, especially when it comes to you,' Lucifer remarked.

The moment Ori's feet touched down, he went to his knees, bent over in agony. Riley shook away her grief and hurried to him, not caring if anyone saw her. When she knelt next to the injured angel and touched his arm, his head slowly rose. The wound in his left chest pulsed blue fluid. Pressing her injured hand against it made no difference.

'Heal yourself!' she urged. 'You did it the last time.'

'Can't . . . not a wound from . . . a Divine.'

Lucifer stomped over, scowling. 'You are a fool, Ori. You know how to heal yourself. Stop being a martyr.'

'No. Not that way,' Ori said. 'I refuse.'

If he dies, I'll be free. He'd not given up her soul. He'd kept his word. *He'd saved Beck's life.* Ori deserved to live. 'Hey, listen to your boss, will you?' Riley pleaded, though she had no idea what they were talking about. 'Do whatever you're supposed to do. You can't give up now.'

The corners of her angel's mouth curved up ever so slightly. 'Riley Anora Blackthorne. My *Valiant Light.*' He swallowed hard. 'I release your—'

Lucifer waved a hand and Ori's body vanished, leaving only a pool of luminescent blue blood on the dried leaves.

'What did you do with him?' Riley demanded. 'Is he—'

A sound burst forth, like the note from a single trumpet magnified a thousand times. Others joined it until it seemed to come from everywhere, even the ground beneath them. High above them, the air split open and radiant white figures dropped towards the earth like missiles. Their wings unfurled, slowing their descent. *Angels.* Their unearthly beauty marked them as being Heaven's team.

Oh crap. Maybe she hadn't stopped the war after all.

One angel in particular seemed to be brighter than the others, clothed not in white armour, but in silver and gold that shone like supernova. More unnerving, his hair was the color of Simon's white gold.

'It's the Archangel Michael,' one of the hunters murmured, falling to his knees and crossing himself. Others quickly followed his lead.

Michael was God's holy warrior, the one the Bible said would slay the dragon. The dragon that just happened to be standing nearby.

As the Heavenly army assembled behind their leader, both on the ground and in the air, more angels appeared on Hell's side. Those were clad in dark silver armour. As Stewart had warned, Riley stood between two immense armies.

Her palms no longer itched, but burned with a searing heat that spread up her arms, into her chest and to her very core. She caught Stewart's eyes. He nodded in return.

This is it.

'Morning Star,' Michael said brusquely. His voice wasn't pleasant, but harsh, hard on the ears, like it held more power than her mind could ever comprehend. 'Your realm is in chaos.' He shot a contemptuous glare at Sartael. 'You have traitors in your midst.'

'My realm is not your concern, Michael,' the Prince replied evenly.

'It is now. We grow weary of your pathetic efforts to purify the souls of these mortals. They do not care. They are arrogant and useless.'

'They are *His* creation. Do you challenge that wisdom?' Lucifer asked smoothly.

Michael's brilliant blue eyes turned flinty. 'Do you put words in my mouth, Fallen?'

'Do not presume to know how I handle my kingdom or the mortals.'

Michael's sword began to crackle now as the legions grew restless. There were murmurs in a tongue she could not understand. The unease rose on Hell's side, as well.

The cosmos was a heartbeat away from total war.

'Oh, no, you're so not doing this,' Riley said, stepping up to the pair. 'I didn't lose my dad to have you guys toast this planet like a marshmallow.'

The moment Michael's eyes touched her she shuddered. Now she knew why people in the Bible always averted their eyes.

'You are Blackthorne's daughter, the mortal designee.' He shook his head in disgust. 'This time it's a child. I have no idea why He bothers.'

Wings or not, this guy was pissing her off. Sure, she wasn't a high and mighty angel, but still . . .

'Look, I know you guys hate each other, but don't bring your war here. We've got enough troubles of our own.'

'So self-absorbed, yet Lucifer argues that your kind is worth saving,' the archangel chided.

'We are worth saving.'

'Have you done all the tasks He has asked of you?'

'No,' she said, her head spinning so viciously it was hard to keep upright. Standing between the angelic hosts felt like a small moon caught in the gravitational pull of two huge planets. Positive. Negative. Light. Dark. All surging through every cell in her body.

Riley steadied herself against a headstone and the dizziness eased. She tried to ignore the fact that the stone glowed at the point where her hand touched it.

'I'll admit we're arrogant and we don't learn really fast,' she said, forcing herself to concentrate on each word, 'but we're getting there. At least we're trying.'

'How many wars plague your planet, mortal? How many

die this day from starvation? You call that progress?' Michael challenged.

This was like being up in the front of a classroom and knowing your whole year's grade depended on your next answer. In this case, the future of mankind.

'It's not your call to tell us our time is up,' Riley said through gritted teeth.

'Ah, child, but it is.'

Riley swore her blood was thickening, boiling off inside her veins. Sweat rolled off her face, down her back and into the waistband of her jeans. She could not stay between the armies for much longer and remain alive.

'What happens if he wins?' she said, angling her head towards Lucifer. 'Then what?'

Michael's sharp bark of laughter was more derision than humour. 'That is not possible.'

'But what if he does? What if you have your infernal war and the only thing that happens is that all us mortals die? Then what? How are you going to explain that to your boss?'

No reply. Maybe she was getting somewhere.

Speak from yer heart. That had been Stewart's advice.

'You don't have a clue what it's like for us,' she insisted. 'You're supposed to be all perfect but you're no better than we are. Maybe that's what God wanted when He made us humans – a chance to do it right the second time.'

The blade blazed hotter. 'Careful, mortal, you blaspheme.'

'I'm not dissing God. I'm saying maybe you don't

have the big picture. I know I don't.'

'She has a point, Michael,' Lucifer replied. 'We threaten to destroy everything He's built. Is that what He wishes, or is this another one of those tests He is so fond of?'

'He would not allow it if it was not foretold.'

'Perhaps.' Lucifer frowned. 'It occurs to me that those in Heaven stand so close to the Light that you must turn away or it will blind you. For some in the darkness –' he looked over to where Ori's body had been – 'they crave that same Light because they remember how warm and loving it was, forgetting His power could scorch as well as heal.'

'And we're in right in the middle,' Riley said, understanding now. 'The angels in Heaven are too close, those in Hell are too far away. That's why we were created, because we balance the Light and Dark.'

There was a muffled rustle of wings on both sides. Then utter silence, the universe holding its breath.

'Please, we've been given a chance to get it right,' she pleaded. 'All we need is time to find our own way.'

The Archangel shifted uncomfortably. 'You think them worthy of His attention, Morning Star?'

Lucifer shrugged. 'It remains to be seen.'

'You will continue the Great Task as He has set forth?'

'Until I am no longer needed.'

'Even if it keeps you from the Light?'

A solemn nod. 'It is my penance.'

'Not all penance, I think,' Michael said archly. 'You enjoy your freedom overly much.'

'My freedom exacts a price beyond your imagining, Archangel.'

Michael's bottomless blue eyes alighted on Riley. 'A mere child,' he muttered, shaking his head. With a wave, Heaven's angels began to disappear in swirling eddies of light, two at a time.

Lucifer nodded his approval and a corresponding number of his Fallen rose in a black mist, then vanished.

Michael unfurled his huge wings as he scrutinized his rival. 'We shall still meet at the End of Days, Morning Star. That *shall* come to pass.'

'So it shall, Archangel. Until then.'

Without another word Michael shot into the sky, twirled once and vanished in a flash of silver and gold.

When she looked back, Lucifer was already gone, taking the remainder of his troops with him.

'What about my dad?' Riley shouted. *He can't stay in Hell, not with the demons.*

He has paid his debt.

But –

You still owe me a favour, Blackthorne's daughter. When that is fulfilled, we will talk. Until then stop whining.

'Whining?' she shouted aloud. After all she'd been through?

Then it hit her. There would be no war today. The earth would continue to turn on its axis while all its inhabitants went about their lives on this sunny morning in February.

Oh. My. God. I actually did it!

Riley draped herself over a headstone and wept in profound relief.

Chapter Thirty-Seven

'Don't touch her!' someone commanded. 'Let the angelic essence bleed into the ground first.'

Ayden. At least her witch friend had survived.

'Look at it flow out of her. It's like a river. I've never seen anything like that.'

Mort. He'd made it too.

It took time, but Riley finally opened her eyes. She was still slumped over the headstone, the granite digging painfully into her ribs. At all points of contact golden yellow light poured out of her body, sheeting down the weathered stone and into the ground just like a battery discharging.

'Ouch,' she said, sliding to the ground and landing hard on her butt. Every cell of her body throbbed, from her toenails to the ends of her hair.

'Now you can touch her,' the witch advised.

It was Beck who did the honours, gently stroking her arm so her eyes moved in his direction. Black demon blood coated his clothes and splattered his cheek. 'Yer alive,' he said, smiling.

'You too.' *Go figure.*

Beck scooped her up in his arms. She was going to protest,

but realized it was wasted breath. She was too weak to walk anyway. He carried her only a short distance and set her on the stairs to the Bell Tower. A scratchy wool blanket was tucked around her.

When she raised her eyes, she found the trapper kneeling in front of her. The wound on his face continued to weep, trailing blood down his neck and into his shirt. He leaned so close their foreheads touched, like he had before.

'Paul loved us both,' he whispered. 'I'll never forget that.'

Neither would Riley. Those last few seconds when her father's brown eyes had met hers she'd seen his endless love, his deep compassion, the boundless pride he felt for her. Those scant few moments were enough to last her a lifetime.

Beck leaned back, then stood. 'I need to see to the wounded. Will ya be OK?'

She nodded in reply. *Don't let anyone else die.*

Pulling the blanket over her head, Riley closed her eyes. The sounds of battle still rang in her ears and she felt the burning flames of Sartael's sword close to her face. She had been able to stop Armageddon, but what about her dad? Was he still in Hell? If so, it was a bitter victory.

'Riley? She peeled back the blanket and found Ayden sitting next to her now.

The witch placed Riley's backpack near her feet. 'Figured you'd want these.' She handed over the key to the mausoleum. 'You left it in the lock. I put the sleeping bag away, but I didn't see the claw. I'm sorry.'

Maybe it was gone, like the demon it came from.

'The knife's inside the backpack,' the witch said. 'You blooded it, so it's yours now. When you're ready, come by the shop. We'll sit in the sunlight and talk of what happened today.'

'I owe you so much.'

'The owing goes both ways.' They shared a lengthy hug, then the witch limped down the road. Along the way she encountered Father Rosetti. They paused, studying each other, then he nodded in her direction and she returned it. They parted company as equals.

Peter. He'd be pacing his room, fearing the worst. Riley dug inside her pack to find her cellphone. To her surprise the self-inflicted knife wound on her left hand had healed with only a faint scar to indicate there'd ever been a wound there, and her cellphone worked despite all the magic that had been thrown around. Maybe it had something to do with it being inside the protective circle. She pushed the speed dial for her friend. No way could she remember his number right now.

'Riley? Please tell me that you're OK and that the demons are history.'

'Yes to both.'

He whooped in her ear. Then he sobered. 'You sound totally wiped. You at home?'

'No. Give me some time . . . tomorrow maybe . . . and I'll call and tell you what happened.' This time she'd tell him all of it.

'It was really bad, wasn't it?' he asked. 'I can tell from your voice.'

'Yeah. It was total Hell. I'll talk to you later, guy.' She disconnected the call and let the phone fall into the pack.

When she looked up, Simon stood in front of her. He clenched a bloody sword like it had been fused to his arm. His usually tidy hair was streaked with sweat and dark circles underscored his troubled blue eyes.

All of them had paid a price for the game between Heaven and Hell.

'I was right: your father was working with the necromancer, making those undead demons.'

'No, my dad was the one who broke the spell. It was Sartael who was behind all this. Weren't you paying attention?'

'That isn't what I saw,' Simon retorted.

'Of course not. You'd hate to admit that a Fallen could get into your head. Well, it happened and now you have to live with that like the rest of us.'

'Why did you stop Armageddon? Was that Lucifer's order?'

'No. It was Heaven's.'

'How dare you lie to me!' he said, his eyes flaring and his hand tightening on the sword. 'So many people have died because of you.'

'No, my only fault was caring too much for you.'

Martha glided up, looking first at Riley and then at Simon. The patron angel of Oakland was still sporting her wings and she wore her *tough love* expression. Someone was up for a lecture and Riley didn't think it was her.

Simon's jaw dropped as he made the connection. 'You,'

he said. 'It was you, in the hospital. You touched my chest and . . .'

'Healed you. Yes, I plead guilty,' Martha replied, her eyes narrowing. 'What did you do with that second chance at life, Simon Michael David Adler?'

He cringed at the tone of her voice. 'I, ah . . .'

'Did you stand by the one who sacrificed her future to give you that chance?' Martha chided. 'When the Fallen came to you with his lies, did you resist him?'

'She—'

'No, you embraced the dark whispers because it was easier than accepting that your faith had been tested and found wanting. You betrayed your girlfriend to the demon hunters to put your own soul at ease.'

'But Riley—'

'Agreed to prevent Armageddon in exchange for your life,' Martha said. She shook her head in disappointment. 'If I was her, I'd be wondering if you were worth all the trouble.'

Simon's face blanched as pale as his hair. 'I didn't know,' he said in a coarse whisper. 'I thought . . . Oh, dear God.' He was on his knees in an instant, his head bowed in contrition. 'What have I done?'

With a tortured sigh, the angel knelt next to the stricken man. 'It is not the end of your world,' she said, patting his arm. 'You'll survive.' When he looked up, his eyes teemed with tears. 'You've learned a lesson – a soul is forged in the fires of adversity, not comfort.'

He swiped away the tears. When his eyes met Riley's, she

saw the unrelenting agony within in his heart.

'I'm . . . sorry,' he whispered.

'So am I, Simon,' she replied.

'Saint!' Harper called out. 'Get your ass over here.' Simon staggered to his feet, then hurried away.

'Go in peace, child,' Martha murmured.

'Will he find his faith again?' Riley asked.

'Perhaps.'

'What would have happened if I hadn't freed Ori?'

The angel puzzled on that. 'It's my guess you wouldn't have been allowed to stand between the two hosts, to plead humanity's case.'

'It's all about sacrifice for you people, isn't it?'

'Of course,' Martha said with a wry smile. 'Which is why your father is no longer one of Lucifer's.'

'What? He's in Heaven?'

'It's getting sorted out. The odds are in his favour.' Martha smiled broadly. 'Very good odds indeed.'

'Oh God,' Riley cried, nearly collapsing in relief. 'He'll be able to see Mom and . . .' Her eyes brimmed with tears.

'Maybe it *was* worth it after all,' Martha replied. She turned her head at the sound of wings. 'Ah, good, they've arrived.'

She marched towards a small knot of angels near the Blackthorne mausoleum and began to issuing orders like a general. The angels scattered, righting headstones, replanting uprooted trees, filling in the holes the Fives had created. A supernatural clean-up crew. When one Divine walked past a paramedic toting a broken headstone, the guy didn't even see it.

I wonder why they're doing this. They didn't fix the place after that tornado went through.

As the angels worked, Riley let her eyes skim over the cemetery, past the industrious angels, the mounds of demon ashes, the bodies covered with blankets. Ori's plinth stood empty, lit by sunlight.

Eventually she'd know if he was still alive. When that day came, she'd either be mourning the loss of the angel or the loss of her immortal soul.

One would be as life-changing as the other.

Chapter Thirty-Eight

Beck wiped the blood on his jeans, then tied off the bandage with a firm tug.

'Ya'll keep the leg, Remmers,' he said. 'Be sure to have Father Rosetti bless the Holy Water so ya know it's good.'

The injured man nodded grimly, his back up against a tree. 'Better than I hoped for.' He swallowed and looked around. 'I don't know about you, but there's no way I'm saying a word about this,' Remmers replied. 'No one will believe me. Not a chance.'

'I hear ya. I'll make sure someone gets ya into an ambulance.'

'Thanks, Den.'

'Thanks for watchin' my back, dude. I owe ya.'

Beck found Master Stewart leaning against a flame-scorched tree, flask in hand. The Scotch came his way and, after a tilt of the container, liquid ran red hot down his parched throat. He handed it back to its owner.

'How's Riley doin'?' the master asked.

'She's . . . talkin' at least. I asked Carmela to check on her.'

'She stood her ground today. If she hadn't, it would have been the end of us all.'

Beck rolled his right shoulder in an effort to stop it cramping, though that did nothing to prevent the muscle twitches: wielding a sword wasn't for wimps.

'I always thought Armageddon was some story they dreamed up to scare kids. I never expected to be right in the middle of it.'

When the flask came his way again, he took another long swig. Stewart still owed him an answer to a question that had been plaguing him ever since the Vatican's team had arrived.

'Back when we first met with the hunters, the priest said he knew who we served. When I asked ya about that, ya didn't answer me.'

Stewart remained silent.

Beck lowered his voice. 'We serve Hell, don't we? The hunters are Heaven's favourites and we're Lucifer's. Am I right?'

'It's not that simple, lad,' Stewart remarked. 'It's not so much a matter of whether we serve the Prince, but that we are the opposite of the hunters. The other side of the coin. Everythin' in this world hangs in the balance between the light and dark.'

'That doesn't make a damn bit of sense.'

'It's not an easy concept. Even the origins of the demons isn't clear. Some think Lucifer created them as a mockery of God's work. Others claim that they're damned souls, sent ta Hell to learn their lesson.'

'Yer sayin' that if I kill a demon it might be someone I knew?'

Stewart hitched a shoulder. 'I don't know for sure. I still don't understand it and I've been trappin' for over fifty years.'

Which meant Beck had little chance of grasping it today.

'Don't let it trouble ya, lad. Yer not a servant of the dark, that's for sure.' The master laid a gentle hand on his shoulder. 'I'm very proud of ya. Ya showed great courage.'

'I did OK,' Beck replied, shrugging off the praise.

'Ya took on an Archfiend,' the master replied, reclaiming his liquor at the same time as he removed his hand. 'That's better'n OK.'

'I didn't kill it,' Beck said. He remembered Riley stabbing it in the butt and then laughed, because it felt good. 'Damn, it's good to be alive.'

'Aye. Now get Riley out of here. Take her ta my place if she'll go. This will hit her hard soon enough.'

Beck hesitated, not sure if he should ask the question. 'What happens to a Fallen when it dies?'

Stewart took another long pull on the whisky. 'Some say that Heaven takes them back if their souls have been cleansed. Others believe they become a demon and start all over again.'

Which meant no one really knew the truth.

There's a lot of that in this job.

Beck found Paul's daughter sitting where he'd left her, the blanket still round her shoulders. Her tangled hair rested on dirt-smeared clothes, her skin unnaturally pale. He sat next to her, waiting for her to speak first.

'How many did we lose?'

'Twelve,' he replied. 'The hunters lost ten. We've got a lot of injuries, but I think most of them are gonna live.'

Riley searched across the stretch of ground around them, looking for someone. Her attention paused on one hunter and she sighed in relief. 'Müller's alive,' she said. 'He has a little boy at home.' Then her face saddened. 'Corsini won't ever get to see his new baby.'

She's in shock. Beck put his arm round her. 'Stewart wants me to take you to his place.'

Riley instantly shook her head. 'No, I want to go home.' She took her time rising from the step, telling him she was in pain.

'The doc seen you yet?'

'I wasn't bleeding to death so she'll check me over later.'

Beck suspected Carmela had said more than that.

Riley looked up at him, her eyes glistening. 'The angel said Dad isn't in Hell any more,' she murmured. 'He's free of the demons.'

Not in . . . 'Yes!' Beck shot a fist in the air. 'Way to go, Paul.' Then he sobered. 'Come on, let's get ya out of here.'

As they walked down the asphalt road past the others, Riley kept her eyes on the path. He knew how it went after a battle. You focused on what you could handle, which was damned little.

She paused only when she found Mort sitting on the kerb. He had a bottle of water in his hand and there was a giant red mark on his left cheek. His summoner's robe was destined for the trash.

'You OK?' she asked.

'I'm just tired,' he mumbled. 'I've never done that much magic before.'

'Did you know my dad was going to be here?' When there was no reply, she stepped closer, her body taut. 'Did you know what he was going to do?'

Beck gently touched her arm. 'Later. I'm sure Mort will be happy to talk to you, but not right now.' He gave the necromancer a look that told him that conversation would be happening or Beck would make it a personal issue.

'I'll tell you all of it. Come to my house tomorrow, after we've both got some sleep,' Mort said.

Riley swung away and moved down the road at a pace she wouldn't be able to sustain. She flagged near the front gate, stopping to catch her breath. Stretchers rolled by them on the way to a street crowded with ambulances and cops.

'Yer hurtin', aren't ya?' A nod. 'Can you make it to the truck?'

'Yes.' Then her eyes flared and she shoved him away. 'What were you doing, you idiot? You don't know how to kill an Archfiend. It could have ripped you in half.'

'I didn't want it to hurt you,' he said honestly.

'Why do you have this insane need to get yourself killed?'

He smirked. 'I'm still alive and it isn't.'

'Only because Ori killed it.'

'Don't remind me. Were ya really tryin' to stab that demon in the ass?'

Riley groaned. 'No, I was aiming for its leg and it moved. I looked like a total dork.'

'Not to me.'

Beck slipped his arm round her waist and they continued on to the truck. So far the press hadn't been allowed anywhere near the scene. That would end soon and he wanted her out of here before that happened.

'I'm sorry about yer angel,' he said, meaning it. 'I figured he was as evil as they come, but now I think he was tryin' to make it right in his own way.'

Riley swallowed hard. 'Why didn't Lucifer take out Sartael himself? Why let it go this far?'

'A leader sends his best man to challenge the enemy. The top dog only gets involved when it goes wrong. Or to claim victory. Been that way forever.'

'It cost Ori his life.'

'Maybe.'

She looked up at him. 'You don't think he's dead?'

'Not sure. Lucifer's a tricky bastard, and if keepin' that angel alive is a way to play with yer head he'll do it.'

'That's what I was thinking.'

Chapter Thirty-Nine

Riley woke to the comfort of her own bed in that muzzy sort of haze that didn't tell her what day it was, how long she'd slept or whether the nightmares she'd had were real or not.

Had to be a dream. That would be good. No rampaging necromancers, revolting Archfiends or epic battles. No dead Ori.

Her eyes opened. The warm light in the room hinted at late afternoon. She rolled her head on the pillow and studied the clock – it was past four. Memories rushed to fill the empty spaces: Beck walking her to her apartment, her heading for the shower, scrubbing herself until the water ran cold. Finding out that Ori had been right once again – she was not pregnant. Never had a period been so welcome.

One thing had changed: the inscriptions on her palms were visible now and looked likely to remain that way.

Then Max had joined her in bed for feline purring therapy. Carmela had zipped in at about noon, pronounced her bruised, but alive, which seemed pointlessly obvious. Mrs Litinsky had followed on her heels, hot chicken soup in hand. After all that care and feeding, Riley hadn't been able to keep her eyes open.

Hauling herself out of bed, she let Max out and curled up on the couch, wrapped in a thick comforter. Though she really didn't want to go there, she began to methodically review all she could remember of the events at the cemetery. Some of the memories made her so sad, like her father's sacrifice. He'd been the hero, not her. As she gazed up at her parents' wedding photograph on the bookshelves, Riley whispered a prayer that her dad was with her mom now. That they'd be together forever.

'I love you guys and I'll never forget you,' she whispered.

Then she buried her head in the comforter and wept until there were no more tears.

It was close to ten that night when Riley's cellphone ran. It vibrated across the nightstand, making an unholy racket. She retrieved it, half-awake. 'Hello?'

'Hey, Riley, how's it goin'?' Beck asked, his voice louder than normal.

She pulled herself up in bed. 'What is all that noise?' Singing, she thought, and bar sounds.

'Me and Elias are gettin' ripped,' he explained.

'It's not only the captain,' she said. Too much noise for two guys.

'Nah, it's a whole bunch of us.' Someone asked him a question and he called out, 'Put me in for five. No way Jackson can balance a pint on his forehead. What do you take me for, some dumbass hick?'

'Hey!' she called out, smiling now. He sounded

happy and it was contagious.

'What?' he asked, and then she heard a long slurp through the phone.

'I thought the hunters didn't do that kind of stuff.'

'Tonight the rules are bein' ignored. We're havin' a wake at the Six Feet Under. Everybody's here, even the priest. Well, except Simon and that jerk Amundson. Too good to hang with us, I guess.'

She didn't know about Amundson, but she was willing to bet Simon was in church, on his knees, praying for all he was worth.

'Do not get yourself arrested, you hear?' she urged. 'I am not going to bail your butt out of jail, mister.'

'Now who's goin' all old geezer, huh?' He snorted. 'I'm gonna get drunk and pass out on my bed at home. Haven't done that for so long I can't remember.'

'Probably a reason for that, Beck. You're killing brain cells and you don't have that many to spare.'

'Yeah, yeah, all you give me is grief, woman. Look, I gotta go. If you want, I can call you later.'

'Not if you're drunk.'

There was a pause. 'Yeah, better make it mornin', then.' Another pause. 'OK, late afternoon. It's gonna take time to get past the hangover.'

'Have fun, Backwoods Boy.'

'See ya later, Princess. Don't forget those cookies.'

Riley growled at the phone, then dropped it on the nightstand. She owed the mouthy Southern Dude those oatmeal goodies. If she was nice, she'd wait until tomorrow afternoon to deliver them, allowing him time to get over his hangover.

Or she could deliver them in the early morning and relish every minute of his head-splitting pain. With an unholy grin, Riley climbed out of bed and headed towards the kitchen and the baking supplies.

To Beck's amazement, Jackson *could* balance an empty pint glass on his forehead. Now he was working on a full one.

'That takes talent,' Beck said in awe.

'I sure don't have it,' Salvatore said, his words slightly slurred in deference to the beer in his system. 'Was that Riley?'

'Yeah, it was,' he said, smiling. 'Rome isn't gonna give her a bunch of crap about what happened, are they?'

'Don't know. Rosetti's talking to Stewart right now, trying to work it out,' he said, angling his head towards the pair at a far table. 'The priest will tell me once they've done their business.'

Salvatore took a swig of his beer, then set his glass down with a pronounced thump. 'About Justine,' he began. 'I know you two have been together.'

'How do you know that?'

'She told me. She likes to stir up trouble.' Salvatore's face furrowed in thought. 'If I'd known you were headed her way, I would have warned you, man to man, you know.'

'She wasn't lyin' when she said you two had a history?'

'No, we were –' Salvatore edited whatever he was going to say – 'close a couple of years back. She nearly destroyed my career to get a scoop on a story. She's beautiful, but she's single-minded and doesn't care who she hurts.'

'I kinda noticed that.'

'Are you two still . . .' the hunter asked.

'No. Like you, it didn't end pretty.' He told the hunter what Justine's article might do to him. By the time he finished, the captain was noticeably upset.

'I'll see what I can do to head her off. She probably won't listen, but I'll try anyway.'

'I'd appreciate that.'

Father Rosetti made his way over to their table, clearly well lubricated. He pulled a chair out and dropped into it. The pint glass in his hand was empty.

'So what's the verdict?' Salvatore asked. 'Is Riley staying here or coming back with us?'

'She's staying in Atlanta. Stewart will keep an eye on her. He promises to take care of any trouble that might arise. I pray to God there isn't any.'

Beck heaved a sigh of relief.

'This has been a rough one for all of us,' Salvatore allowed. 'I can't say that I ever want to see another Fallen in my life.'

'Amen to that. This wasn't what I expected when I asked to come on this mission,' Rosetti admitted. 'I knew things were strange here, but . . .' He shifted the empty glass a few inches. 'If I make a mistake, a life is ruined. If I set one of

Hell's servants free, the world takes one step closer to eternal damnation. It's a difficult call sometimes.'

Maybe this guy isn't such a hardass after all. 'You do have a crappy job,' Beck observed.

'I second that,' Salvatore said, rising his pint in salute. 'This whole mission got to you, didn't it?'

'Yes, it did, ' Rosetti said. 'I was convinced Riley Blackthorne was working for Hell. She was, but she also served Heaven when the time came. She has Lucifer's mark on her, yet she kept us from total war. How do I reconcile that? Is she good or evil?'

'What did Rome say?' Beck asked.

'That she's on the fence. I fear something happened between her and the Fallen, but I'm not sure exactly what. What did it cost her to free him?'

Beck didn't want to know that answer. To change the subject, he pointed at the priest's glass. 'Seems yer beer is empty and so is mine. Another?'

'Make it a pitcher,' the captain suggested. 'I've hunter tales to tell you. Some of the stuff we see . . . it's unreal.'

Beck expected the priest to shut that down, but instead Rosetti nodded his approval. Get a few beers under the guy's belt and he was pretty decent.

'OK, then I'll tell you some trapper ones. We'll see who's the best liar,' Beck replied.

'That would be me,' the captain shot back. 'But we'll have the good father be the judge.'

'You're on, dude.'

Chapter Forty

Riley was up before dawn, unable to sleep. After carefully applying her make-up to cover the bruises and choosing exactly what she wanted to wear to visit Beck – she wanted her trapper guy to see her in something other than ripped and stained clothes – she headed to an unlikely place. This time Ori was calling her in a different way.

The sun was just beginning to rise when she reached the mausoleum. In the distance was the far-off rumble of thunder, hinting that today was going to be more wet than sunny. Kneeling in front of her parents' graves, she uttered a brief prayer for her dad and her mom. Then she retrieved the chamois pouch from her pocket. Inside the pouch was the dirt she'd collected from her father's grave after his body had been stolen. It was to remind her she couldn't trust anyone.

But I can *trust people.* Ayden, Mort, Stewart, Beck and Peter. They'd all come through for her. She upended the bag and let the soil fall back to earth because it no longer held any meaning for her.

Riley opened the double doors and retrieved the red rose the angel had given her. It took only a little hunting to find the spot where Ori had fallen to earth – his brilliant blue blood still caked the leaves. She inhaled the rose's scent one last time, then placed it where he'd last been. Plucking a single petal, she tucked it into the pouch for remembrance of their night together. Then she selected one of the smaller blue-stained leaves and put it in with the rose petal.

If she prayed that Ori survive and it came true, she'd have a horrific debt to pay for eternity. If he was dead, his loss would be with her until her last breath.

'I'll live with whatever happens,' she whispered.

Because sometimes it was best not to fight your fate.

A short time later, Riley left the graveyard behind. Another task called her as urgently as this one: it was time to hear the truth about her father's sacrifice.

Riley sat next to Mortimer on the stone bench in his garden, her backpack on the ground between her feet.

She'd hoped he'd launch into the explanation about her father and why he'd taken Ozy's place in the circle, but the summoner didn't take the bait.

'Tell me all of it, Mort. No more secrets.'

In lieu of a reply, the summoner rose and walked to the fountain where he bent forward to let the water trickle over his fingers. It seemed to relax him.

'I'll tell you what I know and what I think happened.' He flicked the water away. 'Lord Ozymandias had been summoning demons to gain hidden knowledge. He made a mistake with one of his spells and Sartael took advantage of it, manifesting instead of an Archdemon. The archangel gave him a choice – he did what Sartael asked or he would be carted to Hell and tortured for eternity.'

'How do you know that?'

'Ozymandias told me.'

'What? When?' she demanded.

'His lordship was on my doorstep last night at dusk,' Mort said. 'He acted as if he hadn't attacked my house or stolen your father.'

Or helped Sartael push the world to the brink of war.

'Did he apologize?'

'Of course not,' Mort replied, 'but he insisted on telling me his story. He claimed it was so I might not make the same mistakes as I grew in power. I think it was more to assuage his conscience.'

'I don't think he has one,' Riley retorted.

'Perhaps he does now.' Mort straightened up, brushing his wet fingers against his trousers. 'He seemed . . . humbled. He said that Sartael instructed him how to alter the demons and with each additional spell layer he incorporated Ozymandias knew this was heading to a bad end. When your father died, he tried to summon him, hoping that a master trapper might know how to break his servitude to a Fallen angel.'

It all fell in place. 'But Lucifer had summoned my dad first. He knew what Sartael was up to.'

'Indeed. When your father disappeared, Ozymandias panicked. He knew that Sartael was intent on destroying the city, if not the world, so he stole your father from me. Which is why Paul came to me in the first place.'

'Because you were no match for Ozy?'

'Yes. Your father offered his lordship a way out: if Ozymandias did exactly as Lucifer required, he would walk away unscathed.'

'While my dad got disintegrated,' Riley retorted. 'That sucks.'

'It was Paul's choice to serve as a conduit to defuse the spell,' Mort explained. 'He knew it would destroy him, but he felt it was the best way to pay off his debt to the trappers and to Lucifer.'

Riley felt the aching tug of loss once more. 'He looked so peaceful, like it wasn't hurting him or anything. Is that possible?'

'He wasn't in pain. I'm guessing Ozymandias made sure of that,' Mort said gently.

Not all of this had come from the Dark Lord. That left only two possible sources and since Lucifer wouldn't drop by for tea . . .

'When did Dad tell you about this?'

Mort's eyebrows rose in admiration. 'Your father was fairly incoherent until right before I left for the graveyard. Then he shook off Ozymandias's spell like it was nothing. I was stunned. I think he had Lucifer's help with that.'

The necromancer returned to the bench, settling in next to her. 'Paul told me what he knew and what role I had to play. His biggest concern was that you were kept safe.'

Once again Heaven and Hell had played them like master puppeteers.

'If Ayden hadn't repelled the spell when it rebounded, we would have died,' she pointed out.

'I mentioned that to Ozymandias, but he said that he'd carefully adjusted the rebound to exactly how much we could handle.'

'That's bull,' she said. 'No one can judge magic that carefully. It's not that precise.'

Mort studied her with renewed interest. 'I see you learned a few things during your apprenticeship.'

'What? I . . .' He was offering her a compliment. 'I'm happy being a trapper.'

'For the moment. Bear in mind that you have the ability to wrangle magic as well as you do demons.'

Not going there. 'Why didn't my dad tell me what he was going to do?'

'He didn't want you to worry. You know how he was about you.' Mort extracted her demon claw pendant from his pocket. 'It was inside the book of spells. It didn't touch the ground, which is why it's still in one piece.'

Riley took it from him, supremely pleased it had survived. A silver ring hung on the chain, one with a distinctive pattern of ovals cut into the metal. She'd know it anywhere. It was her father's wedding ring.

'Paul gave it to me before the battle,' the summoner explained. 'He knew it wouldn't survive the spell's destruction.'

Dad thought of everything. Riley touched it fondly. 'Mom's still wearing hers. We could have got money for it, but it didn't seem right.' She pulled the pendant over her head, tucking it under her shirt. The demon claw felt cold against her skin, but the ring was warm, like one of her father's embraces.

The ring and the note were all she had left of Paul Blackthorne. No, that wasn't quite right: Her heart still held all those sweet memories of their years together. No matter what, those were immortal, beyond the reach of any demon or angel.

Chapter Forty-One

Despite his head-splitting hangover, Beck found himself in a good mood. Things were finally falling into place: the Vatican wasn't going to mess with Riley as long as Stewart kept an eye on her, and they were doing a really fine job of squashing rumours about exactly what had gone down in the cemetery. The Holy Water was the real deal again, the undead demons were ash and Paul was out of Lucifer's clutches.

He still had the trip to South Georgia to face, along with Sadie's death. That'd be hard, but once he'd done right by her, given her a good funeral and cleaned out the old house, he could turn his back on Sadlersville and his past. He could start planning for the future and determine exactly where Paul's daughter fitted in all that.

'Yeah, things are lookin' up.'

A series of sharp raps on his front door jarred Beck out of his thoughts. He ran a hand through his hair to smooth it, then hurried to open the door. He'd been looking forward to seeing Riley since last night, and it wasn't just because of the cookies.

'Hey, about time you –' he began.

The woman on the doorstep wasn't the one he wanted.

Justine stood with both hands on her hips, clad in tight jeans and a crisp white shirt. Her green eyes were on fire.

He moved into the doorway to keep her out of his house. 'What do ya want?'

'Elias called me this morning. He told me that if I wrote my article about you he would make it very hard to renew my Vatican press pass. Do you have any notion of what that means?'

It meant that the hunter's captain had got a little too heavy-handed.

'It means ya need to back off,' Beck said. 'There are better stories out there than me.'

'That is not the case. In fact, the more I dig, the more I know this will be the best story I have ever written.'

'Justine, you do not want to go there,' he warned.

'Or what? You will strike me like you did your mother when you didn't get your way?'

His mind whirled at the accusation. 'I never hit Sadie. Who told ya that?'

'She did. Since you were not willing to talk about your life, I drove to Sadlersville. Your mother was very happy to tell me all about her delinquent son. About the knife fights, all the girls and the alcohol and drugs.'

'Ya . . . don't know Sadie. She'll lie when it suits her.'

'It wasn't just her, Beck.' Justine's eyes narrowed. 'I was told the only reason you didn't go to prison was because of the county sheriff. That you were exiled to Atlanta because you were in a knife fight with some man whose wife you slept with.'

Ah, damn. She really has been diggin'. As long as she doesn't go any further . . .

'That's in the past, Justine. Just like us. Let it go.' Beck began to close the door, but she jammed a tiny booted foot in the way.

'I am not finished,' she said. A recorder appeared in her right hand and she clicked it on. 'For the record, Mr Beck, tell me what really happened during that camping trip to the swamp when you were fifteen? What happened to those other boys? Why were you the only one to come back alive?'

Oh dear God, she knows. 'You cannot write about that.'

Justine's eyes narrowed. 'Like you urged Elias to ruin my career? Funny how it's important when it's all about you.'

'What do you want?' he said. 'What will it take to keep you quiet?'

Justine's smile showed more teeth than usual. 'Nothing.'

'This is about Riley, isn't it? Yer jealous of her.'

The smile widened. 'I am not jealous of some child. My job is to present the facts so people will judge what is true and what are lies. Your story is important and I will tell it no matter who tries to stop me.'

If she had been a man, Beck would taken her down, but he had no leverage over Justine Armando. She would write the story and his world would collapse.

'Please, don't do this,' he pleaded. 'You will destroy my life.'

'That is not my concern.' She clicked off the recorder and headed for her car. 'Thank you, Beck,' she called out. 'You have been a most entertaining subject. Good in bed and good for the bank account!'

'Ya go to Hell, you red-haired demon!' he shouted.

Justine just laughed at him.

Beck rammed the door shut even before she pulled out of the drive in the fancy rental car.

'She can't do this!' he said, pounding a fist into the wall.

Justine was paying him back for dumping her, no matter what she said. It was his own damned fault. If he'd never touched her . . . If he hadn't been jealous about that damned angel, none of this would have happened.

Once that article was in print, the media would dredge up all the horrors of that trip into the swamp. It'd been a Saturday night in late December: he and a couple of other guys had taken some whiskey and drugs into Okefenokee Swamp to party. When it was all over, he was the only one alive. They never did find the bodies.

Riley . . .

She would be caught in the middle of this hurricane. Would she believe he was a killer? Even those who said they thought he was innocent had that accusing look. He never wanted to see that doubt in her eyes, not like he had with the others.

When he'd been in the Army, on patrol, one of the men in his squad had thrown himself on a grenade. The soldier did it without thinking, willing to die to save the others. This wasn't much different.

Beck knew what he had to do to protect Paul's daughter. He just didn't know if he had the courage.

Riley had expected to find her favourite trapper guy curled up on his couch, bemoaning his Olympic-grade headache. Instead she found a green sports car backing out his driveway. As it flew by her, she caught a glimpse of red hair.

'What is *she* doing here?'

It appeared her timing was good: Backwoods Boy was in need of a sympathetic ear and lots yummy oatmeal cookies.

He'll need a few kisses too.

Just after she knocked, the front door wrenched open and the trapper's furious face glared out at her. 'What the hell are ya – Oh . . .'

'Hi.'

Beck's eyes were bloodshot and the way he squinted suggested his headache could easily level a city. He was tense, his face crimson like he'd been shouting.

'Lovers spat with the stick chick?' she joked.

'We broke up.'

Oh. Though she really wanted to do a fist pump, Riley forced herself to behave.

'Sorry,' she said, though she really wasn't. 'I've got cookies. Maybe those will help.' She held up a paper bag. 'I brought some herbal tea. The lady at the witch store swears it'll help your hangover.'

He grudgingly waved her in. 'I'd eat a dead rat if it'd

help. It never hurt this bad before.'

'Age. It's starting to catch up with you,' she mocked. He frowned at her, but it bounced right off. 'Sit. I'll make the tea for you.'

He dropped on the couch with a groan as she rooted around in his cupboards for a mug. She chose the one with the Georgia flag. A short time later Riley delivered the brewing tea and a plate of cookies, then sat on the couch near him. She waited for his reaction to both.

Beck sniffed the tea experimentally, then shifted the hot cup in his hands, uneasy.

'What did Justine want?'

'Don't want to talk about it,' he replied gruffly.

Ohhkaay. 'Then what do you want to talk about?'

He glowered at her. 'I didn't rip my way out of Sadie's claws just to have someone else dig theirs into me, and that damned reporter is doin' just that.'

Clearly they were back to talking about Justine. 'What happened with you two?'

He took a pensive sip of his tea. 'This stuff tastes weird. Hope it works.' Beck leaned back on the couch, studying the ceiling now. Looking everywhere but at her.

'Beck, talk to me,' she nudged.

He sighed deeply. 'Justine's writin' another article about me. Salvatore warned her to back off and now she's all pissed.'

'Don't worry, she'll just call me a jinx again and then she'll leave town when the hunters do.'

'No, once that story's out my trappin' job is history.'

'Hey, unless you're a serial killer you're good to go, Beck.'

He frowned at her. 'I'm no damn serial killer, ya hear?' he snarled.

'Sorry,' she said, raising her hands in surrender. *What is it with this guy? He was fine last night.*

His expression changed to one of regret. Like he'd come to some decision.

'What are ya doin' here?' he demanded.

Huh? 'What is wrong with you?'

He set the cup down and rose. 'It's time for ya to go.'

'What? I just got here.'

'It's best if ya don't come back. Ya shouldn't be seen with me.'

'But I thought we were . . . I mean . . . the cemetery?'

He instantly grew wary. 'That kiss? I was just tryin' to make ya feel better. Nothin' more.'

It took a second or two to process what he'd said. 'That's not how it was,' she protested.

Beck's frown matched hers now. 'Dammit, girl, didn't ya learn yer lesson the last time? Why do ya insist on daydreamin' about stuff that can never happen?'

Ohmigod. I thought . . .

Had she trusted her heart to something that wasn't real?

Riley was at the front door before she even realized she was moving. Fumbling with the lock, she cursed when it fought back. When she wrenched open the door, the fresh morning air greeted her, reminding her how happy she'd felt driving over to Beck's house. How she wanted to feel like that forever.

She spun and stared at the man who'd driven a stake through her heart. 'Why did you kiss me? Why did you act like you cared?'

'I thought we were gonna die . . .' he muttered. 'It wasn't anythin' special.'

'Nothing special?' she shouted. 'God, I hate you!'

Riley fled the house and down the steps, stumbling over the last two in her haste. She had to escape, run away like the last time he'd hurt her. Never see him again. She'd barely reached the car when Beck's hand caught her shoulder and spun her round.

'Girl, I'm . . .'

'Don't touch me!' Riley shoved him away. 'What is it with you? Do you get off hurting me, is that it? Does it make you feel all powerful, like God or something?'

'It's for yer own good.'

'Oh, right. Silly old Riley isn't good enough for you, huh? Not *Justine* enough for you? Is that it? I gave it up to some other guy now you're paying me back?'

Beck's face went ashen. 'Oh God, girl, it's not you. Don't ever think that.' He shook his head in defeat. 'Yer too special for a loser like me.'

Riley rocked back on heels in stunned surprise. 'What?' she spouted. Where had that come from?

'Do us both a favour and just go away. Ya hear me?'

'Not until you tell me what's going on.'

Beck looked down at his feet, then back up. When his eyes met hers, she swore there was a glint of tears. 'Ya deserve better than some bastard son of a drunk who can't read or write. Ya don't want to be around me, not when people think I'm a . . .'

'Think you're a what?' she demanded.

He shook his head and headed for the stairs.

'Beck! Talk to me! We can work this out.'

He whirled round. 'No! We're done talkin'. Get out of here and don't ever come back. I don't need ya no more. I don't need no one.'

The door front slammed behind him, rattling the front window.

Shaken at his fury, Riley crawled into her car and shut the door. The keys went into the ignition, but she didn't start the vehicle. Instead she stared at the house, trying to understand the troubled man inside. She'd never seen Beck like that before.

He said he couldn't live without me. Now he says he can.

He'd been in a good mood last night, joking around, so whatever had changed had to be Justine's doing. What had that skank done? Why was Beck so worried?

Riley rubbed tears off her cheeks, her fingers coming away black from her mascara.

I should just walk away. Find someone who has it together. I don't need all this drama.

Her conscience instantly weighed in: Beck had stood by her during the worst days of her life. He'd tried to save her father's life. Kept her from starving. He'd bled for her and he would have gladly died for her. If she walked away from him now it would haunt her forever.

Riley turned the key in the ignition and the car came to life. Movement at the window brought her eyes towards the house: Beck yanked his front curtains closed, walling himself off from her and the rest of the world, retreating inside his cave like a grievously wounded animal.

Her heart ached for him, for all the dreams he was throwing away.

Riley slowly backed the car on to the street, her mind in turmoil. She wiped away the last stray tear as she gazed up at the green-and-white house with its closed curtains and its dark secrets. A fierce desire rose inside her.

Blackthornes didn't back down from a challenge. They were strong and resilient like the tree.

'Strife often leads ta a sweeter life.'

Someday, when that sweet life was hers, she wanted Denver Beck to share it with her. She couldn't imagine facing her days without him at her side.

Riley put the car in gear and headed down the street, calmer now, determined to do what was best for both of them. This would be a battle just like the one she'd faced in the cemetery. There she'd stood between the armies of Heaven and Hell. Now it was time for her to stand up for the man who owned her heart, but was too afraid to believe that sweet life could be his.

We're not done yet, Backwoods Boy. No, this battle is just beginning and I'm in it to win.